THE WONDER

Diana Evans was a dancer before she became a writer and critic. Her first novel, *26a*, received a Betty Trask Award, a nomination for the *Guardian* First Book Award, and was shortlisted for the Commonwealth Best First Book and Whitbread First Novel of the Year Awards. It was also the inaugural winner of the Orange Award for New Writers. She lives in London.

www.dianaommoevans.com

DIANA EVANS

The Wonder

VINTAGE BOOKS
London

With thanks to Rebecca Carter (a wonder), Clare Alexander, Jennifer Kabat, Clara Farmer and the Chatto & Windus team, Leon Robinson and his crucial work at Positive Steps, Diane Mitchell, Keith and Elaine Bardowell, Namron, David Akinsanya, Colin Prescod, Wild at Heart and Adam Watson for flowers, Sarah Ee, Tash Aw and Svetlana Scheck-Ramzy for courage, and to Derek A. Bardowell for the title and many other big-hearted wisdoms.

Published by Vintage 2010

2 4 6 8 10 9 7 5 3

First published in Great Britain in 2009 by
Chatto & Windus

Vintage
Random House, 20 Vauxhall Bridge Road,
London SW1V 2SA

www.vintage-books.co.uk

Addresses for companies within The Random House Group Limited can be found at:
www.randomhouse.co.uk/offices.htm

The Random House Group Limited Reg. No. 954009

A CIP catalogue record for this book
is available from the British Library

ISBN 9780099479055

The Random House Group Limited supports The Forest Stewardship Council (FSC), the leading international forest certification organisation. All our titles that are printed on Greenpeace approved FSC certified paper carry the FSC logo. Our paper procurement policy can be found at www.rbooks.co.uk/environment

 Mixed Sources
Product group from well-managed forests and other controlled sources
www.fsc.org Cert no. TT-COC-2139
© 1996 Forest Stewardship Council
FSC

Typeset by Palimpsest Book Production Limited, Falkirk, Stirlingshire
Printed and bound in Great Britain by
CPI Cox & Wyman, Reading RG1 8EX

For Meadow Oshozoway
and Derek

PART ONE

1

When Lucas was a boy, asleep in his cabin on the Grand Union Canal, he had a recurring dream. There was the sound of galloping and a change in weather. Sudden wind shook through the sycamore trees that lined the surrounding streets, then into the room came a man dressed head to toe in black, with coat tails and a hat, and large, priestly hands. He lifted Lucas in his arms and took him out into the night.

It felt very much like flying. They sped up Ladbroke Grove and over the dividing hill and Lucas felt fast and warm in the cave between the man's torso and the horse's soft brown neck. The coat tails whipped in the wind. They passed through barley fields as the pigeons turned to nightingales. Everything was different, the Westway gone, the Portobello Road less travelled; on and on they went without direction or conversation until speed became home. There was not a stretch of canal for miles out here, not an absence or a cemetery stone, so when Lucas woke up, windswept, in the place he called home, in the ramshackle houseboat with its questions and sideways slant against the bank, his disorientation was greater than before. Horseback seemed the surer place, and he'd wait earnestly for the coat-tailed stranger to return.

It came to be that whenever he thought of his father he did not think of Antoney Matheus, but a highwayman, who came for him in the depths of sleep and changed the look of the world, as only fathers can. It was easier that way.

3

One April morning shortly after his twenty-fifth birthday, he was woken by this dream, which had not recurred since the time of his grandmother's death nine years before. It left him with the same feeling of disorientation, the more for its impromptu arrival in his adult mind, and its poignancy increased when he opened his eyes. He was lying on the left-hand side of the queen-size bed he still shared with his sister Denise. His feet were hanging off the end of the mattress as he hadn't stopped growing until he was six foot three. Around him were grooved wooden walls, cool to the touch, inclining on their ascent from the gunwale, masking cupboards built into every conceivable space to make up for lack of it – linen above his head, clothes in a pull-out next to him, a drawer beneath containing Denise's handwritten accounts. The cabin was eight foot two inches wide and the ceiling at its highest point five foot nine. Lucas had a stoop in his upper back from habitually bowing his head.

Most oppressive of all was an antique cherrywood wardrobe which loomed at the end of the bed. The only piece of free-standing furniture in the room, it contained items belonging to his parents – his mother, Carla, who had died when he was a few months old, and his father, who'd allegedly drowned. According to a long-standing rule designed to quell Lucas's childhood fears, the wardrobe was never opened, thereby preventing the vapour of the ghostly, rotting things inside it wafting into his and Denise's nostrils as they slept, causing nightmares. Indeed on the rare occasions Lucas had peeped inside out of curiosity, a bitter tree smell had slunk out from the darkness within, cutting his nerve and making him step away. It was time for a different waking view, a clear, open road, the inside of a girl's bedroom maybe. The twentieth century was drawing to a close. The Conservatives had come and gone, so had Tupac and Biggie. Sizzla Kalonji was taking over the reggae world yet here Lucas still was, staring at the same disturbing inanimate presence inches from his feet, blocking his path to the future. He had recently suggested to Denise that they empty the cupboard and decide what to do with its contents, but she'd responded curtly, saying she didn't see a reason to tamper with things.

Denise, a florist, had left for work hours ago, having neatened her pillow precisely. It was a bright, pink-blossomed morning. Winter had clung to power, and spring had begun that year with high chill winds, lifting the blossom off the branches and bringing it down to rest at road edges, in ravishing pools at the base of the sycamore trunks. Lucas had nothing in particular to get up for other than to finish reading the latest issue of *Touch* magazine, so he closed his eyes and concentrated on the rocking sensation caused by a passing vessel, which always made him imagine he was on an open sea bound for Jamaica. Today it was difficult. In the receding waves of the dream he was more aware than usual of the wardrobe's oxidising brass handle rattling with the movements of the boat, a sound, like the ticking of the bedside clock or the creaks in the walls, he'd become used to not hearing. He turned onto his back, venturing with his long skinny leg across the delicate centre divide that Denise was so astute in maintaining. The bed was a wide warm country when it was all his own. They'd shared it ever since their grandmother had gone (when Lucas was twelve, Denise sixteen), in the beginning as a kind of comfort, especially during thunderstorms, now in the hold of a fossilised, seasick habit. However much he spread out this morning, though, he couldn't shake the feeling of being stifled. Coat tails whipped in the wind. The wardrobe rattled. He got to thinking about Edwin Starr, whom he'd met the day before yesterday in St Albans. In this crowded state of mind, as the Friday traffic passed along Ladbroke Grove outside, he was relieved to feel himself slowly but surely becoming aware of something else – something soothing, a sweet distraction, that thing you can always rely on to take you elsewhere. A lazy, yet willing, matutinal arousal.

Lucas always hesitated at these moments. He was afraid of leaving traces and lethargic at the thought of washing sheets if he did. For a time his hand rested coyly on his inner thigh, but then he decided to go with it, a quick, six-minute ride, to start the day, to settle his head. He'd developed a clever technique over the years that involved throwing off the sheets just before the point of emission and aiming himself upwards towards his chest so that the spray was restricted to that area. For this reason he always removed his T-shirt beforehand. He set out cautiously, with a picture in his mind of Lauryn Hill, whom Denise had refused to let him put on the wall. He wasn't expecting much, not fully committed to the prospect of clean-up, so he was taken by surprise by a sudden shooting, generous charge that made him yelp, necessitating a particularly urgent clearance of linen so that one of his feet got twisted in the sheets. This meant that he missed the best bit. He lay there afterwards, chest-sprayed, cheated, exhausted, wondering as he often did whether it had really been worth it, and whether Denise, somewhere in flower world, had sensed it.

If you passed that spot back then you might have seen it. If you walked eastwards from Harlesden along the towpath almost to the Ladbroke Grove crossing, perhaps sat down on one of the benches there and looked across to the opposite bank, you might have seen a fifty-foot narrowboat of faded green leaning slightly to its left (this was because of the wardrobe). Her name was Silver, written in sloping letters on one side by the previous owner. There were portholes along the saloon. A handrail lined the bow. A pair of corroded ornamental dragons glared out from either side of the dwarfish cabin doors. It was a relic of a thing, with paint peeling off the steel and a useless, rusted tiller at the stern. It looked, in fact, despite the fresh flowers at the windows, as if it might be sinking, it had been there for such a long time. Lucas and Denise did not know what it was to live on land or to have a front door that could be accessed without first stepping onto a deck, and rocking a little. They didn't know what it felt like to open that front door to an Avon lady or a British Gas salesman or a Jehovah's Witness, because the Avon ladies and the British Gas salesmen and the Jehovah's Witnesses did not have the key. Only if you were a water gypsy with licence to moor at that particular spot, or a friend of one of the water gypsies, were you allowed through the high black gate that separated the towpath from the street.

There were obvious advantages to the situation (hardly any junk mail, less exposure to the impertinences of capitalism) but Lucas often wondered what it would be like to talk about gas prices, or the existence of hell, to a chatty stranger on solid ground. He was unlike most boat-dwellers in this respect. The majority of boat-dwellers have one belief in common – water is freedom. When you've tired of a view or you do not wish to be found, when you long to nestle at the shoulder of another urban shore, you simply untether yourself and sail away. You take the murky liquid road at four miles an hour and do a left into Camden, or Bethnal Green, or you go further out, towards the country, and discover new kinds of silence. You go, you go, you disappear. What better way to become invisible than to erase your home, to leave no trace of yourself in sight? What a joy it is to live with just the possibility of such a thing.

This was not how it was for Lucas. This was a permanent, inadvertent mooring with no comparison to a concrete past. He was born on the water, and raised by his grandmother on the same spot. He used to think that all children who'd lost their parents lived on boats, that it was part of the experience of being an orphan – either that or you went to a children's home, where there were probably fewer spiders but no grandmothers or other advantages. Toreth was a caring, garrulous woman of Welsh descent and had helped Lucas through thunderstorms with her dream-inducing story of Peterjohn the highwayman, who'd had nine children and belonged to the bygone age when Portobello Road was just a rough country lane. She and Lucas used to sit

7

on the bow together in fine weather while Denise was absorbed in some kind of gardening activity on the bank. When Toreth was in deep storytelling mode, and if there was a good sunset, she'd sometimes tell another enduring tale, the one about how the boat had got there in the first place, the only story she ever told that featured Lucas's dad. It took place in 1969, in October, on a day whose evening had also seen a remarkable sunset.

Antoney, Toreth would explain, was a man given to 'suspicious' disappearances. On that day, during one such disappearance, he bought Silver from a musician friend of his in Greenford for two hundred pounds, then sailed her down the Grand Union at maximum speed having never driven a boat in his life. He waved at passers-by en route, drinking white rum at intervals from a flask given to him by one of his 'silly little groupies'. Choosing this spot, diagonally opposite the Kensal Green gasworks, he introduced Carla – Toreth's daughter – to her new home with a bleary triumphant look in his eye. 'You want property?' he said. 'Here's property. How about it?' Carla was heavily pregnant with Denise at the time, on the lip of labour. She was hot and dizzy and dangerously in love. She stepped onto the sleepy sunstruck deck and sat down on a metal chair. 'Antoney,' she said, 'you'll be the death of me.'

That was the day Denise was born, in fact, which was what this story was actually about, for Toreth thought that Denise, with her precocious interest in flowers, could be the reincarnation of a much-loved florist of the time called Emily Kirk, whose funeral Toreth had attended that very same day in 1969. Emily, or Em as she was known, had been selling flowers in Portobello Market for more than sixty years ('All fresh, sixpence a bunch!' Toreth would demonstrate) so the funeral was a local event. In the traditional stallholder custom the long and winding cortège travelled down Portobello Road at round about the same time as Antoney was sailing the boat from Greenford. As it passed, the stallholders stopped their work and bowed their heads in respect. Later, as the sun set remarkably and Em drifted into history, Carla was helped up the towpath slope by Antoney in the early agony of dilation. They made it to the hospital just in time. Death had left possibility in the air. There were flower thoughts in the night wind, memories of foliage and further work to be done, and in a miracle of concurrence, Denise pushed her way out into the world with a certain resolve.

'Is that really true, Gran?' Lucas would ask when she'd finished telling the story. 'Of course it's true!' she'd say. 'I'd never lie to a child.'

Those were happier times. Toreth saw out her last years in a nursing home in Hanwell after suffering two strokes, seven months apart. The day she moved in, she gave Lucas a wistful wet kiss and said to him from her crumpled lips, her voice slower than it had once been, 'It's hard for you, sweetheart, all alone in being a boy. Keep your eyes on a straight place.' He hugged her for a while, revising the smell of aniseed off her neck, then he and Denise had returned to the boat alone. Lucas was bereft. Denise was stoical. She closed the cabin doors, leaned against them with her fingertips joined at the small of her back, and accepted her fate with dignity.

'Well,' she said. 'It's just us now.'

'Are we staying here?' Lucas asked.

'Of course we are. Where else?'

They were forgotten, it seemed, like the steps of a dance by people who don't dance. Survival was paramount, and Denise set with increased ferocity to her work. Pretty trips along the summer canal did not come into it. Water was not freedom. The boat had not been sailed in a long time.

They lived on board with approximately two thousand spiders, who wove webs in the window frames and raised children of their own. Lucas was three inches taller than his father had been and of a vastly different physique. His legs and arms were lanky and pole-like, his knees were sharp – in his school years he was known as 'Longboy', 'Highrise', and 'Spoon-in-mug'. He was a bad eater. He liked late-night nachos and sherbet pips. Where his father's sinewy forearms had deemed him irresistible in a short-sleeved shirt, Lucas had thin wrists and elongated hands and, with his large flat feet, dancing did nothing for him. However, he took after Antoney in the eyes, which were brown and birdlike and tended to linger with intensity. He wore his hair close-shaved, bringing out a humble, greasy-nosed prettiness that retreated when the hair grew out. His smile was uncertain. A fleeting girlfriend had once told him he had nice ears.

On Tuesday and Thursday afternoons he worked for no pay at *West*, a local music magazine, but on Fridays adhered to his routine timeless drift, which always began with Scarface. After tidying up the bed he had a complicated bath in the half-size tub and applied Lynx deodorant. Then he entered the saloon through a tattered wine-coloured curtain and went over to the stereo, where Scarface waited with his deep, macabre voice. He was Lucas's favourite rapper of all time. Hailing from Houston, Texas, he was the first one, the only one, to explore the four dark walls of the mind while keeping a hold on the mellow East Coast cool. Lucas had often discussed this summation with Jake, his long-time spar, a friend of a water gypsy, but Jake was wary of showering an American rapper with too much praise, committed as he was to the advancement of the UK scene, which was currently being eclipsed by garage. Listening to Scarface was for Lucas a private glory he never got tired of. Over the years he'd compiled multitudes of tapes with his songs arranged in different orders, different progressions of rhythm and thought, sometimes combining the solo work with the earlier Geto Boys tunes as well as those of other artists, to see how they rolled together. The tapes were labelled in various colours of felt tip and arranged on a shelf according to code and category. In the back pocket of Lucas's jeans was a fold-worn piece of paper containing the lyrics, copied out by hand, to one of Scarface's songs, 'The Wall', on which he now released the play button.

It's fucked up, I'm looking at myself in the mirror
I'm seein' something scary, it's blurry make it clearer
I got a funny feeling that today will be the day . . .

The music filled the space and bounced off the timber walls. Like the bed, the saloon was also divided into two. Here on the left was where Lucas lounged on his giant Moroccan floor cushion, there on the right was where Denise would sit later when she got home from work, in Toreth's side-split bluebell armchair. At one time their mother had also occupied this chair (Denise had memories of sitting here on her lap as a very small child). On a mantel next to the chair, below the spidery window, was a photograph of Carla at the age of twenty-one, a close-up beauty with a narrow face and enormous eyes – 'eyes big enough to walk across', Toreth used to say – and a mass of thick, foresty hair which she'd inherited from her father. She was looking straight into the camera with a satisfied, mischievous expression, her hand at her collarbone, revealing half-varnished, half-chipped fingernails. Lucas and Denise had grown up with this daily image of her. In private interludes, Toreth would take the photograph in her hands and kiss it, or weep over it, and for some years after Carla's death a favourite dress of hers, a scarlet, beaded flapper, had hung mournfully on the side of the cherrywood wardrobe, until Denise had one day snatched it down and thrown it inside. There had never been such mourning for Antoney. There were no pictures of him on display. Apart from Toreth's comment that he'd had 'a hat face', Lucas had had no real idea what his father looked like until he was ten, when Denise gave him a photograph to stop him asking questions. In the photograph Antoney was dancing, a handsome man with high cheekbones, barefoot and bare-chested, posed mid-motion on a parquet floor. The writing on the back said 'Shango Storm, 1968'. Lucas had been in no doubt as to where the photograph, with its bitter tree smell, had come from.

Beneath the gunwale on his side of the room were some of

Antoney's records, artists such as Beny Moré, Sam Cooke and Robert Schumann. In Denise's absence Lucas would sometimes play a scratchy old Sam Cooke song about a man who was born by a river in a little tent, and imagine Antoney soaring gracefully over the canal on Cooke's boundless velvet note. He had always been fascinated by the idea of his father being a dancer. While browsing in a bookshop once on Portobello Road he'd come across an entry about him in an out-of-print hardback called *Stage Explosions of the Sixties*. 'Antoney Matheus,' it read, 'Jamaican-born dancer and choreographer, founder and artistic director of the applauded black dance troupe The Midnight Ballet, which also featured West End star Ekow Busia.' Lucas had asked the shopkeeper many times for more information on the subject. He'd searched through the dance books, the Caribbean books, the theatre books, the video section, but there was nothing else, which in one sense he was glad about. He wanted to know more but was afraid of what he might find. He was afraid of tipping the watery balance of the known world.

Yet lately he had yearned. He wanted guidance. He was in a shaky place. He was becoming aware that something happened to you at twenty-five, when you were no longer twenty-four. He was not sure what, a kind of dismantling, a poltergeist in the mind. He stood on the left-hand side of the saloon, running his eyes over the records, the armchair, the picture of his mother and the cabin doors. Anywhere he was on the boat he bumped into his parents, and unlike Denise he could not ignore them, especially not today. What had been their conversations, here in this room? Had they been happy together, had they been secure in themselves? It sometimes felt as if they might step back on deck at any moment, she in her beaded dress, he in a trilby, and say something ordinary like, Hello, son, look how tall you are. He'd imagined it often, Antoney appearing like that and saying those exact words. He wanted to discuss with him the numbers and the years, the feeling of being braced in this decade of perplexity. At the end of this ten-year stretch was the chasm between twenty-nine and thirty, which many men have not altogether survived. What was it like for you? he wanted to ask. To sit down with his father and say, What did you do when you got here, and didn't know which way to go?

According to an article Lucas had come across in a psychology magazine last week at the Indian newsagent where he bought his sherbet pips, the mid-twenties are, for men, the most productive, decisive, daring and transformative episode of one's life, a time when the leanings engendered during childhood and education reach a point of 'hyperdefinition', which thus guides the man – intellect, body and spirit – into his intended place in the world. He commits to his career. His frame fills out. He usually finds his spouse. 'We might look at it,' wrote this Dr Glenda someone, pictured in the corner in old-fashioned glasses, 'as a brilliant, flag-flying train that comes for him just as he's ripe. But if he *misses* that train – here's the point – if for any reason he is prevented from getting on that train, this is where problems can develop, psychological problems, anxieties, depressions, that can often endure into his later life.' The doctor did not mention whether if you missed the train it came back for you at another date.

On relating this to Jake, Lucas was told, 'That's bollocks, man, train what. Flags? I bet they're talking about the Union Jack.'

'It doesn't matter what flag,' Lucas had said. 'It's about the train, innit.'

'It always matters what flag, blood.'

Jake had then gone on to give a short lecture on colour-coded nationalism. The two of them were passing a joint back and forth in his room in a shared house on Basing Street. They'd known each other since primary school, had spent many afternoons of truancy hanging out in the courtyard of a derelict church round the way.

'Look at you, though,' Lucas said to him, 'You could say you're already on it.'

'On what?'

'The train. You know where you're going, what you want, with your music and that. You've got a plan.'

At this point Jake had sat forward on his usual chair next to his decks. Lucas viewed his muscular arms, so unlike his own. 'Yeah. I've got a plan, certainly.'

'Yeah. So you're safe. You got nothing to worry about.'

'What you worrying for?'

'I'm not worried.'

'Life's short, mate.'

'That's it.' Lucas took a long pull. The smoke hit the back of his throat with a silent thud and a tiny pain. 'But some people don't have a plan. I bet Mikey didn't have a plan.'

'Mikey's Mikey,' said Jake. 'He was always on a peculiar tip. Even at school he was like that, coming out with that cultish shit – remember the stuff about the World Bank? The boy was odd.'

'Everyone's odd,' Lucas said after a pause.

'No, I mean *odd* odd.'

'It could happen to anyone, though. One day—'

'Look, star, I ain't having no white van come throw *me* in the sack. You know what they do to Negroes in those places?'

'Suppose I've already missed it,' said Lucas.

'Missed what?'

'The *train*.'

'Jeez, man, fuck the fucking train – where d'you get this stuff? People write down any old flake and a sucker like you comes along and gets jumpy . . . It's an interesting idea, though, I'll give you that. Definitely a changing time us guys are going through, but I don't see it as no train exactly. I see – what do I see? A racetrack. Yeah. A racetrack.' Jake stood and began using his arms for emphasis, walking up and down the room, the moon at the window. 'We're on the first straight, right, about a third of the way in, we're sprinting along, with shiny foreheads 'cause we're sweating. Ahead of us is the bend where it gets all

14

hairy, and everyone wants to make a mark on things before then, before we start losing the juice, you get me? But listen, Luke – this is Oprah knowledge now so listen. Every guy in that race better be looking at himself and no one else. He can't watch where he is in the race, how far he is compared to the others, because then he's gonna fall back. He's got to concentrate on his *own* stride, and sit with it. All you need, blood, is to find your *stride*, your *thing*, that thing that makes you hot, you know, whether it's the journalism, that furniture thing you were on about last month, whatever it is just *stay* with it. Don't be changing your mind every five minutes.' He put his hand out to receive the joint. 'Now, get your clueless doc to hyper-definitionite *that*.'

Jake's place was one block parallel to Portobello Road where Denise ran her stall. Lucas often ended up there after having spent the afternoon in the vicinity. When he got tired of the boat he would mosey up the towpath slope, let himself out through the gate and cross Ladbroke Grove towards one end of the long, slender market street, West London's Yellow Brick Road, where tattooists rubbed shoulders with bar staff, vinyl junkies, tramps, hostel dwellers, beauties, artists, fashionistas, babymothers, yuppies, students, film crews, tourists, fruit floggers, Caucasian Rastafarians, nuns, drug dealers, art dealers, more tourists, Buddhists, babyfathers, teenage Woolworths employees, psychotherapists, kinesiologists, transvestites, Julia Roberts, OAPs, philanthropists of the Salvation Army, poodles, crack addicts, press officers, homesick islanders, washed-up activists, and sellers of Spanish olive oil. This was where the Grove's heart beat fastest, where the clearest signs could be seen of the sweep of gentrification that was surging across the city, turning ghettos into hotspots and sending them shooting way out of the hemisphere of the average native househunter. South of the Thames this could be seen most of all in Brixton; northside it was here in the Grove, another historic riot site, bordered on the one side – Lucas's side – by Harrow Road, realm of the six

Avenues, and on the other by Holland Park, where life was somewhat shinier. A wavering architectural journey was made between each point, from old discoloured terraces and flat-roofed social housing free of stamp duty at the northern end, to shapely urban mansions with Roman pillars at the other. It was a historical distinction disregarded by pigeons.

Portobello Road was flanked in the streets leading off it by five-tiered ice cream-coloured houses and exclusive communal gardens. A rash of coffee shops was spreading along its length as if England had only just discovered the stuff, as if the return of Labour had given people more to talk about. Lucas was hopeful of the things Tony Blair might be able to do to stop the capitalists poncifying the street with their novelty boutiques and aubergine-décored teashops, their leather watering cans and expensive psychedelic toasters, useless things, the empty offerings of the practice of making money off making money. The place was losing soul, losing its integrity. It was easy to feel, a guy like him, walking along in his skullcap and worn-out Reeboks, as if he no longer belonged here. He was a rough edge, insignificant, useful only in his ethnic contribution to the area's general feel of being interesting.

Most of the time he hung out in the Tavistock Road precinct by the Westway flyover, where his skateboard had been sliced in two by a fat white boy when he was ten. The sherbet-pips newsagent was on the corner. They served the pips in a white paper bag, the traditional way, and weekday afternoons school-children were only allowed to enter the shop in pairs, the owner's nephew acting as bouncer. If not here Lucas would be further up the street outside Honest Jon's, where Jake spent a lot of time flicking through records. Jake had talent as well as drive and vision. So far in his career as a record producer he'd spawned three underground hits (one 'stolen' by a dance act from Devon), which had formed a queue of baggy-trousered rappers wanting his attention. One of these was MC Crow, another Honest Jon's flicker and Portobello hanger, who'd had flings with the tweed-skirt seller opposite Harvey's Antiques, the scented-candle girl, and the Chinese-tops woman who migrated from Camden on Saturdays. There was no denying that Lucas was quite hugely intimidated by this.

The search for Lucas's 'thing', as Jake had coined it, was what had initially brought him to seek employment at *West*, which was based on Talbot Road, a turning off Portobello with a history of soap-box protest that tended to attract these kinds of short-lived cultural ventures. They used expensive rainforest-saving paper that would prove to be their downfall. The five members of staff worked around a large, oval table and were used to listening to each other's telephone conversations. As Lucas had informed Finn, the editor, at his interview in the café down-stairs, he was suited to this kind of career because he could spend a whole day just reading magazines, you know? 'I like the lists,' he'd said, 'Have you seen the lists they do in *Touch*?' The 'Reggae Ten', the 'Hip Hop Ten', the 'Drum & Bass Ten', Trevor Nelson's 'Rhythm Nation Most Played', 'What We Listened To While We Did This Issue', 'The Touch Guide to The Real Spice Girls'. 'You should check it. They did this wicked piece on Mark Morrison once, by a guy called Darren Crosdale – have you heard of him?' Lucas was nervous. He went on to recite a clause from the article – 'languished at her Majesty's displeasure' – and to explain how just that one line had made him want to go into journalism. He used to write lyrics but he wasn't any good at it (this had indeed been confirmed by Jake, who'd implied that his similes were on the same level as Main Source's 'you treat me like a burnt piece of bacon'), so he'd thought that maybe he could write articles, reviews, whatever. 'I could do your lists.' He had many of his own, 'The Ultimate Scarface Compilation', the 'Top Ten Middle School Rappers'. When Lucas had finally stopped talking, Finn, a photographer with long hair and thick eyebrows, the son of an academic, had been tempted to ask him why he didn't just go and ask for a job at *Touch*, but he was afraid this would bring on another rambling monologue, so he'd told Lucas to come back the following Tuesday afternoon.

That was in January. Three months later his role hadn't advanced much beyond the opening of post or the fetching of doughnuts to relieve the five o'clock munchies on deadline days. Denise regularly pointed out that he was too old to be a work experience. In his defence Lucas would remind her that *West* had let him do a list, 'The Five Best Record Shops in the West'. And there was also the occasional important 'mission', further signs of a valued volunteer, a future recipient of salary. Finn sometimes sent him to Subterranea, a local nightclub, to cover gigs (usually the ones no one else wanted to do). Lucas enjoyed the feeling of being 'sent'. He might take Jake along and show off his plus-one, and during the performance he would stand close to the stage, to one side, absolutely still, studying the musicians with a sober expression and scribbling things in his notebook. He was remarkably slow in delivering his reviews. The words never came out as he wanted them to. He had to write by hand, sitting alone on his floor cushion slightly stoned, otherwise it didn't feel right. Two or three weeks later Finn would receive an A4 sheet of lined paper folded into four, providing a thoughtful, esoteric, detailed yet vague, two-hundred-word account of a gig he could no longer remember, signed at the bottom by Lucas Matheus, in green ink. Only one of these had been published. The cut-out was on the wall of the saloon, on Lucas's side.

It was *West* that had 'sent' Lucas to St Albans the day before yesterday to meet Edwin Starr. In composing his magazine, Finn tended to lean away from the commercial music scene (he despised Robbie Williams with a passion) towards the charismatically obscure, the nostalgic, the 'grainy'. Had he had more time during Lucas's interview he might have matched his applicant's enthusiasm for lists with his own for 'Where Are They Now?' features. Motown had been a mighty scene – the force of Berry Gordy, the fizz of the Supremes and Martha and the

Vandellas, the moulding of Marvin Gaye. Edwin Starr had secured his place in history during that time with his anti-Vietnam hit 'War'. And where was he now? He lived in Nottingham. He was a Butlins and Pontin's favourite, still playing up and down the country for lovers of northern soul. He and Martha were doing a reunion concert together at the Alban Arts Centre, so Finn sent his senior journalist, Melissa, to interview him before the show. Lucas was allowed to go along for the ride.

Thinking about it now, there was no reason why Edwin Starr and Antoney Matheus should have known each other. They both belonged to showbiz but different worlds thereof. Lucas didn't even remember thinking about his father on the train to St Albans on Wednesday. He was too busy being prepped by Melissa, a bleached-blonde with a charged and televistic style. 'What I do,' she'd told him, 'before I go in? I have a really strong black coffee, loads of sugar, and I say to myself, "Take it to the bridge!" right? You might want to think up your own catch-phrase' – here, another suggestion of salary – 'but that's the idea, yeah?' Antoney could not have been further from Lucas's mind, or so he thought, as he'd racked his brains for a motto of his own, eventually deciding on a line from *Things To Do In Denver When You're Dead*, which he'd seen thirty-seven times at Jake's (he and Denise did not own a TV). The line was 'For Cynthia. Do it, for Cynthia', as spoken by Christopher Walken. Melissa said he could ask one question and one question only, the rest of the time he should watch and learn. It was nothing but coincidence how Edwin had behaved towards him. He was still embarrassed at how flustered he'd become.

The Alban Arts Centre was a sterile, red-brick building in the town centre. They found Mr Starr in his dressing room, wearing a baby blue tracksuit and pumps without socks. He greeted them both with warm handshakes. Then he looked way, way up into Lucas's birdlike eyes, and he'd said to him these exact words, 'Hey, look how tall you are,' followed by a laugh.

19

A sweat broke out on the back of Lucas's neck. He pictured his father stepping onto Silver's deck with his ghostly feet. Throughout the interview he was convinced Edwin was glancing at him in a curious way. The singer talked about the sixties, what a great time they'd all had back then, a time without limits, where it seemed as if anything was possible, good and bad. Melissa asked him whether he'd known Jimi Hendrix and he said he had, Jimi was a nice guy, one of those freaks of nature. Lucas had calmed down by now and he'd listened, hypnotised, enjoying the older man's sweet and hefty smile, the ease and authority with which he spoke. He began to imagine his father moving through that world. Had it felt like that to him, that life was limitless? Would Antoney be anything like Edwin if he were alive today? Would he still inhabit dressing rooms, wear tracksuits? Would he be kind like this? Just as he was asking himself these questions, Edwin had then paused mid-sentence and said, 'You look so familiar, son. Do I know you from somewhere?' At this point Lucas had dropped his pen.

A deep, shaky breath. Melissa gave him the sign that this was a good time for his question. Peering into the older man's face, the soft eyes and moist skin, feeling foolishly certain that there was some connection between them, he asked, with great trepidation, behind this one question all the others waiting: 'Mr Starr. Did you ever come across, back then – did you know a guy – have you . . .' Melissa ruffled the pages of her notebook. Edwin continued smiling sweetly. '. . . Have you ever heard of a dance troupe called – the Midnight Ballet?'

Edwin's face immediately lit up. Lucas was ready to bawl. Edwin put his hands on his chubby thighs, about to speak. But then he looked away, as if surprised by some other thing. Uncertainty swung to and fro on his face. He scratched his ear, patted his thighs, and looked back at Lucas. 'You know, son?' he'd said at last. 'I don't believe I have.'

*

Lucas now stepped out onto the bow. The noon sun was encased in cloud, the temperature warm. Scarface was prowling through a beautiful track sampled on the Commodores' 'Easy (Like Sunday Morning)', but Lucas's mood remained unsettled. Even out here he was claustrophobic. The cherrywood wardrobe rattled inside his head. He could hear its creaks, smell that bitter smell. Yesterday he'd visited the bookshop again, and had stared at the Antoney Matheus entry for a ridiculous length of time, until he could see faces in the loops of the letters. He didn't want to believe his dad was wicked. He'd never wanted to go along with the general consensus that he was a bad man, boozy, neglectful, his grandmother's subtle insults, Denise's rare echoes. 'He was no good, all right?' she'd told him in a heated moment when they were children. 'He didn't try and look out for us after Mum died. As far as I'm concerned we never had a dad.' It was too easy, too closed. He wanted to believe that Antoney was good.

On weekday mornings before school Lucas used to stand out here on the bow and watch a tall, broad-shouldered man walking along Ladbroke Grove, holding the hand of a little boy. He would never forget them. The boy was in uniform and carrying a satchel. They'd looked like each other, more than in their faces. Even though the boy took quick, fidgety steps, with the occasional bounce, and the man's strides were calm and extended, there was a point at which they'd met and reflected one another. They were two different stops on a single journey. The man had a proud disposition and long, neat dreadlocks, always tied back. He would pass himself on to the boy, who wore the beginnings of this pride, suggested in the way he frequently looked up at his father. Lucas used to gaze at them until they were out of sight, imagining himself in the boy's place. He found it difficult to accept, in the light of their perfection, that the man might not want the boy, that there could come a situation where he might not look out for him, unless there was something that prevented him doing so.

21

In a private drawer in the bedroom, where he kept the photograph of Antoney dancing, there was a gift, a toy bus made of wood, which he'd had since he was a baby. It was a present from his father. Giving it to Lucas was Toreth's single act of kindness in the sketching of Antoney's character. This was what made him want to believe.

Sitting on the bank as usual at the bottom of Denise's garden was the yellow-eyed cat that lived somewhere nearby. The cat and Lucas were used to one another, united in their lives of non-pressing business. They stared each other down as the sun strained to come out from behind the clouds. Then Lucas looked southward, beyond the two dark discs of the gasworks, beyond the vast expanse of railtrack bound for Paddington, to the twin tower blocks on the horizon that, unbeknown to him, his father had helped build in the 1960s. Lucas had no knowledge of this small piece of family history, but he often imagined himself living in one of those blocks should he ever escape the water – he'd go somewhere high up. Closer to where he stood, running across the Grand Union, was the Ladbroke Grove Canal Bridge that at the end of every summer bore the glittery march of carnival kings and queens. Denise's garden was a neat harlequin pause next to the boat on the upward sloping bank. She grew tulips, her hallmark flower, and delphiniums and roses. There was a temperamental pear tree against the back wall, a high, cold, top-spiked wall, stretching all the way to the other end of the cemetery.

And here was the greatest reminder of all. In these fifty-six acres of undulating land, in this sprawling mass of epitaphs and bones that had been called on in 1833 to relieve the overcrowding of London's churchyards; here, on the other side of the wall from where Lucas and Denise ate, slept, bickered, gardened, and took complicated half-size baths serviced by a cistern they had to refill every month from the towpath tap, here was their mother, their dead mother, buried beneath limestone in a cluster of other graves, adjacent to a family plot of Ethiopian monarchs.

Denise laid flowers here fortnightly. Lucas visited less often – his proximity made it seem unnecessary. At one point in her life, Carla might also have wanted to be buried like the Ethiopians, in the communal way, with Antoney lying next to her, but she was very much alone in her plot. There was no epitaph in this necropolis for Antoney. His was elsewhere, in some other place. It had always troubled Lucas that he did not know where his father's grave was.

Usually he managed to block out the cemetery, like the ticking clock and the creaks in the walls and the rattling of the wardrobe. But not today. Today, when he remembered it was there, with its one presence and other absence, it sent him a little wild. It was a loud, vivid thought that dangled in the house of Scarface, and then Scarface spoke back to it. 'He greets his father with his hands out, glad to be the man's child.' Lucas turned his head towards the music. As he did so the sun escaped the clouds and the deck brightened. He'd heard the song many times. He knew every last word, but he'd never heard the words like this. Scarface went up and down the stairs of the song with his deep voice, sometimes three at a time, sometimes jumping right down to the bottom and walking slowly up. Lucas went with him:

> *So you standing in the tunnel of eternal light*
> *And you see the ones you never learn to love in life*
> *Make the choice let it go but you can back it up*

'If you ready, close your eyes, and we can set it free.' The yellow-eyed cat walked back in the direction of Harlesden. A bird shadow passed quickly across the surface of the bow. Lucas was held in an instant of pure clarity, in which all his questions faded to a single point of entry. The sun was warm and spurring on his neck. He wasn't scared any more. It was time for change. With no more hesitation, as if ejected from a very long pause, without thought of vapours or nightmares or

23

Denise, he ducked through the cabin doorway and went with feverish steps back into the saloon. He threw aside the wine-coloured curtain and entered the bedroom. He did not linger this time or peep inside. He stepped up to that old cherrywood thing. He lifted its oxidising brass pendant in his hot hand, and he pulled, hard.

2

It started with Katherine. She came and split the twentieth century in half. He saw her under the sea with ribbons in her hair, and after that he was not the same.

It was a windy day in March 1951 and in the afternoon Antoney took the Goldtooth bus to Kingston with his father, Mr Rogers. They were going to the Carib Theatre to see an African-American dance company. Mr Rogers had acquired their tickets through a deal with a fellow non-profit-making saxophone player and he allowed Antoney to hold them for the duration of the journey. He held them with both hands, thumb and first two fingers, his legs swinging forwards and backwards with the movement of the bus, which went upwards, upwards then downwards into the city. It was a winding mountainous road with bush valleys and pimento trees on one side and nothing but precipice on the other. Some of the passengers preferred to look down into their laps rather than out of the window, but not Antoney.

He had been to the theatre once before with his mother, Florence, to see a *Jack and the Beanstalk* pantomime, but because he'd shown indifference she had never taken him back. He was too old for pantomimes now – he was nine. Mr Rogers understood this too. Katherine Dunham (she sounded like something expensive) was a world-famous dancer and a Broadway star. She'd worked in Hollywood movies, had her own touring company, and was renowned for bringing African and Caribbean dances to the stage in grand style for the first time. She was also an anthropologist, so all in all she was not a waste of time. 'She nice-looking too,' Mr Rogers was saying. But more importantly than this, she was out of the ordinary, like Mr Rogers himself. He was a lithe, effeminate man with extremely slender hands and a prettyboy face, who always wore a flower in his hat. He was sometimes here and sometimes not and everyone, including Florence, called him Mr Rogers.

Antoney hoped they'd be sitting near the front. He declared that he'd like to sit right in the front row but Mr Rogers replied that these were not the best seats. 'A few rows back is better,' he said. 'You get it better from a distance. Or if you get a balcony you luckier still. From there you can see the side of the stage, into the wings, and if you crane your neck you can watch their faces when they're waiting to come on. That is a fascinating thing.'

'Where did you see that?' Antoney asked.

Mr Rogers tipped up his chin, trying to remember. 'Ah, some while back, some place in Trinidad I think it was.'

Antoney was not generally a talkative child. He'd already decided that if he ever had to choose between a body and a voice he would choose to have a body. However, he was often talkative when he was with his father.

'How many places you been to, Mr Rogers?'

A lot of places, he didn't count them all. America, Mexico, of course Cuba. Mr Rogers was born in Cuba and had moved to Jamaica with his aunt when he was little. His mother had stayed behind. She lived in a town far in the east called Baracoa. 'If you stay in one place for too long you start to dry out,' he told Antoney. 'You need a little stretch of sea between the years or the months.'

They ate from a bag of stringy Number 11 mangoes. On one side the wind blew backwards two aimless billygoats. On the other side the cliff displayed the heavens.

'Mr Rogers?' Antoney said without shyness. 'Will you be around more when you and Mama get married?'

'I believe so,' his father replied. Antoney's legs swung higher at this answer.

'And once you both married, what happens when you need a little stretch of sea?'

Mr Rogers became thoughtful. He took time picking a mango string out of his teeth. There was a wide gap between the front two, as there was between Florence's front two. This, according to Antoney, was the evidence that his parents were meant for each other.

'The way I see it is this,' his father said at length. 'The sea must always be available to you, no matter what the circumstance. If it's in your nature to swim then you must swim, otherwise you liable to fall sick. Your mother knows what I mean. Marriage is not a jail, son.'

'No,' Antoney agreed. He'd seen a jail once. It had hardly any windows and was made of unpainted brick, definitely not the same thing as a marriage. 'You're right,' he said.

The Goldtooth bus was driven by a man called Juicy. His right arm hung out of the open window next to him and he leaned with relish into each perilous swing along the turning road. No one ever asked him to slow down. There was no point. He was lord of the Goldtooth. He began the long descent into Kingston, where the dancers, in the warm back rooms of the Carib, were getting ready.

Or perhaps it started earlier than this. Perhaps it started, as dreams often do, in bed, in a cryptic hour of the night.

Two years before Katherine, Antoney dreamt that he could fly. Probably it was a very ordinary flying dream – you are suddenly and amazingly airborne – no different from anyone else's flying dream. But what makes one flying dream stand out from another is the response of the dreamer. Antoney did not simply wake up the next morning and begin another day unchanged. He could not forget it, what it felt like.

It was easy. Wings were not necessary. There he was, in the bendy crispy world of a dream, standing in the sitting room of their little tangerine-fronted house in Annotto Bay, St Mary, deep in the Jamaican countryside, and he heard a voice that was not as such a voice, more of a tiny arrival in his brain. It said to him, Let's try this. He began to wave his hands at his sides. Then he applied a trace more effort, felt a fluttering sensation in the soles of his feet, and sure enough, up he went, a strong-armed boy already, adrift and at ease just beneath the ceiling. He laughed and said to the voice that was helping him, I'm flying! I'm flying! Look at me!

The dream recurred, increasing in size and stature. He went beyond the house and rose up higher than palmtops, as high as he wanted for as long as he wanted, to shift and turn, to glide and dip, arms outstretched and body tipped forwards like a real sky creature. It was blissful up here, hotter and cooler at the same time. He was spacious and more and less than a boy.

Antoney took these dreams very seriously. They were real to him. He acquired from them a distrust of the concept of the impossible. It was all a trick, he realised. Don't believe it. Look around the corners of tricks.

In the waking hours he searched for ways of staying off the ground. He ran instead of walked, jumped from this place to that and exhausted the old rope swing across the mud pond. He climbed ladders. He languished high in trees. He wondered whether he would fly a plane one day. These were the best things: to run, leap, float, turn. It was difficult for him to sit down on an indoor stationary object such as a chair for extended periods of time, like in the classroom (this, to his mother's chagrin, was reflected in his grades). He just didn't like to do it. He preferred to sit outside on the grassy slope near Miss Enid's shop, where one day while looking skyward, as was his habit, he saw a prancing red and white kite with bows on its tail. He watched it for a long time as it looped

28

and spiralled, he watched it dance, until it made a quick diagonal exit into the trees.

He went immediately to find his mother. He found her walking back along the path from Mr Chambers's place in the hills where she did housework. This would be followed in the late afternoon by a shift in the bar next to Miss Enid's shop, where Irish Moss, a supposed aphrodisiac made of seaweed, was a popular drink; the seaweed was collected from the straggly coast that ran the length of the town, then washed and hung up to dry on the market stalls and shopfronts.

Antoney went up to his mother and said, 'Mama, I want to be a kite.'

Florence did not understand. She was stern with her son and didn't like to indulge in vague or dim-witted conversation with him. It encouraged him along a deviant, beckoning path. 'What do you mean you want to be a kite?'

He skipped about her, making her tired. It was Eliza's fault, the way he was. Eliza was the name of the hurricane on the eve of which Antoney was born. She was not a particularly calamitous hurricane, one or two trees and fences had been felled, but Florence remembered how she'd felt holding the infant in her arms as Eliza had charged through. What a terrible vulnerability a child was, nothing but a leaf in the eye of a storm! Florence believed there was a little bit of Eliza left over in Antoney now – she'd got inside him and whisked him up like fritter mix and that was why he couldn't keep still.

His arms swung to the left then to the right. Two jumps and another skip. 'I want to be on the air,' he told her strangely, 'blowing in the wind. I want to be dressed in all the bright colours.'

'That's nonsense. Come here, boy, that's wotless talk.' She gave him her bag to carry and they walked up the path towards the house. 'You be something better,' she said. 'You be a doctor or a pharmacist. Get yourself a decent living. That's why you have to work harder in school.'

Antoney made a wrinkled, fruit-like shape with his face that his mother didn't see. He was noticing that there are two kinds of people in the world: those who have flying dreams, and those who don't.

Florence's wedding dress was waiting beneath a plastic cover in the tangerine house. It was her aunt Ivy's dress, used twenty years before to unite her with a local mason. They had endured. They still lived in his place by the river and Aunt Ivy still cooked ackee and saltfish for his breakfast on Sunday mornings before church.

It was an olden-white dress with lace at the hem. At twenty-seven, a tardy bride, Florence was smaller than Ivy had been at her age so the dress had to be taken in. It was not the dress Florence would have chosen for herself if she'd lived in a big house with a glass door in Stony Hill or Fort George. But she didn't, at least not for now. For now the most important thing was to walk to the altar with Mr Rogers and marry him. Then the rest could take place.

She believed him, secretly, about the saxophone. Florence was the kind of woman who seemed like a different kind of woman from the kind she was. Where it seemed, even to her, that she wanted one thing, she wanted another. She wanted the unknown where she thought she wanted safety. She wanted hot jerk chicken when she thought she wanted mild chicken curry. She wanted a man who wore a flower in his hat, played a saxophone all day in his cousin's backyard and walked with a blasé sideways slant, while she thought she wanted someone sensible. Thus whenever Mr Rogers told her that one day that saxophone of his was going to make him rich, she believed him but expressed otherwise. She told him he was dreaming. He told her about the jazzmen making big bucks, maybe he could be one of them. You have a son, she said, you need to take care of your family. He replied with America, with England, that there was a better life elsewhere than the two-mile, banana-leafed length of Annotto Bay.

Florence didn't know about England, but Stony Hill would be nice.

After years of stalling, Mr Rogers had finally made his motions towards a matrimonial life. He hadn't proposed as such. It would be more accurate to say that he had agreed. It was a starry night, he was rum-dizzy, Florence, in a pretty slip, was standing in the doorway that led out to the veranda and one of her arms was raised up near her face and folded around the doorframe, her eyes darker than he'd ever seen them, she smiled with that same-size gap as his and said, 'Mr Rogers, I've missed you. Why you don't come lie down and put your feet by my feet?' Mr Rogers had a calm and beautiful feeling then beneath the rum-stars, that this girl would always be this girl, that with this girl he could go and then return and she would always say something like this, put your feet by my feet, and then it had struck him what a good and perfect thing the steady family unit was, what a joy it was to have someone to return to, what a fine son they'd made together, how sweet and rich it would be to people the hills of St Mary (and beyond) with more little Antoneys. Fifty minutes later, with his feet by her feet and his hips still pressed upon her hips, he sighed into the warm right ear of his woman, 'You are my safe and always one', to which Florence had whispered back a not unfamiliar suggestion, 'Well, Mr Rogers, we might get married.' And this time Mr Rogers said yes.

Two weeks from now, Florence would put on that old white dress. She'd put on her one silver bracelet. She would wear a flower in her hat like her safe and always one, and together they would face the cross.

The Carib Theatre was the largest building in Jamaica. It was egg-shaped and designed to give an impression of what it might feel like to stand at the bottom of the Caribbean Sea. All over the walls and ceiling there were West Indian sea creatures, starfish and barracuda, feathery crinoids and fireworms, an

31

enormous turtle beside a flat-eyed peacock flounder, even a shark. Antoney imagined it would be a very good setting for a flying dream. As they sat in their seats amid all the noise waiting for Katherine, he asked Mr Rogers not for the first time whether he'd ever had such a dream.

'Of course,' his father said as usual. 'More than once.'

They were four rows from the front. The Goldtooth bus had pulled into Kingston with all passengers intact, and on the walk to the theatre Mr Rogers had tipped his hat at passers-by. It always seemed to Antoney that his father was a famous man. Everywhere he went people of all ages seemed to know him. The smartly dressed women who worked in Woolworths had waved at him as they'd passed by. Today the flower in Mr Rogers's hat was red with an orange centre. His shirt was a dark shade of purple, with a shine around the collar-edge. Antoney was wearing a pair of navy slacks (his best pair, pressed to death by Florence) with a red shirt that, although slightly too small for him, worked well with his nimble, ripening waist. They made quite a sight. Antoney had taken his father's good looks, the lush and definite mouth, the sculpture in the cheeks and the roguish eyebrows. As for the eyes – both Antoney and Mr Rogers, they had the thinking eyes of sparrows.

The posters outside the theatre confirmed for Antoney that Katherine Dunham was indeed a fine-looking lady, with good posture. She was pictured mid-dance with her hips bumped playfully against her male partner, her arms swung out in the other direction. But nothing could really prepare him for the impression she was about to make on him. Mr Rogers having his connections, they jumped the queue at the entrance and went right in. This was a far cry from *Jack and the Beanstalk*, which had taken place beneath a zinc shelter in Richmond. Antoney loved the theatre's nooks and secret recesses, the big echoey space. He loved the bold decoration on the walls and the hum of anticipation. He had the feeling that a whole other earth could exist here, that you could be one thing when you reached the door and another when you went inside. It was like magic, a cave full of magic, a spellbound place. Throughout his life thereafter, whether he was in London or Paris or Copenhagen, it would be just like this: you come to the theatre, you enter that smell that is the same in every theatre in the world, a smell of possibility and breath held in, and everything earthly falls away.

He did not share these impressions with Mr Rogers, who carried on shaking the hands and tipping his hat like the Humphrey Bogart of Kingston. He remained quiet, watching the seats fill up with the chattering crowd. People seemed less real in here than they did outside, more like children, even the older folks. They all looked as if they were pretending.

The stage was withheld by a heavy scarlet curtain with black tassels at the floor. As darkness fell swiftly outside, the dim lamps around the sides of the auditorium added more suspense to what was beyond the curtain. There was an occasional movement from behind it that excited Antoney. He wanted to touch the mysterious velvet.

'When will it start?' he said.

'It soon come,' said his father. 'Be patient and wait.'

Mr Rogers crossed his legs, leaned back in his chair, held up his chin and placed his slender hands one above the other on his lap. Antoney did the same.

A few moments before the lights began to descend, Mr Rogers leaned over and said, 'Hey, I might have an avenue to get us backstage afterwards. What you think?'

'No,' said Antoney in alarm. 'I don't want to go backstage!'

'How you mean? You don't want to meet Miss Dunham?'

'No, Mr Rogers.'

His father moved back again into his chair as the lights fell. 'Let's see,' he muttered. 'You might.'

The auditorium was completely silent now, as though someone had taken a wand and hushed it. When the curtain rose Antoney's stomach rose with it. He disappeared, he and

Mr Rogers, the rest of the audience, and what remained was an already moving stage gently lit by glowing footlights. To the beating of drums and robust singing a host of dancers swept and side-stepped across the stage, the women in long white dresses, the men bare-chested in white knee-length pants. The central point of focus was a tall and powerful-looking woman with a large striped ribbon on her head that flapped about as she danced. She had the brightest face Antoney had ever seen. She wore her power all over her, not just in her face, but in her legs and arms, her bobbing shoulders, her hands which made careful shapes. She had enthrallingly bright eyes that promised themselves and the world that they would always be bright, and a lovely, obstinate mouth. Mr Rogers whispered to Antoney in the dark, 'That is Katherine Dunham.'

For the entire performance Antoney could not take his eyes off the stage. He was enamoured of the beauty and confidence of the male dancers, brown and agile like him, the shuffling, sliding and skipping of their feet. He hunted himself within them, eventually spotting himself, with a gasp of delight, during a fight scene in which two men took long, running jumps over one another, making fast flights and riveting tumbles and spinning each other around. But Katherine was the one he followed most devotedly. He watched her move, sometimes like a ballerina, sometimes like the folk dances he already knew, other times both at once. He watched her roll her neck and send up her legs. He saw the constant ripple in her tight torso. She wore a white, ruffled dress with a broader skirt than those of the other women, and dipping this way and that she held the skirt between her fingers so that she gradually began to look like the wind, like she could blow two billygoats backwards. Watching her dance made him feel urgent, that he had something imperative to do. He wanted to stand up right then and do it, but he didn't know what it was. This woman, he felt, was of a greater element than he was, even than Mr Rogers was. She was a wizard.

Antoney learnt an important fact in this instant, a fact that would stay with him always. He learnt that dancing can make you more than yourself.

Katherine and her troupe performed a number of different pieces. It was dramatic dancing, with stories inside it. The story Antoney liked most of all was of a boy who turned into a serpent, in a piece called 'Shango'. While killing a white cock during a sacrifice to Shango, the boy was possessed by an evil serpent spirit. He hissed and slithered about the stage in a snake-like groove, until he was possessed by Shango himself, at which point his movements became stormy and fierce. In the seduction of young boys by superheroes, here Shango was, rolling his head, stamping his feet, thrashing his arms with tremendous strength, sending his congregation into a frenzy. At the climax of the piece the boy stood on the altar with outstretched arms, receiving worship. Antoney was mesmerised. He wanted to be that strong, that fearless. He wanted to take a serpent into his power, and for the people to call out his name.

'So,' Mr Rogers said, 'you want to meet her?'

The audience was rising and filing out. The curtains were closed. Antoney took some hazy travelling seconds to relocate himself and arrived back at his father.

'What's wrong with you, boy? You look like you been boxed in the head.'

'I'm not sure I want to meet her, Mr Rogers.'

'You look to me like you do.'

'She doesn't know me. I might get embarrassed.'

'Look, I know for a fact she's a very nice lady – just make yourself big and come.'

They went out to the lobby where Mr Rogers found the theatre manager, through whom he sometimes managed to arrange shows. He was an enormous man with matching sunglasses. Mr Rogers told him that his son wanted to meet Miss Dunham.

'My boy likes to move about a lot,' he said, 'same as those dancers there.' The manager laughed and said, yes, he had a boy like that too.

They had to wait for a long while, standing in the lobby by the door to the auditorium. The lobby emptied; it got late. Antoney began to worry that he might not meet Katherine after all, at which point he became desperate to meet her. All his fear was upstaged by one crucial question he needed to ask her. If he didn't get to ask this question, he wouldn't know what to do next.

At last the theatre manager, still wearing his sunglasses, led them through a side door into the backstage area of the Carib. He and Mr Rogers chatted and laughed (how could Mr Rogers be so casual and limey at a time like this?) while Antoney looked around him at the gloomy dark space. It was the back of magic. This was the place, if you made a magic trick, you might come to get your rabbit or your tall black hat. This was where you could make the trick so that the lady would not be sawn in half. It was extremely untidy, a dusty, winding, tricksy kind of a place, with smoky black walls and random objects lying around – musical instruments, ladders, a straw hat, an English tea-dress on a hanger. It lacked completely the grandeur of the auditorium, but it was the thing that made the auditorium possible.

The theatre manager talked about how Miss Dunham liked her dressing room to be a certain way, she liked to be surrounded by fabrics, fruit, books and such, so he'd had a bit of a job preparing for her. She was a woman who knew exactly what she wanted and expected to get it. This talk only increased Antoney's trepidation. As they neared her dressing room, located by the bottom of a shallow flight of stairs, he had a mind to run off. There were loud voices coming from within. Before he could make his exit, having forgotten all about his question, the door was swiftly opened by Katherine Dunham herself.

'Did you see my slipper through there, an orange slipper?'

She turned back into the room, which was full of flowers, and crouched down next to a wicker trunk that said 'K. DUNHAM' on the side.

'Miss Dunham,' said the manager, 'Mr Rogers is here to see you.'

'Mr Rogers,' she murmured. 'Mr Rogers? . . . I don't believe I—' She stood up, almost as tall as Mr Rogers, and took a good look at him. 'I'm really not certain where we met, but you do look familiar. Was it back home somewhere? Hold it, here, I'll wear these.' She bent to put on a pair of mules, sighing with relief as she did so.

There were three other people in the room, two women and a man. They were leaning against the dressing counter, wide-shouldered and supremely confident, their collarbones gleaming. They dropped their chatter and studied the visitors.

The room was indeed draped with vivid fabrics and lush hangings, as if the experience of the stage was meant to continue when it was over. At one end of the dressing counter was a basket of fresh Jamaican fruit. Mr Rogers spoke to Katherine all ease and charming smile; he mentioned the saxophone and a show in Baltimore, and whether she remembered him or not it didn't seem to matter after a while. It was clear that she liked him, all of them liked him, and Antoney realised that this was why his father was famous – he had a gift of personality. The room filled up with voices and laughter. At first Antoney tried not to look directly at Katherine, but she had such a warm and gentle manner it was difficult to stay terrified of her. He raised his head, looked up into her marvellous bright-eyed face, and viewed her seriously. She seemed smaller than she had on stage.

'And who is this fine young man?' she said.

Mr Rogers touched Antoney's back, pushing him forward. 'This my son, Antoney.'

Katherine sat down on her trunk. She'd changed out of her

costume into fishnet stockings and a silky mid-sleeved dress. She leaned towards him. 'Well, Antoney,' she said. '*You* are an early beauty.'

He was not entirely sure what she meant by this but he thanked her anyway.

'Did you like the show?'

'Yes, thank you, Miss Dunham. It was better than *Jack and the Beanstalk*.'

Katherine laughed and held her hand briefly across his face. 'That's good to know. Do you live in Kingston, Antoney?'

'No. St Mary, in the country. You can get a bus there from here.'

'Ah.'

She looked warmly and frankly into his eyes, giving him courage. This was his chance. As his father had often told him, a chance might happen only once. So he took a deep breath and reached for his voice, which seemed to have slipped down the back of his throat. He found it eventually, though it was quieter than he knew it to be. 'Miss Dunham?' he said.

'Yes?'

'What would I have to do to – to be a dancer . . . like you?'

Antoney felt his father's eyes on him for a brief, intense moment. The other conversations in the room carried on, not much had changed, but he felt as if he'd suddenly lost his clothes. He wished he could go with Katherine somewhere secluded, just the two of them, and talk about this alone.

Katherine simply smiled. She raised one foot up on the trunk and hugged her leg. She spoke clearly, as if used to the question, pausing at times to allow him to absorb what she was saying.

'It takes dedication, Antoney, and a lot of hard work. Do you understand the word dedication? . . . Good. Because you have to be dedicated. You must dance every day, whenever you can, to keep your body strong. Listen, sit down here. Would you really like to be a dancer?' He nodded vigorously. 'In that case,'

38

she said, 'you have to be so dedicated, that there is hardly *anything* more important to you than your dancing. Now, that's really not an easy thing to do. Sometimes you'll get tired, things will be difficult and you'll feel like giving up. You're still a growing boy yourself, so you'll know what I mean when I say that you have to treat the dancing like something that is growing inside you, like a child, or a plant. You give it food and water. Do you understand?'

'Yes,' he said.

She paused, and something sad went across her mouth. 'Most of all,' she concluded, 'you must not be fearful or lose your way.'

They sat there on the trunk talking for a long time, until it seemed as though they were alone after all. Katherine told him that she'd come to Jamaica years ago to do research and had spent time living in Accompong, the Maroon village in the Cockpit Country. She'd also been to Haiti, Cuba and Martinique, the latter, it turned out, the origin of the male fighting dance Antoney told her he'd especially liked during the show. She'd been to so many places, she said, had seen so many different kinds of dancing that she felt she still had a lifetime's worth of dancing to get through, and still more of it to see and collect. Antoney held on to her every word, another important question formulating in his mind.

'Miss Dunham,' he ventured, 'who is Shango?'

'Shango? You liked him? Lots of people like him.'

Shango, she explained, was a very powerful god, an Orisha, from Yoruba folklore, who still had many worshippers around the world in places such as Cuba, Haiti and Brazil. He was originally an earthbound deity but his people had got fed up with him one day and he'd risen up into the sky to become the god of thunder and lightning. During slavery Africans were not allowed to practise their own religions, so they disguised their gods as Catholic saints – Shango was St John the Baptist. He was fierce and determined, with an iron will. His signature colour was red, and he carried with him a double-headed axe that defined his thrashing, menacing dance. He really wasn't someone you'd want to mess around with, Katherine said.

'So he's still alive?'

'Oh, yes, sure,' she laughed. 'Some say yes, then others just don't care.'

By now they were sitting very close together. Antoney was no longer aware of the other people in the room, including Mr Rogers. Katherine pressed one hand to the base of his spine, the other palm down underneath his chin, lifting it. 'The top of your head shall touch clouds,' she said. 'Straight and tall. There. Yes. I can see you're going to be mighty strong one day.'

Sitting there next to her in his red shirt, he knew she was right. She added, almost in a whisper, 'I think you'll make a fine Shango.'

The two-mile stretch of Annotto Bay was dotted with fourteen churches, the oldest of these the red-brick Baptist church on Main Street that slaves had destroyed during the 1831 Christmas rebellion. In the process of rebuilding, the stained glass windows had been fitted by hand and clauses from the scriptures inscribed into yellow trim along the walls. A brown-haired, blue-eyed Jesus looked down at his disciples, who all agreed that it was high time Florence and Mr Rogers were wed.

They were getting ready, the congregation. They were humming and hemming and making jerk. Antoney was lectured by Florence. 'Don't jump, don't run and *don't skip*. You walk *slowly* down the aisle behind myself and Mr Rogers, you hear?'

'Yes, Mama.'

She slipped into Aunt Ivy's dress, which was still a tad loose at the hips. Antoney stood behind her and pulled up the zip. They paused before the mirror. 'You look nice, Mama,' he said.

He was wearing the navy trousers he'd worn the day of Katherine, this time with a stiff, freshly ironed white shirt.

Mr Rogers was at his friend Martin's place getting ready separately. They'd arranged that he would meet them at the church door.

On the way back from Kingston the night of Katherine, Mr Rogers had put his arm around Antoney on the back seat of another bus, this one empty (its name, Rat Attack). They'd had the whole bus to themselves because it was in the power of Mr Rogers to find a bus-driver friend who was going that way and didn't mind driving them back to St Mary in the middle of the night. They went round and round, up and down the mountain terrain. They could see nothing out of the window but night, a milky half-moon that disappeared and came back. They talked about Mr Rogers's mother, which was something Mr Rogers rarely spoke about because she wasn't well. Sometimes he would talk about Cuba itself, in short, geographical details, about shade, for instance, how you could walk from one end of the island to another under the shade of trees, or about distance, that on a clear night, if you stood at the bottom of Cuba and looked out to sea, it was possible to see the lights of Jamaica.

But tonight Mr Rogers wanted to talk about his mother. She was a quiet and feline lady. What does feline mean? said Antoney. She was like a cat, said Mr Rogers. She moved so softly, she hardly disturbed the dust. She'd lived for a while in Havana, which was in the west of Cuba, but now she lived in Baracoa, her home town. There was no road to Baracoa. You couldn't get there by bus. It was a cut-off town cradled by mountains and shark-infested ocean. Mr Rogers's voice had become low and hesitant. Antoney had not heard this tone in him before. He told Antoney that he couldn't remember the sound of his mother's voice any more, partly because it had been such a quiet voice, but also because she rarely used it. While she was in Havana, she had fallen in love with a seaman. This seaman had loved the sea so much. Whenever he set sail, Mr Rogers's mother would walk up and down the Malecón, the Havana sea wall, waiting for him to return. Then one day he did not return. She walked up and down, up and down the Malecón for seven days, in a long skirt and a pair of old shoes, looking out for her love. She was carrying his child. Every day she walked until the sun fell down and the night creatures flew up, and on the seventh day, she sat down on the stone wall and took off her shoes . . .

Mr Rogers trailed off there. Antoney was close to sleep, waiting with his grandmother for the seaman to return. When he realised that Mr Rogers had stopped speaking, or perhaps that he could no longer hear him speaking, it was too late. He and his grandmother lay on their backs on the pale wall, then they closed their eyes and rolled off into the sea.

Florence and Antoney arrived at the church at eleven o'clock. Florence, with a flower in her hat, held her bouquet of orchids with one hand, her skirt with the other, and they mounted the two circular steps to the door. Inside, the congregation was gathering, fanning themselves, straightening their children's skirts, finding the best seats, discussing all the promise and future of the Rogers family unit. To Antoney the church was an unsettling place. It was a jumping-up, squeezy-eyed, weeping and wailing, handclapping place where he'd seen Aunt Ivy lose a hold of herself, and now, as they came in sight of the waiting crowd, a dreadful feeling came over him. There was Aunt Ivy, just inside the doorway, bundling Florence up into her arms. There was all of Annotto Bay, from here to Boot and Stocking Bridge, in their best Sunday clothes. There was the polished wooden cross to which his mother and Mr Rogers would walk. Someone was warming up a tambourine. Antoney turned his back and stood outside on the step. He put his hands in his pockets, watching a tight grey cloud make its way towards the sun.

Behind him his mother said, 'Antoney, come here and stand next to me. Your cousin wants to talk to you.'

As he stood next to Florence, nodding and not quite listening, he imagined his father walking along Main Street towards the church. He was wearing his black shoes and a white shirt the same as Antoney's. The flower in his hat was yellow. He was about to come into view. He would stand at the bottom of the steps and look up, ready as he ever could be, into the face of his imminent wife. 'Florence,' he would say, 'you look better than your seventeenth year,' then he'd stride up to her, take her arm, and the walk would commence. It was simple.

'You see your father coming?' said Florence.

He went back out on the step. He looked up and down Main Street and came back inside. 'No, Mama.'

She smiled. There was just a hint of worry in her eyes.

'I told him not to be late.'

She resumed her conversation with her older sister, though she had less to say and glanced at intervals towards the open door. Antoney stayed behind her, one foot in and one foot out of the church.

As time went on, Florence also moved nearer to the door. Her face began to close in and she receded further from conversation. She asked Antoney one more time, 'You see your father coming?' They waited and waited. They waited until they were both standing on the round, shallow step outside the church, their backs to the congregation. The voices behind them were becoming hushed. Florence held the orchids with both hands in a double fist, her elbows sticking out. She was stone still, like the bricks of the jail walls, unable to walk forward down the steps, unable to go back into the church.

Aunt Ivy came out shiny-cheeked in her floral suit to speak to the unfolding event. 'Oh Lord, Florence,' she said. 'If Mr Rogers is a righteous man he is coming at this minute and he better beg for forgiveness when his eyes look pon you. He is late, very late, still not *too* late. But so help me, God, if he doesn't come soon he'll never be able to show his face in Annotto Bay again. Wait.' She leaned back into the church and plucked out a lanky nephew. 'Joseph, here. Run now to your uncle Martin's house and check they done left, and hurry up, boy, we've waited too much already.'

'Ivy,' said Florence, lifting her head, 'Joseph, stay where you are. Nobody is going to fetch Mr Rogers. Mr Rogers must come by his own feet and his own will.'

'Mama,' pleaded Antoney, 'let me go and look for him.'

Florence repeated, 'Nobody must fetch him.'

Fifteen minutes later, she bent down. Her movements were slow and deliberate, as though previously rehearsed. One arm – bare in the sun – placed the orchids on the shallow red pool of the step. She paused there for a few seconds, collecting herself. Then she brushed off her dress, stood again to full height, looked straight out in front of her, and walked down the steps alone. Antoney watched all of this, the hands, the shoulders, the position of her head.

Shortly afterwards, he followed her.

3

Oscar Day believed that there are two types of dancers: ugly dancers and beautiful dancers. Both of these are compelling to watch. The ugly dancer is often stocky, wide-necked, can have large hands. He or she may appear heavy when dancing (although it is not heaviness, it is substantial lightness) and drawn to the earth. An ugly dancer can sometimes be uncomfortable to watch, but never tedious, while a beautiful dancer is easy on the eye and loyal to expectation. This other kind of dancer is soft-limbed and slender, airy and light on the feet. He or she is tall in many cases, with a long, animalistic neck and delicate hands. These are types, and types are rarely absolute, but this was what Oscar Day had surmised over the years.

What could he have said of Nijinsky? If he'd ever seen that Russian dance, what would it be, ugly or beautiful? He thought about this a lot. He guessed, from photographs and the things he'd read about him, that he transcended the distinction; it was too simplistic. The body, for example. Vaslav Nijinsky, at only five foot four, had the thigh and calf muscle of a sprinter but his arms and torso were petite. He was bulky yet sinuous, stout and broad-necked yet weightless, and rumour had it that he could fly. If only there were time travel. If only it were possible, Oscar would stop all this hand-to-mouth philanthropy and go back to the ballet on Theatre Street in St Petersburg before the

First World War to watch Vaslav Nijinsky fly. It went like this, the famous leap: he goes up, up up up. The audience gasps, some of them stand. He stays up there for what seems like minutes travelling through the air and then, and *then*, when it looks as if he's about to come down – listen, he goes *higher*. And *then* he comes down.

Some of Oscar's students (you could also call them followers, you could maybe call them protégés) did not believe the account of the Nijinsky leap. You're adding stuff, they said, that bit about him going higher before he comes down, you're exaggerating. No, said Oscar, it's true. Let me explain. Nijinsky's body could do it because he'd made it possible. He spent hours every day strengthening his leg muscles and Achilles tendon, he learnt to control his breath so that he could turn in flight – he *made* it possible. Believe more often the things you can't see, Oscar would say, it'll get you further in life.

Oscar had first become aware of Nijinsky as a dance student in his hometown of Mandeville in the US, and had taken to collecting photographs of him. Having accompanied Oscar on his subsequent travels in Europe and Latin America, these photographs now lined the walls of his school (you could almost call it a commune, most people simply called it 'Oscar's place'). The greatest selection was in the entrance hall, the anteroom to the tiny kitchen, the cramped office and the dance studio. Here were two old leather sofas, rarely vacant, and a worn-out carpet that Oscar had stopped sweeping because of life being too short. In one photograph Nijinsky was doing a playful side-on skip with his head thrown back. In another he was sitting next to a piano studying a score. There was Nijinsky in *Scheherazade*, in earrings and a headwrap, and Nijinsky in *Giselle*. One of Oscar's favourites was of a very young (1911 or 1912) pretty-eyed Nijinsky, with a high white collar and middle parting. Here you could see his pronounced cheekbones and slanted, mournful eyes, the slyness in the mouth. He was softly and defensively looking out at the world.

Also in the vestibule, above the kitchen door (Oscar could not recall why he'd put it up there – probably because he didn't really like to look at it), was yet another Nijinsky, hideous and quite unlike the others. He was in costume for Michel Fokine's puppet ballet, *Petrushka*. His face, collapsed into a warped and wretched grimace, was covered with powder, and he wore an oversized white ruffle around his neck. The photograph was taken in the dancing years, but it seemed to speak of everything that happened after Nijinsky's dancing years had stopped. Oscar didn't like to dwell too much on that, though it was important to remember.

There were other portraits besides. Isadora Duncan, the woman who freed the ballerinas from tiptoes. Josephine Baker with the banana skirt in Paris. Gene Kelly, Tamara Karsavina, Martha Graham, José Greco. Oscar himself as a wavy-haired young man in a pair of shorts, standing with his Six Eight troupe by a lily pond on Hampstead Heath. Six Eight in its time, Oscar liked to think, had done their bit for free expression. They were daring and eclectic. They had challenged the boundaries of performance by bringing the work off the stage and into the audience. They were no Isadora and they'd never been famous, but they had done their bit.

On settling in London, Oscar had studied ballet for a time at Marie Rambert's school in Notting Hill before later forming his troupe. When Six Eight disbanded he focused on teaching, eventually choosing the basement of a disused church off Portobello Road for this purpose. He lost his home in the 1954 Acton tornado so now he also lived in the basement, beyond the weathered door at the bottom of the old church steps. It was not legal – nothing about his place was legal. Occasional letters arrived from the Royal Borough of Kensington and Chelsea threatening eviction, but nothing ever happened. St Bernard's was a large, austere building with crumbling stonework, Gothic windows and an intricately carved wooden door that on first impression had reminded Oscar of Notre Dame in Paris. To the right-hand side of the steepled nave where Jesus wilted from his stained glass cross and the dark pews remained fixed to the floor was a good-sized hall, positioned directly above Oscar's studio. No one seemed to notice the school gradually take root down there, the studio being scrubbed smooth for barefoot safety and the wall-length mirrors erected. No one noticed when Oscar, the day after the tornado, still in shock, descended the steps with his surviving possessions – astonishingly, his spectacles among them – and lay down on his back in the middle of that vast floor to dream of tigers (a gentle dream, of lying in his old bed in a roofless room, four tigers calmly sitting down around him). No one noticed either that Oscar stayed in the basement night after night after that dream, and by the time anyone did, getting him out was a matter of bureaucracy. In certain situations, bureaucracy was a beautiful thing.

The tornado, Oscar had concluded that first night on the studio floor, was a kind of message. He was disposable by himself, he was sport for freak weather. His life now was for the younger ones, the ones who wanted to dance, to be either great or free.

Eight years on, he was currently experiencing the beginnings of rheumatism, a morning pain in his legs and lower back. With all the draughts the church was freezing in the winter, so cold that the warmer months were cooled by memories of winter, so he was usually wearing a sweater, sometimes a blanket. Last thing at night, when the young had all finally left, scattered into Ladbroke Grove and beyond like rain trails, Oscar gathered his tartan blanket around him and went out into the church back-yard to smoke his one cigarette. It was usually around two a.m. He acknowledged the stars and took in the decent smoke, thinking about the day gone by, a particular student's progress or an idea for a new phrase of movement. When this was finished he came reluctantly back inside.

He used to sleep in the office, when he'd first moved in.

There was a little mattress and just enough space on the floor alongside the desk. But he'd found sleep difficult there. He no longer trusted beds, predictable comfort. He found that his insomnia responded to a more nebulous arrangement. Each night after his smoke, he went into the dance studio and closed the door. He positioned two horse vaults at the appropriate distance, placed a large plywood board on top of them, a pillow on top of that, and there he lay down with his blanket. Sleep came at length. It lasted no more than three hours. Morning slipped cool and white from the high-up windows along the studio wall, and as he rose he caught himself in the mirrors, bald-headed, almost old, struggling to get upright. The final betrayal of every dancer is that the body is mortal. Every morning in those mirrors, Oscar was surprised at himself.

If there was a place in London in 1962 that was in need of this kind of social enterprise, Ladbroke Grove was one such place. Outside Oscar's walls were slum digs, rubbish heaps, frontiers. The church, tucked away behind a gated courtyard at the junction of Talbot Road and Powis Square, was situated in the heart of one of the city's poorest and most neglected wards, as yet showing scant sign of its approaching rise to glitz and fortune. This was not the kind of place you would come to buy a psychedelic toaster or a leather watering can. This was not where you would stop for aubergine tea. It was a last place, an only place. It was tumbling down and covered in coal-fire soot. Rats and mice stalked the streets, feasting amid the demolition scrap piles left by the cranes of '58, when large patches of the Grove had been bulldozed to make way for boxy council housing, creating apocalyptic scenes that, to any local, to Toreth walking by with her shopping for instance, were not unlike those seen during the Second World War. Those five-tiered terraces overlooking Colville Square had no conception at this time of their ice cream futures, but were irritably inhabited by multiple family units who put up with leaking roofs, rising damp and 'Keep Britain White' graffiti. The area's proximity to the West End had also rendered it a playground for runaways, rogues and the stalkers of Soho, who along with the local hustlers and partygoers, frequented the cantankerous pubs, shebeens and gambling joints dotted around Westbourne Park Road and Portobello. Along nearby Bayswater Road prostitutes still leaned moistly against the Hyde Park railings, shortening their skirts at slowing down cars. This was a place that said yes, if you'd come from some way off, with holes in your pockets and children at your heels, or if you'd crossed the sea in your best suit and a blue-feathered Kingston hat, brimming with expectation. This was where they just might let you in, not with kindness, but with scorn.

Most of Oscar's students lived locally or in the surrounding neighbourhoods. He was bad at charging the correct rate for his tuition, making only what he needed to get by, because he knew that they didn't just come here to dance. They came for the same reason he himself had come after the tornado. They came to retreat, to get away from the soot. They descended the crumbling steps to the basement and stepped into a purer moment. That was why they spent so long lounging on the sofas after class as if they didn't have homes to go to. It didn't matter they might have seen a mouse or two shooting across the dance floor, or how damn cold the place was. It was a purer mouse, a worthwhile cold. Hours went by on those sofas as they discussed different genres of dance, shows they wanted to see, music that inspired them, as they listened to Oscar talk about his travels, his dip into the Latin-American dance scene in Paris during the thirties. They talked of performance psychology and the choreographic experiment, of 'hits', which occurred between the body and the music when the two elements joined together and made each other shine. These gatherings were loud and punctuated by frequent laughter, the students often getting up to demonstrate a move they'd seen or test each other's skills.

They fell broadly into three categories. There were the stalwarts, like Ekow – he lived two streets away, he had a smile as broad as landscapes – the ones who'd attached themselves to Oscar, who were concerned about what he ate, his sleeping arrangement, and sometimes even swept out the entrance hall for him. There were those, like Simone, who came once a week, having already begun a serious dance training or career elsewhere to which Oscar's place was merely a supplement. And then there were the elusives, those who came for one or two sessions and disappeared. They resurfaced, disappeared again. Sometimes Oscar didn't recognise people.

One October afternoon just after five o'clock, half an hour before the evening class was due to begin, he was coming out of the kitchen with a cup of three-sugar coffee when he saw a tall young man standing in the entrance hall. He was studying the photographs, his back to Oscar. There was something about him that made the teacher linger. He had an extremely long, sturdy neck, was wide-shouldered, powerfully built, but there was a quality of lightness in him that gave rise to illusion. If you were not looking down at his feet, it was possible to suspect that he was afloat, that he was suspended just above water. Oscar took him to be a professional ballet dancer but then he wasn't sure; his posture was slightly bent and his shoes were blockish and filthy (ballet dancers, however poor, are usually precious about their feet). The stranger was staring with particular interest at the skipping Nijinsky.

Oscar sipped from his cup, half waiting and half watching, as he moved on to a photograph of Katherine Dunham in a satin dress with a feather in her hair, leaning against a column. Oscar was about to head across the hall to the studio when the young man finally turned round and noticed him. Well, look at him, thought Oscar, What a face. A boyish smile was just arriving at the mouth, as if remembering something, yet it was also beginning to leave. This smile, of arrival and departure, the snatch of boy, offset a harder, more constant expression presiding in the eyes, which were clear, cautious and brown, birdlike eyes, set well back in the shade of cocky velvet eyebrows. The mouth was smooth and tender-looking, more like a woman's mouth, with a faint vulnerability at the corners. It was the kind of face you wanted to talk to someone about. It had chisel and grace, russet skin, lofty Nijinskian cheekbone. Oscar realised he was staring.

The youngster said definitively, 'That's Katherine Dunham.'

'Indeed it is,' Oscar replied. 'Quite a picture, isn't it?'

'I met her once'.

'Did you really? Where?'

'In Kingston. She was exactly like that there.' His voice had a soft, Caribbean tune to it and was low-pitched. He glanced at Katherine again before asking, quite unrelatedly, 'Is it some type of religious dancing you do here?'

Oscar laughed. 'Religious? Me? No. Religion, in my humble opinion, is nothing but a perverse form of optimism – we've no use for that here. We just hijacked the place for our own sordid purposes.' He realised he hadn't answered the question fully so added, 'I suppose you could call it modern dance, for information's sake. It's a vague enough term – Martha Graham despises it, understandably.'

The visitor studied Oscar for a moment, his eyes hard and direct. Oscar was quite a short man, only five foot six, though he somehow never gave the impression he was looking up at people. He smiled encouragingly. The visitor seemed unsure, his coat still buttoned, his big scruffy bag still shouldered, of whether he wanted to stay or leave. He was perhaps hoping to be persuaded by something Oscar might say at just the right instant. There was an awkward silence, broken by Oscar, who was still somewhat dazzled by the aesthetics of the boy.

'Are you from Kingston?' he asked him.

'No, from country. What about you?'

Oscar wasn't sure whether by 'country' he meant Jamaica or its countryside, but he left it there and answered that he was from a small town near New Orleans, though he could hardly remember being there any more because he hadn't been back in light years. While he was talking the voices of some of the early-arrived students drifted out of the studio as they stretched and loosened up their bodies, chatting among themselves. The aloof Simone showed up and went on in, greeting Oscar as she passed and glancing briefly at the newcomer.

'You haven't been before, have you?' Oscar said. 'I don't usually forget a face.'

His reckoning was correct. 'I haven't danced since time,' the young man said, rather too proudly and thereby failing to hide his nervousness.

'And where did you used to dance, if you don't mind my being so inquisitive?'

But he seemed to be losing interest in the conversation, returning half his attention to the photographs as if they, not Oscar, were the thing that might persuade him to take off his coat. 'Back home I did ballet,' he said distantly, 'but I didn't like it too much – it was too . . . straight, I guess. And then I did—'

He was looking above Oscar's head at the hideous Petrushka Nijinsky. He gazed at it as he had at the skipping Nijinsky, then turned back to look at this first one again, along with the *Giselle* and *Scheherazade*. He moved from one impression to another having apparently forgotten all about Oscar, until he finally settled on a smaller photograph positioned immediately next to the studio in which Nijinsky was tiptoeing towards the right with his arms outstretched, as if walking into the hall.

'Who is that guy?' he asked at last.

Oscar came and stood next to him. They studied the image together.

'It's Vaslav,' Oscar said, and they gazed another while.

'Vaslav Nijinsky. Star principal, the Ballets Russes. The greatest dancer of all time.'

Oscar had never been content with the term 'modern dance' either. He agreed with Graham about its lack of precision, but he stopped at using her preferred 'contemporary dance', which was closer but still not quite right. He usually said 'free dance', if forced to define it, referring to a loose and fluid, Latin-edged style of movement intended to foster individual creativity and daring while also employing some of the technique-building elements of classical ballet. To dance with integrity, Oscar believed, and with bravery, was not possible without freedom from within. His classes were driven by a concept of dancing as personal exploration, as a liberating avenue into self-connection and self-confidence. Although he wanted his students to do well as dancers, he also wanted them to be well as individuals. Look at you, he'd tell them, look in the mirror. Your time is short. Each minute inside of you is a creative minute, an invitation to encounter your own greatness. Don't be scared, don't fear it. Stay open. Be courageous yet humble in the face of your unknown ability.

Before the official warm-up of pliés, floor exercises, adagios, some work on the barre, each session began with fifteen minutes of improvisation during which the students were encouraged to tap into the accumulated emotions of the present moment – private angers, jealousies, anxieties, the something good that happened yesterday – and dispel them through unmediated movement. They'd run, lunge and cartwheel across the hall, spinning and colliding. It was designed to eradicate shyness, which Oscar had once suffered from, and to bring everyone to a single unified point of readiness.

Oscar watched Antoney closely during this first class. They were dancing to a jazz score. He had an unusual way of moving. Evasive and cat-like, it argued with something underneath it that was much more flamboyant, that wrestled inside the broad, eager torso, the long sinewy arms branching out from his white vest (what Oscar would have given once, for such arms). When Antoney first started dancing that floating quality Oscar had seen in the entrance hall almost completely disappeared and he was really somewhat heavy. He obviously wasn't used to public classes. He stood right at the back, the haunt of the novice, and during the improvisation he walked and fumbled around in a small patch of floor, at one point folding his arms. He did however look directly at Oscar from across the room for most of the session, with a fierce and searching concentration.

'Untie your posture,' Oscar told him on one of his rounds, checking feet, adjusting arms. Sometimes he lost track on these walks. He would end up in a deep exchange with one student about the inner thigh tension or the psoas muscle, about the breath in relation to the ribcage, so that the others would have to continue the class uninstructed, at which point they'd usually look to Ekow to lead. Oscar told Antoney softly, his hand upon his lower back, 'Use the posture as the foundation for the movement. Be aware of it. You don't want to give it full control, but use it to your advantage.'

He might be wrong – he wasn't usually wrong about these things – but this boy had the makings, Oscar sensed. The makings, the factor, the watch-me, the grace note. If he could just get that fear off his back (it was a very large fear, like Dracula's cloak), something special might happen. A beautiful dancer he could be, with all the charisma of ugliness.

But then, like all the elusives, he disappeared.

Florence and Antoney docked at Southampton in April 1958, after travelling five thousand miles on a steamship made in Italy. Florence suffered seasickness throughout the journey, but on the day of their arrival she put on her new suit – hand-sewn, light grey – with a white shirt, light blue gloves, and a hat with a matching blue feather. Antoney found it amazing how his mother always managed to ensure that their clothes were ironed no matter what. There was not a crease on her skirt as they came down the crowded gangplank, her head even higher than usual, her handbag over her forearm, nor on his own dark grey suit that she'd also made with help from Aunt Ivy. Now sixteen, he'd grown another inch since the measurements were taken so the trousers were slightly too short for him, and flapped around his ankles in the cool English breeze.

They had with them their best and warmest clothes, Antoney's disappointing schoolbooks (because learning never ends), some crockery, the remainder of all the money Florence had ever saved in her life, and a Bible. Everything else had been given away or discarded. Unlike many of their fellow passengers, she intended this as a one-way trip.

Florence had been aware for a long time of the opportunities available in England for Jamaicans like herself. She had a cousin, Gregory, who'd enlisted in the British Army during the war and had never returned. He was now a bus conductor in London. Mr Chambers, the pharmacist whose housework she did, had a son who worked in carpentry in Birmingham and had sent for his wife and child to join him. People were leaving from every corner, lured by Queen's-English wireless announcements and newspaper ads for vacancies in nursing, the railways and manufacturing. Some were even taking a chance and jumping on the ship when no one was looking – a local man had spent a whole day in '53 saying farewell to the district, to Miss Enid in her shop, to Florence behind the bar next door, to the pastor, his cousins, his parents, saying he was leaving for England the motherland tomorrow, only to return the next day a failed stowaway. It didn't occur to Florence to join the exodus until it slowly began to dawn on her that Annotto Bay would never find itself able to forget that groomless day in 1951. She was famous for her incompletion. She was a pitied soul offered a pineapple juice refreshment and the best post at any talkative neighbourhood stoop, in order that she might uncage her thoroughly interesting pain and feed the fountain of gossip. She couldn't even go to church in peace. And she was tired of mustering a ten-shilling here and a six-shilling there. What about a one-job situation? What about a brave new district? Now that Stony Hill and Fort George were out of her reach, England became an attractive option.

To her inward embarrassment on her visit to the labour office she discovered that she was beyond the eighteen-to-thirty age criterion for nursing training (which she would've been no good at anyway as she was blood-squeamish) so she applied for a job as a National Health Service domestic and got a loan for part of the passage. Antoney had only one concern about their leaving, which he couldn't voice to his mother: how, if not by looking in the tangerine house, would Mr Rogers find him?

During the night of the day after that day, Mr Rogers, like a shadow on a wall, had made a fleeting appearance. As Florence was sleeping the competent, resolute sleep of the shamed, Antoney was woken by a sound at the window. He looked out and saw nothing, so he went onto the veranda where he heard the sound again, a hiss. The grass rustled. The far stars blushed. His father stepped into view, dishevelled, his thumb hooked in his pocket, his hat for the first and only time unflowered. Throughout the brief exchange that followed he stayed near the bushes seven or eight feet away.

They did not greet one another. Mr Rogers said simply, 'Son, I'm going to see me mother.'

Antoney remained silent. It was taking all his concentration to keep his anger intact, when actually, out of relief, he wanted more than anything to go and embrace his father. His body made a strained forward lean that deepened when Mr Rogers eventually took a small step back. Sparrow eye to sparrow eye, they checked each other, and Antoney remembered riding the Rat Attack bus back from Kingston the night of Katherine, listening to the story of his quiet, feline grandmother. It was the same sensation as then, as if he and Mr Rogers were the only two people who existed and everything else was a story to be told. Before turning away and disappearing into the darkness, Mr Rogers raised his right hand, took off his hat, and said this:

'I'll come back for you.'

Casual like that, as if he was going to play a game of dominoes first. This was the promise that resounded in Antoney's head through his twelfth, thirteenth and fifteenth Christmas, the day he left school, whenever he was on a bus, whenever he walked past Woolworths in Kingston. In the lead-up to the departure for England he became more and more anxious that it was a promise that could not now be kept, and when they finally set sail across the Atlantic he felt himself sinking, growing thinner and transparent until he became completely invisible, so that searching for him would be the same as searching for a piece of glass at the bottom of the sea.

Antoney carried his mother's surname now, Matheus, at Florence's doing.

Cousin Gregory put them up in London until they got settled. He had a dim, frowsty room on the first floor of a coal-blackened house on the corner of Portobello and Faraday Road. After three nights on the floor he asked Florence for his bed back, onto which he often collapsed full of cider at four a.m. in his London Transport uniform. Antoney was impressed by Gregory's carefree bachelor lifestyle but Florence had them looking hard for somewhere else, only to find that they were either too strapped for cash or too West Indian, which was the same, apparently, as coloured, black and African, all of which could in some cases also be the same as Irish, child or dog. They eventually found a place for a steep two pounds ten a week on Bassett Road, one of the wide, tree-lined avenues off the western side of Ladbroke Grove with a history of Edwardian splendour. Now it was just another dark, litter-strewn street with children playing half naked amid the debris and the occasional drunk lying across the pavement. The house was owned by a Dutch woman who lived alone on the top floor. She was very strict with the electricity and only allowed tenants to use twenty-five-watt bulbs. Those with radios were charged extra, as were those with children under the age of ten. The front yard, once a lawn, was overgrowing around the wreckage of an orange Bentley that the landlady had meant to turn into a novelty taxi. A few doors down an abandoned house had become a dumping site for broken sinks, mattresses, prams, suitcases, unwanted flooring and dead animals, emitting a rank, vermin-assisted smell that was evident from halfway up the street. Florence, who still couldn't believe that this was England, had to walk past the scrap heap every morning on her way to work at the hospital in Paddington, cursing under her breath as she went – until she took to doing what everyone else did: a left, a sharp right, then another right to the bus stop on Ladbroke Grove, serenaded en route by the perpetual sound of the workmen's drills.

She and Antoney had a room to themselves but they had to share a sink and a stove with the other people on their landing. On the floor below was a divorced woman called Sheryl who was from Oracabessa, a town not far from Annotto Bay. There was only one toilet. With the coming and going of so many people through a single front door it felt a lot like living in a shop or a railway station; there were voices in the walls and footsteps in the ceiling. Every time the front door slammed (the landlady forbade slamming but people slammed it anyway), a strip of beige wallpaper curled up a fraction more from the corner above Antoney's bed.

He spent a lot of time that first English summer walking around the brave new district, through the jail-like chimneyed terraces that had given him on arrival the ominous sensation of passing through a series of tunnels, the true ground level existing not at your feet but somewhere above your head. He walked along Portobello, past the moody pubs and shopfronts, up Talbot Road to Powis Square where he sometimes hear music coming from the old stone church, through the tense back-streets leading up to Westbourne Park that Sheryl told him to avoid because of 'white trouble'. He missed home. He missed the busmen. He missed mango distinctions. He'd walk, with his light step, with his slight right-side bounce, sometimes as far as Oxford Street, maybe not returning until long after Florence was back from work. She wanted him to apply to the local college to do pharmacy but he told her one evening that he wanted to get a job in one of the theatres in the West End, as an ice cream vendor or something like that. (How colourful the lights, the rim of the Shaftesbury's awning. Imagine the feeling of stepping out from a Covent Garden stage door into the London street, whose paving stones were made purple in places by the glow from the lamp posts . . .) 'Now listen to me,' his mother said – she had just placed before him at their ex-casino felt-topped dining table a plate of gravied rice and green banana but she took it away – 'and listen to me good. I spend the whole day from morning mopping and scrubbing, and all you got to say to me is West End and ice cream? When I can't even cook on my own private hob? Just about nothing I've seen of this country so far has made me partial to it, but one thing I know for sure is that there is opportunity here for you to make something of yourself, you hear? You better think again if you planning on getting into that dancing activity at my expense.' Here Antoney interrupted her to say that he could make his own money, outside of pharmacy, but his mother took this for insolence. 'Take your head out of the sky,' she said, still holding the plate. 'I did not get on that boat and come all this way for you to be a kite, and blow about in the dyam wind.'

Three months after the move to Bassett Road the riots happened. They were neither sudden nor grand in scale, but an escalation of existing hostilities heightened by the blacks retaliating. The father of the Vincencian family across the hall arrived home late one night with his head in bandages, having been attacked in the street by a gang of boys carrying iron bars and throwing bottles. 'White trouble took another step closer to the devil,' Sheryl said. If Florence was not in her room during the four days in which they were confined to the house, ironing over and over again the light grey suit she'd worn on the ship as if she were reboarding it tomorrow, she was in Sheryl's room below, which took the large bay window and was covered with doilies. Sheryl read out passages from the Bible to pass the time. When evening fell they looked out of the window over the district and might see the occasional orange petrol bomb flicker, but aside from that it was a period of clear, shimmering dusks in which the sun sank down like molten jelly behind the black slate roofs. 'Is a pretty sky,' said Antoney, whom Florence would not let out of her sight.

'What is this place we come to?' she said, unhearing, and she would continue to say this, days and weeks after the return to impermanent peace, when she was still too afraid to walk out into the open air and slam the front door behind her.

Some Saturday nights in a house on Tavistock Crescent, nearby to Oscar's place, the Marshall brothers put on a blues. There was not much blue about these parties beyond the name and a little nostalgia. They were red-lit and sweaty, pink-punch, white-rum and whisky happy. From the ceiling of the living room hung a huge glowing red disc studded with aluminium beads beneath which an impossible number of people gathered and danced until dawn, until the place was musty, ska-wrecked, soul-shook and blue-beat haunted. The Marshall brothers were from Trinidad, Coby and John, both in suits, Coby bigger than John, bachelors in their thirties. Most girls went for John because he was the DJ. (It's a kind of intuition, when a man can play the right music at the right moment.)

By '62 Antoney was a regular here. He was working not in pharmacy but in the building trade, mostly locally on new blocks of flats. He'd been unsuccessful in getting a job in ice cream vending and had sorted letters for a while at the post office, until he'd realised that he could only abide work of a physical nature. He enjoyed the lifting and flexing, the hammering and shovelling. It was bad for his hands but he could work to his own rhythm. When the week was over and the Marshalls were holding a dance, he arrived always after midnight, sometimes with a workmate, usually on his own in order to concentrate on the dancing, and would hold up a wall in the red room. He watched what the shoulders were doing during the blue-beat swing, the different ways of executing the roach or the twist. To the sounds of Prince Buster and Lord Tanamo he studied all the idiosyncrasies of skanking, a new thing in which one knee was lifted in tandem with the raised foot coming forward. If a girl came up to ask him for a dance he would oblige out of politeness, then drift back after one or two songs to his wallflower post.

It was ten days before Christmas and the north star was visible. Tomorrow was sleepy Sunday. What better time was there to find a bluesy shirt or a sexy dress or a pair of trousers that changed colour halfway down, to moisten up your hair, head down to a Marshall dance and pay your three bob at the door? The party was in full swing when Antoney got there. He shook hands with Coby and went down the passage to the living room. The furniture had been moved upstairs to make way for the speakers, which were stacked one on top of another so that they were bigger than man. The turntables took the centre wall, vast black soundscapes that John was hunched over, lovingly, blissed inside his headphones. Baba Brooks boomed into the hemisphere, Derrick and Patsy, the Mighty Sparrow, James Brown. The only free spots left in the room were right next to the speakers. After half an hour Antoney had to shift to relieve his eardrums, so he went to find a drink.

Back in the passage the front door opened yet again and a group of people arrived, laughing and joking with Coby, making a lot of noise. Antoney recognised Ekow straight away.

He was with another guy and a couple of pretty girls, one of whom he also vaguely recognised. They all had an ease and an air of confidence about them, a goodtime buzz. They made him think of the dancers he'd met in Katherine's dressing room.

Surveying the scene, Ekow noticed Antoney and smiled at him in his broad, effortless way. Antoney nodded back, continuing on into the kitchen to get his cup of punch. There was a loud conversation going on about the cricket, a bored, big-shouldered girl standing by the sink holding her drink with both hands. She raised her eyes surreptitiously at Antoney as he headed back for the living room. Ekow intercepted him. 'Hey,' he said. 'Where you been?'

They were just about the same height. He had on a tight yellow shirt with a kind of gloss to it, which made Antoney feel plain in his short-sleeved cotton polo. 'Nowhere special. I been about.'

'Oscar was asking for you.'

'Yeah?'

'Yeah, you should come around.'

One of Ekow's girls got hold of his arm and leaned against him. 'Darren's getting drinks, darling – punch?' She looked different out of her dance gear, in her party clothes and makeup, rouged dark skin, thick mascara, long straightened hair going down her back.

'Simone,' Ekow said, 'remember this fella? One class and jump ship. You must've scared him off.' (This was partly true. She'd sauntered about in her leotard and ballet slippers in the front row with a perfect symmetry, and during Oscar's private consultation with Antoney about posture she'd actually glared at them over her shoulder.)

'Please,' she drawled, giving Antoney a swift up and down inspection and extending her hand, 'Why would anyone be scared of *moi*? It's very nice to see you again.' She turned back to Ekow. 'Michael's here, he's all *over* Carla, so keep an eye on it. Punch it is,' and with that she went back to her friend, who was pine-skinned, turquoise-booted, haloed by sensational hair.

'Good shirt,' Antoney said, trying to make conversation.

'It's from the market, you like it? Hey, man, come on!' Ekow slapped hands with a fellow in a cap. Jimmy Cliff's 'Miss Jamaica' came sailing out of the red room so Antoney made an exit, returning to a better spot this time away from the speakers. Not long afterwards Ekow's crew spilled into the crimson space and proceeded to take over the dance floor. Ekow started with a two-step, which would advance towards the complicated and the flashy but not yet. At first you take the dance slowly, you settle into the atmosphere, nod at the beats, shake the hands – unless of course you're Coby, who shoved his way in and started the capricious stuff straight away, blade-rolls in the shoulders, fists up, the knees bent low, Ekow getting ready to catch him up. Simone and her pine-skin friend, whom Antoney guessed was Carla, danced together, Carla balancing her cup of punch in the air with her long, ribbony arms. Half the men in the room had their eyes on her. She was a swaying, turning starlet, a bouncing turquoise-dipped nymph who broke often into laughter, flicking about a shaggy evening scarf that jumped around her calves. As Ekow dragged Antoney into their centre she took a good look at him, lingering for longer than she might have meant to, until she was distracted by Simone. They all danced on. Gaps appeared in the frosty night sky.

When there are just fifteen or twenty people left and it's close to dawn, that's when the second party starts. The philosophy in the kitchen deepens. The dance floor gets misty. The DJ starts playing slow joints, love songs that send yawning dancers towards each other, or the weird tunes that don't go down well in a crowd. Carla had taken off her boots, revealing contoured, sensuously weighted ankles. She shimmied up to Antoney in the middle of a repeat of Sam Cooke's 'Chain Gang' just when he was about to slump down against the wall, and said, 'Oh no you don't', so they danced together. Antoney was infected by her vivaciousness, she put him at his ease and he started getting down hard, causing quite a stir with his complex moves, his unveiled panache. She came into his arms for a sultry slow one, thigh to thigh, he smelt the shampoo in her hair, then finally, on the opening of another ska tune, they slumped down against the wall. She sat cross-legged, like a kid, angled towards him.

'I get this funny feeling,' she said, she was a little drunk, 'when I hear a ska track. The record starts, right, and I'm listening to it, but I just can't tell what it is at first, know what I mean? It sounds kind of – impossible, like the sounds don't fit together. D'you ever get that feeling?'

'Not really,' he said. In the paler light she was planetary-eyed and smooth of cheek, with slightly crooked teeth. She had a slow blink as if there wasn't enough lid to cover the expanse.

'No? Well, after a *while* I see it, a few bars in. After a while the track sort of . . .' she wriggled her fingers like a magician, '. . . untangles, you know? *Then* I get it. Why do you think that happens?'

'Maybe it's meant so,' he said.

'I like your eyes,' she said.

'I like your ankles.'

She lived, he discovered, with her mother. With all the dancing she said her hair was wet and dry at the same time, which she seemed to see as a problem. She told him without a blink or a halt that her father was dead. She was tactile, touching his arms and shoulders innocently as they talked. When he asked her whether she was one of Oscar's people she said, 'On and off. I'm not much of a dancer, really.'

Simone came back into the room after a long sojourn in the kitchen while John was playing Louis Armstrong. Carla leaned back onto her friend's lap as she sat down with them, spreading out her arms so that she was half lying on the floor. 'Where's my boots?' she said sluggishly.

'They're over there,' said Simone.

Carla drew up her hand near Simone's face. 'Simone's the real dancer,' she said. 'I just hang around a bit, don't I?'

The second time Antoney went to Oscar's place, a few weeks later, he took his position one row nearer to the front. The time after that, another row, but he was usually late in order to miss the opening improvisation, which he found humiliating and ridiculous. Oscar was not impressed with lateness. 'Dancer,' he shouted, 'your timing is lousy. Buck up or get out.' Soon Antoney was there once, twice, sometimes three times a week after work, having lied on occasion to his mother about where he was going. This was the first place he'd felt he belonged since moving to England. Carla also started coming to classes more often.

They danced to Paul Robeson and Mendelssohn's piano concertos, to Ray Charles, to an Egyptian flute player Oscar had bought a record from in Alexandria (a sound like birds singing up through tree trunks; you could hear the player's breath when he drew it in). Oscar had all kinds of music. There were hundreds of reels, in towers in the office, a city lining the desk, Felix Baloy, Keely Smith, Igor Stravinsky (who, Oscar informed Antoney, had worked with Nijinsky on an X-rated ballet). In Oscar's place music was like weather, it would change always but it was always there, holding sway over what it witnessed. 'The music,' he said, 'even when it's silent – there *is* music in silence – is what brings the body forth. It is your lamp, your genie. It's the prince's kiss.'

The more Antoney danced the more he wanted to dance. It was like the flying dream, as they moved across the floor. The dancers looked so lovely when they threw back their heads and put one palm flat on the small of the back and held back the connecting shoulder and went proudly forward. Different from him, better than him, somehow more meant. When he caught himself in the mirrors his confidence shrivelled up. He

66

seemed so awkward, like a distortion of himself. He watched the way Ekow put a flourish on things, the way he could take a phrase and have it seem as if it was made for him, as if that was how it was meant to be done, the proper execution. Antoney often found himself imitating Ekow instead of looking for his own version, then would catch himself again in the mirror, warped through imitation, the arm cast out too far or the shoulders too taut, and again he'd become discouraged, which in turn made him appear more awkward. At such times he had an urge to stop dancing al-together. He and Ekow were becoming good friends, but he couldn't help feeling jealous of him.

From Oscar's point of view, aside from these struggles with inhibition, Antoney stood out as potentially one of the best in the class. One evening the teacher stopped the students in the middle of a session and did his call, 'Come round, dancers, come round.' He dragged his three-legged stool to the centre of the floor. Although the studio was warm from the dancing his sweater was still draped over his shoulders. The students sat before him in a semi-circle, some lying on their fronts, others upright, legs splayed, twelve or thirteen of them. Times like these they always made Oscar think of the tigers.

'Today I want to talk about before,' he began, 'because there are some of you who seem to have forgotten.' He scanned their faces, settling for a few seconds on Antoney, who was sitting behind Simone and Carla towards the back of the gathering. 'Before,' he said. 'Way back. When we were young. I mean really young, not like you or I – we all know I'm not a day over forty.' Some of the dancers giggled. 'But seriously, remember what we were like back then? We were loose, that's what we were. Don't you remember? Weren't we just wild, when we were five or two or seven? At least *I* was. I was full of the shiny stuff. I used to think rainbows were painted by fairies and nutshells were their carriages.

'I'm not sure when all that stops exactly,' Oscar continued. 'It depends on what you get given. But at some gradually evolving point it stops, and this is a terrible thing, terrible for all of us. We've started to grow up, to learn about ways to behave, obligation and responsibility, the concepts of danger and pain. I've always believed that adolescence is not a difficulty in itself. It's only made that way because of its approach to a life of constraint. What I'm getting to is this.' He leaned forward, one elbow on his knee, like a grey-eyed grandfather holding court to his descendants. 'When we dance,' he said, 'it's possible to get back to that state of looseness. It's probably the only way back to what we were before we got given what we were given, right? It's all still there, waiting for you, but only on one condition – and this applies to everyone.' He now looked squarely at Antoney and said sternly, 'You have to be willing to let yourself out into the playground. You've got to find the courage to *lose* yourself.'

There was silence in the hall. Oscar stood up. 'Now. In such nostalgic spirit, we're going to spend the remainder of the session attempting the Nijinsky leap.'

One by one the dancers rose to their feet. They began to jump. There were wild, high guesses and clumsy landings. Oscar mentioned the leg muscles and controlling the breath through the mid-flight turn but right now it didn't matter, he said, just let it loose. It became simply a matter of height. Who could reach the windows, who could stay up the longest, who could achieve height and length at the same time. They ran into the jumps making silly leg shapes. They shrieked and fell. Oscar bellowed and laughed and threw off his sweater. 'No no *no*, Ekow, he went *higher* – before he came down, he went *higher*!'

'What was it,' Antoney asked his teacher, a couple of nights later, 'that made Nijinsky the greatest dancer of all time?'

The basement was empty except for the two of them. They were stretched out on the sofas in the vestibule, the photographs surrounding – the powdered Petrushka face, the androgyny, the beautiful bone-coloured legs. Antoney was quite reserved during the noisy evening hang-outs with the other students, but alone with Oscar he was inquisitive and relaxed. When it came to talking about Nijinsky, Oscar was always ready.

'I often wonder about that,' he said. 'It was the leap, partly, the raw rocket energy. But it was also the stuff behind all that, the kind of person Vaslav was. He was practically mute, you know, as a kid. He could hardly string a sentence together.'

'So . . .'

'So, it's significant, don't you think? . . . He needed to dance. It was the only way he could fully express himself so he applied himself to it entirely. That's what gave him his dynamism. Oh, he had the wonderful body and the face and all that, which counts of course, if you can turn the heads to take a look at you in the first place. But most of all it was the *need* that made Nijinsky great – that, and the fact that we won't ever see him again.'

Antoney asked whether he'd been married. Oscar said he had, to a Hungarian beauty called Romola, a society girl. He had a tendency to speak of Nijinsky as if he'd known him intimately. 'I don't think it did him much good, though. I don't think marriage does anyone much good for that matter.' When Antoney asked him what he meant by this he explained, 'Settling down with one person like that, it shrinks your view of life, you know? You reach for less, you stop taking risks. That's dangerous for artists. Look at Vaslav – first he gets married, then he gets fired, then he goes crazy.'

'You mean Romola drove him crazy?'

'Not just her, his mother-in-law, his director, financial grievances, the war, himself. Things accumulate, I imagine, when you're in that place, and I do think that greatness can lead to a sort of floundering abyss. During the war he and Romola retreated to a villa by a lake in Switzerland. Vaslav did his exercises every morning, played with his kid – he was happy for a while, surrounded by mountains, glittering snow. But his stage career was practically dead by then. That was all he knew. He had no routine of rehearsal, performance, touring, nothing for his mind to hold onto. I suppose he just . . . unravelled.' Oscar glanced towards the office where he kept his books but decided against getting up. 'In the last couple of months before they took him off, Vaslav kept a diary. I'll lend it to you some time. It puts you right there with him, right in his head. Those were his last free words, because for the next thirty years he was pretty much institutionalised. He had every treatment going, straitjackets, iron beds, insulin, opium, you name it, until he was the weirdest creature imaginable, huge and cackling like a little girl's nightmare.'

In Annotto Bay, Antoney had known of someone like that, a mad thing, though she was never taken away. She had lived in a hut by the beach and it was rumoured that she'd killed her husband. Everyone said she was mad. They said it with such conviction that its status as rumour had come to nestle without remark in the realm of fact. Florence said it, Aunt Ivy said it, the reverend, who touched the woman's forehead with a holy wet finger one day when she appeared in the church in a torn skirt, praying and singing. The poor mad soul, the reverend had said. Antoney had always wondered what that meant, to be mad in the soul. Was there a point, he wondered, when the woman (her name was Jennifer Gates) knew that she was mad? A definite switch between not crazy and crazy? And if so what was it? Because probably, if you could remember the exact place where you'd lost your head, the right address, the turning back to it, then maybe it was possible to make yourself unmad. He'd tried to discuss the issue once with Florence but she had frowned at him – That is a strange question, Antoney, she'd said. That is not something to spend the time of day thinking about.

He offered his theory to Oscar. Maybe if Nijinsky had been able to remember the right way back, his 'address', he might have been able to save himself. Possibly, said Oscar, but perhaps the nature of madness is such that you can't remember.

'Anyway,' Antoney said, 'I'll never be as good as him. I started too late.'

'Let's just see about that,' Oscar replied.

He'd drawn up his legs and tucked his blanket into the space beneath his knees. One side of his face was visible in the light coming from the naked bulb in the kitchen. The skin was loose around the jaw, the nose prominent. His spectacles were on the armrest of the sofa. Neither spoke for a while, until Antoney asked him, 'Don't you get lonely living here all by yourself, Oscar?'

'I get by . . . It suits me.'

He threw a quick look at Antoney as if debating something in his mind.

'I was married once, too.' he said. 'Hard to believe, I know. It seems like a century ago.' He spoke slowly, without nostalgia. 'She had this gorgeous, long, fabulous blonde hair. She was really quite a catch, but somewhat wasted on me. I lived with her for seven years and all that time, Antoney, I never felt like myself. It didn't make me happy. Slowly but surely, I found out what it feels like to be with someone you thought you loved, then to stay with them because you're afraid – it's an awful way to be alone.'

'Did dancing make you happy?' Antoney said.

Oscar pondered this. 'At intervals,' he answered, 'yes, it did.' 'For the durations of leaps.'

In the autumn of the following year, 1964, Antoney went with Oscar to see Alvin Ailey's company at the Shaftesbury Theatre. He lost all hope for himself during 'Revelations', a spellbinding series of dances set to gospel and spirituals. It stunned him, the ship of arms at the beginning, the windswept white umbrella, the speed and splendour of the male trio and the funny leaning women with their fans. As they stood amid the endless applause,

71

Antoney stiff with longing and the burning of being so much less, Oscar inclined his head towards him and said, 'That's something you could do. It's not magic. It's just the movements in your head.'

4

'Louis, I take it. *West* magazine?'

Simone de Laperouse stopped one step short of Lucas's table. He got up, not because he was well versed in the proper greeting for a lady at a swanky brasserie, but because there was something about her – a melodrama in the shoulders, an austerity in her lipstick-drenched smile – that commanded him to rise. She was extremely petite, wearing a hot-pink spring coat with squared buttons and a rounded collar, as if she had indeed just stepped out of 1969. Her jet-black hair was tugged off her face into a shop-bought ponytail so that her eyes went upwards at the corners, the way Denise's did when she plaited her hair too tight. Stooping, Lucas shook her diminutive hand, aware that his own was damp, and thanked her for coming all the way from Battersea.

'I must blame my lateness,' she said, removing one finger at a time a pair of sheer black gloves, oddly placed for May, 'on the Hammersmith and City line. We were stranded on an open track.' Her hands unveiled were a carnival, rings on every other finger, long fuchsia nails to match the coat, a sound system of bracelets round the right wrist. She dropped the gloves on the table and slipped off her scarf. She looked to Lucas to be in her late fifties.

He'd found her in the cupboard, a white-feathered bird in a pile of barely readable newspaper cuttings, bending her thin

73

neck towards a darkened stage floor. 'Bird', according to the caption, was one of the Midnight Ballet's signature works. Lucas found it disorienting, having studied the photograph for so long in its grainy black-and-white spell, after so many solitary hours spent picking through the soggy, wood-smelling memorabilia (that he felt now had been waiting for him all this time, his 'train', as Dr Glenda might have put it) to see this over-bejewelled lady in front of him, in three-dimensional form. He'd expected a plainer, slightly withered version of the white-feathered girl. She was garish by comparison, like a middle-aged Chaka Khan or Naomi Campbell's mum. After attempting a witty return about the Hammersmith and City line that didn't work out, he asked her whether her chair was okay, addressing her as Mrs de Laperouse.

'It's Miss.' She handed him her coat, revealing a pencil dress with a zip-up 1980s belt. 'We're quite near the door, aren't we? Never mind. I'll sit over there,' and with her shoulders in their constant performance she moved round the large circular table towards the sumptuously cushioned bench that lined the edge of the brasserie. All the tables were nestled against this bench, adorned with thick white tablecloths and confusing silverware, as well as glasses, side plates, two-flower vases and napkins – there didn't seem enough room left to actually eat a meal, Lucas had thought as he'd sat there waiting, going over his opening question. Antique gilt-framed mirrors deepened the walls alongside moody pictures of film personalities. Further seating spilled out onto Portobello Road. The real-life Simone de Laperouse located her desired spot on the bench, dusted it off with the back of her hand, raised her little aquiline nose in the air, her strict spine an example to slouchers around the world, and slowly, impeccably, sat down, with all the grandeur of a queen descending to her throne.

'I've never liked having my back to the audience,' she declared.

Lucas had spent an hour and a half at home deciding between

jeans or combats, the Stevie Wonder T-shirt or the Rhythm Nation. He'd finished up with Stevie and jeans, a last spray of Lynx on top, but had disembarked feeling flapped and badly aimed. The opening question, according to Melissa, should be wide yet solid, possibly humorous, personal but not *too* personal, intelligent but not profound. It should also be spontaneous if you can manage it. 'Interviews are like sex,' she maintained. 'You've got to relax into it but show you know what you're doing.' After some befuddled sessions on his floor cushion Lucas had come up with two options for kick-off, planning to decide between them at the last moment as a stab at spontaneity. But right now he couldn't remember either of them. It had just occurred to him that his real name was printed below the 'Worst Five Pop Songs of All Time' list on page six of the latest copy of *West* that he was passing across the table. Louis Miguel (the surname was taken from Sizzla's Christian name) had seemed an appropriately poncey name for a Notting Hill-based journalist; its similarity to 'Lucas' made it seem less of a lie. He had practised the scenario of telling a stranger over the telephone that he was Antoney Matheus's son, but it had felt wrong, as if the words weren't coming out of his own mouth, so he'd decided to tell Simone who he was face to face. She was flicking through the magazine with interest. In an attempt to divert her from page six, he stretched across the table and directed her to the 'Where Are They Now?' page, on which Finn, lured by her obscurity, had agreed to feature her.

'Ruby Turner?' she said. 'Well *she*'s still around.'

Lucas started to explain, 'Yeah, but the page is for artists who were successful at—'

'But aren't any more, yes, I know . . . Relax, I'm just joking. All things come to an end.'

The cuttings had noted Simone de Laperouse as one of the Midnight Ballet's hottest attractions, 'a creature of considerable promise' and 'spirited, effervescent technique'. These days she taught dance part-time at a community centre in Lambeth, where

Lucas had tracked her down. 'I won't say I wasn't surprised to get your call,' she said. 'It's been years since anyone's even mentioned the Midnight Ballet to me. I thought we were long forgotten.'

'Not around here,' said Lucas. 'The editor's into – local stuff.' He checked his notebook, gathering himself. (For Cynthia. Do it, for Cynthia.) Then Simone said nostalgically, her hand on her cheek, her skin an elegant, powdery kind of dark brown, a ghostly brown, 'This place brings back so many memories. We used to watch films here on Saturday afternoons.'

Lucas said in freefall, 'You mean, with the others?'

The Grove Brasserie had not always been swanky. Before it was swanky it was café to a rundown cinema, the Grove Picture House, which had initially, during Toreth's youth, been a music hall. The picture house had changed hands several times over the years, falling in and out of operation. During the early nineties it had specialised in black cinema, rejoicing in Spike Lee and John Singleton, nostalgic for Jimmy Cliff in *The Harder They Come* and Gregory Isaacs in *Rockers*. The projection room at that time was at the top of a winding staircase. There was just one screening room, where things had not always gone well. Sometimes the duty manager doubled as the projectionist and the film would black out at reel changeover. Lucas had tasted the bad, chewy popcorn, salt indecipherable from sweet. He'd witnessed, with great sympathy for Jake, the frequent pattie complaints that were thrown at him behind the kiosk. Not surprisingly, that version of the picture house had also closed down, then along came a rich Swede. It was him who'd made it swanky.

Now it was called the Grove Screening Rooms. There were footstools in the auditoriums, good armrests. In the brasserie lettuce standards had been revolutionised (down with iceberg, hello baby mesclun and rocket). They did not sell crisps at the bar, only nuts (but not peanuts), and all the previous staff had been sacked apart from one, who had commercial and interesting hair. Jake found that his dreadlocks either really came in handy or really didn't. Under the new management he was given white trousers to wear, a white shirt, a long white French apron and, worst of all, a white bowtie. To add to this he was instructed to twirl his silver tray around on the tip of his finger in spare moments rather than stand about looking bored, which was bad for capitalism. 'I look like a dick,' had been his first words to Lucas when seen in this new get-up. If it weren't for Jake, Lucas's meeting with Simone de Laperouse would have been taking place at the Breadfruit takeaway.

Jake arrived at their table, notepad ready, looking sheepish and distant in his uniform. He and Lucas had arranged to act as if they only knew each other in passing, to make it seem like this was just one of many places Lucas might frequent of a Tuesday afternoon in his journalistic toil. Denise had not been told of the meeting, on account of her surly reaction to the opening of the forbidden cupboard, so Jake was the only conspirator in the Louis Miguel disguise. 'How's it going, Louis?' he said.

'Yeah, safe,' said Lucas, preferring to keep chitchat to a minimum. Jake was a lousy liar. He was checking out Simone. Lucas knew exactly what he was thinking: not bad for an aunty.

'Have I seen you somewhere before?' he had the gall to ask her.

'I don't think so, young man,' Simone replied, but she threw a girlish smile to one side and played with her necklaces.

'We get loads of famous people in here. D'you know who came in the other day? Annie Lennox. Serious. No lie. She was—'

'So what are you having?' Lucas returned the focus to the menu. Jake had granted him freeness on certain items: bread, green salad, the cowpat olives and one of the fish dishes. Free drinks were limited to pineapple juice and the house wine. 'Would you like some bread?'

'We do a mean seabass,' Jake helped. 'Luc – Louis. You come here a lot. I know you're familiar with our house bottle.'

'Oh, it's far too early in the day for me,' said Simone. 'Just water.' She ordered the wrong salad. Jake told her they were out of tomatoes. Lucas would break it to him later that he should never consider getting into acting.

Along with the newspaper cuttings, some photographs, a man's square-tipped snakeskin shoe and his mother's flapper dress, Lucas had also found in the cherrywood wardrobe a 1969 diary, belonging as well to his mother. It was leatherbound and flimsy, the kind allowing more space than needed for noting the day's appointments but not enough for an essay. Sitting in the clearing further up the bank to avoid being discovered by Denise, he had tried reading it. A child's felt-tip scrawl trampled across the pages (was it his? Denise's?). In the first few months there were brief, occasional entries, 'tour meeting', 'Rushwood Simone'. In spring and summer she'd written more. She had a neat, schoolgirl hand, which he ran across with his fingers. The seventh of June: *I'm a slave to the ground. It's a crime. I drag myself through the streets.* With her gravestone only on the other side of the wall he found reading full sentences chilling. Instead he'd skimmed for names – 'A' he assumed, for Antoney, Simone was mentioned frequently, as was someone called Bluey. The overall effect of the diary was that he was placed somehow further away from his father, while Carla, her voice almost audible in the slopes of the writing, became newly present, wandering around the boat in her scarlet dress. He was reminded of her when the sun flashed against the cabin walls, the way it used to flash against the beads of the dress when it was hanging up on the side of the wardrobe. He dreamt of her, of waking up to the sound of running water to find her washing her hands at the bathroom sink.

He was being sent, he felt, an open road. Over Breadfruit rice and peas he'd asked Denise matter-of-factly, seated at their dining booth, 'Do you know anyone called Simone?' 'Simone who?' she'd said, like a knock-knock joke – she was in a good mood as the Salvation Army had asked her to flower a luncheon. He gave the surname but she was none the wiser until he added, 'I think she was a friend of the family or something.' Denise swallowed her brown stew chicken displeased. Her lips tightened like her hands would tighten the earth around a new bulb. The boat rocked. She said, 'How do you know that?' in her coldest voice, then before he'd finished with his dodging, rambling answer he was told, 'I'm not interested in that junk you found. I don't want to hear about it. Is this really what you do all day while I'm out there working – rummage through a cupboard? Lucas, get a life. Rent is not free. I'm not doing this for much longer. Christ, if we were ever to sink you wouldn't even be able to swim to the top of the canal on your own!' Lucas reminded her that in fact he could swim, it was she who couldn't swim. 'Yes, I know,' she'd said drily. 'I was being metaphorical.'

Simone de Laperouse took an olive on a toothpick from a mosaic saucer and popped it into her mouth. He watched closely, every move she made, as the dining lips lost their lipstick, the stony fingers scintillated. Her earrings had passed a golden age. She was a vessel between then and now. She had the knowledge, the key. 'I'll start from the beginning,' she said.

The tape recorder was switched on. The brasserie was awash with ambient come-down music and Lucas worried that this and the knife and fork sounds would drown her voice, which was sharp, muscled, attempting, he came to discover, to hide itself behind someone posher. Despite all efforts, 'mean' came out as 'main'.

When Simone de Laperouse was five years old she saw a picture of Josephine Baker with her curls slicked onto her temples. She was so dazzled by her beauty, her glamour, her power that she wanted to be just like her, so she started taking

79

ballet classes in Kilburn. She knew she was going to be a dancer in the same way old people know they're going to die. At nineteen she auditioned for Ballet Rambert but didn't get through, 'even though I had a better line than half those girls there'. She did a spell in cabaret. 'Let me make this absolutely clear, Louis, because some people mistake cabaret for stripping. I have never removed my clothes in a professional setting apart from in the dressing room. I'm not that type.' She listed the highs and lows of cabaret – bussing home from Baker Street in the middle of the night, the perils of dancing in heels. Meanwhile to keep herself 'in tune', she was also doing the occasional 'serious' performance at fringe festivals with Oscar Day, who taught cutting-edge contemporary at a church not far from here. 'You may have heard of him. I mean, he was quite well known at the time. Eccentric. Bisexual, I might add.'

Lucas hadn't. She added with a short laugh that he was Nijinsky's number one fan.

'Nijinsky?'

'The ballet dancer. Russian. You can read about him. Anyway, Oscar was a fantastic teacher, the best I ever had. He took dancing right back to the core, so that you came away feeling . . .' she searched for the right word, her fingers glinting '. . . *vital* and *brazen*. He helped me to *locate* myself in the movement, you know? If it wasn't for Oscar the Midnight Ballet would never've happened.'

'Is that right?' said Lucas. 'Is he still around?'

'I've no idea, he could be dead for all I know. Are we doing photographs today? I wasn't sure.'

Finn sometimes sent a photographer along to interviews to get the conversational shot. Thankfully he hadn't considered this one worthy enough, so Lucas had de Laperouse all to himself. He could trip up, mess up, embarrass himself all he wanted and no one would know about it but him. 'We wanted to use a shot of you in action back in the day,' he said.

She informed him she had lots of those at home. She sipped

her water but did not continue with her account until prompted, as if put off by the snub of not being photographed, or perhaps the earlier shift in spotlight towards Oscar's whereabouts. The way she sat so erect, like her back was a fence, made Lucas feel sloppy underneath the Stevie T-shirt. He straightened himself as she elaborated on Oscar's interactive style of choreographing, his particular regard for her skills, his 'innovative vocabulary', which Lucas didn't really get. He wished he was more like Jeremy Paxman. He does it so well on *Newsnight*, he thought, when the person being interviewed is flaking around in uninteresting territory and he brutally hauls them to the nitty-gritty with a question like 'What makes you think that the party is ready for a man of Transylvanian heritage?' Just as he was thinking this, Simone came out mid-sentence with 'Then Antoney came along.'

A highwayman flew across a backspace in his mind.

'Antoney – Matheus?'

'Right, the artistic director. You've done some research, I see.'

Jake appeared with their mains and Lucas used this pause to re-establish his footing. The wide-yet-solid-intelligent-but-not-profound opening question, option one, of how Simone came to be a member of the company had led to a crucial spot, but now that they were here he was unsure whether he wanted to go further in, or walk back out onto Portobello Road where the avocados glittered in the sun and the Spice Girls ad leered beneath the Westway, leaving the past in the cupboard and himself in the present where they both belonged. He realised that until this moment he had never thought of his father as a once breathful, three-dimensional being. The questions burned beneath. Did he wear tracksuits? Did he live his life limitlessly?

'What was he like?'

'Antoney?' She had an olive stone in her mouth that needed to be taken out. 'Antoney was . . . hm—' She removed the stone. 'He was ill-equipped, shall we say, for where he landed. He was

81

a lesser man, a lesser leader by far – but Oscar was quite taken with him.'

Here there was silence. A spray of laughter broke out at a neighbouring table. Lucas said with a hint of defensiveness, 'How d'you mean he was lesser?'

'In order to win the world a director has to win his troupe first,' she said. 'That takes a certain kind of skill, which Antoney lacked.'

Oh, she had got along with him well enough. She'd never been one to indulge in conflict in a situation like that, when you're spending vast amounts of time with one set of people. Professional diplomacy should be maintained at all times. But there *were* some times . . .

Lucas began to suspect that Simone was jealous. Antoney turned up and became her beloved teacher's pet. She dwelled on how Oscar used to single him out during classes and make him demonstrate movements for the other students, 'when there were more experienced dancers preceding him'. 'He *did* have a unique style, I'll admit that. He was always doing something different, like his arms would be in the wrong place or he'd roll out a move rather than pull it back. The problem was that Oscar would then *change* it to fit with *that* way of doing it, which of course wasn't *everyone's* way.' She leaned forward conspiratorially, with the same girlishness she'd shown with Jake. 'My theory is Oscar was sweet on him.'

'What, because he was bisexual?'

'Of course not *just* that . . .' She fixed on Lucas her stretchy-upward eyes for a second, seeming embarrassed. 'It's just a theory.'

Oscar Day made the premature gesture of appointing Antoney – the 'lesser', the 'oddball', 'shyer than a newborn donkey', 'always in scruffy shoes' – as his co-choreographer for a festival showcase at an arts venue called the Sphinx in Earls Court. This was something he'd never done before, not for Ekow, who in Simone's opinion was much more deserving of it (personally she had no interest in choreographing – she was all dancer, made to be made for, to execute not arrange). Antoney apparently had some kind of Midas touch, but Ekow had fine ideas. 'He knew a lot about African dance, jazz dance. He was technically very astute. He'd been nagging Oscar for ages for an opportunity like that.'

'What was the Sphinx piece like?' Lucas asked. He was aware of the need to keep her in the frame. 'Were you in it?'

'I was. This was more than thirty years ago, I can barely remember it. What . . . repetitive, Caribbean-influenced – amateurish, really. No, wait, I do recall one phrase – it was such murder on my thighs.' Her shoulders flicked in a subtle mirroring of her description of it. 'Crouching down, to a rhythm. The right arm goes out to the side and taps the floor . . . yes, and a pause.' Her bracelets jingled as her psychedelic fingers found a keyboard. 'Then the hands stroke the lap, faster and faster, you shoot up and trip forwards with the arms following over the head, like falling down a flight of stairs. Gosh, I didn't know it was still in me. The body never forgets, that's true. I did that phrase so damn often. It was all over Antoney's work, like a signature.'

'What did it mean?'

'Beats me.'

'Who else was in that dance?'

'Antoney, Ekow. The core Midnight Ballet members.' Simone looked briefly down into her lap. 'And a friend of mine called Carla Bruce.' There was a frightening sign of recognition in her face as she again fixed her eyes on Lucas.

Now was the time to tell. Step aside, Louis, and let Lucas take the stage. Carla drooped in a heavy, beady mist over their table, she swayed over his seabass like a water balloon waiting to be burst. 'Sadly she passed away,' Simone said, deepening the onus to unmask. Lucas felt sure by now she'd seen through him, but what was in his head did not come out of his mouth. Louis spoke first.

'Sorry,' he said.

'Don't be, it was a long time ago.' They bent over their food, he with the same sensation he'd had in the clearing before the opened diary, that he was somewhere he should not be, the felt-tip scrawl trampling over the secret world. He wanted so much to tell her that he'd dreamt of his mother last night washing her hands, to ask whether she'd ever seen her wearing that dress when it was still scarlet, yet he couldn't find the language.

'I bet you tore up the place,' he said, believing himself to be at this juncture idiotic. Jake approached to perform his task of asking the diners whether all was good, if they needed more bread, more liquid. 'Actually,' Simone decided, 'I will take some wine, just a small glass.' Five minutes later Jake was bent beside her, placing a pearly white bulb at her right. Winking at Lucas, he went to stand by a dumb waiter and did not twirl his tray.

'It's strange,' she said, taking her first sip. 'You remind me of Carla in a way.'

'That is strange. What sort of way?'

'There's something about you. I don't know, my mind's playing tricks. I haven't talked about all these people in years and I'm seeing their faces now in front of me. Being here, Portobello Road . . . I spent a long time living in Paris, so it all became very distant.'

Carla and Simone had gone to school together, she told him. They used to go busking on Harrow Road when they were twelve. Carla sang Christmas carols on an upside-down bucket and Simone used to tap-dance. Always carols, no matter what time of year it was. Whenever they got a penny Carla would put the bucket over her head. Simone chuckled weirdly as she related this. 'Yes, that was Carla. A wonderful, natural dancer. Pure and rippling. She never believed it.'

'How d'you mean?' said Lucas.

'She always used to say that she had no talent. The rest of us were 'real' dancers and she'd just landed in it by accident, which was *partially* true, I suppose – Carla wasn't a do-or-die type of

84

dancer. She could just as easily have done something else.' Simone brought the glass to her lips and took a thoughtful swallow. 'She didn't like being in the spotlight. That surprised me. I mean, I'd known her most of my life and I never saw that kind of timidness in her before she got together with Antoney. The way she used to dress? Uh! That girl gave that boy style where he didn't have it!'

Simone seemed to relish this opportunity to reminisce about her friend. She gave a catalogue of Carla's clothes, all from second-hand shops, scarves and old boots, mini skirts, blouses, vintage dresses – the flapper included. She'd throw outfits together in the most outrageous ways, colours that just didn't match, orange tights, furry coats. She was a woman before her time. 'The girls I see walking around these days, they think they're so trendy, but Carla could've taught them a thing or two. As for Antoney! He used to wear these *awful* Laurel and Hardy slacks with creases at the front, I mean *seriously* creased, dull, standard shirts, the filthy shoes, oh it was shameful. I'd never've let a son of mine walk the streets looking like that. If a man's assets were in his clothes—'

'Yeah, I get you—'

'Well, by the time Carla was finished with him the man was wearing pink. She got rid of those mucky shoes and found him a pair of snakeskins. Drainpipes, good-fitting jeans. It was one of the most radical makeovers in fashion history. I'm sure if it wasn't for her guidance Antoney would never have found the nerve to pursue his other – interests, as it were . . . Presentation is everything.'

Lucas took a big swig of water and asked her what other interests she was referring to. He really wanted to go down the back alley and have a smoky respite from Mr Miguel with Jake, but no salaried journalist would do such a thing when the talk was hot.

'I don't like to gossip,' Simone said. 'Lots of men find it hard to stay loyal.'

85

'Are you saying he cheated on her?'

'As I said, I don't like to gossip.' She turned away from him towards the back of the brasserie, appearing to drift into her own thoughts. He got the feeling that she wasn't to be trusted, she was only telling him part of the story. The ambient comedown music had been replaced by a French singer, which Lucas found depressing, or perhaps it was the conversation that was depressing him. He refrained from asking any more questions about his mother for fear of not knowing what to do with the answer.

'She left two kids behind,' Simone said distantly. 'I should have kept in touch with them.'

The interview moved on to the point when the Midnight Ballet had actually formed. Simone explained that Antoney's boldness as a dance-maker was deceptive; it gave the impression he was further advanced than he was. Everything happened very quickly. Following the Sphinx project he did more joint ventures with Oscar in which she had a starring role. This was the beginning of her rise to become the troupe's 'principal dancer' (which Lucas hadn't specifically read anywhere in the literature). She claimed to be his father's 'muse'. 'No matter what I may have felt about Antoney's deficiencies as a director,' she said, 'I did like dancing his work. I liked its fluidity. It was voluptuous and eclectic. There was a childish conviction to it, something of Oscar's brazenness.'

In 1966 ('Lord, I'm ancient') an audition was held in Oscar's church basement to find more people to take part in a show they were putting on at the Ledbury Theatre, a local venue whose manager was a close friend of Oscar's. 'See, it started with a show. Initially there was no intention of forming a company.'

'Where exactly was this church you're talking about?' Lucas asked.

'Round the corner from here by Powis Square. St Bernard's. They must've knocked it down by now, it was derelict.'

'Did it have carvings on the door and stuff?'

'Yes, like Notre Dame, Oscar used to say. Is it still there?'

A chill, a spider-tingle had arrived at Lucas's shoulders and upper arms. He and Jake, climbing over that high gate into the courtyard, Jake with his big teeth in braces, he in his mashed-up boat-foot trainers. Six stairs down to the basement. Who can jump them all? *You hear something?* says Lucas. He puts his ear to the basement door. *Hear what?* Jake joins him. *Can you hear a bell? What bell? I can't hear no bell.* They listen harder, and now there are many sounds, voices, drums, laughter, footsteps, Simone. On that cloudy winter's day in 1966 Simone de Laperouse with her glossy lips and probable leg warmers, Carla with her foresty hair and vintage boots, Antoney with his drainpipes and a new artistic frown, Ekow of the unhailed talent, and a stream of hopefuls descended on Oscar Day through this very door, twenty or thirty of them, from all over, west London, north, south of the river, a couple from Birmingham ('Don't ask me how word got that far'). Some were British born, some not long here. There were several Nigerians and a few sly-looking Jamaicans ('You know that sly look, Antoney had that look,' Simone said). They were students, factory workers, dance enthusiasts, night-jobbers. Women outnumbered men for the dancing try-out, vice versa for the music. The atmosphere was one of pure excitement. Anything seemed possible. 'Back then, Louis, it wasn't like nowadays where you've got Adzido and Kokuma and Phoenix and all those guys. Black dance companies were a rarity here in the sixties. You'd sooner try and get work in the West End or in a contemporary or ballet troupe, though you had to be trained to get that type of gig. None of these people were trained by the way. No. There was only ever one trained dancer in the Midnight Ballet, and that was me.'

Simone's father was a scientist, one of the first Bajans to graduate from Oxford University, she hastened to note. When she was a young girl, after the Josephine picture, this scientist father had told her something she would never forget. He told her that human beings are made of stardust. That's right. We are hydrogen and oxygen and many other things, but we are also light atoms created in the bellies of ancient stars. 'Can you imagine that?' (Lucas warmed to her again with this.) 'That the universe is inside us, that we're so much more than what we think we are, or what society says we are?' (Hell, yeah.) 'I always despised the idea of leading a common, mediocre life. I wanted to be bright. I wanted to be shiny.'

'You are shiny.'

'No, I'm not! I'm not any more! I'm dusted over. Seized up. Look at me, I'm old and stiff. Back then I *glowed*. You should've seen me – I was as bright as the north star, a completely different person. I hardly recognise myself now.' She was close to tears, holding onto her serviette. Without her lipstick she did look older. There was a red smear of it on her chin.

'Everyone in that basement that day,' she went on, 'no matter who they were or where they came from, they were exactly the same as me. We all felt the same way. All of us wanted to shine.'

So there they all were in Oscar's basement. The high windows were misted up with body-heat. The drums were tapping, the hearts beating, the dancers stretching, the bell ringing. 'Who played the bell?' asked Lucas. 'The bell,' she said. 'You mean the cowbell? That would be Bluey. Bluey wasn't there that day.' Oscar spoke up, the mirrors at his back, and brought the hall to silence. Antoney was standing next to him looking demure and terrified. The project was a three-night run at the Ledbury Theatre, Oscar explained, a one-off experiment that he hoped would see recurrences. No one would be paid for rehearsals, but they would receive a grace-fee if the box office came back good. He'd been teaching for a long time, he said, and he had been lucky enough to see enter into his fold a very talented individual who went by the name of Antoney Matheus, a name he was convinced the dance planet would be hearing a lot in the future. Antoney studied the floor. The girls checked him out from his cocky eyebrows to his floaty feet. A couple of latecomers arrived and shuffled around at the back getting changed. It was quite rare, Oscar continued, for someone this early on in their career to have such an authoritative and innovative understanding of the choreographic process. He praised Antoney for his 'special mind', his exciting vision of weaving together modern, Caribbean and African vocabularies (here Ekow straightened in his position leaning against the mirror). 'But let me bore you no further,' Oscar concluded. 'I'm sure Antoney would like to say a few words himself. Antoney? Anything you'd like to, er . . . ?'

The fidgetings, mumblings and tinkerings stopped. This was the first time Antoney had addressed a crowd. He took a small step backwards, his hands clasped behind him. He looked as if he was praying for a sudden trapdoor to plunge him into the ground. When he finally found his voice he was told by one of the drummers to speak up. 'My teacher's got better words than me,' he said. 'I don't really have much to say.' A long pause ensued. Finally he went on, in short sentences, a speech utterly without fluidity. 'I was born in a hurricane. Movement comes from everyday life. This thing we're doing here, we just following the wind. Let's find out where it takes us. No walls, no bars, no categories. That's it.' He turned quickly back to Oscar. He really wasn't one for a speech, but he was sincere and compelling in his own way.

'So,' the teacher said. 'Without further ado.'

As Simone de Laperouse finished her glass of wine, then another, as Lucas joined her, as the Grove Brasserie got busier and Jake finished his shift at which a bill payment was pretended, she recollected all the people who'd eventually made it into the Midnight Ballet. She said that when you're part of something like that the studio becomes your home, the dancing your breath, your colleagues your brothers and sisters. You don't forget those people, she said.

Milly Afolabi (dancer)

At the time of the audition, Milly was studying bookkeeping at night school while working as a chambermaid. She lived in Harlesden, having arrived in the UK from Nigeria in 1960. Driven by her concern about the lack of West African food-stuffs in the neighbourhood (Where is all the yam, the egusi seed? Where is the gari?), she was looking into importation. Milly was an electrifying dancer. Oscar and Antoney noticed her immediately, the girl in the second row with the red vest, large earrings and close-cropped hair. She danced in a full, big-hearted way. She had strong legs and her shoulders had phenomenal shake capacity. Her experience included perform-ances in Lagos and Accra, and she would come to share with the Midnight Ballet much from her repertoire of West African moves. Milly often said that dancing should not have an age limit like it did in England. It's something you should do throughout your life, whether you're old or young, fat or thin. In the late 1970s she and her husband would open an import-export grocer on Victor Street in Harlesden, which still survives to this day.

Alphonso 'Fansa' Fontaine (drummer and percussionist)

Alphonso – the loud-mouthed guy at the back of the hall with the wristbands and firm drummer arms – had met Antoney at one of the Marshall brothers' blues where they'd got talking over punch about Kumina, a devotional dance and music orig-inating from the Congo and practised by the Maroons of eastern Jamaica, particularly in St Thomas. The Kumina was a backward-leaning, forward-creeping type of dance that Antoney had always loved to imitate, while Alphonso himself had learnt the Kumina rhythm, as well as the Dinki Minni and Brukins, on drums inherited from his grandfather. Alphonso grew up in Kingston and used to play in folk ensembles there before coming to the UK. He left his struggling ska band, the Hot Tones, for the Midnight Ballet. He was used to the showbiz life and enjoyed late nights and Guinness punch (a concoction of Guinness, nutmeg, cinnamon and condensed milk that Simone described as vile). He also liked to take full advantage of groupie activity. Girls waited by stage doors, fluttered in lobbies. Alphonso was never standoffish or superior towards them like Antoney was. Instead he told them he was not married and had no children as yet, and gave them his absolute attention.

Ricardo and Rosina Morris (dancer, dancer and photographer)
These two, hailing from Kennington in south London, were supposed to be twins but Simone had never been convinced. They looked nothing like each other. Her theory was that they lied about it in order to seem fascinating and mystical, which seemed to work with Antoney. Ricardo had a low forehead and a kind expression. His initiation into the dance planet had occurred through a girlfriend called Polly-Cinder. The story went like this. She was half Spanish, a quarter Irish and a quarter French. She had height and finesse, long swishy hair. She and Ricardo had locked eyes across his first dance class ever, which he'd attended having been told by a fellow painter and decorator that this was where the girls were at. Just think, he told Polly-Cinder later, entangled in a daisy field near Guildford, our children will be a quarter Scottish, a quarter Egyptian, a quarter Spanish, an eighth Irish, and an eighth French. Their relationship didn't last, but Ricardo had discovered himself to be quite an addicted mover. Big-built and stocky, he was what Oscar would call an ugly dancer. He would later embark on a career as a wrestler.

The alleged twin, Rosina, with the high forehead, joined the Midnight Ballet as a dancer and also became its photographer. She was tomboyish, much louder than her brother, and could sometimes be quite nasty to him. Of all the dancers in the troupe she was the weakest, always slow in picking up the movements, to Antoney's impatience. Most of the surviving photographs of the Midnight Ballet, including the ones Lucas found in the cupboard, were taken by Rosina. She'd started taking pictures in her teens and had always wanted to capture beings in motion.

The Wonder (singer and understudy drummer)

Originally from Ghana, The Wonder was a restaurant worker in Bayswater at the time of the audition and was craving a return to the stage, having previously spent many years working as a freelance fire-swallower in Spain and the Canaries. He'd been a talented and vivacious fire-swallower, bringing imaginative nuances to his act – such as, say, if a honeymooning couple were watching his performance after a sunset beachside meal, The Wonder (always spelt with the capital T – he was sensitive about it) would give his burning baton to the lady and invite her to set fire to his foot. He didn't actually swallow the fire, he'd once revealed to Simone. No. It was a special baton that extinguished as it entered the mouth, though sometimes the edges of his lips did get charred. The Wonder was large of belly and had a wide and pockmarked face. Despite his maturer years, he quickly grasped the intricate Senegalese footwork Ekow demonstrated.

Benjamin Omotunde Ojo (drummer)

This was the guy who told Antoney to speak up during his speech. The oldest of the troupe, and perhaps the least liked, Benjamin was working at the Heinz factory in Park Royal at the time. He hated baked beans and all things Heinz. He wanted to go back to Nigeria with his wife and children but was worried by the political unrest there and also lacked the funds. His djembe was the only thing that made him feel better about life. Whenever he disapproved of something his nostrils expanded and he rubbed his right knee vigorously. He once unleashed a damning tirade on Simone de Laperouse that went something like this: You think you are the Queen? You think you are better than me? You are not better than me. You are shit, you dance like shit. You are just like a broom. You have spent so long doing *ballet* and this modern nonsense stretching thing they call dance, there is no Africa left in your body! Simone was so upset she missed rehearsals for a week. However, Benjamin *was* a competent and commanding drummer, and would sometimes launch into impromptu, staggering solos at the top of the beat. After these moments, said Simone, he always seemed like a nicer person. But most of the time I hated him.

It was eight forty. Simone had now drunk three glasses of wine and was slurring her words. She and Lucas walked out beyond the glitzy awning of the Grove Brasserie into the purple Portobello evening, which for Lucas was now peopled with a wristbanded drummer, a pockmarked fire-eater, fraudulent twins and a bald guy called Day. Antoney and Carla were in the oxygen he breathed, which would incidentally encounter stardust. The church at Powis Square rang out like a Sunday morning with its new history. All of this was more prominent to Lucas than the funk and chatter coming out of the Market Bar, Scary Spice's thighs underneath the Westway, or the silhouettes smoking on the Falafel King stoop.

The journey to the tube station was unsteady. Simone was visibly tipsy, then there was Lucas with that drift of his. If you went for a walk with Lucas you would soon come to realise that instead of walking in a straight line alongside his companion he takes a vague, diagonal route, wandering towards you so that you have to sidestep into the road to avoid him. It was a huge source of irritation for Denise, who always walked ahead of him. Jake's way of coping with it was to stop still just before the point of collision in silent reminder of straight-line etiquette. Tonight Lucas was particularly drifty.

'Oops, we are a wobbly pair,' Simone said. 'I'd better hold onto your arm,' which she had to do upwardly, because of the difference in height.

They were coming down the deserted market alley that led

from Portobello Road to the tube station on Ladbroke Grove, now rendered gloomy and greenish in the absence of its Saturday mayhem. Nicotine voices rose up from Meanwhile Gardens running alongside it, which was frequented most evenings by homespun drunks. Lucas was feeling sordid with deceit. As they reached the end of the alley, just about to emerge onto the busy street, he had another strong urge to unveil himself – perhaps in return Simone might tell him what she was hiding. But he was deterred by a violent flapping of wings from one of the pigeon nests beneath the railbridge running across Ladbroke Grove (there were two, one on each side of the street, which directly below was spattered with black and white mess like an oil on canvas). Louis Miguel had got him in too deep. He somehow doubted that he'd ever see Simone again. There was little more she could give him. Except.

West, Louis told her in his quick-thinking, on-the-pulse journo gab, might be interested in doing a larger piece on the company. If she had any more contacts, could she let him know? There was a silence. Simone told him she wasn't in touch with anyone any more from those days. 'Everyone's scattered, upped, died, or got old and unsociable,' she said.

'Why was it called that?' They were just about to say their final goodbye. 'The Midnight Ballet?'

She looked up at him against the tinge of the streetlight behind him. Once more that searching, suspicious stare. 'Carla came up with it,' she said. 'It was a joke. We used to rehearse late.'

He watched her walk towards the ticket barriers fishing in her pink pocket for her ticket. Her back was steely straight, her head high, yet there was something raggedy about her. The withered hem of the coat, the old-fashioned evening shoes, it was around her like a vapour, and Lucas got to thinking about how you can see the expanse of a person when they're walking away from you, their entire life, the sum of all they've experienced, like an anthem or the credits at the end of a film. As a train

flew overhead he saw the expanse of Simone de Laperouse, and
there was melancholy in her song. She went through the barriers
to the stairs. He was about to walk away, then suddenly she
stopped mid-climb, her hand on the rail, and spun back round.

'Louis!' she called out.

He met her at the barrier.

'There is someone else,' she said breathily. 'He was a good
friend of Antoney's. A critic. He used to write a lot about us in
the newspapers.' She looked for an instant as if she couldn't
remember his name, but yes. 'His name was Riley. Edward Riley.
But all of us called him Riley.'

5

Looped onto the five-tiered houses of Ladbroke Grove, onto the ice cream terraces and the ten storeys of the twin tower blocks that Lucas can see from Silver's bow, are hundreds and hundreds of balconies. Those on the tower blocks are small and box-like, shielded from pigeon shit by green council netting. Towards Holland Park they tend towards the curvaceous and ornate. In some spots whole rooftops are assigned to the act of looking out, a pastime that has become intrinsic to Grove custom. The people, the pigeons, the loose-gowned lovers, they look out on the mousy bend of the Grand Union Canal, the numerous neighbourhood churches and the sycamore-lined stretch of the dividing hill. They pull up a chair, set beside them a glass of red wine or a beer, and some may still remember a Sunday in September 1967 when the children came out into the streets, which at that time were being obstructed by the building of the Westway highway, upon sinister titanic stilts, the biggest road project London had ever seen. Against a backdrop of motionless machinery and dusty mountains of rubble the children skipped and chattered, some of them wearing bonnets and Regency dresses, others top hats, or pipe-cleaner butterfly wings, or Arabian waistcoats. Batman and Robin were present. Another pair sat cross-legged on a travelling float at the feet of an Ethiopian king flanked by stuffed lions. Those children who were not in costume came as they were, in fallen socks and scuffed shoes, shorts and patterned jumpers, anything bright they had in their cupboards. They gazed at the Bulgarian dance troupe. They accosted a high-eyebrowed clown for his sweets and his collection of assorted curly balloons.

Along with the children came their mothers; their fathers, uncles, older sisters and lipsticked aunties, who carried tubes of glitter in their handbags for replenishing the cheeks when the sparkle was sweated away by dancing and the intermittent sun. More people gathered from further afield, many of whom had been exiled by the roadworks from their now demolished homes to Siberias such as Burnt Oak and Ealing, and wanted to catch up with friends. Music was provided by Calypsonians inside street-corner speakers, or beaten out live from the silver bellies of Trinidadian steel pans. It was getting to be a lucrative time of year for Emily Kirk and her fellow florists. Horse-drawn landaus and open-top cars were frizzy with garlands, wreaths, bouquets, and if anyone could turn a corn cob or make a good jerk thigh they'd do well to get a grill out on the pavement and fire it up. This noisy procession slithered up Ladbroke Grove all the way to Holland Park Avenue, along Notting Hill Gate, left into Pembridge Road, back down Chepstow. Two years before, the fayre was just a scruffy little bus-dodging ragtag parade to release slum frustrations and let the world know there was more to this district than drugs, colour clashes, concrete mixers and scrap heaps. Now it was turning into something to grab a balcony for.

Meanwhile at Oscar's place in Powis Square, the Midnight Ballet were rehearsing for their show at the Ledbury Theatre, which was two weeks away. They'd taken over the hall on the ground floor alongside the nave as their own designated space. The church door was ajar, the sound of drumming wafting out into the courtyard. Any Kensington and Chelsea civil servant might walk by and hear them but Oscar was long past caring.

St Bernard's was built in an age of community spirit where

the local centre of worship also served as a venue for jumble sales, youth clubs, women's meetings and tea dances. The hall had a canteen hatch at the back that Carla liked to sit on, and a storeroom now being used for costumes. One of its grimy alabaster walls still bore a poster for a china and crockery bazaar that had taken place there in 1948. Two of the sash windows were broken, there were no mirrors, the floor displayed black flushes of ground-in dirt that had proved impossible to scrub out, and a neighbour had already complained about the noise. But none of this mattered. Heinz, for Benjamin, was far away, the cabaret club for Simone, for Antoney the building site, for Milly the hotel. As Simone described it to Lucas at the Grove Brasserie, they were 'charged and supple and alive', sweating in the hollows of their necks. Nothing could make a day sweeter than the waking recollection that you'd be spending at least a few hours of it engrossed in music and vigorous physical exertion, and given the work still to be done on the material for the show, the pressure was on.

The sounds of the fayre were audible as the group watched Antoney and Milly (who was secretly his favourite dancer) attempt to blend together elements from a Nigerian dance called the Apepe with some contemporary movements. It wasn't going well. Antoney had learnt that the movements in your head were not as simple as they seemed. They jumped away from you if you reached for them. Sometimes when he was operating a concrete mixer or triggering a drill down on the Westway site, whole phrases would come to him fully intact, perfect, flowing cadences, and he would stop what he was doing to try and record them in his notebook. But as soon as he did so they'd disappear. Maybe the movements in his head were just that, the movements in his head – they weren't meant to go anywhere else. 'Don't be so defeatist, Antoney,' Oscar had responded to this. 'In creation there is destruction. The original concept never survives in its imagined flawless form. You lose a bit of it, and there's no shame in that.' Antoney was not convinced. He still wasn't sure Oscar hadn't overestimated him. He'd been having worrying dreams about falling off the stage and being laughed at by the audience.

There were four dances in all ('ballets', as Oscar called them). Two of these were developments of his and Antoney's previous projects – a version of Shango inspired by Katherine Dunham and a jubilant salute to the Marshall experience called 'Blues House'. The other two were new, a modern piece based on Jamaican Kumina, and this tricky one they were working on now. The ballets were amalgamations of generic knowledge collected from various members of the group, Oscar's expertise, and Antoney's gift for creating fluid and dramatic arrangements across varying vocabularies. He boldly combined burlesque throwy shoulders, Senegalese jumps and Merenge hips with gestures he'd seen in the street, a classical leap here, a little skanking there. He'd already made a name for himself on the fringe circuit on account of his audaciousness, which seemed to know no limits, but at this moment he'd apparently hit a wall. Milly had been repeating the same phrase for ten minutes.

'Look,' said Oscar, eating an overripe pear, 'think of it simple and it *will* be simple – a walk across a floor.'

Antoney threw a sideways glare at the old master. Carla was sitting nearby in her hatch, barefoot, her ankle-chained calves dangling in mid-air. Despite his irritation, he couldn't help being beguiled by her rampant copper-brown hair, which was tied back off her face making her eyes look larger still. Even on a hot day like today, Carla always turned up to rehearsals in her moulting six-shilling fake-fur coat and ankle boots then stripped off to a pair of shorts and some kind of flowery hippyish vest. Her attitude towards the dancing was light-hearted and could easily be mistaken for indifference. She didn't work quite as hard as the others, never got involved in the petty disagreements that broke out. Instead she watched things from the edge, sometimes interjecting an irrelevant, frivolous comment that would lift the atmosphere and dispel the bicker. Watching her as she grinned at Simone, Antoney wondered again whether he'd been wrong to let her go. She used to be his girl. He remembered the warmth of her body close to his and experienced a surge of yearning.

Simone was hovering close to the action in her ever-present legwarmers. 'Let me try it. I think I've got it. Play it.'

Antoney gave Simone half a minute to try out the sequence, during which he walked round her in a tight circle, then he stopped abruptly, listening. 'It's the music.' He approached the drummers. 'The music's wrong, it needs something . . . Fansa, play the Brukins.'

'You want Brukins now?'

'Yeah, try it.'

Fansa and Benjamin had their quarters at the other end of the hall by the storeroom. Fansa liked to play topless, his wristbands flipping and his long thin head tipped back as if he was trying with all his might to hear the faintest of sounds. Attached to the rim of his drum were three amplifying metal sheets with holes in that made a hissing noise as he played. Benjamin didn't know the Brukins so he looked on, stout and bulbous-headed by contrast, his own djembe at attention. The rhythm wasn't an obvious match. As Benjamin listened and watched the dance proceed, his nostrils began to expand. His right hand started rubbing that right knee.

'That's it. Better,' said Antoney, looking relieved. 'We'll slow it down. Oscar, what d'you think?'

'I'm liking it.'

It was intended as an all-girl piece with Milly taking a solo in the middle. Antoney beckoned for Carla and Rosina to join in; Simone was already in position. As the Brukins resumed and the dancers followed Milly's lead, Benjamin stood up, making a deliberate scrape with his chair. It wasn't the first time he'd brought things to a halt. It was obvious he had something serious and annoying to say. He directed his point towards Antoney.

'You should present the Apepe in the original way Milly taught it to you.'

The drum tapered off; Antoney asked him what he was talking about. 'Can we just get on with this?' Simone said hands on hips. 'We're trying to work?'

Benjamin went on in his strong Yoruba twang. 'Yes,' he said, 'I am watching you work, and sometimes I don't like what I am seeing. This is a traditional dance. You cannot just take a little bit here, a little bit there and throw everything together as if you are making soup. What does the Apepe know of the Brukins?'

'Is he serious?' Oscar said to Ekow under his breath.

'I don't give a shit about that,' replied Antoney without thinking. The music was still lacking something. He knew they were short on percussion but it had got too late to do anything about it. 'Fansa, continue.'

Benjamin's nostrils flared to full capacity. 'Listen,' he said, 'you are just a boy and you don't understand.' Carla saw Antoney tense at Benjamin's condescending tone. The drummer was always eager to remind people of their director's limited experience in relation to his own. 'Some of these dances you like to play around with here, they were created *centuries* ago. Hundreds and hundreds of years. Even before slavery, before this country even existed. They are artefacts of African civilisation. They should be protected and preserved.' He looked around the hall for possible allies. 'Is it not so?'

Rosina was yawning. Fansa was stretching. Milly shrugged and mumbled that the music was all right with her, while Carla gazed longingly out of the window towards the sound of the steel pans (Whose idea was it to rehearse on Sundays anyway?). When she turned back from the window, she found that Antoney was standing right next to her. He touched her wrist as if about to guide her back to the work at hand, though she got the feeling that this was only an excuse. Recently he'd taken to doing this, absently holding her shoulders while clarifying something

101

with another member of the troupe, taking her hand to lead her into a new position. He'd complained to her one beery night at Fiesta One (a Midnight Ballet nightspot) of feeling out of his depth, that he wasn't cut out for this kind of leadership, he was a quiet man with a whispering soul. She tried to ignore it, but every time he touched her the old feelings came back, a warm fear mixed with childish happiness.

The Wonder spoke next, having followed the conversation while massaging his foot and chewing on a piece of ginger (he smelt strongly of the stuff, it was said to be good for the kidneys). Face down underneath his stool was a book of essays on Zen Buddhism. 'Maybe there is something in what Benjamin is saying,' he said thoughtfully. 'What is it we're trying to do with this show? What exactly are we trying to say?'

'I'm not trying to do or say nothing!' Antoney broke off from Carla in a temper. 'What is this, dancing or politics?'

'Right,' called Oscar. 'Come come, boys, no time for heated debate.'

'But you are tampering with tradition!' cried Benjamin.

'Tradition? Jesus, what's that?'

'You, the oldest person among us, are asking such a foolish and ridiculous question?'

At this Ekow started across the hall towards Benjamin. He wouldn't have Oscar put down in his own damn place. 'Oh, sit down, Ben,' said Fansa. 'Don't be so old-time.' He came back in loudly with the Brukins, muffling the aggravation, 'Come on! Follow me!' and gradually the dancers resumed. But Benjamin was still furious and Antoney was still scowling. He was making flight, that was all. Run, leap, float, turn. What did it matter, a Kumina walk or a jump from Senegal? Why did it matter the languages he chose? He found it difficult to concentrate after this, so was among the first to notice a thin-faced, dark-haired white boy staring into the hall from the open doorway.

Carla noticed him as well. He looked as frightened and determined as a brand new soldier. It wasn't unusual for curious strangers to look in on what they were doing. People were always poking their heads through the windows, kids sniggering at the entrance – he was probably a stray from the festival (there was a tell-tale whistle around his neck). But unlike the average voyeur, this boy seemed to want something. He stood as if glued to the spot, looking hungrily into the centre of the room, not settling on any one person or object but venturing small glances at the drums, the various people scattered about. His childish, suntanned arms poked out of an oversized T-shirt. He attempted a smile of greeting. Once more the drumming ceased.

'Can I help you?' said Antoney.

'I want to join,' the boy said.

'Join?'

Simone and Fansa laughed. Antoney and Oscar exchanged a muddled look. The boy simply nodded.

'Well, what can you do?' Antoney asked him.

'Anything.'

Even Benjamin was looking tickled.

'Can you dance?'

'Nah.'

'Can you sing?' said Fansa in jest.

'Dunno,' the boy shrugged. 'Don't think so.'

The drummers roared with laughter. Carla told them to be quiet. 'Darling, what's your name?' He couldn't be more than sixteen or seventeen. He had the bluest eyes she'd ever seen.

'Bluey,' he said.

She laughed. 'Really?'

'Now what's funny?'

'Sorry. It's just that it suits you. Is that a nickname?'

He told her it was. He was drinking her in with his eyes, speaking only to her. 'Can you play something, Bluey?' she said softly.

103

'I can play piano. My dad's an organist, at church. It was him taught me.'

By now Benjamin and Fansa were holding on to their stomachs and slapping their flanks. 'But we don't have a piano!' Benjamin cried.

'I'll try drums then.'

'Guts he's got,' Oscar muttered to Ekow.

After some hesitation Fansa, coaxed by Carla, shifted off his seat to let this Bluey boy have a go on his djembe. He approached the instrument full of intent with an accelerating, loose-jeaned walk, but he obviously hadn't straddled a drum before because he lifted his leg over it, almost losing his balance, instead of sitting down first and pulling the thing towards him. Benjamin played an over-complicated rhythm that only an experienced drummer would be able to follow. The boy went red in the cheeks as he got lost in it again and again, eventually giving up and stiffening in his chair. He looked so destroyed that Carla couldn't stop herself from going over and ruffling his dark, tousled curls, which seemed to embarrass him further.

'There must be something,' she said.

'So anyone just hanging around outside can board the ship?' said Benjamin.

'Nah, you're all right.' Bluey started getting up the same way he'd sat down. 'I'll be off.'

'Wait a minute. Can you keep time?'

This was Antoney. He scrambled around in Fansa's duffel bag and found a set of wooden claves, hitting them together, but he wanted a higher sound. Benjamin was complaining that obviously the boy could *not* hold a rhythm, he'd just *demonstrated* that, and was told to shut up once and for all by Carla and Rosina simultaneously. When Antoney found what he was looking for – a cowbell and stick – he rose with it and handed them to Bluey, telling him to keep a straight two-four time. The bell was made of brass and attached to a coarse red strap.

'Fansa. Play the Brukins.'

They all watched. Hope had returned to Bluey's face, combined with a life-death concentration. In his new standing position next to the drums he regarded Carla for a last moment before taking up the beat. He played firm, enfolding the music with his own constant metre, smiling even, revealing a set of tiny, nicotine-stained teeth. The bell rang out through the windows and up through the eroding steeple. He didn't slip once, even when Benjamin began to accelerate. He kept up – then *they* kept up with *him*. His was the last shining sound, bringing the music to a close. Silence reigned.

'He can keep time,' Fansa said, flabbergasted.

'Yeah,' said Antoney. 'Yeah.'

The introduction of the cowbell solved the Apepe dilemma. Bluey was invited to play with the group at the Ledbury, with a view to further engagements if there happened to be any, and was told to return on Wednesday at four. Before he went back out into the festival (floating, lifted) he was given a gruff lecture by Benjamin on the philosophy of rhythm keeping.

'You are responsible for the beat, understand? If you lose time, someone else can lose time. You will make a mess.'

Carla put it differently. She felt such a powerful liking for the new recruit it could be said they were friends already. His nervous eyes seemed to pull her head first into their sea-framed pupils. 'You're the centre,' she told him. 'Without you, Bluey, remember, everything falls away.'

'What a striking boy,' Simone said when he'd gone.

After the rehearsal Oscar, who usually went walking on Sunday afternoons anyway, was dragged into the festival by the younger ones. He, Antoney, Simone, Carla and Ekow trailed together for a while behind a float, on the tail of several youngsters dressed in white leotards and red-rimmed butterfly wings who were unperturbed by the indecisive drizzle wetting their foreheads. Carla and Simone capered around doing ad hoc dance routines. They drank from cups of Coke-chased rum. There were all kinds of folks about. Whistle-blowing teenagers, spacy Mediterranean students in stripy tops, big-haired Jamaican girls in mini-dresses, old black men slurping pints outside the pubs, shopkeepers, policemen, open-shirted steel band skivers, a well-known barmaid in her famous leopard-print coat. There were fragments in this district of the Sahara Desert and the Irish Sea, the Panama Canal and the music box of Kingston, and the happy and terrible commotion that had developed from this was that you could find a good party as easily as you could a good fight. Portobello was not an English name. It was the result of an argument between the English and the Spanish in 1739 (and buried beneath the tarmac along Notting Hill Gate were the bones of Roman soldiers, who'd failed to make it home from some other battle). The parade contained a message to the type of iron-bar-slinging, riot-rousing character who wanted rid of all the different colours in the area: Like it or not, the steel pans sang, we're staying.

On the corner of Chepstow Road and the Westbourne Grove antique strip, Simone and Ekow went off to get some food and Carla was left alone in the crowd with Oscar and Antoney. By now she was merry from the rum, but there was an uncomfortable instant when Oscar turned away to chat with an acquaintance, leaving her and Antoney to their own devices. They both spoke at the same time and tried to style it out. Something about the scene with Bluey had made Antoney miserable. Normally it didn't faze him when Carla was hit on by other guys, but lately, he didn't know why, he'd been missing her if he hadn't seen her for a few days, picturing what she might be doing at any given time. She was the only person he felt he could talk to about things. She listened to him without judging, would stroke his shoulder in her easy, tactile way, or rub the back of his head with the same gentleness and understanding she'd shown to Bluey today. He could do with someone like that, someone sweet and decent, a girl who would always be this girl, who would wait for him at the end of adventures.

It was starting to occur to him how important companionship could be in keeping a man's feet planted on steady ground.

As for Carla, in the sudden absence of Simone she found it difficult to feign nonchalance at the fact of Antoney's recent passing touches, the heat of which seemed to be nestling and glinting in his face now while they avoided each other's eyes. As the procession made its way across the Chepstow junction the crowd thickened and they were shoved against one another on the pavement. The easiest thing to do would have been to interlock their arms and weather the bend as one unit, but instead Carla tried to recover the slice of space between them and stumbled backwards off the edge of the pavement. 'Careful,' he said grabbing her. 'You might get carried away.' He gave her such an adoring look with those sparrow eyes of his that a rapid smile took over her whole face. He was so handsome, she thought, so fine; the finest guy she knew. For a second she thought he was going to ask her back. He kept his grip on her, but unnecessarily firm – he seemed to have got stuck. They were both relieved when Oscar appeared again, coming between them, and started talking about the chance of getting an ad for the show in one of the papers. This led on to a discussion about stagefright – Carla was afraid of forgetting her steps.

'You look above the audience to the black space at the back and focus on what you're doing,' Oscar said. 'That's what I used to do when I was nervous. Pretend you're in an empty room. It works, really.' He took a handkerchief out of the pocket of his creased linen shirt and wiped his face with it. Carla used to feel intimidated around Oscar but she'd come to love his company. 'If you do forget steps just make sure you style it well. Don't look scared, whatever you do. Right, Antoney? Now why don't you two young things go and have a strut?'

An old calypso track by Lord Kitchener was drifting on the breeze amid the ripple and tinkle of the steel band up front. Carla started bopping again, her slim body moving effortlessly to the music. Antoney wished Oscar hadn't come back to walk along with them because he was putting him on the spot, smiling at him in sly encouragement. What he really wanted was to be on a bus, sitting alone with Carla on the top deck of a 52A. He should have told her what was on his mind when he was holding her back there and she was gazing into his face with that glorious, crooked-toothed smile. She might never smile at him like that again. Feeling glum and downcast, he danced next to her past the Chepstow balconies and the dilapidated houses, with possibly the stiffest gait a hoofer has ever adopted. All his old shyness leered at him, stopping him enjoying himself, or responding when she ventured to hold his hand. Eventually she bade them an awkward farewell and went home.

'Oh for Christ's sake, man, why don't you just lay it on the line? You two are driving me nuts!' Oscar and Antoney headed back to the church.

'You don't understand,' Antoney said. 'I like her, man. I mean, I *like* her.'

'You don't say.'

They were walking at the slow pace of beer mixed with rum. Antoney's speech was slackened by the booze. 'Why do I feel like this all of a sudden? I'm embarrassed around her, I don't know how to behave. I'm starting to look fool. We took that road already, Oscar.'

'Just talk to the girl. Tell her how you feel.'

'But say she's not thinking about me like that? I'd have to live it down. I still have to dance with her.' (He and Carla had a duet at the end of Blues House.)

'Antoney, look,' Oscar said. 'She's obviously crazy about you. If one is thinking, the other is usually thinking too. Just have a good time with her, why don't you? Live a little. It's all material, and the more of that you can get the better.'

They'd come up Talbot Road to the square. Antoney didn't notice the way Oscar steadied himself on the church gate for a few seconds before opening it, or how slowly he proceeded through the dim, weedy courtyard. He was too busy thinking about whether or not he was in love, and if so was it with the *idea* of Carla (good-looking, good dancer, pine-skin, nice personality) or Carla herself? He used to find her immature at times when they were dating, girlish and superficial, her obsession with clothes, always having to be dressed up like she was going somewhere hip. She wasn't on his wavelength the way Oscar was when it came to discussing anything to do with dance. What if they got back together and these things put him off again? How was he supposed to know which instinct to trust? On top of all this his mind was so full of the coming show he could hardly think straight.

'She makes me feel calm,' he said, less a statement directed towards Oscar than a shred of his darting thoughts.

At the railing over the basement stairs, Oscar held on and swung one backward step down trying to appear nimble. He was forced to clutch the area above his left knee afterwards as it was giving him considerable pain.

'These legs,' he joked. 'They used to do pirouettes, you know.'

'Stop pretending, Oscar – your party days are far from over.'

'No,' he said more seriously. 'What I need is a walking stick. That was the longest walk of my life.'

Antoney leaned over the rail. 'So what you think, about me and her?'

'What do I think? Hey, the girl's a dream.'

'You think so?'

'Yeah, she's . . . what's the word I'm wanting?' Oscar looked up into the indigo evening, saw the Big Dipper and the white half moon. 'Ah. Yes. Luminous,' he said. 'She is luminous.'

Antoney returned home to Bassett Road with a smile on his face, thinking all the way, *She is luminous, luminous*. He was no longer sharing with Florence but had the box room on the ground floor, though his mother still cooked for him. Florence was in Sheryl's room, where they'd passed much of the afternoon watching Bette Davis in *Mr Skeffington*, stepping out once or twice to stretch their legs. The two women looked out at the litter on the streets, the remaining loiterers and homebound stragglers. They talked about how much the parade had reminded them of back home, everyone out and about, the dressing up, the children – it brightened up the place. Look at all that rubbish, though, said Florence, and they won't clean it up till next month, said Sheryl. The steely silver music wafted in the night breeze. The footsteps of the walkers carried on, perhaps in anticipation of how they would continue to walk, at the close of every summer, in greater and greater numbers, of what dazzling concoctions of masquerade they would show off in the future, when the music trucks joined in, and soca had sprung from calypso, when the Latin beats and hip-hop sound systems got in on it too and the hot grills took up whole streets, and people started coming in their hundreds of thousands, from all over the world – when that scruffy little bus-dodging ragtag parade had turned into the Notting Hill Carnival.

Carla also lived with her mother, in one of the new four-storey blocks of flats round the back of Harrow Road. They were Westway refugees. Toreth blamed Antoney for it. He was one of *those* men in the orange hardhats who'd destroyed her little house down Latimer way, her vegetable patch, her south-facing sitting room that yes could've done with more space and yes had suffered a leak here and there, but it was her long-time place, wasn't it, the house whose threshold Carla's father had carried her over on their wedding day. He was all in the air in that house.

His name was Freddy Bruce. He was from the Windward Island of Dominica. He and Toreth had met in 1943 while he was on leave from the air force – Toreth had dropped an egg on his foot coming out of the grocer on Portobello Road. Her flour, her biscuits, her sugar and what-have-you were all wrapped in greaseproof paper in her basket, and on top of that was her cone full of eggs. She rushed out of the shop having had to queue for forty-five minutes just as Freddy was walking past with a mate. They collided, the basket tipped, out fell one egg onto his polished black shoe. You can tell a lot about a man from his shoes, Toreth would comment when she told this story. Your father had nice feet. He was proud of them.

Toreth gasped. 'Oh God, oh blimey, what've I done, oh look!'

Freddy was somewhat miffed, evident from the look on his face. Some of the yolk had got on his trouser leg, which Toreth frantically brushed at with a handkerchief without even realising what she was doing. His friend was laughing so hard that Freddy lightened up and cracked a joke that went something like 'Well, I was thinking I needed to get that left shoe shined with something special', which his friend also found hysterically funny. Soon all three were chuckling away, Freddy and Toreth eyeing each other up and getting all coy, and before walking on with his eggy foot he asked her if she wouldn't mind taking a stroll through Hyde Park with him some time. She said, 'I'll have to ask my dad.'

Carla's grandfather had moved from Llandudno to London in 1929 with his wife, three children and a laundry plan. Laundry's the thing, he used to say. Whether you're Welsh or English, rich or poor, everyone needs to get their washing done. He'd originally had ideas for a fancy kind of laundry where you could get a cup of tea or a slice of Battenburg cake as well, but he was a bit before his time on this and ended up with just a straight down-the-line establishment on Scrubs Lane, which he ran with a dictator's ferocity, as he did his home. On Saturdays they cleaned house, on Sundays they went to chapel. Toreth was the only girl, and even at twenty-one when she met Freddy she wasn't allowed out with just any old shanooble or Humphrey. When it came down to it she couldn't quite bring herself to ask her dad if she could go for a walk with a Negro, so she went behind his back to see if it was worth the trouble first. It was. Freddy took her on one of those boats. 'I don't know how he could afford it, Carla, those rowing boats in Hyde

Park. They cost the earth!' That was pretty much when she fell for him. He was broad and well built, 'like men are supposed to be'. It was the most romantic moment of her life, Freddy in his white shirt, she in a yellow frock, the two of them drifting across the lake. The only thing missing was a parasol.

Ten months later they were married, then ten months after that Carla was born, a war baby. Freddy didn't come back for six months once and Toreth thought he was dead. When the war was over he got a job as a coach driver. Carla's earliest childhood memories were of sitting next to her mother on that most important seat right behind the driver and staring at the back of her father's head. The journeys ended at Blackpool beach, Great Yarmouth, Brighton, and Freddy would be able to move his head again, lifting Carla up, biting her cheeks with his crowded beige teeth. She was the image of her mother with her large-eyed narrowness but she had her father's teeth and thick, Indian-descended hair. His arms were one of her favourite places, his voice one of her best sounds. When she was six and a half he did a long trip down to Penzance and never returned. December. The icy homeward road. Freddy's coach collided with an overtaking lorry and was sent skidding into the ditch, killing the driver and two of its thirty-one passengers. Carla remembered standing in her nighty at the bottom of the stairs listening to weird sobbing coming out of the sitting room. Her father had gone away, she was told. He had joined the flowers. He was sitting by a pear tree in heaven. 'Did he drive there?' Carla asked her mother on one particular occasion. 'Yes,' Toreth began again to weep, 'he did, but a bit too fast.'

After that Toreth developed a phobia of transport. She would not take a boat, a coach, a train, preferably not even a bus, and therefore neither would her only child (she and Freddy had been trying for another). When the family began talking about moving back to Wales she said she was staying put. She got a job at the Soap Land laundry on St Helens Gardens, taking in lodgers when times were tough, and Carla grew up with the many reminders of her father around the house – the photograph of him in his Royal Air Force uniform on the mantelpiece, the threadbare Dominica tea towel on the wall above the kitchen table, an island that seemed about as far away to her as Jupiter. When she met Antoney at the Marshall brothers' blues in 1962 she was eighteen and still hadn't been any further than Llandudno. Throughout her school years she'd spent her extra-curricular afternoons helping her mother wash linen. In times of excruciating boredom she would crush the hot sheets to her face and breathe in until she was full of loyal heat, which may have gone some way towards bestowing on her a gift for contentment. This was a fundamental difference between her and Antoney. Laundry had taught Carla that whatever the restlessness or discontent you might be feeling, you could always get satisfaction from fresh sheets.

If there was anything in Antoney's smooth, low-pitched, see-saw voice that made her think of a long-ago best sound, she wasn't conscious of it. He was broad and strong the way men are supposed to be. He was just her type. 'Tell me, how did you cope losing your dad like that?' he asked her on the 52A from Ladbroke Grove to Victoria. 'It was all right,' Carla shrugged. 'You know, it happened. We just got on with it.'

He had this thing about buses. One night after a class at Oscar's he'd asked her whether she fancied going for a ride. They took the 23 to Oxford Circus and walked down to Piccadilly. The week after that it was the 18 followed by the 30 and they ended up in Hackney. He said a journey was better than the destination, and she did notice he was always more jovial when they were on the bus than when they were off it. Lights, trees, turns. Regent Street to Kennington. Upper Street to Archway. Night stars on the river and the marvellous mannequins of Knightsbridge. His favourite food was ackee and saltfish cooked with Scotch bonnet peppers. Hers was toast. She asked him about Jamaica. Steep, round roads different from these, he said, proper sun, mountains, but a

113

small place. He had more to say about Cuba, whose lights he said were visible in clear weather from the northern Jamaican coast. It was a place that seemed to fascinate him. Once he had enough money he planned to go there and see the Afro-Cuban folk dances for himself. He also wanted to go to Paris, America. He was so full of worldly thirst and curiosity that Carla felt plain by comparison. She'd find herself nodding and listening as he talked, studying a dent in the skin on his cheek-bone, perhaps the remains of a terrible pimple, not being able to think of anything worthwhile to say. He asked her once if she'd ever been to Dominica, and when she said she only had the tea towel he studied her with a lingering, emptying surprise.

She was drawn by his intense, inward stare. She liked the mystery of looking for him when he was looking right at her. His boyish smile, the worry at each corner. The way he always sidled off on his own with an air of solid absorption that made one think that whatever he was deserting was far less inter-esting than the entertainment he could create in his head. It wasn't exactly shyness she saw in him. It was a confidence in his own world. He liked to smoke, to sit alone with a nice-sized joint and reflect, but he didn't mind if she sat with him. He said she was one of the few people he could ease along with when he was lifted. Everyone at Oscar's thought they were coupled up. Then one day they were. He put his arm around her on the top deck of the 2B and they kissed. They were both a bit dry-lipped, the bus smelt of curry, but their second kiss was better, almost as good as a good first kiss. All they did for the next five months was kiss. They were as chaste as children. Antoney would massage her leg, rub her waist, she'd squeeze his back. Simone said maybe he was a closet queer, but Carla knew different. He was being respectful.

'I bet you've had loads of girls before,' she'd said to him, crossing Waterloo Bridge with its sweeping arches. 'I bet you're a real stud.'

(Only Cordelia, Maxine, Susan back home who popped his cherry when he was fourteen, and Nancy up St Mark's Road where he went sometimes for belly pork.)

'No one as fine as you,' he said. 'I like to keep myself clean.' (It was true. He didn't go all out with just *anyone*.)

'That's good.'

'What about you?'

'No one special.' She gave him a golden, secret smile. 'I'm saving myself for a proper man.'

Although it impressed Carla that he was being so gallant, she wouldn't have minded an attempt at third base just to know he was anticipating something. She didn't want them to get cool before they had even got hot. She became quite preoccupied with it. Then one night in November of '64 they went to the funfair at Shepherd's Bush Green, where two things happened: the first, a fortune-teller; the second, a vision.

They took the 94. The ferris wheel waited. Gypsy tents were lit from within by many coloured lanterns. Together they made a charming sight as they drifted through, Antoney in a long leather coat they'd found while browsing at the second-hand shop (he wasn't completely out of the Laurel and Hardy phase by then but things were looking up), she fizzy-crowned in a thick-belted trench. Antoney said it had been a long time since he'd had his fortune read, so they entered a tent with a blue light showing through the gauze and sat down side by side before a plump, two-chinned Romany woman in a headscarf.

'Together?' she said.

'Yep, why not?' said Carla.

She used cards, turning them in her hands at the darkened table. First of all she told Antoney that he had a secret admirer and he should look after his legs and the side of his roof, which he smirked at. Then she said she had a message from his parent far away.

'What do you mean my parent?'

115

'Your mother or your father, in a far-away place.'

'His mum only lives on Bassett Road,' said Carla.

'It is a very important message,' the fortune-teller said, straight-faced and slightly bored.

Antoney asked her, in an unstable tone Carla hadn't heard before, 'Is my father dead?'

'That is not my area,' said the woman, pausing. 'But I do not think that the parent is dead. Do you want to hear the message or not?'

'Okay, what is it?' Antoney leaned back scornfully, trying for his usual detachment.

'Well. Here,' she said. 'It is short. I will explain it. You are tender, I can see, in the subconscious place, and there is darkness in you. The parent says that if everybody goes in one direction, you always want to go in another, and that you must not change this.'

'Is that it?'

'Almost, yes. The other thing is that if you do not follow your feet, the darkness will eat you like a big fish – a shark, I think he said. You must follow your stretch of sea.'

At these last words, Antoney got up and walked out of the tent.

Carla was left sitting there, bewildered, her own fortune yet to be told, which was almost as odd, it turned out, as the one she'd just heard. The woman looked deep into her eyes. She worked the cards then looked again into her eyes, this time with a slight shock. She didn't say much except that she, Carla, was such a pretty girl. 'When you are asleep at night, my dear, try to sleep on your side, instead of on your back.'

'That's it?'

'Yes, I'm afraid so.'

'Can I have my money back, please?'

'Hell no, what you think?'

'Who the fuck was that?' Antoney said as Carla emerged from the tent.

116

'You tell me. Are you all right?'

He looked as though he wanted to hit something. He wouldn't say what was wrong, only that the woman had given him the creeps. Carla embraced him, so vulnerable he seemed all of a sudden, and at first it was a bit like putting her arms around Nelson's Column. He'd only ever mentioned his father to her once, that he'd taken off when he was young, but he hadn't shown much sentiment about it at the time. She led him away from the tent. They walked about together in the frosting grass.

Then the second thing. Fireworks. Gazing up, holding hands, the carousel tune drowned out by the explosions. Carla saw greens, pinks and silvers making shoots. But Antoney saw something else, which he described to her later in detail. While he was looking up there into the black world of night, with the lavender clouds just liming here and there and the moon not quite full, he was thinking about how the fireworks made a pattern like a dance, and that maybe he should try and make a dance like fireworks, when he saw a bus. 'A bus. You saw a bus, in the sky.' 'Yes I did,' he would confirm. It was just cruising across the moon, cool as cucumber. 'What, like a 23? Double decker?' said Carla. No, single deck. He couldn't see what colour it was because it was in silhouette. But he could see, he *knew* somehow, that there were dancers inside it, and they were all going somewhere fabulous. 'I should think so, taking that route.' He watched it as it made a shallow arch from the left side to the right side of the moon. The windows were open, the passengers facing the front, up and down it went, and then it was gone. 'See it there, a real-life flying dream.' 'You're so weird,' said Carla.

Actually as Antoney was relating this to her they were lying undressed and entangled in her bedroom, Carla having niftily sneaked him in while her mother was asleep. That was the third thing that happened that night. In a magic mood fuelled by the bravado of stealth, they fell silently onto her strawberry and

117

stem eiderdown and went all out. They couldn't make a sound in case Toreth woke up, and they were shy with each other due to the circumstances, so everything was slow and tentative. When he took off his vest she marvelled at his triangular shape, the way he shot out of his waist. He spent some time kissing the insides of her ankles which eventually started to tickle, making Carla giggle too loudly. 'I don't want to hurt you,' he said. 'You won't hurt me,' she whispered, and the pain was only small in comparison to the big moist warmth of it, the feeling of being surrounded and transported. After the bus conversation they fell asleep for too long and were woken at six by Carla's mum going about her morning toilette in the bathroom next door. It wasn't just because of the Westway that Toreth and Antoney never hit it off. It was because that ankle-tickled giggle had pierced her sleep, and she saw him from the bathroom window escaping up the front path, struggling to put on his shoe.

Three months later they'd broken up. The bus vision made Antoney take his dancing more seriously. He said it was a sign, an omen, and if he ignored it he'd be bringing on bad luck. He spent more evenings at Oscar's place discussing God knew what. Carla got quite bored sometimes when all he wanted to talk about was whether he really had what it took to be a choreographer and how you had to 'let the dance be what it wants to be'. If Carla started a conversation about window-shopping on King's Road or how much she wanted to see Otis Redding, he'd find an annoying way of navigating the topic back to dance matters. All she wanted to do was run her hands up the backs of his thighs, to lie so close to him that their noses were touching, to fall asleep in the crook of his arm, her first proper man. But it was hard to find somewhere to lie down, what with Toreth not allowing him upstairs, and he didn't seem to like taking her to his place. They lost a rhythm. There was distance in his touch, so she wound up feeling like one of the mannequins in Knightsbridge, exquisite, but cool as porcelain. He practically ignored her during classes; hanging out with Ekow, Simone and the others in the vestibule he treated her no differently from anyone else. She also found him arrogant at times. Walking her home from a party he expressed the opinion that real artists were above 'everyday people' and they had to live in an unconventional way, like Oscar, with minimum distractions. They had to make their work the most important thing. Carla strongly disagreed. She stated in a breezy tone flecked with sarcasm, 'Bad idea to make one thing your be-all and end-all. It's bound to come tumbling down.'

A week later, when she asked him whether she was his girlfriend or not, he said, 'Baby, why do we need to define what we are? Let's just be.'

'Ok,' she said. 'See you about then.'

She often thought of him when she was in bed in the new Harrow Road place. Unlike her mother she was glad of the move. They had a balcony instead of a garden. The ghost of Freddy was thinned. In the corner of her bedroom was a pipe that went down through all four storeys so that everyone shared one heat. In this pipe she could hear many things, domestic quarrels, drunken mutterings, the moans and mattress-squeaks of dawny sex – which always made her remember the magnificence of him lying on top of her in rhythm, looming triangular above, his hands holding his weight on either side. She used this image in her own particular way to see if she could get to the moon.

The Ledbury Theatre was not seafaring like the Carib. It was without barracuda. There were no starfish or turtles on the pale green walls, instead mounted teardrop lamps, then a high, arched ceiling below which spotlights marched across on metal beams. The stage curtain – recently washed and rehung – was wine-coloured, as all good stage curtains, according to Oscar, should be.

The Midnight Ballet gathered there on the afternoon of 6 October 1967, a month before Antoney's twenty-sixth birthday. He had a strong recollection as he entered the building of that windy day on the Goldtooth bus to Kingston – the billygoats on the mountain ridges, the sharks on the ceiling of the auditorium, the orange-centred flower in Mr Rogers's hat. His chest was tight with nervousness. He'd hardly slept the night before because he was so anxious about things going wrong, the dancers forgetting their steps or not enough people turning up. When Carla walked in with Simone – they were radiant from the previous night's egg facials and she'd done something different to her hair – he went straight up to her with that piercing gaze of his and kissed her full on the cheek as if she was his wife, so relieved he was to see her. It bugged him how Bluey always planted himself beside her like a stray dog who'd found a home.

Milly and 'the twins' were late. Fansa brought along his latest chick and kept winking at her during the sound check, so that Oscar eventually asked her to leave, provoking a scolding from Benjamin to Fansa about his marital failures. Ekow and Antoney charged about in the otherworldly daylight-darkness of the auditorium. Ekow was the more composed of the two. Antoney snapped at people. He shouted at Milly for being late. He couldn't seem to settle himself down – it was as if a hurricane was starting to blow inside him. Things came to a head during the light check, which he wanted complete control of. He trusted no one with the responsibility of casting the amber beam stage left four minutes and twenty seconds into 'Shango Storm', or a full red spotlight on the lifting of Carla by himself in the Blues House duet. He yelled at the technician and when Ekow told him to calm down, that the lights would be cool, he shot back, 'Lights are everything, lights are everything! Why are you so damn blasé about matters all the time?' Ekow told him to go and have a joint.

Carla didn't catch this dispute because she was backstage on a bottom step talking to Bluey, who'd lost time during the Brukins sound check and was fretting about the responsibility on his shoulders. 'It's like the atomic bomb, right. If they set it off everyone's buggered. I'll mess up the whole thing if I go out there. I'm scared shitless.'

Carla ruffled his hair, enjoying the feel of its soft curls. In the preceding fortnight she'd learnt that at thirteen Bluey had run away from home in Shropshire intending to join the circus, but had ended up living with an uncle in Ealing and working in his bakery for his keep. He looked younger than his years. He was eighteen going on nineteen.

'I'm scared too,' she said.

'You ain't. You don't look it.'

'Seriously, I've never done anything like this before. Only school stuff.'

'I feel like running off.' Bluey fixed her an amorous look. 'Let's run off, you and me.'

The closer it got to curtain-up the more frantic and unreasonable Antoney became. At one point he grew convinced that the stage had shrunk since the dress rehearsal, and was drily told by a stage hand that it was an immobile structure. He didn't leave himself enough time to eat. The Shango cutlass was temporarily lost. His red waistcoat seemed threadbare. There was no talking to him. Half an hour before the show was due to begin, the lobby out there peopled and starting to rumble, he rushed out of the men's dressing room in a total panic. '*Why* is it so blasted hot in there? I don't know what I'm doing. Where the hell has Oscar gone?'

A voice replied from the gloom. 'He's gone to stand at the back.'

The Wonder was sitting in shadow on a wooden box outside the dressing room. He was just sitting there, in his orange musician's robe, doing nothing, like he was waiting for a bus. It made Antoney want to laugh and slap him at the same time.

'What you doing, man?' he asked him.

121

'I'm having the minute,' The Wonder said. 'Why don't you join me?'

'Wonder, we're—'

'*The* Wonder, Antoney, please, I've told you this before. Wonder is a girl's name.'

To this Antoney could think of no response except to stare at the musician uncomprehendingly. With a grunt he sat down next to him on the box, which was reminiscent of Katherine's trunk. He kept his back to him, leaning forward elbows on knees, shoulders like cement, wringing his hands together and tapping his foot.

'Big night,' said The Wonder.

'Yep.'

'When I was working as a fire-swallower, I used to worry sometimes that my appearances would not go well. Especially at first. You always want it to go well.'

'Yep,' said Antoney disinterested.

'I used to think to myself, what if I set myself on fire? What if I burn somebody and I'm locked up in jail or something horrible like that? What if I fail to satisfy my audience, or I embarrass myself?' He nudged Antoney, who had ceased tapping his foot. 'You know what I used to do?'

'What?'

'Before the show, I used to take my drink – I was a brandy man back then but now as you know I don't drink, it's bad for you, but really you can use whatever spirit you like, it doesn't have to be brandy. So I used to take my drink, just a small amount, and pour it onto the stage for good luck.' The Wonder had a warm, slightly high voice.

Antoney shifted round. 'You mean, kinda like a libation?'

'Exactly that, yes. A prayer to the gods to fend off any negative energy. I believe it worked for me. My audience was never disappointed . . . Also,' he added, as Antoney was contemplating this information, 'the quiet minute to yourself is very important. It's not good to get so worked up before a show. It's bad for the heart.'

Shortly afterwards Antoney sent Ricardo to the bar for a shot of rum.

Shortly after that, he lost his voice.

Drinking wine with Lucas at the Grove Brasserie, Simone remembered the opening night in minute detail, as vividly as if it had been last week. She remembered standing barefoot in the wings behind Carla as the auditorium unexpectedly filled up, her hands on her friend's waist, both of them wearing red rayon skirts and sleeveless leotards. Carla told Simone she felt unlike herself. Their faces were heavily made up. She looked like a startled brown doll. Every few moments as they tried to peep past the curtain at the audience, Simone went up onto the tips of her toes, a habit left over from ballet.

The audience were local Grove folk, curious others, fascinated middle-class liberals, a dance and arts in-crowd with smoky eyes and James Dean haircuts. Toreth was there, sitting dubiously with the other family members of the cast in the front row. Florence had made a point of not coming. She'd attended the dress rehearsal but had been embarrassed by Antoney parading around in his Shango skirt and makeup. The drums, the deity theme, to her it was nothing more than a form of Obeah dancing like that practised in St Thomas back home, and she'd said as much. The two of them were not speaking, a state of affairs that would worsen over time.

The skins of the drums had been spread with talcum powder to create a mist as they were played. The Wonder's opening chant stilled the final rustlings from the crowd. Overall there were few hiccups. Bluey had his robe on back to front but he kept time. Forgotten steps were mostly well styled, and Antoney was a star as Shango, blazing across the stage his arms gleaming (*You'll be mighty strong one day, you'll make a fine Shango*). It was a mystery what had happened to his voice. Every show they did from then on he lost it fifteen minutes before curtain-up and didn't get it back until somewhere during the interval. It was better for everyone that way, Simone said.

She remembered that the electricity between Carla and Antoney that night was almost visible. You felt that should you pass between them you might trip over something – it was as if the apprehension and the cave-like atmosphere of the theatre had put a spell on them both. Any time Carla came near Antoney his eyes would soften. While she and Simone were standing there in the wings in their Shango costumes Simone became aware of a certain charge behind her, and turned to find Antoney lurking a few feet away from them. However strong this chemistry was, though, it seemed to act as a barrier between them because they hardly spoke to one other all evening. It wasn't until the closing dance, Blues House, that they were finally able to communicate.

This was everyone's favourite ballet. Six dancers (Antoney, Ekow, Ricardo; Carla, Simone and Milly) the men in fedoras, the women in gold-sequined tops and white chiffon scarves, jiving and skipping through a series of dizzying, eclectic vignettes set to a soundtrack comprising the Maytals, Lord Tanamo and Nina Simone. There were sculpted hands and statuesque heads, loose hips and rustic arms. In the middle of the piece was a full-group sequence using a glittered aluminium disc as a tossing prop, featuring Antoney's signature motif of tapping the floor, the accelerating stroking of the lap, then the rising up and tumbling forward, here in a festive mood. He and Carla closed the piece with their duet. It was the high point of the evening. As soon as the two of them were alone together on the stage with Nina's mournful voice, having sloped Kumina-style from each wing to meet in the middle, that chemistry they'd been skirting around for days, weeks, months, took over, and it seemed as though they actually were in an empty room, aware of nothing else but each other, and the audience was looking in through a keyhole. As Oscar would describe it, from his position standing at the back there was something mildly pornographic about watching them. In all his years in dance he'd never seen anything quite so erotic, so tangibly passionate. Toreth looked away. Their bodies slid against each other always in contact, in various renditions of an embrace. They appeared boneless and sublime in the haze of heat that rose up from the footlights, Carla's arms long and hypnotic. They were greater than themselves. When he lifted her up in the red light and pressed his face into her ribs it was the supreme moment, the point where Carla knew, she later told Simone ('the poor misguided darling'), that this was the man for her.

It was the best they'd ever done it. Oscar was overjoyed. The applause that followed was rich and aromatic. It sounded to Antoney exactly the same as when his mother was cooking and she lost the thread of what she was doing and the onions fried short of oil so she added water. You know that sound I'm talking about?

'You're so weird,' said Carla, lying in the crook of his arm at four a.m.

There were two journalists in the audience that night. One was from a local newspaper. The other was Edward Riley, who was reviewing the show for an influential journal called the *Dancing Eye*, and wearing a salt-and-pepper coat which he kept on for the duration of the performance.

6

It was one of those lime tree shaded houses off Holland Park Avenue with the long front gardens, the kind of front garden where you could prepare a speech on the way to the door. Lucas hadn't moseyed through these parts in a while, but Toreth used to take him for walks here, explaining that the only difference between the people on this side of the hill and their side was money, which was a pipsqueak in the book of human merit. Over on the main boulevard was the local excellent patisserie, the top-quality dry-cleaner and fancy burger joint, two streets away the sumptuous city park. The house wasn't flash, though, like some of those neighbouring it. There was no manicured hedge, there were no flowerbeds, lanterns or hanging baskets. It was somewhat run-down, with a rusty gate and calf-high weeds languishing around the stepping-stone path. Dirty windows and climbing ivy gave off an eerie abandoned mood. At first, sheer trepidation prevented Lucas opening the gate. He'd found it necessary to have a noon smoke before coming and was therefore chewing Wrigley's. The closer he got to the black front door the less he could remember of what he'd intended to say.

He knocked. (*If you don't eat fear the fear will eat you.*) His notebook and recorder were in his record bag in case he got as far as an interview. The city was in the grip of a late-spring heatwave. Today he wore his only white shirt to make a good impression – he didn't have an appointment, or any idea what, or whom, to expect.

After the second knock there was still no answer. He was thinking about leaving a note, which brought up the puzzling Lucas versus Louis question, when out of the corner of his eye he saw a curtain flicker, then a grey and white cat sitting in the window watching him. He tried one more time and waited for what seemed like a full five minutes, until he heard movements behind the door. It was opened cautiously, by a sallow, bearded old man with joyless eyes, wearing an ill-fitting corduroy jacket and house slippers. He peered out at Lucas with hostility in his face.

'I'm not interested,' he said. 'I'm reporting you people for harassment, you're disturbing my privacy.'

He seemed more upset than the situation might have called for, if Lucas *had* been a British Gas salesman or an Avon lady, which he wouldn't have himself mistaken for.

'I'm not selling anything. I'm looking for someone . . . Mr Edward Riley?'

From the way he stiffened (as if being accused of something) Lucas knew straight away that this was the guy. It threw him for a minute. He hadn't expected him to just rock up and answer the door like this.

'Well. What do you want?' the old man said.

No mumbling or fumbling, get straight down to it. For Cynthia. Do it, for Cynthia.

'I'm a journalist. Louis Miguel, *West* magazine?' His offer of a handshake was not accepted. 'I was going to leave you a note – What it is, I'd like to talk to you about some research I'm doing on the Midnight Ballet—'

'What?'

Lucas thought Mr Riley couldn't hear him so he said it louder. 'The Midnight Ballet. I've been reading your articles.'

'Which articles? Where did you get them?'

The man seemed utterly confused and somewhat paranoid. His grave left eye twitched. As Lucas reminded him of the existence of public libraries, he turned his head a fraction as though hearing something in the darkness behind him. From the masterly style of Riley's articles Lucas had envisaged a more confident person, someone outwardly pompous, with a big belly and maybe a moustache, not this small, tense, washed-out character standing before him. His right hand was holding a fountain pen which he clenched and rolled in his palm. He kept his other hand on the door ready to close it at any second. In a last-ditch attempt to keep the door open, Lucas delved into his bag for a copy of *West* and mentioned the feature he was writing (four weeks had passed since his meeting with Simone, however, and despite some effort he hadn't yet produced anything presentable). He thought he was going to be sent on his way, but then the critic said sternly, with a hint of suspicion, 'What's your angle?'

Louis thought quickly. 'Retrospective.'

'How did you get my address?'

'From the internet.'

'You should've written first. I won't tolerate hacks.'

With that he motioned to close the door. Scrambling for another approach, Lucas remembered the way he'd felt reading Riley's descriptions of Antoney and the troupe in the British Library. In that far-ceilinged silence, life going by on the Euston Road outside, he'd almost heard the dancers breathing – Carla, Simone, Milly – the swish of their red rayon skirts. He'd felt the vibrations of his father's quick footsteps on the library desk.

'I liked what you wrote,' he said in a newly intimate manner. 'His "bassy signature turn". That's a nice description.'

The June sun shone on Mr Riley's eyes, which were poised at odds between grey and blue. They seemed to say, 'Flattery won't work with me, young fellow.' But as they lingered on

Lucas's face the brandy-red lips trembled faintly. He was obviously frightened of something, yet not enough, or perhaps too curious, to shut that door.

'I was about to go out,' he said. 'I don't have long.'

The house was divided into two flats of which Mr Riley had the ground floor. When Lucas stepped inside June disappeared. The hallway was dim, sombre and cat-smelling, the atmosphere so tinged with heaviness that he instinctively bowed his head the way he did at home. It wasn't exactly that the place seemed dirty. It was just that everything in it, the carpet, the walls, the tasselled light shade, looked so old that dust must have seeped inside it never to get back out. Still, he was pleased to have got this far and congratulated himself on good doorstep work. Mr Riley led him slowly down a wide corridor with rooms leading off it, the first door open only by a slit, the second revealing an old-fashioned Formica kitchen, the third closed. At the entrance to the fourth room at the end, Mr Riley paused. His pace had become slower as they'd advanced down the corridor and all the while he'd been looking furtively behind him. His back was curled with age, sending his chin in towards his neck. He said to Lucas carefully:

'Don't touch anything in the study, please.'

They entered a large, ugly room. The brownish octagon design of the wallpaper was distinctly retro without intending to be, the carpet a dulled blue. Against the opposite wall was a bulky mahogany desk on which sat an old-fashioned typewriter, surrounded by several fluorescent Post-its, mug stains, books, paper, and to one side a settlement of cardboard and green leather boxes. A paisley-covered sofa was slumped in a corner. The adjacent wall of bowed bookcases cried out for a carpenter, one of the shelves devoted entirely to ornamental paraphernalia – glass elephants, chipped porcelain dancers, miniature ballet shoes, paperweights and framed photographs. The contents of the room seemed to have been gathered here over decades – an antique magazine rack, a metal filing cabinet – with no other thought but to satisfy incidental requirements as and when they came up. Lucas felt he'd stepped back in time, into the private den of someone who had little contact with the outside world. The room, like Mr Riley, reeked of melancholy and solemnness. Lucas could imagine him sitting at that desk for hours on end writing his detailed, lyrical articles, hardly looking up from the page, his lips dry and pursed from solitude. The only relief from this oppressive atmosphere was a set of French windows leading out to a garden, thus making the study seem brighter than the rest of the flat. One of the windows was open, the warm breeze toying with a pair of floor-length muslin curtains.

After a moment of indecision, Mr Riley ordered Lucas to sit down on the sofa. He watched him do so, one hand in his pocket, the other still fiddling with his pen, standing a tad too close at first then backing away towards the desk. All the time he inspected Lucas like an unknown specimen he'd just found.

'Is this where you work?' Lucas said, aiming for normal social interaction.

The question was ignored. 'What's the precise reason for this piece you're doing?'

Mr Riley finally sat down on his leather writing chair.

'Well,' said Louis/Lucas. 'It's an untold story, innit, a piece of local history no one knows about. Plus,' as Simone had mentioned, 'there's a lot going on in black dance right now, so it's timely.'

'Oh. I see.'

The lying was becoming quite draining for Lucas. He didn't know how long he'd be able to stay undercover in such a stifling situation. It reminded him of the time he and Jake had gone into a pub in Maida Vale when they were fifteen pretending to be from Sheffield and were asked for ID – their northern accents had crumbled in trying to convince the barman they were old enough to get cider. He told Mr Riley he'd met with Simone de Laperouse, which wasn't actually a lie.

The worry in the old man's face increased as he spoke of what she'd told him about the Midnight Ballet's history, their rise to success, their particular vocabulary and exotic appeal. Mr Riley stood and practically shouted, looming closer again, 'Exotic! How ridiculous. They were a serious company with a sophisticated repertoire. Well-crafted, intelligent choreography. They were one of the most important troupes of their time, not some monkeyish cabaret act.'

'Er, yeah,' said Lucas. Here in his study Mr Riley seemed larger and more energetic, even predatory. His ashen proximity was unsettling.

'I forbid you to use that word in your write-up,' he said.

'You mean monkeyish?'

'Exotic.' There was a brief pause. 'It's important not to misunderstand them.'

The way he said 'them' struck Lucas as strange, because at the same time as he said it, he glanced at the door, as if he thought the Midnight Ballet cast could be huddled out there in the corridor with their instruments and costumes and duffel bags. The notion was so strong that Lucas also looked over at the door. He decided to get to the point and get going.

'Simone had quite a lot to say about the artistic director,' he said. 'We're focusing on him in particular – seems like an interesting guy. Did you know him well?'

Mr Riley said quietly (he was now seated back in his chair), 'I did.'

'Could you tell me what you remember about him most? Do you mind? Anything special you remember?'

Lucas was getting out his notebook. Mr Riley remained completely still, watching him, his pale, withered hands resting neatly on his knees, again that accused expression on his face. He gave off an intense dislike for his visitor in this instant. After a long, uncomfortable silence he said:

'His voice.'

'His voice.'

'It was anxious. It murmured.'

In order to avoid Mr Riley's stare Lucas bowed his head and wrote.

'He would incline his head suddenly, as if he was listening for rare birds. Do you like that description?'

Looking back up, Lucas saw hatred in Mr Riley's eyes. He couldn't understand what his problem was. He was about to speak, but the old man hadn't finished.

'Who do you think you are coming here like this? Coming here asking me questions you don't understand?'

'Look, I didn't—'

'Do you think that reading a few articles makes you an expert on something? That by stealing someone else's memories you can make it seem as if you were there?' Lucas slowly rose from the couch. Mr Riley rose with him. 'I'll have you know, I've been working for a number of years on a much larger project than this pith of yours. Antoney Matheus was a complex—'

Just then Lucas was startled by Mr Riley's cat slipping into the study from the corridor, preceded by a ghostly movement of the door. A sweat was breaking out beneath his shirt. Denise was right. He should forget all about this and move on, it was getting spooky. The cat, groomed and well fed, ignored both men and went to the bookcase, where it rubbed itself tail-up against a shelf. It was at this point that Lucas's eyes fell upon a photograph of his father, a few rows up amid the ornaments.

There were two photographs, in fact, neither of which he'd seen before. In the first Antoney was standing in the street with a matchstick held between his lips – a winter's day, given his heavy coat and layers beneath it. There were two deep lines in his forehead. (*What did you do when you got here, and didn't know which way to go?*) In the other he was dressed in a suit and trilby, younger-looking, leaning in a doorway beneath a STAGE DOOR sign next to another, lighter-framed man also in a suit. They both looked satisfied and happy, their arms folded identically, their heads tipped towards one another in an air of friendship.

They looked as if they could take the world in their palms and mould it to any shape they wanted.

Mr Riley's tirade had lapsed as the cat nuzzled and purred at his leg. Lucas moved closer to the bookshelf.

'I can't help you,' he heard Mr Riley say. 'Please leave, you mustn't touch anything.'

'Is that you?'

'Who?'

'In that picture.'

The man next to Antoney was healthy-looking and sweet-eyed, a full head of wavy light brown hair and a small chin. He was sporting an apricot tie. There was a certain elegance about him, an elegance Lucas had noticed in Riley himself when he'd first sat down in his writing chair. 'Is that you when you were younger?'

The critic came and stood behind him. They studied the image together. The atmosphere in the room loosened.

'Nineteen sixty-eight,' Mr Riley said. 'He'd just been nominated for a choreography award.'

'I read about that.'

'That's him at his peak. See how happy he looks.'

'Yeah. He does.' Lucas turned so he could glimpse the critic's face. 'Mr Riley,' he said, 'what happened to him?'

'I thought Simone de Laperouse told you everything,' the old man smirked.

'Not the whole story.'

'He – well – he left us, didn't he?' There was a faint tenderness in his voice.

'But can you tell me about it?'

Mr Riley paused, once again becoming stern. 'Be frank with me. Is there a personal interest here that you haven't yet mentioned?'

Lucas said it at last. 'He was my dad.'

The project Riley was working on was a book entitled 'Antoney Matheus and the Midnight Ballet.' It was a long-standing

133

exercise, not very far from completion, meant as a testament to the company's work and a biography of Antoney's life. The boxes by the desk were full of manuscript pages, progress notes and Midnight Ballet source material such as concert programmes, photographs and posters. In addition to these were copies of every article and review ever written on the company, a significant proportion of them by Riley. The book-shelves contained an extensive dance library with which he could contextualise and support any premise, any minor fact. He became excited as he explained this, that it was crucial to know your terrain to the last detail. Here in this room was an archive of a forgotten moment and he was the only one qualified to do justice to it. He still wouldn't allow Lucas to touch anything, but he did eventually, during the long talk that followed, show him a few pages of his book. The last item he mentioned, guardedly, as final proof of his inside knowledge, was a green leather box containing a collection of letters written to him by Antoney himself.

Riley had met Antoney in June 1968 at a pre-show press gathering, having seen him dance many times before. Shortly afterwards he interviewed him for the *Dancing Eye*, and they instantly became friends. Even before they met, Riley felt that he knew Antoney already, in his soul, because a dancer dancing well is a heart made apparent on a body. They were the same, the two of them. 'What I mean,' he told Lucas, 'is that we were very different but we understood each other precisely.' Antoney had a special respect for Riley because he was the one critic who showed real insight into what he was doing. The company was an immediate hit and was covered widely in the press, but many journalists put too much focus on their ethnicity, their 'exoticism', how beautiful and vibrant they all were. Antoney did want to make something beautiful, but he also wanted to be taken seriously. He didn't want to be seen as a fireworm or a unicorn, he once put it. He told Riley that moving to England had made him over-conscious of the painful distraction of colour, that as a boy in Jamaica he'd had a clearer view of things. 'Blackness is more than black,' he used to say. 'Life is so much bigger than black.'

He was 'a dusky Adonis'. Girl hacks took a shine to him. '*Shango Storm* is a storm of a show!' 'Mesmerising,' wrote *She*. Even, 'the most ravishing thing to have danced on a British stage in years'. Simone de Laperouse was admired for her dexterity, Milly Afolabi for her bristling energy, Ekow for his charm, but Antoney was undoubtedly the star of the show. Short, chirpy interviews with him featured in the arts pages of the London papers, in the burgeoning underground gay press. A *Times* critic announced him as Britain's very own Alvin Ailey with a Caribbean twist. It wasn't all sleazy, but Riley nevertheless took it upon himself to write long, rescuing reviews in the *Dancing Eye*, focusing always on craft, the theatrical value of the company, Antoney's precociousness as a choreographer. Even back then he'd made a project of it – for something very peculiar had happened to him the first time he'd seen Antoney dance. It had never happened to him before, in any of the hundreds of shows he'd reviewed. The rule is that you keep your eyes up and your pen down. You record everything you're seeing in a kind of sensory, illegible narration to be deciphered later, of events in torsos, nuances of arms, turns and backdrop shades. You never look down. You never stop writing while the curtain is up. But when Antoney first appeared on that stage in the Ledbury Theatre as Shango, in his red waistcoat and skirt – after watching him for just a few minutes, Riley had stopped writing. It lasted six or seven minutes. He explained it to Lucas with a halting in his voice. Every critic needs an angel to keep them fair, he said. Maybe this was his.

Riley was once a hack himself. He had worked as a news reporter in the fifties but had lacked the brashness for it; he asked the wrong questions too late. As a child his mother used to take him once a month to the theatre in the West End (his grandmother was a ballerina, there were putty-coloured tutus and a flounced satin crinoline in the attic of their house in Finchley). Eating figs in the dark in the velvet pews he'd watched the swans cross the lake on ballet feet, the Nutcracker flight to the kingdom of sweets, and he'd eventually begun to feel, especially during duets, that the watching belonged to something, that it needed an accompaniment aside from figs. The feeling moved to his fingertips and made them tingle. To allay the tingling he started taking a pen and paper with him to the theatre. Doodles became words, words became sentences, about the heavenly stage and the winged creatures who owned it.

This early fascination with dancing never left Riley. During his stint in the newsroom he mentioned to a fellow reporter that he'd like to write dance reviews. The reporter, known for his tactless manners, said that Riley wasn't suited to writing reviews because to write reviews you had to know what you think, 'and you don't know what you think,' he said, 'you're a common man with a common mind. No offence, but you don't have an awful lot to say about much.' Riley left that newspaper soon after to scrape a living as a freelancer for the dance press. He saw three or four shows a week on free watcher tickets, was sitting three rows back from Antoney and Oscar at the Alvin Ailey show. He developed a notebook system whereby his scribbles in the dark were arranged in alphabetical order and colour-coded according to genre and company. Everything he wrote was a journey, like sitting on a train and seeing rooftops, sheep and yellow grass go by, then finally arriving somewhere with a clear head. You don't have to know what you think, he would have told that reporter if he'd been able to at the time. You only find that out after. All you need to know is what direction to take.

Given the amount of material Riley had written on the Midnight Ballet before meeting Antoney, and if words likewise are a heart made apparent on a page, it could be said that

Antoney also knew Riley already. Riley was the older by ten years. Antoney confided in him and sought his opinion, about creative insecurities, working relationships, dealing with his sudden and bewildering fame. They had long talks moving from coffee to brandy in a Spanish café opposite the 20th Century Theatre on Westbourne Grove, their favourite table positioned next to a small stained glass window that they both looked up towards when they were thinking. Antoney was the talker. Riley was the listener, the quiet observer. He was invited to sit in on the company's rehearsals whereby he got to know the other members of the troupe, Ekow the compulsive marketeer, complaining Simone, suspicious Bluey, Carla ('It amused your mother to call me by my surname'). In the autumn of '68 Riley followed them on a tour around Britain, already mindful of this future book of his. It was remarkable how successful they'd become in a very short time, yet it was typical of the age. A month after the Ledbury they'd had a second run at the Jeannetta Cochrane Theatre in Holborn, then more shows following at the Commonwealth Institute and Sadler's Wells. Riley had watched their performances grow tighter and more polished, their bows become neater and less alarmed. They were welcomed into the experimental crowd that was shaping contemporary dance at the time and were also popular with the general public. Now only a year on from their début they were pulling in crowds at respectable venues around the country. Those were marvellous, whirlwind days for everyone, not least for Riley. Rusty train rides through the southern counties, sun-splashed promenade walks watching diamonds frolic over the sea. In some of those places, Cardiff, Oxford, Devon, the dancers were treated like visiting dignitaries. They'd descend on a quaint guesthouse or a smart hotel as a mass of noise and raucous showbiz glamour, their posters up in lobbies, libraries and shops, the best eggs in the house for breakfast. They were thrilled by what was happening to them. There were invitations to parties, small-town girls fluttering by the stage after curtain, pictures of them in the newspapers. Antoney and Ekow would stroll into the theatres like rock stars at the helm of their entourage. That stage door Antoney had once dreamt of was now a familiar late-night step-through.

'Your father believed he'd been blessed,' Riley told Lucas. 'He felt that he'd been chosen – the moon-bus, the flying dreams. He liked Albert Einstein's quote about dancers being the athletes of God.' As a result he had always found it extremely difficult to come back down to earth after a show. That was his best self, up there on stage. He wanted the applause to go on forever and would fill the silence that followed it with his own chatter, talking on and on in the dressing room about the highlights and mistakes of the evening's performance. He was first through the door of the nearest drinking hole, where he'd lap up the attention of the locals, a permanent Pall Mall on his lip, his trilby slanted on the back of his head. The next morning he would wake up reserved and moody, eager for the next gig, and often the only person he'd want to hang out with would be Riley.

Back in London Ekow and Oscar, who dealt with the company's administrative issues, began mapping out the possibility of another tour, this time in Europe, having already received an invitation to perform at a theatre in Paris. Proposals were sent out to venues in Holland, Denmark, Belgium, places where Midnight Ballet press coverage had seen syndication. Meanwhile Antoney set about creating a new ballet. It was inspired by a conversation he'd had with Riley about whether dance should strive to become its music. He wanted to experiment with reflecting specific instruments through different parts of the body. Could a navel be a piano? Could the shoulders achieve the same purity as John Coltrane's tenor sax? But he had a lot of trouble with the piece. He couldn't get a grip on it. 'The beginning of every new dance is the same,' he'd revealed to Riley during their first interview together at the café. 'I am wholly inadequate and full of fear. I can see *something*, like a leaning, a hit between body and music, but I don't know what's going to happen. I'm searching. I'm feeling, and for a long time I can't find it. It's terrifying.' (Riley had watched him here as he paused and inclined his head upwards towards the stained glass window, like a listening bird.) 'So when I finally get it,' he'd continued, his eyes flashing, 'when I take it forward by just a little, I feel as if I've done a whole day's work, like I should just get my coat and go and have a pint. Those first few steps of the dance are perfection. They shine. I wish I could show them to the people just like that, on their own, before they get messed up by the rest of it.'

Ekow criticised the idea for the new ballet as basic and pretentious. Antoney told him it wasn't his business. Oscar had been encouraging him for some time to give Ekow a chance at the choreography but Antoney was unwilling to. He was even reluctant for Oscar to have a hand in this one. He wanted to prove to himself that he could make something on his own. The company was still performing regularly around London, which provided a distraction from what was turning into a creative block, but the animosity between Antoney and Ekow increased with Antoney's refusal to relinquish any control. Light and sound checks became battles in which Ekow now insisted on his right to take charge, seeing as Antoney's expertise lay elsewhere. On one occasion before a gig in Greenwich Antoney threw the Blues House disc across the stage in a temper, just missing a passing technician. Likewise rehearsals were tinged with conflict. Simone would side with Ekow by seconding any suggestion he made and challenging Antoney's word on things. She complained aloud about the meagre sums of money the dancers were being paid, adding fuel to an all-round underlying dissatisfaction with the discrepancy between the company's success and the financial gain of its members. Simone was a malicious, conniving character, in Riley's opinion, and he also found Benjamin very unpleasant. He was there when he accused Antoney once of stealing. 'Tell me the truth-o. You have never dipped into the pot to get yourself a meat pattie or a little bottle of rum?' Milly walked out of that particular rehearsal as she was so tired of people arguing. If it hadn't been for the more calming elements in the group – Oscar, The Wonder, Carla – the whole thing might have faltered.

Riley's dislike for Simone increased the more he got to know her. She always had to be the centre of attention and would do everything in her power to get what she wanted, even if it meant betraying her friends. Antoney didn't get much past those first leanings of his Coltrane dance until one night, about a month before the European tour, when Riley happened upon an encounter between him and Simone at the church.

He'd gone to Powis Square looking for Antoney, who had failed to turn up for a drink they'd planned at a pub along Notting Hill Gate. He always looked forward to their time together and was disappointed he hadn't shown. It was an unusually warm, still evening in mid-March. He drifted along Portobello hoping he might run into him, and nearing ten o'clock his footsteps turned up Talbot Road towards the square. The church door was ajar. He slipped inside. Jazz music was playing, Coltrane's 'A Love Supreme'. He was about to proceed into the rehearsal hall when above the music he heard voices, first a woman's, then Antoney's. The woman said, 'I thought you might like some company, that's all. Don't be unfriendly.' Riley recognised the voice as Simone's. When he peeped into the poorly lit hall he saw her from the back, standing by the window a few feet away from Antoney, wearing a short crocheted dress in two different shades of pink and a pair of strappy high heels that sharpened the muscles in her flexing, well-oiled calves. She was dressed as if for a party, while Antoney was bare-chested and barefoot in only his flimsy black dance pants. There was a light sweat on his skin. Riley stayed in the porch and listened.

'Have a shot if you want,' Antoney said. 'I'm not the unfriendly one around here.'

140

'Why don't we forget about all that?'

Simone took from the table a plastic cup set by a rum bottle, keeping her eyes on Antoney. 'You know,' she said, 'you look that much finer dancing with your shirt off. You should dance like that all the time, the fans would go wild ... Is there something to chase this with?'

'You see a bar anywhere in this room?'

'Never mind, I'll pass. It's just that drinking alone's no fun.'

'I'm done anyway. I was about to step out.'

'Still working on that Coltrane thing?'

'What do you want, Simone?'

'I know you've been having problems with it.'

Antoney went to the centre of the room and impatiently picked up his T-shirt from the floor. 'It soon come.'

'It would be nice if it was ready for Paris, wouldn't it? Oh please don't dress on my account,' Simone said, in quite a seedy tone, Riley thought. 'It's nothing I haven't carefully examined before.'

She went towards him catwalk-style, each foot circling and landing in front of the other. Riley saw now that her lips were well glossed, her cheeks sharp with rouge. She looked rather disgusting to him, the way women could. The two ends of her collarbones protruded from her thin shoulders, so inferior to Antoney's sleek desert planes. 'Don't,' she said, halting his arm, touching the soft cloth of the shirt.

'Why not?'

'Because I don't want you to.'

There was a silence in which they appeared to be just looking at one another. Riley took in Antoney's magnificent russet back, the chain around his neck as he looked down at her. Perhaps she whispered something to him, Riley wasn't sure. But he did see her move her hand to Antoney's waist. 'I've always been sweet on you, you know that.' Trailing her fingers downwards she said, 'I hope Carla's as – appreciative, shall we say, of her privileges ... as I could be?'

'Come on, stop messing around,' Antoney said brushing her off.

'Have you noticed she's been kind of moody lately? I don't know what's up with her. She barely talks to me these days.'

'Maybe that's because of the way you act.'

'The way I act?'

'You and Ekow, the two of you causing trouble and such.' To Riley's relief Antoney put on his T-shirt. They talked a while about Ekow, Simone said she could try and make him stand down – after all they only wanted what was best for the company – but Antoney could maybe be a little less possessive about things. He appeared to see her logic.

Coltrane was advancing into the 'Psalm' section, Antoney's favourite part of the album. Simone said, that seductive aim creeping back into her voice, 'So why don't you show me what you've been working on tonight? I might surprise you. I might be able to add a little something to it, something special, you know? Something no one else on this earth would be capable of giving you.'

She approached Antoney again, this time running her undeserving hands up along his arms to make a loop around his neck. 'We could work on it together,' she suggested, pressing her body against him. This was not a comfortable stance for her, offering herself like this – she was awkward. Riley wanted to flit her away like a fly from an al-fresco steak.

Antoney was amused. 'Simone,' he said. 'You're making a fool of yourself. I don't think about you.'

At this, with a tiny flick of her head – one hand rubbing the other elbow as if it had been hurt – Simone took a single delicate step towards the door, causing Riley to shift out of sight. But instead of advancing she angrily swung back. All the seduction was gone. She was Simone de Laperouse as everyone knew her, haughty, demanding and self-centred.

'Antoney,' she said, 'I am the only trained dancer in this troupe. I'm good enough for Rambert but I chose you. I work harder than anyone else, I give my very best at every show, every rehearsal – I deserve principal status. You're damn lucky to have someone like me on your ship and you know it. So why is it, Mr Artistic Director, that after all this time you haven't yet given me a solo?'

'A solo?'

'Yes, a solo.'

'Is that what you want? A solo?'

'I'm not about to choreograph one for myself,' she said indignantly.

Antoney laughed. 'Well, why didn't you just *say* so, girl? Could've saved you getting all dressed up like you're off to the Marshalls!'

He laughed again over the music, leaning backwards and bending forwards. He went on for quite a while with it. Riley almost joined him.

'You really know how to flatter a girl, don't you?'

'Don't worry, baby,' he said, calming down and swigging from his cup, 'I'll make you a solo some time. All you needed to do was ask me straight. We'll do it, I promise.'

She gave him a filthy look with her small aquiline nose in the air, then took that same delicate step towards the door, her hand clutching her elbow. As Antoney would explain it to Riley later that night, he was suddenly struck by the profile of her face, the gently hooked nose, the upset mouth. The space around her seemed to shine, to come alive, most of all down by her feet and around the neck. He had a funny sensation that his blood was quickening, that he was speeding up inside in a kind of heightened excitement. Coltrane's sax in the background. The woman, the bird, equal in the instant with the sax. The first few steps of the dance miraculously came clear to him. He went towards her, jittery and tunnel-visioned.

'It doesn't even need to be a sax,' he muttered. 'It could be something else.'

143

'What?' she snapped.

'Do that again. What you just did.'

Lucas listened to all this sitting back in the dip of Riley's ancient sofa. His questions throughout became more exacting, more sparse. Did Carla find out about this? Why was she moody? How did Antoney take his coffee? His notetaking eventually ceased as Louis Miguel released his grip and Lucas son of Antoney sank deeper into his father's story. For the first time since opening the cherrywood cupboard he could see himself in it, in Antoney's restlessness and insecurity, his melancholic mornings. Riley's study changed from an ugly neglected hovel into a precious absorbent dome in which Antoney had once slept, here on this sofa, in which he'd once stood, over there by the French windows where Riley remembered him most, the white curtains swelling in the breeze around his tall, broad shape. It was like standing on solid ground. And Riley himself, during his recollections, had lost his earlier hostility, was kinder and forthcoming, evidently pleased to have someone close to the story to share his knowledge with. He made Lucas tea, in a chipped mug, and offered him stale bourbons. 'It's remarkable you should turn up now,' he said. 'I've been experiencing something of a block myself.' As a kind of nervous habit he picked a lot at his beard. There was a permanent remoteness to him, despite his softening.

Riley wrote for the dance press but little these days. The *Dancing Eye* had folded in 1982. The *Stage* newspaper occasionally sent him to The Place in Euston where the chairs were uncomfortable, but his fingertips did not tingle; he came away with emptying pages. He'd reached the conclusion that life should amount to more than a few pages of a magazine or a column of text. Mostly he worked on his book, now a seventeen-year project. He had no publisher lined up but hoped for outside interest on completion. Riley appeared on the face of it to have none of the accessories to old age, a late wife, children

144

or grandchildren. He'd lived in this same flat since the sixties and apparently hadn't decorated. When probed about why he'd spent so long on the book, he simply said, referring to Antoney, 'He didn't want to be forgotten.'

Lucas pictured them, Antoney and Riley, two men who could mould the world to a shape they wanted, walking up the Ladbroke Grove hill to its highest point on that warm, still night in March 1969. It was four in the morning. After leaving the church unseen Riley had gone home, to be woken in the small hours by Antoney, wearing an emerald suede cape he'd got from the costume trunk and a flickering smile. He asked him out for a walk 'with the night creatures'. Riley felt like a child accosted by a wizard. They walked for hours, along the Holland Park boulevard, round the huge Shepherd's Bush roundabout, down Wood Lane all the way to Harlesden, Antoney talking non-stop about the creation of 'Bird', his first independent piece. He'd never realised before how evocative Simone was. All he'd had to do was watch her. She did exactly as he asked but more, just by being herself. 'It was as if the dance was already there for us to move into, and we moved into it together.' At one point he pranced into the road to demonstrate a sequence, ridiculous in his cape, and was barely missed by a passing car. He was reckless, on fire. He was going to conquer Europe. Life was limitless.

At the top of the hill the two men stopped. They looked down on the sleeping violet streets, the trees half nude in their first spring blossom, the armies of chimneys and the amber lamp posts. Antoney put his arm around Riley's shoulders, bringing his face close to his.

'You see that shine out there, Riley, down by the edge of the land? That layer of something shimmering? Like a secret force? A shine? See it there?'

'You mean the lights?' Riley said.

'Yeah,' said Antoney smiling, 'the light. That's what I love about you. You always know what I'm talking about.' They stood silently in the quiet, Riley's heart beating fast, Antoney gazing at the horizon, its distant, yellowish glow. 'That thing there,' he said, 'that's what makes me believe in myself.'

Loser, thought Denise. Slacker. Lazy, selfish git.

She was waiting for Lucas. He was supposed to have been there at four thirty to help her take some stock down to the Salvation Army for the luncheon tomorrow. While the stock wilted in a pile of boxes on the ground her seasonal sunflowers were displayed in slender metal pails along the front of her stall, her orchids next to where she stood in her carpenter jeans and sensible shoes. She looked for him in the distance, no longer expecting to see him. A sea of shoppers picked at stall-tops, fingering the Afrocentric jewellery, the tie-dye babysuits and second-hand CDs. Today Denise had had one attempted robbery and a Nigerian man asking for a black flower, which she hadn't been able to provide. There was actually no such thing as a black flower, she'd explained to the man, there were only illusions of black, such as hollyhocks and calla lilies, but she didn't have any of those. It always troubled her when she was unable to meet a customer's request. All in all she was in a lousy mood.

That morning she'd risen at four as usual while Lucas was still snoring. She'd undented her pillow and taken her complicated bath, then set out for the New Covent Garden Flower Market, which wasn't in Covent Garden but in a warehouse on the other side of the river. This was where Denise's day began, in Battersea, while it was still dark. She cruised down Park Lane in her dewy mustard-coloured car bewildered by the magic of dawn. This was her singular point of abstraction, and in it she noted her favourite tree, the one outside the Dorchester with the lights on it. That tree, she always thought, had a special air of conviction in the way it held itself. It was always Christmas, in a passing moment at the beginning of the working day, in the presence of that tree.

Once she was there, emerging anoraked from the gloomy car park, her hair – greying at twenty-nine – centre-parted into two French plaits, all else faded. She approached the heavy rubber doors and pushed them open with her own secret flourish. The flowerheads rushed brilliantly towards her. Little lawns of yellows, all the possibilities of pink, the unequivocal smell of travelled roses. She dived into the beautiful industry. As a trader she must account for every occasion. She must imagine all of it, the wedding, the funeral, the lover; the giver as well as the receiver. She must try to envisage the very flower the old man would buy, newly lonely, to place at the stone of his dead wife, what the last romantic would choose for passion in November, or the sister of a bride who hates white. There are those like that. There are people who come to Denise's stall at nine o'clock in the morning and tell her they want a flower without any green in it, preferably not even a stem. She had to provide for all of it. So every morning she whisked through the warehouse with a trolley collecting her well-thought-out goods, watched by the rows of glassy garden gnomes that Lucas had once tried to tell her were alive, then drove back along Park Lane to her patch beneath the white canopies on Portobello Road, a prime spot, the hub of the market. She was next to an Algerian silk scarf dealer who ate falafel every day from Falafel King on the corner and always gave her the orange that came with it. She was quieter than Em. Denise was not a shouter. She was coolly attentive, gave advice where needed, but let the flowers take centre stage.

Where the hell was he? She hadn't seen Lucas at all today. She knew he went to 'work' on Thursdays, but usually even then she would spot him at some point hanging around outside Honest Jon's and drag him over for half an hour to help her out. Not that he was much help. He didn't wrap well and wasted brown paper, he was like a bad chip server, but at least it meant he was engaged in something useful, something salary-related. The Salvation Army lunch was Denise's first big job and she felt she'd already made a bad impression. She would have to take the flowers there herself. But Lucas should do it. He didn't help her. He didn't wash up. He was like a kid, a pigeon – he looks down, he sees the strange electricity of human life. He was getting worse. He smoked too much of that foul-smelling stuff. She'd ban it from the boat completely so he'd have to do it on the towpath. He had no direction, no sense of ambition. He didn't dust. He left biscuit crumbs on the counter. He squeezed the toothpaste at the top end, the selfish end, instead of at the bottom. Did he think she was his mum? Did he seriously think he could live off her for the rest of his life? Even if she *was* his mum she wouldn't let any son of hers take liberties like that. From now on she was giving him no more money. She'd *make* him get a life, instead of prowling through that bloody cupboard, those old things, like a retired person or some kind of untrained archaeologist. That was probably where he was right now, in the cupboard. He was probably listening to Sam Cooke or Nina Simone, as he had been lately in place of the usual shouty hip-hop, and sitting in the cupboard. Denise hated hip-hop. She found it violent, arrogant and over-testos-teroned. She had no particular musical tastes and preferred silence. But at least Scarface or whoever was present-day, living in the now. Even with the gunshots in the background it was probably the better option, given what he was getting into. Questions. Every other day questions. Awkward questions. How old was 'Antoney' when he drowned? Did she have any memories of him and their mother together? Did she know their grandmother's address in Jamaica? 'When I told you to get a job I wasn't talking about joining MI5,' Denise had told him last week. He was shaking their foundations, turning over her careful stones. He made stupid clichéd statements such as 'You can't go forwards until you've been backwards' and 'You don't know who you are unless you know where you're from.' Was he about to join the Nation of Islam? Was he cult-susceptible? She didn't know. Even the way he walked was getting more exasperating.

If she admitted it, she was worried about him. No, she was not his mum, but ever since that day in 1986 when she was sixteen and Lucas twelve and Toreth had gone into the nursing home, Denise had felt responsible for Lucas – and like a parent never quite able to see their grown, hard-back child as an adult, she could never fully refrain, despite all her fury, all of her expectations, from seeing her brother exactly as he'd been that day; as a pole-limbed twelve-year-old boy.

Denise had the narrow face and prominent eyes of the Bruce side of the family, but she was similar in mannerism to Florence, whom she faintly remembered as a harsh, sharply spoken woman. She had never had much to do with her paternal grandmother. She'd learnt from Toreth that Carla had found her too stern with children. She was probably dead by now, like everyone else. Death had courted Denise throughout her life, beginning with her mother's when she was four and had first sensed that she was in some way responsible for Lucas. From behind her screen of foliage, Denise had come to see that life was somewhat burdensome.

There were certain stark images that sat like unwanted furniture in her memory. The strongest of these was that of her mother lying on the grass, one shoe on and one shoe off, with daisies stuck in her hair. Toreth used to talk to Denise a lot about the daisies when the two of them were alone together. Lucas was still a baby when Carla had 'passed by', as Toreth used to put it, so he was spared. In a distant, rambling tone that made Denise feel uncomfortable, Toreth would recall standing in the off-white hospital room and pulling the damp flowers out of her daughter's hair. Toreth herself came from a different world of hair, and she'd always loved Carla's kink, her great soft mass. 'I used to imagine myself walking about in it like in the woods,' she would ramble, 'and it did feel a bit like that actually, picking out those stems, like I was walking through a forest, and it was very quiet. It's astounding, Denise, how much you come to

149

understand about your child when they pass by you. It's the moment when you know them fully, better than you ever did. Do you understand, love?'

'No,' Denise would say bluntly. 'I'm too young.'

So Toreth had picked all those daisies out, and they fell to the sterilised floor, and she went back to look after the children because a mother and daughter have to be interchangeable in such situations; they know each other's ways. Toreth knew, for example, that Carla used to make sure she taught her children something every day, the name of the blue-berried buckthorn bushes along the towpath or the distance between here and Dominica. She knew that when Denise wouldn't eat her vitamins, Carla had chopped them up to nothing or caramelised them, so that at least she'd take in the spirits of vegetables. But it wasn't the same, not for Denise. She didn't cry at the funeral because she still believed her mother would get up again and walk, even though they'd put her in a box. Instead she comforted Lucas, at one point lifting him ludicrously in her elfish arms.

Her father did not attend the funeral, but Florence did. She was living in a flat on Silchester Road at that time, where Denise remembered being taken on visits. She stood by a tree a little apart from the gathering with a veil from her black hat hiding part of her face. Before leaving the cemetery she approached Toreth. They exchanged no words, only a long look both cold and compassionate. I try to understand, Toreth seemed to say, but not now, bitch. When Antoney came down the towpath slope a month later, Toreth was less accommodating. This was another stark image in Denise's memory, her grandmother's lumpy figure opening the cabin doors holding a petite kitchen knife. She, Toreth, had been chopping vegetables to turn them into spirits. She had seen Antoney coming down the slope, and when he knocked she went to the door with no malicious intention but to tell him never to come back. On seeing his face, though, she couldn't find the words. All she could see in his unwanted presence was her daughter's irreparable absence, the discontinued hair growth. So she reached up, this changed, driftful expression of herself, and she scratched him on the side of his head with the utensil she found in her hand.

That was the last time Denise had seen him. Her recollections of her father prior to this were scant. He was a suggestion at the corner of her sight, a waspish blur past the foam of her mother's embraces. Toreth coloured this vague outline with a gradual, rambling character defamation, that he was 'bad seed', 'bad blood', she should never have let Carla get involved with him in the first place, that he was the reason she'd been taken from them before her time was due. As always Denise was the sole audience. She often got the feeling her grandmother wasn't fully aware of what she was saying during her monologues, or of whom she was talking to. Denise didn't want to talk about her mother's woody hair or her father's evil gene. She didn't want to talk at all, and eventually she wriggled out of earshot and retreated to her garden.

As far as she knew, Antoney had returned to Jamaica with his mother in the seventies. Over the years, Toreth and Florence maintained a sporadic contact centred around the children. Toreth would sometimes mention Florence to Denise, that she'd had a difficult life and she deserved our sympathy. One day when Denise was twelve, Lucas eight, Toreth sat them both down in the dining booth and announced to them that she'd heard from Florence that their father had died – not 'passed by,' but died – drowned in a boat accident. There was a confusing silence. Lucas as ever was the more enthusiastic in his questioning. What kind of boat was it? he wanted to know. Was it a ferry or a big ship? Could he swim? Were there any sharks in the sea? Toreth said she didn't know exactly but it was more than likely a little boat because if it was a ship they might have heard about it on the BBC. 'Don't be upset,' she said. 'It's not worth getting upset over.' They could now go on with their lives without loose ends. Then she got up and started making coleslaw.

151

Denise observed as Lucas carried the story around in his skinny palms. He decorated it to his taste and understanding. It was a dark night in Jamaica. There were rainclouds in the sky. A man got into a boat. He was a good swimmer, but not good enough to win against a storm. So he sailed out, and when he got far into the ocean it started to rain. The man thought, Oh no. It rained and rained and rained, and then came thunder. He was soaking wet. He lost one of the oars. Then a great big storm wave came up and turned his boat over. He swam for about twenty minutes until he got tired, and finally, he sank to the bottom of the sea never to be seen again. There were no sharks though, so that was something. For Denise on the other hand, the news was just a drop of water on an island behind her back.

She might have managed to forget about Antoney altogether if it hadn't been for Toreth's last words to her. Two days before her grandmother passed by, Denise and Lucas went to visit her at the nursing home. She was sitting in her wheelchair. The second stroke had left her paralysed down her right side, but she didn't seem particularly unwell that day compared to any other, except that she was talking strangely. She said she wanted to see her Llandudno hills, the sea stretched loosely out. She said, 'I can't hold back the man. I've seen him walking towards me for a long time now, but he keeps on stopping, because he sees things along the way that he finds distracting.' Lucas held her hands. She cried. Before they left, Toreth called Denise back into the room for what would be her last private monologue. It wasn't actually a monologue, this one. It was short, but it was very heavy, the usual case of too much information.

'Denise,' she said, with her close, stale breath, her sickly aniseed smell. 'Write and ask your grandmother in Jamaica about your father.'

That was all. Six months later Denise did so. More months went by before Florence replied, on blue airmail paper, post-marked St Mary. The tone of letter had the same harshness

Denise remembered of her. 'Your father is gone from us,' she wrote. 'It's best you forget about him and get on.' Florence then revealed something that caused Denise to put the letter down for a few moments before finishing it. She could not quite bring herself to pass the information on to Lucas, so she hid the letter away among her work papers and never looked at it again. She got on with the job of guarding her brother without loose ends.

The letter was still there, shoved to the back of the drawer underneath the bed. When Denise thought of it, waiting there at her stall, it struck her with a panic that Lucas might have found it. Maybe that was why he was asking all these questions. Maybe that was why he hadn't turned up. Maybe he'd found it and hadn't been able to digest it and – what? She didn't know. She had to get home. She asked the Algerian to watch her stall while she took the stock down to the Salvation Army, then closed up quicker than she ever had before. The buckets, the cast-offs, the orchids, the takings, she fetched and carried to the car and took a shortcut to the canal avoiding the traffic on Ladbroke Grove. She was no longer angry, only flustered, which was rare.

Lucas wasn't home. She rushed through the saloon to the bedroom and pulled open the drawer where she kept her accounts. She hunted through the reams of paper, feeling to the wood underneath, in the corners, around the sides. She almost cried when she couldn't find it. Only when all the papers had been emptied out of the drawer did she see it. Yes, right at the back, still in its blue airmail envelope. A loose end. A confusion. A backward trip. There was only one thing to do. She went and got a match.

7

Djembes in the back. Sun roof open. Wide clear road through pearl French light in a fixed-up, golden-winged bus. The wings had been painted by Bluey at the motor yard in Cricklewood, one on each side, on a royal purple background. If you happened to be standing by a cornrowed field on the route from Calais to Paris in May of 1969 you might have seen it fly by, the size of a large caravan, one brake light missing, windows down, The Wonder at the wheel in a baseball cap chewing on ginger. The others were eating fruit pastilles. The back was brimming with stuff – costumes, props, instruments, emergency food, Simone's high-maintenance luggage, bottles of rum for libations and other moments, two tents in case of breakdowns. It was not a smooth ride. There was turbulence. But when is there flight without turbulence? Also there were sleeping bags and blankets, including Oscar's faithful tartan donated at the last minute before he waved them off. Carla had already taken possession of it.

She was seated not at the front, not at the back, but in the middle by the window, which she found was the most comfortable she could get. The blanket was draped over her lap though she wasn't cold. Bluey was sitting next to her as usual, while Antoney was in the passenger seat in front with his foot up on the dashboard talking to The Wonder over the big-band sound of the Supremes. Neither Carla nor Bluey contributed much to the surrounding chatter (Rosina: 'Don't the telegraph poles look different here?' Simone: 'Josephine Baker's got a leopard . . . She *has*. I wonder if I could get to meet her'). If Carla was quiet, Bluey was quiet. Since Calais a force field of quietness had built up around them so that people stopped making the effort to draw them into conversations and half forgot they were there. They might as well have been sitting on another bus – going in the opposite direction, Carla would have preferred, back to Calais, back onto the ferry, back past Marble Arch, back through the familiar streets all the way to Harrow Road. She was realising on this her first trip abroad how much she loved London. Home was the only place for a woman with her particular form of travel sickness. Every five hundred yards she wanted to throw up. Every mile she wanted to use the toilet, so she'd minimised her drinking, which wasn't helping with the nausea, the turbulence, the piercing smell of petrol smoke and cows' bums. The further the bus sped on into the adventure ahead the more she regretted not deserting at Dover while she'd still had the chance. What was she thinking of? Dancing. Six weeks on the road. In her condition.

The Wonder pulled over. Elongated clouds lay across the sky in the shape of human ribs. It's a crime, she thought, the slave a woman is made to the ground when she's pregnant. Gravity is the master. Every step she takes belongs to it, and her feet are not enough. It wants the knees, the hands, the back, the stomach, so that the most amenable position for her is actually lying down on the concrete, or better still the grass. This was what Carla wanted to do as she climbed down off the bus to vomit in the ditch. This was what she'd wanted to do every time she'd got on stage in the last three months. She wanted to just flop to the floor like a set of clothes at the vanishing of the person inside them. It took all her will to jump, to spin, to lunge, and she was always paranoid during the Blues House lift that Antoney would notice a gain in her weight, which she was trying to fend off for as long as possible. She was using as a model a ballet dancer she'd heard of once who'd had five children and had danced through each pregnancy, the foetus helpfully staying out of sight until the seventh month. So far it was going all right. Her clothes fitted her the same. Even without her clothes her stomach gave nothing away. She had to be careful though. She wanted to eat all the time. She dreamt of fried egg sandwiches. If she ate a fried egg sandwich she would have to follow it with another; that was why they were banned. During the first trimester she'd regurgitated most of what she ate anyway, but the nausea had recently come to an end. Until now.

Antoney knew nothing. She climbed back to her seat, cutting her eye at him on the way. Off they went. He reassured her they'd be there soon, then resumed tapping to the beat on the dashboard with his snakeskin shoe. He was wearing purple drainpipes, presumably to match the bus. His shirt was open to the navel, his hat a side-cradle for when his head tipped back against the headrest in blissful reverie at the open road. Who did he think he was? Jimi Hendrix, a Beatle? How was it fair that a man could just plant his seed and breeze on as normal while the woman had to incubate, and suffer, and swell? If he told her he was tired she wanted to shout, What do you know about tired? If he said he was hungry she wanted to punch him in his hard, solitary belly. He'd actually had the nerve to tell her at a rehearsal not long ago that she needed to put more effort into her dancing, that she was 'stepping too low'. What did he know about gravity? What did he know about anything?

It wasn't his fault. It *was* his fault but it was her fault too. She'd tried to tell him, but each time she'd been obstructed by something she remembered him saying while walking along the Grand Union Canal. 'Kids make you old,' he'd said. The implication was clear. There was a family unit up by the gasworks ahead of them featuring a pram and a toddler. Just before he'd made this remark, Carla had jested – maybe with a hint of suggestion – that the family could be them one day. His expression had changed to one of disgust. She was insulted.

156

That horrid phrase (she actually thought the opposite was true) stalked to the forefront of her mind now whenever they were alone together, making her hate him more, so that even general conversation between them was strained. She loved her foetus. She loved its secret absorption of her body's food, the feeling that she was never alone. Her little mystery. No one else in the troupe knew, not Simone; not even her mother knew. The day before departure she had tried to tell Antoney again, intending to suggest that maybe it would be best if she stayed behind, but there was such a burning excitement in his face that she couldn't bring herself to spoil it. So she would have to tell him somewhere en route. Maybe the Parisian wind would shake loose a paternal wish. Maybe Amsterdam, Hamburg. The multiple bus journeys would set him in permanent good temper so that he could take anything in his stride. He would do the right thing. She knew he would. He'd stand by her – because of what they were. She was his empress, his luminous ankle queen.

The theatre that had booked them was in Montmartre in the north of Paris. Both Antoney and Simone seemed put off at first by its humble exterior and its distance from the epicentre. Perhaps they'd been expecting something like the Royal Albert Hall. They were pleased, though, to discover that both nights had sold well. This was the 'world première' of Simone's Bird solo. A costume composed of white feathers had been sewn by a Chinese woman in Clerkenwell (apparently the quickest and cheapest back-street tailor in theatre). Simone was now calling herself the company's principal. Carla secretly hoped Bird would go badly to bring her back down to earth, but it didn't. It was mesmerising.

The piece was set to a single wooden flute played by The Wonder. It had a very specific central posture of the upper body tipped forwards and Simone's thin arms extended along her back, the joined hands resting lightly on the sacrum. She made quick, flitting head movements, taking feathery steps and eccentric leaps about the stage. Carla was watching from the wings, and when Simone lengthened her slender neck and dipped her nose almost to the floor to the otherworldly sound of the flute, sending the white feathers up behind her, she hardly recognised her. She was spectral and delicate, as if she could be lifted in the palm of your hand. Oscar always said that watching someone you know well on stage is a bit like seeing them naked. Carla hadn't grasped what he'd meant until now. She was looking at the creature inside Simone that had always been fluttering to come out – her specialness, her extraordinariness, her Josephine. It was worrying that Antoney alone had been the one to let this creature out, but Carla was happy for her friend – that is until she saw the way Simone jumped into Antoney's arms amid the crashing applause when she came off stage, as though she weighed nothing. Carla by comparison felt like a ton of roof slate during her lift. Antoney seemed to wobble underneath her. She was not worthy. She had no right to be there.

The run was extended by a further two nights. Flowers were thrown at Simone's feet, at Shango's thundery exit. Antoney strode through Montmartre in his suede cape, the applause continuing in his head. He told Carla that he liked Paris because it was the kind of place you could live sideways, whatever that meant. They were staying in a cheap hotel a few blocks away from the theatre. Simone was in with Milly, Carla with Antoney, though by the time he got back from trying out the late-night bars with the boys, the jazz clubs, the Left Bank cafés, she was fast asleep, having spent the come-down after the show drinking chocolate out of sachets with Bluey. Simone and Ekow had paired up. They were all over each other, as if the Parisian wind had finally blown them together. 'She's changed,' Carla said to Bluey – he had asked her why she and Simone weren't as close as they used to be. 'She's so full of herself these days, it makes me sick. I liked her better when she was a nobody.'

Antoney questioned Carla one afternoon when he woke up, hung-over and bloodshot, about what was going on between

Ekow and Simone. She was getting ready to go to the Louvre. They were supposed to be going together but he'd ducked out. 'Isn't it obvious?' she said. 'They're fucking. Why, what's it to you?' 'They're not compatible,' he said, and disappeared into the tiny en suite.

It was something Carla had come to accept about Antoney that he could not only physically disappear – he would tell you he was going out to buy cigarettes and come back five hours later offering no explanation – he could also disappear when he was standing right in front of you. He might be looking straight at you, even having a conversation with you, but his voice, his manner, would be monotonal and slightly hostile, as if you were standing in the way of a glorious and necessary view. This was becoming more frequent. Where in the beginning Carla had found his self-absorption seductive, now she found it irritating. Success had made him jumpy and obsessive. He drank more than he used to. His outbursts during rehearsals, his theories of shrinking stages and lightbox conspiracies were becoming more extreme, and in the absence of Riley she was realising how much her influence over him had lessened since they'd become friends.

Standing before the *Mona Lisa* she was reminded of him. She studied the strange, airborne feel of the head and shoulders. The noncommittal smile; the elusive, sandy eyes. It occurred to her that Antoney's eyes were the same, looking inwards and outwards at the same time, at nothing and everything, at too little and too much.

The wardrobe mistress at the theatre was sweet on Carla. She was a loud brunette with an amazingly high waist; she touched Carla's hair as if it were a moonbeam. After the final performance she donated to her a glossy, olive-coloured vintage ballgown that Carla had noticed, with a gasp of appreciation, hanging up on a clothes rail backstage when they'd arrived. '*Prends-le*! Take it,' the wardrobe mistress said. 'I want you to wear it. I don't mind I get into trouble.' Carla insisted she could only go for a walk in it. To the heavy-lidded sighs of the wardrobe mistress she glided – yes, glided, she conquered gravity – to Antoney's dressing room, where she assumed he was still changing. In this dress she was capable of anything. She was Cleopatra, empress of Egypt, with child, proud of her fruit. She would present herself to its father with a thousand trumpets ringing. He would hold her up to the heavens in his mighty arms. She knocked firmly on the door, the sumptuous fabric rustling, her forearm dripping with the ribbons from her sleeve. 'Enter,' she heard him say, so she pushed open the door – to find him sitting before the mirror rolling a joint. And whom should she find sitting next to him on the counter, her un-feathered legs bare in her mini and brand new lattice sandals, her powdery collar bones sharp in the bright light, but Simone, expectantly beholding her.

'Wow,' she said. 'Look at you.'

Antoney turned. He was still wearing his makeup. 'It suits you,' he said. 'We were just talking about you.'

'What about me?' Carla now felt inappropriate and out of date.

'I was thinking maybe you're doing too much in Blues House and you should save more energy for the duet.'

'I'm fine with it the way it is,' she lied. Simone quickly looked away.

'We'll just do some minor reshuffling in the first half, all right?' said Antoney.

Anything for less dancing, really, but Carla was, again, insulted. She stood humiliated in the doorway, staring at the back of Antoney's head, Simone smiling at her in fake reassurance. 'Fine,' she said. 'Do what you want,' and she swept away, tears hotting her eyes, desperate beneath her anger that they mustn't touch the duet, because it was her only link to him when he disappeared.

Hurrying through the empty auditorium towards the exit she ran into Bluey in the lobby. The second she saw him she felt better. 'You look incredible,' he said, a rare and irrepressible joy in his face. She cried into his ear (for his shoulder was too low down) and pulled him out into the street to get some air. Bluey was the one person, apart from her mother, whom Carla felt utterly safe with. He was the kindness that waited for her. She could always communicate with him even when she couldn't stand to talk to anyone else. The way he looked at her made her feel immortally beautiful, and it often seemed that they were looking directly into each other's souls – though this, so far, was not what she understood love to be. As for Bluey, walking beside her like that with her hand resting in the loop he made with his arm, like a gentleman should, even in his jeans and sweatshirt he fancied himself as nothing less than the luckiest and most envied cowbell player on earth.

They walked through the streets, taking narrow turnings and quiet alleyways. They had no idea where they were going and were unconcerned about getting lost. If they preferred the look of the right turn to the left they would take it. There was a simple pleasure in bends and slopes, the possibilities of corners. They were not in Paris, but a place inside Paris, which would be exactly the same in any other city, in any other country or neighbourhood in the world, because they were the place, the contentment they spun together. Eventually they changed tack and began to take the busier boulevards, energised, lured by the activity of the night. For the first time since leaving London Carla was aroused rather than troubled by the foreignness surrounding her, the alien chatter, the different river, the unknown faces full of mystery and intrigue sitting at patio tables outside the bars and nocturnal coffee houses. At some point after midnight they found themselves on the Champs-Élysées, a symphony of lights and traffic and supreme mannequins. Passers-by stared at Carla as she floated along in her bulging olive skirt, even the haughty Parisian women in their heels and stylish coats couldn't help smiling. She was getting tired by now. Just as she thought she could walk no

161

further they came across a pretty square surrounded by trees and berry bushes, with benches and a small brick-framed flowerbed in the centre. It was deserted, which was strange given the buzz going on outside it, and it had a thoroughly rural feel, as though it had been transported there just as Carla needed it. They entered along a slim footpath almost hidden from the boulevard by bushes.

'It's nice here,' she said. They sat close together on one of the benches. The temperature was slightly cooler than outside.

They hadn't talked much about what had upset her at the theatre, but now that they were seated she revealed her problem, which Bluey took uneasily. She was relieved to share it with someone at last. 'Don't tell anyone,' she said. 'This is between you and me.'

'How come you ain't told him yet?' Bluey said.

'I keep trying. I'm scared.'

'What for?' When Carla shook her head he objected, 'You shouldn't have to be scared of your fella like that. What's he done for you to be scared of him?'

'It's not anything he might do. I mean, not like that – It's more the way he'll look at me.'

'I don't get you.'

'He likes me the way I am. If I change – you know, I'll get fat and stretched and all that – maybe he'll feel different about me. He'll have to change too. I feel like I'm inflicting something on him.'

Bluey glanced at her with disapproving bemusement, finding his cigarettes. He looked quite dashing for an instant with his powerful eyes and freckled cheeks. It struck Carla as it sometimes did how attractive he was. 'Isn't he supposed to accept you whatever?' he said. 'Anyway it's none of my business, as long as he treats you all right. He should've seen it for himself by now without you having to spell it out.'

'*You* didn't,' said Carla.

'Yeah well. I ain't your fella.'

A woman entered the square, reminding them that they were still in the centre of Paris. She nodded in their direction, then walked solemnly along the opposite side of the flowerbed. She was about forty, with dark curls like Bluey's, dressed in a black coat and court shoes, and gave off an air of loneliness.

Carla asked Bluey whether he planned on having any kids himself. 'That depends on a lot of things,' he said, adding when coaxed, 'The circumstances an' that. The bombs.'

'The bombs? Why are you always going on about bombs?'

'Because the bombs are gonna kill us all, that's why. It takes one button, one bastard, and that's it. They'll use it on Vietnam and one day they'll use it here too. I don't know if I wanna be a dad to a mite if he's only gonna get blown up.'

'God, that's depressing.'

'That's the world.'

As Bluey finished his cigarette the other woman in the square approached them and asked in French, gesturing, whether he had one to spare. 'Yeah, course,' he said. She bent to get a light. Rising back up, she stood over them as she took her first few puffs, studying Carla seriously through the smoke. As if satisfied by something, she said au revoir, and walked on at the same slow pace in the direction of the exit.

'It depends on the family set-up as well,' Bluey continued. 'I don't like families. They're dangerous – bunches of people living in the smog of each other's moods.'

'I take it you had a moody family,' Carla said.

'And you never?'

His face had taken on that murky expression Carla sometimes caught during rehearsals, when the cowbell was on stand-by and he was sitting waiting, lapsed into his own thoughts, or when there was an argument going on. His eyes were deadened. An absence drifted off him. She would sometimes approach him in these moments and tickle him, but this time she didn't. He had never talked much about his family.

'Is that why you ran away? Because of moods?'

'Maybe,' he said, lighting up again. 'Then maybe I went looking for a bird in a ball dress.'

'You're a funny boy, you know that, Bluey Ellis?' Carla said as they left the square. 'I wish I knew what goes on inside that head of yours.'

Back along the Champs-Elysées they went, her arm inside his loop, her skirts abound, and she was just a little bit taller than he was.

Carla didn't find another Cleopatra moment after Paris. Her demotion in Blues House erected a wall between her and Antoney, exacerbated by the collusion between him and Simone, which if Simone hadn't had a thing going with Ekow she would have suspected was an affair. Antoney seemed delirious on the constant motion, the driving and dancing and packing and driving, past the sundried mountains near Rheims, through the small provincial towns where people stopped in the street to stare at the gold-winged bus going by with near-black smoke coming out of its exhaust. The air inside the bus was tinged with the smell of exposed male feet. By way of in-house entertainment Fansa, Ricardo, Rosina and Antoney took sips of the libation rum, having loudening discussions on topics such as cricket, marriage, the authenticity of the Bible, the superiority of French Polly-Cinders over English ones and the assassination of Malcolm X. The rest of the troupe were relieved to disembark at the end of each journey, Simone commenting that she hadn't realised how smelly men were until now. As was his way, Antoney was always less jovial once the bus had stopped moving.

He was particularly disappointed by Amsterdam, a trip that ended with Milly deserting. Everything was bad, the theatre shabby, the accommodation dirty, bad-smelling sheets (who did they think they were putting up?). The show itself was also weak, which Antoney put down to the fact that he hadn't been present for the libation. His way of dealing with it was to let fly a rant immediately after curtain, his voice still hoarse from its recent return to itself during the interval. He laid into Bluey especially, who'd lost time twice, and Milly, who'd forgotten steps, berating her for failing to style it out like a professional, for dropping focus and being sloppy. Milly lost her temper and called him a hypocrite, a tyrant and a hysterical dictator, ripping off her chiffon scarf and throwing it into the bin. The next day she walked. She was still his favourite dancer. He glimpsed her from the hotel window crossing the road with her rucksack, her big plastic earrings swinging against her neck, that perfect moving neck, those fantastically shakeable shoulders. She'd rejected his unapologetic attempt to make her reconsider. Ekow said he was in a class of his own of idiocy, but he refused to take all the blame for it. He found comfort that night in a rumful multi-bar swagger through the red-light district with the fellas. In the cherry-coloured gloom of the generous girls in the windows along the Singel canal, Fansa found one to put his money on, in a zebra corset and black wig. Not Antoney. He liked to keep himself clean, even if his woman didn't seem much bothered about that these days.

Swaying in the dark by the water he thought about how different Carla was from how she used to be. She wasn't fun any more. She brought him down, sitting behind him on the bus with Oscar's decrepit blanket on her lap like an old woman – in the summer! Travel didn't excite her, didn't exhilarate her. She favoured the smaller world. Nowadays she was always siding with anyone else but him, be it Bluey, Milly, Ekow. Why was it that when anything went wrong it was always down to him? Why was he expected to hold everything together when he had to think about making new ballets as well? It was too much to put on a guy. It crossed his mind sometimes to go solo. He could do that now. He was well known. He could go to any number of theatres and get a slot. He was Antoney Matheus, celebrated dancer-choreographer-director. He'd come from a tangerine house in the bush and here he was touring with his own troupe. But he could hire dancers instead, as and when he needed them. And the beauty of it would be that he'd only be in charge of his own boat. He wouldn't have to deal with Ekow, all of his antagonising demands and his muscling in on areas that weren't his place. Hadn't he ever heard the saying about too many cooks spoiling the gumbo soup? Ekow used to be such an easygoing, good-natured type of brother. He remembered him just liming into the Marshalls' place in his shiny yellow shirt, how welcoming he was at Oscar's and how inspiring Antoney used to find his optimism and lightness of heart. Now he could barely have a conversation with him without wanting to knock him out. He made him feel bad about himself, as if he was inferior, not just to Ekow but to everyone. People could do that to you – Benjamin did, his mother did, Simone used to but not any more. If a person made you feel like that you could never fully trust them, you could never hold them close. He told himself he'd write this down in a letter to Riley, that being alone was better than being in a bus full of people who brought you down; he'd rather stare into nothingness and despair and gain strength from the exercising of his courage. That was the right way. That was where the meaning was, in accepting that there was no meaning, and building from that point.

He knew what was wrong with Carla. She wanted to get married. She wanted him to propose. That was another area where they were different. As much as she made the effort to go along with his unconventional ideas, as much as she liked to pretend she was down with the hippies, she was a traditional girl with the conventional desires for comfort and stability. During the discussion on the bus about marriage a few days before, he'd felt the weight of her silence behind him when he'd said – more strongly than he might have meant to owing to the drink being passed round – 'Marriage is not natural, right. It's two people clinging to each other because they're scared of the world and scared of being themselves.

166

That's what tradition does to people. It tells them what to do, and the only reason it gives them for why they should do it is that that's what people have always done.' 'But there are different ways of being married,' Rosina had put in, to which Fansa had joked, 'I only know one way – and it's a rocky, brimstone place!' Most people had had something to say on the subject but Carla kept quiet throughout, her face to the window. Antoney was terrified at the thought of getting trapped, like Oscar had been while he was married, of shrinking, of being pinned down or disappearing into someone else. He would be compromised. He would be giving himself up, and he didn't want to do it.

He watched the boats moored against the banks of the Singel with a deep frown in his velvety brow. He was drawn in by the flickering sight of their decks rimmed with Christmas lights, the glow from the misty marine windows emitting a sense of peace and tranquillity. He watched one sliding through the navy water leaving behind it a trail of limpid silver. How right, how right and wide it must be to live like that, in solitude, detached from the burdens and interferences of land, free to move off whenever you felt like it, with no one to answer to but yourself. No dancers jumping ship. No woman scratching to be wife.

'Hey, Ric,' he called across the road, 'how much you reckon those boats there cost?'

The next morning they set off for a major show in Hamburg, a six-hour drive crossing the Dutch-German border. The loss of Milly had put a dampener on things. Ekow and Antoney were seated as far away from each other as was possible, Antoney at the front underneath his hat, Ekow at the back with his arm around Simone. Carla was in her usual seat, utterly miserable. Even Fansa and Benjamin were silent. The Wonder, however, was fresh, positive and alert, sprightly from ginger and an early night preceded by a few verses from the *Dhammapada*. He loved to drive. He kept an eye on the petrol gauge, filling up when necessary, but he was no mechanic, so failed to take heed of the now pure-black smoke chugging out from the back of the bus and the higher octave of the metallic squeals accompanying it. The route followed dappled country roads alongside dikes and waving grassland. When they stopped by a field somewhere between Oldenburg and Bremen for people to relieve themselves, the bus finally died. On trying the ignition The Wonder was met with a hopeless cough. They were miles from anywhere, nothing but fields, trees, deserted road and German telephone lines stretching all the way to the horizon.

'Why're we stopped?' Antoney said, waking from his sleep.

Simone updated him. Ricardo, Bluey and Ekow were tinkering around at the front of the bus, Rosina was getting out her camera. Carla looked on with increasing alarm. They needed to be at the theatre by four and it was almost noon, though this was the least of her worries. She was more anxious about the prospect of being stranded pregnant in the middle of nowhere with no shelter to speak of but tents and a bus.

Antoney came out onto the roadside. A soft wind was rolling through the grass. 'What's the problem? We need to get moving.'

'We ain't going nowhere for now,' Ekow informed him. 'Engine's gone.' Ricardo and The Wonder were preparing to hitchhike to the nearest place to find parts.

'But that could take hours,' said Antoney.

'You got a better suggestion?'

He stared foolishly into the bonnet. He didn't know brake fluid from fan belt. 'Ric, weren't you supposed to be responsible for keeping this thing in shape?'

'Don't lay it on me, I wasn't to know. The machine's old, that's all.'

'And there's no point dishing out blame.' Ekow and Antoney bickered until Simone told them to give it a rest. The group watched as Ricardo and The Wonder walked off with thumbs at the ready into the landscape ahead, rust-coloured and bright green in the midday sun, the dark grey road bending at the furthest point to the right. Antoney sucked his teeth. A missed show was almost as bad, if not worse, than a bad show, a missed opportunity to hear many hands making the sound of onions fried short of oil. The theatre would be waiting. The Germans would be going about their Saturdays in anticipation of the evening's entertainment. Antoney felt his blood quickening in that hot, mounting way it could. By three o'clock when the boys still weren't back he needed a drink to ease himself out, so he uncapped the three-quarter bottle left of the current supply and shared a listless toast leaning against the back of the bus with Fansa, who said there was nothing they could do so they might as well make the most of it, enjoy the likkle interlude. 'Look at all that space,' he said. 'Look at that sky. You know, it does remind me of the countryside back home a bit, the feeling it gives you, nothing blocking your view. It makes me think for a minute that the world is not divided.'

Antoney couldn't quite get into a philosophising frame of mind. No one else apart from maybe Simone seemed put out by their situation. Ekow and Benjamin were asleep. Rosina was taking pictures of people's feet. Carla and Bluey had decided to use Oscar's blanket as a picnic mat and were eating apples among the dandelions as if they were Adam and Eve. It infuriated him. *He* should be sitting with her, not him. The sight of them like that drove home to him that he and Carla were on the verge of finishing, that possibly she had stopped loving him, which by itself was a lonely, disturbing thought. She made him feel like an outsider, his own girl. To put it out of his mind he carried on trying to flag down passing cars – they were few and far between – but none stopped for him. It got so he couldn't stay in one place unless he was drinking something. His thoughts were heightened, sharpened, his vision stark. He was afraid. The wind roamed over the land like low-flying angels. An abandoned hut in the far distance was a stout man beckoning. Alcohol was a kind of truth, he believed that. It gave you the full, rounded actuality that was denied you by the shallow grind. The real picture. In a blue shift of light marking the closing of the afternoon, he saw Simone climb down off the bus, stretching her arms, her corduroy skirt riding up her thigh, her ever-glossed lips. He saw her exactly as he'd seen her in the church hall during the making of Bird, when she'd glowed for him, shone for him in her two-pink dress, materialised in his hands. The temperature in the air had dropped from its earlier warmth. Dirty clouds were gathering. He went over to her somewhat hungrily, not clear on what he wanted to say. He suggested that the two of them should try and track down the others, that he couldn't stand to wait there any more.

'Antoney, dear,' she said, 'are you going to be drunk all the way back to Dover? Your eyes are melting. We best wait.'

'No,' he said, 'come on, I wanna talk to you.'

'Why can't you talk to me here?'

'Because it's private . . . I've got an idea.'

'What's your idea?' Ekow appeared behind her, leaning out of the bus with his sly face and cold manner.

'I wasn't addressing you.'

'You are now.'

'Simone, I don't always know what it is you see in this fella. You her keeper now?'

The others were looking over at the bus. In the dulling light, as gentle spots of rain started to fall, there was a collective nervousness at the prospect of being stranded for the night in bad weather. They had little food (the emergency supply had not been treated as such – Fansa and Ricardo enjoyed that universal peanut game of throwing the nut into the air and catching it with your mouth). They were also low on water, and Rosina was worried about Ricardo.

Ekow surveyed the skies. 'I think it's time to put up the tents,' he said.

Antoney called after Simone but she followed Ekow to the back of the bus. Carla was watching him cautiously from a little way off with the blanket wrapped around her shoulders, her tall, lean figure reassuring against the dusk. In his growing misery and fear he would have liked so much to be held by her, but he didn't know how to approach her. He couldn't make out whether her expression was kind or cruel. He felt that he was being swept away, turned off his feet, that everything around him was becoming devilish and sinister. He'd never felt so bad, so frantic. He couldn't bear to talk to anyone but he couldn't bear to be inside his head. The clanging of the tent poles agitated him. He put on his cape to make himself feel better but it didn't help. People huddled inside the tents sheltering from the rain with sleeping-bags and blankets, eating fish out of tins and stale biscuits. He couldn't join in with them. They all seemed to sneer at him, Fansa too, their eyes full of hate, so he went to sit on the bus by himself with the last of the liquor. At some point, walking up and down the aisle, he thought again of the waiting theatre in Hamburg, a good thought – the audience, come to see him fly.

With a wild hope he tried the key in the ignition several times. When it failed to work he started beeping the horn in a frenzy, finding that each minute going by was easier that way. Ekow soon came out of his tent and flung open the door of the bus, shouting and cursing, grabbing Antoney's arm roughly. Unable to restrain himself any longer, Antoney lunged at him out of the driver's seat, smashing him to the ground. He began hitting him anywhere he could with his fists, in the face, the torso, kicking him, but Antoney was no fighter. He'd always avoided fighting at school and when forced to he'd never won. He got tangled up in his cape. Ekow overpowered him, but instead of using his fists in return he used his palms, slapping Antoney upside the head and telling him simultaneously that he was going to quit, that he, Antoney, was a calamity and a lunatic. Carla and Simone had come out of their tents. Antoney heard Carla somewhere above him screaming at Ekow, 'Leave him alone – *Ekow*! Get off him!' As soon as he was released, he took one breathless look around him then ran off without a word, mindless of the storm, while Carla shouted after him.

He went in the direction of that hut, the stout man beckoning. It seemed like a very long way, he had no real conception of time or distance. Wet through from the rain and smeared with mud he eventually veered off the highway down a long narrow path, which was darker than the road, with stinging nettles on either side of it. The sense of claustrophobic terror he'd been experiencing gradually began to subside as he walked. The thunder in the distance became muffled and unthreatening, as though it belonged to another world. He went further and further along the path feeling more at peace in his own company. When he finally neared the hut, which was indeed stout, too low for him to stand up in, he heard a different sound coming off the rain, the sound of waves breaking on shore, within that a faint knocking.

He imagined that the landscape before him changed dramatically. He could see the aqua ocean, coconut palms as high as the moon, a yellowish shine around the edge of things. The hut itself was brighter in colour on closer inspection, no longer grey but a rich brown, the air warm and still. Next to the hut, a few paces from where he stopped, he identified the source of the knocking sound. A short, thick-built woman was crouched on the ground hammering a nail into what looked like a child's stool with a piece of wood. There was something about her that Antoney recognised. She hummed to herself as she worked, an old song in a minor key – suddenly he remembered.

Mrs Gates? he said.

She used to hum that tune on the beach, sitting in the water with her dress on. After lessons the schoolchildren would go and spy on her, Antoney among them, and whisper to each other about how creepy and magnificent it was that mad old Mrs Jennifer Gates had killed her husband. She looked exactly the same as then, though her dress was dry.

How are you, Mrs Gates?

Oh, she replied, not looking up, just passing the time of day.

He asked her out of interest, Have you found that thing yet?

She knew exactly what he was talking about. The right address, the turning back, the exact place where she'd lost her head.

I haven't come across it as yet, she said, but I know it's around here somewhere.

Do you know what the building looks like?

She said she believed it had a whitewash front, and could he let her know if he saw anything? Then she looked up at him for the first time since he'd seen her, and he noticed with alarm that her eyes were sunk well back into her face so that they looked like black caves. She offered him something to eat. A strong breeze started pushing him towards her.

No, thank you, Mrs Gates, he said, stepping back. I better be going.

Suit yourself, she shrugged. But you just remember to take care of *your* address. We don't want *you* getting lost too. Then we'd both be in a fix!

Unbeknown to them, the Midnight Ballet had a large following in Denmark. Their pictures were in the newspapers preceding their arrival, and they were met at the theatre in Copenhagen by a cluster of excited dance lovers, some of them bearing flowers. After the final show of the run, which had been watched two nights in a row from the balconies by a once genuinely blonde baroness called Kristine Ploug, they were asked to give a private performance at her 'house', which was located north of Copenhagen in the scenic Zealand country-side along the Kattegat coast. It was actually a castle. The baroness, a widow, lived there alone with her staff and occa-sional nieces and nephews. A voluptuous, quick-reflexed woman with a powerful presence, she insisted the troupe stay on and relax for a few days, as she so loved being surrounded by the beautiful young dancers, Antoney in particular, whom she regarded as a genius.

You entered the place along a gravelled avenue and climbed a slope to a spacious driveway with breathtaking views of the countryside. The castle had a copper roof and three towers at the north wing, tall windows looking out onto lushly manicured lawns, a fenced meadow in which two horses flicked their tails in the raw Baltic breeze, and to the south a stretch of dense forest that eventually dispersed into a private beach. There were more than thirty rooms in the building, decorated in rich reds, lilacs and mustards, including a wicker-furnished sunroom with a glass ceiling (rarely empty during the troupe's stay), which led out onto a pretty garden. The baroness had lived there all her life, she told them. She loved it so much that she'd never been able to move away. 'But where's your man?' Fansa asked her. 'You mean to tell me a beautiful woman like you is resting here all by yourself?' 'Ah, I'm afraid so,' the baroness was visibly flattered – she spoke English with a guttural Danish swing, 'although I have many visitors, from America, Russia, England, all over the world, such as your wonderful darling selves. I'm so glad I managed to turn your arms to stay.'

Simone reckoned this was about the standard of accommodation they should have been enjoying throughout the tour, and jumped right in. Everyone was elated, contented, like children delivered into an astounding nursery, but no one was more grateful for it than Carla, who was still traumatised from Antoney's flip in Germany. She was so relieved after the final show to lay her head on the Egyptian cotton pillows in the luxurious bedroom set aside for the two of them, that she slept solid for nineteen hours, waking up to him sitting on the end of the bed studying her.

That evening the baroness gave a lavish dinner in her enormous dining room, where an entire wall was devoted to a portrait of her late father with his dog. The troupe were in good spirits; the comfort surrounding them, the warm colours, the

174

candles, the copious food and the prospect of no more shows had weakened barriers between people. Even Antoney and Ekow were being civil to one another. Several conversations flew across the table at once, about dance institutions in Denmark, Ailey's company, Les Ballets Nègres and the contemporary scene in the UK. Carla contributed little, enjoying the feeling of being close to Antoney, their shoulders touching, his hand at one point resting on her leg. He'd been very quiet since that night. He'd returned to the bus at dawn, humbled and aloof, and had taken to giving her those soft looks like he used to. She observed him as the baroness asked him in a fascinated tone about his choreographic process, the kind of topic he would normally thrive on, but tonight he was disinterested. He sipped his wine and offered short, vague explanations, trailing off and glancing at Carla. She started to wonder whether he knew, whether he'd guessed, like Bluey said he should have. Whether he had or not, she decided that this, finally, was the place to bring it out into the open.

Fansa was sitting to the left of the baroness, who was at the head of the table wearing heavy green eyeshadow and a turban-style headwrap inspired by Isadora Duncan. He took every opportunity to compliment her on her fashion sense, her delicious cuisine, her 'melodramatic' furniture, which did have a lurking, animalistic feel. 'Yes,' she said, 'I have been lucky to be encompassed always by nice things and possessions, but I'm sure your lives are much more exciting than mine. I've never done anything so *melodramatic*, if I can take your interesting phrase' – she gave a coquettish flick of her lashes in Fansa's direction – 'as taking the stage and travelling around the world with a group of fellow artists. I would make a disappointing storyteller. I have no tales, you see. I have not done the sensational things.'

After coffee Carla excused herself to go to bed. Antoney did the same. They went slowly up the curving marble staircase, beneath a scintillating chandelier, joining hands halfway up, and stepped into their room, which looked out on the meadow and seemed dreamy and secluded in the blush of low lamps and the gleam from the crimson bedspread. The rugs were so thick that when they took off their shoes their feet sank down. He was gentle with her in a new way, as if she was brittle, walking her to the bed, slipping off her beaded dress. Dancers and pregnant women have one thing in common. They look at themselves. She looked at her fattened breasts as he covered them with his mouth and hands, her unlonely stomach which had developed a discreet mound. He paused there with his cheek, lying on top of her.

'Baby,' he said darkly, 'I'm scared of myself.' 'Don't be scared,' she said. 'I'm here. Everything's fine.'

This is the place you sink back into, thought Antoney. All his underlying fear and emptiness fell away like water flowing down the creeks in the hills of St Mary. This is the place, if you made a magic trick and the trick got you lost, that you could come to to get yourself back again. They had never been this close before. To Carla everything hidden was spoken, with their bodies and their souls.

They fell asleep wrapped up, and woke in the small hours at exactly the same time. A full moon was shining in through the window. The tips of their noses were joined. There was nothing to be said about it. They would make plans later. For now Carla just wanted them to bathe together in the idea of their third person. She reached for his hand and guided it to her stomach. He pressed it, half closing his eyes and smiling sleepily. 'Can you feel it?' she whispered. He mumbled yes, you feel so good, and rubbed up and down over her breast. Turning onto her back she looked up at the ceiling, happier than she'd felt in months, clutching his arm across her. 'Soon we'll be able to feel it moving,' she said. His breathing had deepened. She also closed her eyes.

Ten seconds later he said, 'Moving?'

'Yeah, and kicking. Just like you.' She held him tighter.

More alert now he said, 'What's that?'

She thought that maybe he didn't know about babies kicking, which was actually just like him, but the atmosphere in the room was changing. She wasn't sure how to respond so she said nothing. Neither of them moved.

'What are you talking about?'

'Don't you know?' He slid his arm away a bit. 'Do I have to spell it out for you?'

'You're pregnant?'

'*Yes!*'

'No.'

'What do you mean no?'

'You can't be.'

'Why?'

'Because – Jesus, Carla.' He sat up in the bed. She said coldly, 'I don't see it as such bad news.'

A dialogue followed, clarifying the facts of the situation, the slow revelation for Antoney of the real reason behind the travel sickness, the aloofness, the low stepping and the refusals to dance.

'*Four months*?' he said. 'Four months and just now you're letting me know?'

'I tried to tell you, loads of times, but you—'

'Jesus.'

He kept shaking his head. Yet again he was insulting her.

'Who am I to you?' she said putting on her nightgown. 'It's not as if we just got together, is it? I don't know why you're acting so upset.'

'I am in no position to start raising pickney!'

'*We!*'

'We never even *talked* about this.'

'Well sometimes, Antoney, things just happen by themselves and there's nothing you can do about it. You just get on with it.'

There was a fretful silence. Antoney was having visions of prams, dummies, milk bottles, women wading along Portobello

Road with thickened ankles, ruined postures and echoes in their heads of nights full of screaming. An alien concept. A drab, pinned-down existence.

Carla eventually came and sat next to him, in a calmer manner, laying her chin on his shoulder. 'Can't you imagine it?' she said. 'A little creature that's ours, looking after it together? We can get a place. I've thought about it. You wouldn't have to give anything up, things will be just the same as they are now – only we'll have a little person to look after . . . I don't mind not being married.'

He was silent. Without looking at her he said accusingly, flatly, 'So you want to be ordinary.'

'What?'

He didn't elaborate. She stood in front of him at the foot of the bed, her hands on her stomach, and shouted, 'You think *this* is ordinary?' In a swift action she went to the armchair by the window, grabbed the robe she'd been wearing earlier in the day and shoved her arms into it, tying it at the waist. Then she stormed off into the adjoining bathroom and slammed the door.

He tried to run it over in his mind, the prams, what she'd said about getting a place and things not changing, but he couldn't see it. It couldn't work. All he could see was dullness and finality. He thought of his mother and her big disappointment over him. He'd never asked her to give herself up for him but she was always blaming him for it anyway. He wouldn't be put in that position. He would not repeat. Dancing and pickney did not match. *One* most important thing. Not two, one.

But there was a solution, which when it came to him made him rise from the bed. Yes. The power of disappearance. Look around the corners of tricks. He put on his briefs, forming the right wording carefully in his mind. He felt quite lighthearted as he knocked on the bathroom door. She was sitting on the toilet seat, looking very small all that way away past the mirrors and the free-standing gold-tapped tub. She didn't look up.

He knelt at her feet, taking hold of her hands, which she resisted. 'All right,' he said.

Her eyes moistened.

'We'll deal with it.'

She was nodding, a hint of a smile, tears falling down her cheeks.

'It's legal now,' he said. 'As soon as we get back – We'll do it, properly. It's not too late. I'll be with you every step of the way.'

Carla took a moment or two to get his drift. At first her mind could not accommodate the idea, and when it came clear she kicked him in the balls with her foot.

'Hey, *watch* that!'

Her eyes were murderous. Her hair was wild. 'So you want me to kill it,' she said, mirroring his earlier phrasing.

'It's not killing, it's—'

'Don't you get it, you bastard? I love this child already!' She picked up a soap dish from above the sink and threw it at him. He ducked. 'Get out.'

'Carla—'

'Get out!'

'Wait, let's—' Then came a bottle of luxury shampoo and a bottle of something else.

'I said fuck off!' she bellowed.

So what else could he do?

He sat in the sunroom trying to think. The more he went over it the more irate he got. He was sure she'd done it on purpose to trap him. She had no right. She was messing him up. He didn't feel like a drink so he smoked cigarettes instead, and when it started getting light he went out for a walk, first on the lawns then into the shoreside forest, which was spooky but not unpleasant. Dawn creatures flew up in tall blue trees. He stared

179

to the top of an ivory birch as if it had all the answers. Following the sound of the sea, he eventually came out into the baroness's private bay. *The sea must always be available to you*, he heard his father's words in his memory. *You need a little stretch of sea between the years or the months*.

And what a big open place is this earth. The sky out there was boundless, striped with lanes of luminous morning white. The sun was emerging from behind violet mountains on the horizon, forming a slithering film on the water. He felt mildly better. Kicking off his shoes he went to the water's edge and let the Baltic cool massage his feet. Some two hundred yards to his left there was a narrow jetty stretching into the sea, concluding at its end with a stone-walled circle against which the waves collided. It was while sitting on the sand and looking out at the jetty that he caught sight of someone else on the beach, a man. He was dressed in a thigh-length dashiki, jeans, and a pair of incredibly white trainers. The Wonder. He was drifting over in Antoney's direction, raising his arm in a cheerful salute.

'A wonderful day!' he called. Arriving closer he said, 'I love to walk as the sun is rising. It's the best time.'

Antoney didn't say much, not being in a chatty mood.

'Ah come on,' The Wonder said. 'What's the matter with you again? Didn't you sleep well? I slept like a baby. This place is just great.' He sat down.

'It's all right,' said Antoney flatly.

'Who would've thought when we started out that we'd be one day staying in a castle? You know what this reminds me of, Antoney?' He didn't need an answer. 'It reminds me of a place I once visited in Portugal. I was there with my wife having a break from work, and we were staying at her relative's house in the town – I can't remember the name of it any more, this was years and years ago. But there was a very impressive building that I could see from the upstairs window, a lot like this, with a bay next to it just like this one. Maybe it was a premonition, eh?' The Wonder leaned in and motioned a nudge. 'Maybe it was fate that got us here . . . My friend, you don't look well this morning. Are you sick?'

'Look, I had a heavy night. I don't feel like company.'

'I've been meaning to say to you, Antoney, that you should try and cut down on your drinking.'

'How you mean? I haven't had a drink!'

'Really? That's good . . . good. Well, no more shows. You can rest now.'

They were silent for a time, taking in the view.

'Where is your wife now, Wonder?' said Antoney.

'Let us address this problem. Why is it that to this day you cannot call me by my proper name? It's important to get a man's name right. How would you like it if all the time I was calling you An*tho*ney, like the Americans? You wouldn't like it . . . Oh sit down, boy, I'm not angry with you.'

'Why does it matter to you so much?' Antoney said. 'Wonder's – for fuck's sake, *The* Wonder's not your real name, is it? Were you born with that name?'

'That's not the point.'

'What's your real name?'

'I can't tell you that.'

'Why not? Come on, it might help me get it right.'

'What's yours?'

'You know my name.'

'What's your father's name? Your ancestral name?'

'It's . . . My father's name was – Rogers . . . I'm not sure. I carry my mother's name.'

The Wonder looked questioningly at him, noting some discrepancy. Antoney couldn't hold eye contact with him and they were suddenly embarrassed.

'So what is it?' Antoney said.

Staring straight ahead, The Wonder said quietly, 'It's Brian.'

'Brian?'

'Do you find it funny?'

181

'No, no, it's just – different from what I expected. What's your surname?'

'You don't need to know my surname.'

'Have you got someone after you, The Wonder? See. I told you it would help.' Antoney nudged him back, the Carla problem virtually forgotten.

'I'm glad we've finally reached the desired objective,' The Wonder said. Turning seriously to him, he added, 'Keep it to yourself, though. Is that clear? I'd be very upset if you revealed this to anyone else. All right?'

'All right, man, I understand.'

'Good.'

Leaning back on his elbow, The Wonder's thoughts returned to the interrupted juncture.

'My wife left me,' he said. 'For another guy.'

'Did she?'

'Yeah. I was a young man then, good-looking like you. Maybe she was bored, I don't know.' With a stamp of his foot on the sand he scared away a fuzzy spider. 'She thought that my profession was unmanly.'

'What, the fire ting?'

'Exactly. What could be more manly than swallowing fire?'

'Did you have any kids with her?'

A daughter, who now lived in Portugal with her mother. He saw them only occasionally, funds permitting. Antoney asked him cautiously, 'Did it change things for you, being a father?'

'You're full of questions this morning. Of course it did. Everything changes unless you're a stone man.' He glanced at Antoney. Then he said with equal discretion, in his warm, airy voice, 'I thought she looked different. Her colour is higher.'

Antoney got to his feet and started down the beach.

'Ah, you're not pleased! Is it so terrible?' The Wonder was getting up. 'Where are you going?'

Ignoring his shouts Antoney approached the jetty, rummaging

in his pocket for his cigarettes. He found them and took out a dishevelled Pall Mall but he had no match. The Wonder was closing in on him. 'Have you got a fucking light?'

'No I have not, and that's bad for you. Do you want to get cancer of the lung?'

'Will you stop acting like my fucking father! What the fuck is it to you if I smoke?'

'It's nothing to me,' The Wonder said. 'Nothing at all.' He backed away and walked off, which Antoney found disappointing.

'Does everyone know about it?' he called out. 'Come back here.'

'Say please.'

'Say what?'

The Wonder turned, his very white trainers with him. 'Say please.'

Antoney had that urge again to laugh and slap him at the same time. He laughed, but only for a quarter of a second. 'You're insane.'

'You too.'

'Jesus.' He readied himself. He was reluctant. 'Please.' And The Wonder sauntered back, in a conversational mode. 'Humility is a wonderful thing, you know. Much more impressive than manliness in my opinion. It doesn't matter who else knows. I hope you haven't upset her. She is such an adorable woman.'

'I'm not ready, The Wonder. I don't want my life to go small.'

'Let me ask *you* a question. It's my turn. Come with me.'

Passing him, he stepped onto the jetty. Antoney followed sooner or later. They went halfway out until The Wonder came to a stop, the waves shifting on either side of them.

'Now,' he said. 'What do you see at the end of the jetty? Look to the very end.'

'The sea. What about it?'

'Yes, yes, I know it's the sea. But imagine for a minute that the jetty is the course of a man's life. It carries on it your child-hood, your dreams, your formative experiences, the passions that drive you in whichever career you choose for yourself. That little circle at the end there, for our purposes – just for a minute, Antoney, you don't have to be so cynical – is a stage, right? Ah, I've got you now! And on that stage are all the things that must exist in addition to your dreams and your passions, the necessary elements of love, companionship, family, guidance. So tell me now, what do you see at the end of the jetty?'

'Ok. I see a dance.'

'Who is dancing?'

'Me.'

'All by yourself?'

'Yeah.'

'Is there no one close by? Look harder.'

Antoney went forward and looked. He saw the same thing. 'There's nothing else. I don't even understand what you're talking about.'

'Well if there's nothing else there,' The Wonder said gravely, 'I'll have to pray for you, because right up until the time you fall over that wall to your death you'll be alone.'

From a few feet away he studied Antoney with such sadness, such pity and disappointment, that Antoney turned and stared again at the jetty, bewildered. The Wonder was retreating back towards the shore. It was curious, but this time Antoney did see something else. There appeared on the stage the outline of another picture, an old, old memory. His mother and father were with him on the beach at Annotto Bay where they used to take him to swim. The three of them were looking down. His mother said, See the funny crab, Antoney? The black-eyed creature flitted in and out of sand holes. Why does he move like that? Antoney asked. And his father said, Because he has too many feet, which his mother found funnier than the crab itself. Sitting above them on the stone wall was Carla, in her scarlet dress, looking out on the glistening sea. The image on the other side of the stage, the one of him dancing, had faded to the same transparency as this new picture.

'The Wonder, hold on,' he shouted. 'How do I know which picture's right?'

'You don't know,' The Wonder shouted back, his dashiki flapping against his jeans. 'You're young. Didn't anyone ever tell you that?'

I am a selfish man, Antoney wrote to Riley. I've always thought only of myself and what I want, without realising what I get from others. Carla told me yesterday that we're subjects of nature, that we have to follow the natural course set out for us because that's what everything means. So that's what I'm going to do – and I do love my girl.

When the baroness heard the news of Antoney and Carla's engagement she was overcome with emotion. Having kissed them repeatedly from cheek to cheek, she explained that she'd hosted her daughter's wedding in the castle grounds five years before and still cried whenever she remembered it. She first suggested, then gradually started to insist, that *they* should get married here too. They had everything they required, didn't they? She could arrange whatever they wanted, the catering, the dress, the rings, music. Didn't they already have their own photographer, as if it was meant to happen? Oh please, darlings, there's no better time than the present to make a love solid, and there was nothing she would like more than to see them take their vows in her garden. As she whipped up this absurd vision, other people around her began to join in, Rosina, Fansa, Ricardo, coaxing them on, getting excited, even Simone said go for it why not, *I* would. The only person who showed no enthusiasm at all was Bluey, who nervously caught Carla's eye.

Carla took more persuading than Antoney because of her mother. How could she get married without her mother there? She'd be too upset, she couldn't do it to her. 'Yes, I see,' said Kristine, 'of course. But not to worry. We will fly her to us.' 'My mum doesn't fly,' said Carla. It was impossible. No. 'But then

185

talk to her,' the baroness urged. 'Talk to your mother and see. Perhaps she will give you her blessing . . .'

Toreth was tearful. She was sitting in her third-floor tenement living room on Harrow Road craving her daughter's return, amid the busy leafy wallpaper, listening to Frank Sinatra on the radio, while Carla, also tearful, was sitting on the end of a chaise longue with walnut feet on the Kattegat coast. Toreth said Carla should accept the baroness what's-her-name's invitation if it made her happy, if it was right, if she was absolutely *sure*, more importantly (which Toreth wasn't) that Antoney was the man for her, that she wouldn't dream of standing in her way just because of her problem with flying – but as long as she could have pictures. After further thought Carla decided with dwindling reluctance to let it happen, to follow nature's course. The wedding was on.

The castle was spun into a cyclone of activity. It was now Tuesday. The wedding was set for Saturday. Every corner, every windowpane, every fork and knife was polished to a sparkle. The baroness took charge of the invitations, the ordering of flowers, the assessment of the gazebo in the garden where the ceremony would take place. Ekow finally got the chance to choreograph a piece, a duet to be performed by him and Simone to a gospel arrangement by The Wonder and the other musicians. The baroness was mindful of the bride and groom's wish for a low-key event, so she only invited the essential people, who were spread across Zealand, into Copenhagen and Funen: fellow members of the Danish aristocracy, a close-friend film star and her husband. Yes yes yes, she said, we will keep it small, but not *too* small as to be insignificant, only one member of the press (of course you must be in the newspaper!), a visiting Russian count also very dear to her. Make sure there are enough chairs, she told the butler, make sure there are enough drinks; we mustn't run out of drinks, these coloured boys drink like fishes! Oh, a wedding, a wedding – twinkling silver icicles hanging from the roof trim, the national flag atop the third tower. With dancers stretching beneath trees, Kristine charging about waving her arms, the drummers tightening their skins and beating out rhythm on the lawn for the hell of it, nobody noticed, at first not even Carla, Bluey on the outskirts, disappearing for long periods, his cowbell left forgotten in the duffel bag full of percussion.

'There you are. I haven't seen you all day,' said Carla, when he suddenly appeared in the doorway of the sunroom on Thursday. 'I was looking for you. Where've you been? This thing's getting out of control, Bluey. The baroness has turned into a jumping bean. Have you heard about the Russian count? Do you think Jimi Hendrix is coming to my wedding? Now *him* I wouldn't mind.'

'Listen to her.' Simone was standing behind Carla doing her hair, cosy again, the bad vibes between them gone. 'If I had a count coming to *my* wedding I wouldn't be complaining. Let him bring the whole damn entourage.'

'I mean, I would've been happy with a vicar and a few pork pies. A bit of Otis – rest his soul. It's too much.'

'Carla, you're forever underestimating yourself. Just think, when you're sitting back at home with a crying baby in your arms and bags under your eyes,' (the foetus was now common knowledge), 'you'll be able to look back on this and sizzle over it. It's not fair. Why wasn't I born rich? Why do I have to go back to Kilburn?'

'You'd still be complaining if you didn't.'

'Can I talk to you for a minute?' Until this point Bluey had been standing silently in the doorway. His request came out abrasively.

'Who, me?' said Simone.

'Carla,' he said. His hair appeared greasy. He was wearing the same clothes he'd been wearing yesterday.

'Of course you can, darling. Go on.'

'On your own.' He glowered at Simone.

'Well, excuse *me*, I'm sure. A little delicacy wouldn't go amiss.'

187

She wiped her hands on a towel over the back of Carla's wicker chair and left for the grounds, throwing a dirty look back at Bluey. He closed the doors behind her, faced Carla for a moment, sat down on an adjacent wicker, then immediately stood up again.

'Are you all right?' she said.

'Nah, I'm not.'

'What's wrong?'

He sat back down. 'I dunno. I dunno.'

'Bluey?'

'This wedding. It ain't you, Carla.'

'That's what I've been saying. But it doesn't matter, it's just decoration. The heart of it's the same.'

Bluey lit a cigarette, his hands trembling as he did so. 'But I don't know why you're marrying him, that's the thing. He ain't good enough for you. I don't like him. You could have any fella in the world.'

'That's your opinion,' she said, sounding hurt.

'I don't wanna upset you.' He stood up and went to the door to see if anyone was looking. Satisfied they were absolutely alone, he rubbed his hand on his jeans, walked over to her frantically, right to where she was sitting, and knelt down. As he grabbed her hand he made her think of a hamster or a mouse, a little scratching thing brushing at her knee.

'Marry me instead,' he said.

She laughed, a short laugh. The raised beauty spot next to her eye moved upwards then came back down at the end of the laugh. The damage was already done.

'Are you being serious?'

'It ain't a joke.'

'Um—'

His scratchy childish hand, his skinny forearm. The smell of nicotine all over him. 'Look, I ain't much,' he said, 'I know that. But I'll look after you. I won't ever hurt ya.' The desperation in his face increased. 'I promise you won't regret it.'

'This is weird, Bluey.'

'Please. Marry me. Not here, we'll go off somewhere else.'

She shifted her knee to move his hand off as it had become disgusting to her. It fell to the floor. She shook her head imperceptibly. 'I love you,' she said, 'you know that – but you're my friend.'

His blue eyes went dark. He rose and stepped back. 'So you're not gonna have me?'

'I'm sorry. No.'

He hesitated, looking blackly into the garden.

'All right,' he said. 'All right then. I'm off.'

'That woman is fine,' said Fansa, lying meanwhile in the shade of a cypress tree. 'Look at how she moves – so quick. I have never seen a mature woman move with so much spunk.'

'I've seen better-looking older Polly-Cinders than her,' replied Ricardo. Fansa shared a moment of waving with the baroness as she whisked by in the distance.

'Not me,' he said. 'Look at that. She set up nice. Got good structure. Good skin, not rashy or moley.'

'Wrinkles, though.'

'But hardly any, only around her eyes. Aaah, this grass is so green. The air so clean. London is such a filthy place.'

Fansa and Ricardo got sleepy. The lunch had been extravagant.

'Her husband liked to fish, you know. There's a cabin by the beach with the equipment still there. She told me. Nets,' Fansa sighed, 'hooks.'

'Hm.'

'I've always dreamt of being a fisherman.'

'Yeah,' Ricardo said, opening one eye, 'right.'

The baroness's wedding dress had been well preserved over the years in leather sheeting. It was crisply white and studded with diamonds, the skirt composed of five layers of fabric that gave the impression the wind was underneath it. The bodice dipped

189

at two embroidered arrows into the cleavage and the navel, the puffed satin shoulders erupting from the outer edge of each collarbone. It fitted Carla with uncanny exactitude.

The eve of the wedding was a party in itself. The men drank booze and lolled about in the sunroom listening to Doris Day (the baroness's favourite artist) and Prince Buster, under strict orders assigned to Ekow by Simone to keep inebriation to a safe and civilised level. Maid of honour, Simone spent the evening in the drawing room in the north wing with the other women, a less raucous affair involving mint tea and slim champagne that Rosina, bored, departed from when the baroness swept back into the room to fetch Carla for a final fitting in the master suite.

Kristine's bedroom had its own lounge, a hulk of a salmon-tapestried sofa, a towering Oriental chest containing intricate drawers, next to the biggest bed Carla had ever seen. She put on the cleaned and winking dress behind the changing screen and slowly emerged. Kristine gasped, starting from the sofa.

'You are astonishment,' she said, 'a vision of perfection!' Her eyes welled up, sending a charge of uncertainty rising to Carla's throat. 'Come,' said the baroness. 'Come to the mirror.'

Kristine stood behind her in the reflection. 'We were the same size. I feel that this was meant to happen. You were sent to me, you and darling Antoney, to begin your life together, hm?'

The dress was a starry cloud, permeating the space around it.

'It's lovely,' Carla said. 'I look like I'm magic.'

'You do, you do!' Kristine squeezed the tops of her arms. 'And there's something I want to give to you.'

'No, please, Kristine, you've given us enough.'

The baroness nevertheless went to the chest and took a jewellery box out of the second drawer, then returned to the sofa and patted the space next to her.

'This was given to me by my grandmother the day I was married.' She lifted out a bracelet of large, oval rubies. Each ruby was laced with a ring of smaller white stones, also diamonds. She passed it to Carla.

'I can't take it.'

'I want you to.'

'I can't. No.'

'Please. Please take it. I want you to have it.' On the tail of this Kristine's tone became determined.

'But it belongs to *you*. I've only known you since Saturday!'

'Well if you don't like it,' Kristine said, offended.

'It's not that. I *do* like it but—'

'So then have it, *please*!'

'Oh God.'

It was heavier than it looked. Carla stared at it in her hand, feeling a twinge at the base of her stomach. 'Let me help you,' said the baroness, and clasped the bracelet around her wrist. 'There. Now you are ready. You're going to amaze him.' Carla covered her face with her hands.

'My dear! What's wrong?'

Carla sobbed.

'But *why* are you crying? You don't like it—' Gasp. 'You don't like the *dress*! Oh but I told you, I only want you to wear it if you *wish* to wear it. We can go out in the morning and get another.'

'It's not the dress.'

'The bracelet.'

'It's not the bracelet!'

Kristine was exasperated. Carla brought her hands down and gave a champagne hiccup, a vast, shaky sigh. She noticed that the baroness had exceptionally tiny feet.

'It seems like I'm always crying these days,' she said. 'I didn't used to cry so much. I'm overwhelmed. They do say it affects your moods.'

'Your moods? What is wrong with your moods?'

Unable to contain herself, Carla burst out laughing. She could not believe that with all Kristine's chattering, her running

191

about, her liaising, interfering and flirting, she didn't know the situation.

'Are you . . . in the motherly way?' she asked.

'I sure am.'

Kristine tucked in her elfish chin and shifted in her seat. 'Oh. I was not aware of this.' (The de-inviting of guests, the cancelling of flowers, the count, the *embarrassment*. No, it's too late, it's far too late, but this is not proper, goodness me, the young of today.)

'Shall we call it off?' Carla thought of the sweet simplicity of pork pies and Otis Redding.

'No no no, impossible. It's not in the least an issue for me. I'm an open-minded person. What a – *wonderful* addition to the occasion . . . Only we wouldn't want our guests to share in the news. A child is private, a very private knowledge between a man and a woman, and I wouldn't like – the count, for example, to disturb its peace with his awareness of it. Are we together? Do you see? No, we must go ahead.' She peeped at Carla's abdomen. There was a pause.

'It's a shame my mum can't come.'

'Is that the reason you're upset?' Kristine turned towards her. 'If there is something else, apart from . . .' her eyes descended '. . . I would like to offer you my earlobe, even though you have only known me since Saturday, as you said. I can't replace your mother, but please don't hesitate to try me if it will make you feel better, so that your mind will be free of worries tomorrow.'

Carla decided to give it a go. She hadn't been able to get the things Bluey had said about Antoney out of her head. 'Does Antoney stroke you, I mean *strike* you, Kristine,' she asked, 'as the marrying kind?'

'Yes, of course. He has all the qualities.'

'Really?'

'Yes.' Silence. 'Is that *all*?'

Carla leaned back listlessly against the sofa. 'So why do I feel like I'm putting a bird in a cage?'

(What is the matter with this girl?) 'I don't understand you,' said the baroness.

'Forget it. It doesn't matter.'

But Kristine wouldn't have it, the bride so glum and creased on the seat. She returned to speedy silly wedding mode, brought Carla to a stand and manoeuvred her back to the mirror. 'Don't worry,' she said with mounting melodrama, 'Your nerves and your moods, that's all. There's no need to worry about Antoney. He loves you. I can see it when he looks at you. You are his music, his diamond. You are his one and only love, and tomorrow you will marry your one and only love!'

Yeah yeah, calm down, thought Carla.

'Just one thing, my dear,' said Kristine. 'What are we going to do about your hair?'

They studied her great frothy crown.

'I'm going to leave it like this.'

Half an hour before midnight the conversation in the sunroom had descended to blow-jobs. Fansa was leading. 'I gave up the mouth,' he was saying. 'I don't want no woman chewing on my tings.'

'Someone shut him up. The Wonder, talk to him,' said Ekow.

Third beer, second rum in, Antoney asked out of curiosity, 'Why'd you give it up? C'mon, let the man speak.'

All of them sprawled out on the wickers, Fansa explained red-eyed, 'But just imagine it. She down there doing the business and everyting sweet, then one day – because there is always a day – she in one a dem funny tempers, right, she vex about something you did last week that you can't even remember.' So the man is lying there (the abstraction went on in this vein) in the most vulnerable position a man could be, defenceless, laid back, approaching ecstasy, and at some point in her work the woman suddenly recalls her vexation with him, bringing on a previously unannounced form of epilepsy that results in the biting off of the man's donkey-rod. The others fell about. Ekow

193

tried not to join in. Only The Wonder remained unmoved and thoughtful. 'Fansa, you shouldn't make such unkind jokes.'

'Has anyone seen Bluey yet?' asked Ekow.

From within the castle Simone appeared at the door with a towel wrapped round her head. She sniffed the liquored air. 'Ekow. Are you drinking alcohol?'

'Baby, when have you ever seen me drink? I'm a clean-living brother.'

'Good. I'm trusting you now. It's almost twelve, you should all turn in soon. Antoney, you want to be fresh for tomorrow, don't you?'

'*And* frisky,' Fansa sniggered amidst the leftover giggling.

Carla then appeared next to Simone in a bathrobe, looking serious and fearful, and absurdly young. The men fidgeted, glancing from her to Antoney, who made no great attempt to put her at ease.

'Take a minute,' said Ekow.

Bride and groom went into the hall. They had a brief, thick hug, which reeked of booze but momentarily erased Carla's doubt. Before leaving him to go upstairs she fixed him with a hard look, her fist holding onto his vest strap. 'I have to say this one thing,' she said.

'What is it, baby?'

'If you ever hurt me, Antoney, if you ever betray me – I won't forgive you.' Her tone left him terrified.

Just as he returned to the sunroom shouts were heard from the garden. Simone went to the door and saw two figures zigzagging into view, one ran to the left, the other to the right. Each time they crossed they did Nijinsky leaps. She would later explain to Lucas that the time Ricardo and Rosina did LSD together in Denmark was the only time they ever seemed like twins.

'The Wonder!' said Rosina. 'You look like the sea! Simone! You look kind of – witchy.'

'Who wants to go swimming?' Ricardo asked in amazement.

'Don't you hate it when people change and start acting stupid when they're drunk? Ekow, round it up or there'll be hell to pay. And no swimming.' Simone's nose went skyward and she disappeared into the belly of the castle, followed soon after by Benjamin and The Wonder.

'All right, folks, party's over.' Ekow began collecting glasses.

'That woman's got you stamped for true,' said Fansa.

Ekow studied the groom, who was leaning back in his chair with his eyes shut, listening. Rosina pranced back out onto the lawn calling for Ricardo to follow her. Passing Antoney, Ricardo said slowly, zoning in on him, 'You've got to see the ocean, mate, it's *bea-uuu-tiful* – silver, goes on and on for miles.'

'No swimming,' Ekow shouted. 'No one's going swimming here tonight!' But Fansa struggled up and bolted after the twins.

Two men left. Antoney sat forward in his chair. Ekow was breathing heavily, forbidding him, daring him, upright across the room with a bottle in his hand.

'Maybe a little night walk,' Antoney said lightly.

'Don't do it.'

Antoney made to stand.

'Leave this room through that door and it's over.'

'Stop ordering me around!'

As Antoney came full upright Ekow pushed him back into the wicker chair, bringing the bottle near to his face. He used it for emphasis as he spoke. 'Listen to me and listen hard,' he said. 'I meant what I said about quitting. When we get back home I'm out of here. I've had it. I'm doing this one last thing for you in being your best man as a leaving present, because you asked me, because you're my brother, but most of all because Carla's your saving grace. You're a prick without her.' Antoney was scowling at him, his mouth screwed up like mango string. 'In fact,' Ekow said, 'I'm doing this more for her than you, because for some strange reason that I just can't configure she loves you. I don't know why but that's it. Now, whatever oddness you've got going on up there, boy,' he tipped Antoney's head with the bottle, 'whatever it is, you need to do something about it, see a shrink or something I dunno – but if you fuck this up, Antoney, if you fuck this up for her I'll break you in two. You won't know your face from your feet. I'll break you. Are you understanding me?'

Antoney's scowl had lapsed. He was looking up at Ekow frankly, with a clear, inquisitive expression. The others were shouting and laughing in the garden.

'How do you do it, Ekow?' he said.

'How do I do what?'

'How come you get through so easy?'

Ekow's hands fell to his sides. He dropped his head to the left with his answer, which was slow in coming.

'Easy, bro?' he said. 'Nothing's easy. I just know the things to tell myself.'

And he let him have a little night walk. No sea, no swimming, no longer than an hour, no further than where the forest trees began. They shook on it. Ekow sat down on a comfortable chair in view of the garden. He put his feet up on a footstool and as the temperature dropped drew a blanket to his knees. He imagined the coming day, Carla descending the stairs in the morning to a hush from the hall. He wondered whether there would be a day when Simone would come down the stairs for him. Looking up through the glass ceiling at the night sky, he remembered something he'd read once about light years and the view of the stars. The stars are not the same as how the human eye sees them. The faulty human eye sees only the lemony shine of the familiar time zone, but light years away from here the stars are red and many other colours, held away from us by galactic secrecy. A picture emerged of what the actual night sky might look like, a sea, full of naked, winking colour. Burgundies, greens, glowing, turning, just quietly turning in the astrological chill.

'Mr Fontaine. Unstick your eye.'

Fansa was having a dream about fishing. He was sitting on a

mound of rocks in the middle of the ocean with his line extended, about to catch the biggest fish in the world, when he heard his wife's deep voice calling him from an advancing steamer.

'Mr Fontaine!'

The rocks beneath him started to feel soft. He felt the surface of them with his hand to discover that they'd turned to grass, which meant he was sinking. He scrambled upwards and tore open his eyes. A powdery blue sky. The edges of trees. Simone in a hairnet looking ready to spit.

'Alphonso. Where's Antoney?' she said.

Fansa found himself sitting on the lawn about twenty yards from the sunroom. He searched around him, patting the grass as if a tiny Antoney was misplaced somewhere among the blades.

'Do you know what time it is?' Simone said.

'What time is it? What day?'

'Saturday. Eight a.m. There's a wedding planned for eleven.'

'*Shit*.' Fansa staggered to his feet. 'Where me shoes?'

'No, more's to the point, where is *Antoney*?'

'Me nunno!'

She slapped him hard across the chest. The bride, he was informed, was upstairs preparing herself. The baroness was fully switched on. The count was on his way, the aristocracy, the movie star, the press, the registrar. Fansa became aware of activity to the side of the castle, chairs coming out, people darting back and forth. 'Tell me what happened before I slap you again.'

He tried to remember it. Shards came floating back in a watery mist. 'We were on the beach,' he said.

'The beach.'

'And those guys were going to swim—'

'I strictly said no swimming!'

'And Rosina was—'

'What was *Antoney* doing, you fool?'

Rubbing the back of his head, Fansa muttered, 'I think I remember him messing around with the boat.'

'The boat? What boat?'

'The boat out of the hut. He was dragging it.'

'Alphonso, please tell me he didn't go sailing.'

'Well, I can't remember exactly if he did or didn't. I don't *think* he did, because otherwise I'd remember it, but I'm not sure.'

'Thank you. That's extremely helpful,' said Simone.

A search ensued, which was still going on when the guests began to arrive at a quarter to ten. Some ageing ministers, the bee-hived actress in an Ossie Clark dress with her boyfriend, a large woman in a very high, very wide hat, dancers from the Danish Ballet, the journalists (four of them), then Kristine's rowdy sister from Funen and a swarm of nieces and nephews. It turned out in the end the count couldn't make it.

Chatter and civilised laughter gradually filled the gardens of the castle. The event was granted a perfect sunny day – though the atmosphere was somewhat cool, the way a wedding will be if hardly any of the guests know the bride and groom, and this was an extreme case of that. The baroness, in a lambish dress with side split, flitted about with her champagne, clutching people's hands, checking the children's collars, pointing out the members of the Midnight Ballet – first of all Fansa, now showered, as he was never very far from her side; Benjamin, assisting in the search for Antoney while also enjoying the canapés; The Wonder, not assisting but waiting quite still underneath the cypress tree, proving when approached by the actress to be a perplexing and reticent conversationalist. The twins were looking for Antoney. Simone and Ekow were also transient sights, positioned as they were at the helm of the search.

They looked in every one of the thirty rooms. They looked under beds, behind curtains, in the forest, behind the bushes. There was no one in the beach-hut. There was no boat. All they found were his snakeskins with the socks inside them at the beginning of the jetty. Simone thought he was drowned, but it was in her line of duty to pay regular, reassuring visits to Carla in her suite – she refused to come out until she was convinced

198

Antoney was in the vicinity. At the same time Simone felt it would not be right if she didn't try and mingle with the glamorous guests, using her acting skills to hide her concerns. Despite everything, she managed to sense what she saw as the guests' admiration of her dancer's slim grace and her thin, dainty neck. With all the going up and down stairs, the scanning of the landscape for the groom, the fleeting private conferences with Ekow, and the effort of trying not to look like she was lying to the diamond-studded bride each time she said Antoney was close, well, she was just sweating through her sunflower dress.

By half past ten he still hadn't shown. Carla began to take off the baroness's gown, telling herself it was for the best, it was right, that she'd known it all along. 'Where's Bluey?' she asked again. 'Where is he? I want to see him.' Simone didn't know where Bluey was, but she begged her not to take off that dress. Please, she said, just a few more minutes.

They waited and waited. As the guests began to hush the baroness became inwardly hysterical and informed people that Mr Matheus was detained on a sudden matter of life or death to do with his mother. Wine was sipped, glasses were twiddled. The registrar waited, the brooched and ribboned tuberoses hanging from the gazebo roof trim waited. Ten minutes to eleven. Five minutes to.

At five minutes to, Carla's face closed in. She took off the dress, left it on the floor, and went to the window to look out on the meadow. The two horses flicked their tails, as they always would. She refused to cry any more. She massaged her little mystery with a slow, circular motion and told it they would be fine, just the two of them. In the distance beyond she saw a figure emerging over the field. It was tall and broad and had a walk that reminded her of the way Antoney used to walk, like he was floating. He was wearing a stone-coloured suit. She watched him come towards the castle, believing she was daydreaming. She smiled, despite everything, at the memory of what they were.

In the garden the guests also saw the figure approaching. He moved so slowly that it seemed to take an eternity for him to arrive. When he did he ignored everyone apart from The Wonder. He was clean-shaven.

'Where is my wife?' he said.

'She is coming down now.'

'Am I late?'

The Wonder checked his watch.

'You're more or less on time.'

PART TWO

8

Vaslav Nijinsky had an old grey winter coat and a Tyrolean hat. What is a Tyrolean hat? It's a type of velour, cord-wrapped hat originally worn by dudes who lived in the western mountainous region of Tyrol in Austria. During the Second World War Nijinsky and his wife Romola spent a lot of time apart due to his ongoing treatment in psychiatric hospitals. The time they did spend together they dodged bombs and Auschwitz trucks, and one snowy day, after being detained by an air raid in Budapest while trying to get a fuel permit, Romola returned to the inn they were staying at to find Vaslav standing covered with dust in a roofless room, gazing at her silently. By this time he was flabby and white-haired and was said to have developed a cackle. The Who's Who of doctors had tried morphine, neuroleptics, bromides, opium, scopolamine, barbiturates, and a series of insulin shock treatments that had left him unable to tie his own shoelaces. Romola decided he was safer at the hospital so she took him back. Then one evening in 1945, when Hitler was after the mad – not *just* the Jews, homosexuals, Gypsies, Ukrainians, Jehovah's Witnesses, blacks, brunettes and other dissidents – she was sitting at the table having her dinner when she was disturbed by a knock at the door. She went to answer it. It was Vaslav, Vatza, as she called him, in his old grey winter coat and Tyrolean hat, carrying a bundle of his things. With him was an attendant from the asylum who informed Romola that they'd been ordered to exterminate all their mental patients by morning.

'Why are you telling me this?' said Jake. 'I thought this was about your dad.'

'D'you know how old he was when he flipped it?'

'Who, your dad?'

'No, Vaslav.'

'Should I give a shit? How old?'

'Twenty-eight.' Lucas revealed this with foreboding.

'The train again.'

'The train's just a symbol, Jake.'

'You gonna eat that sausage?'

S & M (Sausage and Mash) was the premier specialist joint for bangers in the western hemisphere, situated in the line of eateries beneath the Portobello canopies. The dish was served as a white mountain with one, two, or three gourmet sausage tracks ascending, amid a pool of gravy, red onion being the most popular. The tables and benches were deeply worn from years of service. From where Lucas was sitting he could see Denise's stall. Six weeks from now, on the last weekend of August, her income would see a seasonal boost at the feathery hands of the Notting Hill Carnival.

'Anyway, the guy sounds like a weirdo to me,' said Jake, having taken the sausage off Lucas's plate.

'Who, Vaslav?'

'*Riley.*'

'He's all right when you get to know him.'

'Why's the man sitting in his house for two decades writing a book about someone no one's ever heard of? Doesn't that strike you as a little bit psycho? How d'you know he ain't one of those dudes with bones under the house? Nah man, it happens all the time, the hermits are the worst. How do you *know*, blood – let me just put this to you for a minute, no disrespect – how do you know your old man's not in a bag underneath this guy's kitchen as we speak, and he's trying to make up for it by writing this book?'

'Don't be fucking stupid.'

'It's a worst case scenario – but it's possible.'

'That's just wrong.' Lucas was shaking his head, appalled.

'But that's what you're letting yourself in for, Sherlock,' said Jake. 'The truth. And the truth could be ugly. You don't know. Do you see what I'm getting at here?'

'He's not in a bag, all right? That's not what this is about.'

'So what is it about?'

'It's about details. The full picture.'

Lucas watched Denise compiling a bunch of flowers. She lifted a stalk here and a couple there, in a brisk action like a throw, holding them away from her so that the water didn't splash her shoes. Her customers, two women, were watching her appreciatively; she said something brief to them as she wrapped. She had excelled at the Salvation Army. She'd since been asked to adorn a sixtieth birthday party at the Amadeus Centre in Little Venice, for which she'd offered to employ Lucas as an assistant, though he'd found this both unappealing and patronising. He was not a flower boy. He was not her boy.

He and Riley had become associates, he would call it, partners in retrospection. He went to his flat twice a week sometimes more, instead of going to *West*. If he did ever show up at *West*, in a lame attempt to maintain his interest in salary, they treated him like a visiting ex-employee whose absence they'd had no trouble adjusting to. Finn had stopped asking about the Simone de Laperouse 'Where Are They Now?' piece.

Each time Lucas went to Riley's place it seemed different, brighter. As he'd been saying to Jake, the corridor leading to the study still had the same sombre atmosphere, but the doors into the other rooms, apart from one, the one next to the study, were usually open now, letting in more light. The air, also, smelt clearer and less stuffy, and the old man had bought himself a new writing chair. Riley slept in his living room, on a futon by the window in view of the obsolete TV. He ate his meals at a table in the kitchen and everything else revolved around his study and his garden; (he wore gloves and a blue overall when tending it). He was still remote, always guarded, but he seemed to like having Lucas around. He let him read sections of his book, which was written in the same elegant style as his articles and made Antoney take on for Lucas a mythical, heroic quality like a character in a novel. He could feel him breathing and thinking in the formal intimacy of ink. He read and reread, so that the words lifted off the pages and the air spoke to him in Antoney's voice. Combined with the many photographs there were to look at – one of Antoney and Carla with a young Herbie Hancock, others with Joan Plowright, Josie Woods – as well as the press cuttings he hadn't previously seen, Lucas sometimes had the sensation, as Antoney was being coloured in, that he himself was being rubbed out. At such times he would leave the archive and browse Riley's bookshelves. This was where he'd come across the Nijinsky biography, and remembering what Simone had said about Oscar's admiration for him he'd taken it down off the shelf. He was drawn in by the descriptions of crinolines and peg-top trousers, of frills and highway frock coats, the snow in St Moritz. He read it lying on the grass in Riley's garden. It provided an engrossing accompaniment to Antoney's story.

While Lucas was reading, Riley would be close by, sifting through the archive, selecting elements for him to look at, studying things he himself might not have perused in a long time. He said that he, too, was making new discoveries, brought on by Lucas turning up, but Lucas could tell that he was also supervising him, censoring what he could and couldn't see. The box of letters had disappeared after the first couple of visits, after Lucas had asked if he could read one. (This was where Jake first started to get suspicious.) Riley had said the letters were private, not to be shared. He never worked on his book while Lucas was there, but he said he'd got through his block and was making advancements again. His tendency to stand too close to someone, as if he'd lost the etiquette for personal space or was worried about not being heard when he spoke, Lucas put down to a lack of contact with people. As he'd reckoned on meeting him, Riley had no children and had never been married, apparently no social life. Sometimes Lucas would look up from his reading to find the old man scrutinising him with a cryptic, almost hurt expression. He told him he had his father's eyes, but everything else was different. They hardly ever talked about Carla. He said he hadn't known her very well and there wasn't much he could recollect, except that he'd always found her quite impressionable. Lucas was learning more about his mother from her diary, which by now he had found the courage to read. He didn't think of her as impressionable.

Riley showed little interest in Lucas's life outside his search, but he did ask him one day in the garden what plans he had for himself, whether there was a particular publication he wanted to write for. Lucas turned Nijinsky face down on the grass, and was promptly told to please mark his page with a bookmark or a pencil instead so as not to damage the spine. 'I'm not sure about journalism any more,' he said. 'It's just a few pages of a magazine, like you said.'

'I was referring to quite a different situation,' Riley said derisively. He was pruning roses in his gloves and overall, which he did with his lips clumped together amid his beard so that he resembled a monkey.

'I know,' Lucas said. 'But I'm not much of a writer, really. I don't have a thing, you know? I don't have a passion, something I was born for, my own thing – like Antoney did, or Denise.'

For a second Riley looked perplexed by Denise's name. 'Ah, the florist.'

'Yeah. She thinks I should be working in a building society. She doesn't get it. We weren't put on this earth to just scratch out a nine-to-five and then die – there's more to it than that. That's what I'm always saying to her.'

'But one must do something with one's time,' said Riley snipping. Lucas did mention that he'd like to travel. He'd never been to Jamaica. He'd never been out of the UK except to Calais on school trips. When Riley reminded him that in order to travel he would probably have to save up first, which might involve getting a proper job for a while, Lucas got annoyed and said, 'What, like yours? Sitting by yourself all day writing about people dancing?'

At this Riley accidentally chopped off a perfect yellow rose from the bush. He came slowly over to where Lucas was sitting, during which time Lucas apologised, but he came nevertheless, silent and focused with his soft tread, and again stood too close.

'You mentioned passion,' he said. 'You don't have a passion, an interest. Then naturally you wouldn't understand what it feels like to be claimed by something, to be engulfed by it and incapable of refusing, of following where it takes you, even if it takes you to a blank wall. Maybe you'll find it one day. All of us have one, only we allow ourselves to lose sight of it. Perhaps you'll discover something when you go travelling.'

He said this drily, as if he didn't expect that Lucas would and didn't much care anyway.

'Passion creates memory,' he added, 'history, which is the most important thing of all.'

God, this dude's uptight, thought Lucas.

'I'm telling you, he's a nut,' said Jake. 'He ain't the kind of person you want to be hanging out with. How old is he, what, ninety?'

They were having after-sausage tea with toothpicks. Jake had always been fastidious with his teeth on account of their ample size and squareness.

'Sixty, seventy – so what? Would you be worrying about how old he was if you were me? It's like I've struck gold,' Lucas said with widened eyes. 'My whole life I've been wondering who and what, and all of a sudden here's this guy lifting up the curtain so I can see inside, like he'd been waiting for me. It's destiny. It's taking me somewhere, I can feel it. It's a stroke of luck I found him.'

'Star. You don't know how lucky you are to have missed your old man.'

Lucas completely lost his train of thought. This was more outrageous than the body bag.

'Excuse me?'

'See you there wondering,' said Jake. 'Well, I knew my dad, innit. He was there living in the same house, dropping me off at school, all that. But he was also an original arsehole. Sixteen different women any one time, rolling in whenever. I didn't know who was who when he picked me up at the gate – all the other kids asking whether that woman was my mum and how many mums I had anyway. It was *embarrassing*, man, I swear, he had no shame. Worked when he felt like it. Mum's paying all the bills and compromising herself due to the fact she loves the bastard, and that's what gives him the right to boss me about like he was worth shit as a father. He was there all right, but he wasn't there for me. I couldn't even stand the sight of him.'

'Something's better than nothing,' said Lucas.

'No it's not. You're saying that because you don't know.'

'How can you cuss out your dad like that?'

'Because he was *there*, and the only thing I got from him was the right to cuss him out.'

Jake motioned to a passing waitress for the bill, greeting a girl he knew, who was standing at the counter, with unusual seriousness, a nod, no teeth. He shook his head at some internal thought he didn't share. 'I might not be wondering,' he said, 'but I'm dodging. I'm second-guessing myself all the time so I don't end up like him. You've got a clean slate, Luke. No shadow over you, no template, nothing to repeat. You're free – why spoil it for yourself? Personally I think you're getting into all this stuff too deep.'

Lucas had three pounds on him that he tried to contribute to the bill but Jake wouldn't take it. He shoved the money into his hand anyway, insisting, and Jake submitted to save his feelings. They parted underneath the Westway with a touch on diagonal shoulders. Jake went northwards for a flick through Honest Jon's. Avoiding Denise, Lucas went southwards, up through the Tavistock Road precinct where he had a brief afternoon smoke in the sun with MC Crow. They watched a large woman with a paintbrush ponytail herding her four little boys around her pram, the queue of schoolchildren outside the Indian newsagent. As Lucas headed off, he thought about repetition, whether repetition also was fated. He didn't agree with Jake. It was better to know. And maybe what you didn't know you repeated anyway, because of genes, because of generations unfolding in their particular unchanging fabrics. He was hardly aware of it as he came to Oscar's place. His footsteps took him there of their own accord, and he found himself gazing through the gate at the weedy courtyard, the ancient church door. Reality began to slip away again. He was a thin space, evaporating. The pigeons on the gate spikes couldn't see him because he was after their time. He was an absence in the present of his just married father, who'd returned from the Kattegat coast to a new disappearance. Without a word, Oscar had gone. A notice on the door of the basement had read, 'Classes suspended. Contact the Midnight Ballet for further information.' The horse vaults and board were stacked up against the wall in the studio as always. The reels of music were still in the office, the photographs in the entrance hall, minus two (the skipping Nijinsky and Oscar with Six Eight). There was coffee in the cupboard, sugar, as if he'd be back any minute. Was that where it had started? Lucas wondered. Was that the moment where Antoney himself began to disappear?

Ekow stuck to his word and left the company when they returned home. Fansa stayed behind with the baroness to lead a life of fishing as a kept man. In the tide of departures, Benjamin also jumped ship, eventually returning to Nigeria with his family.

Carla stopped dancing to become a wife and mother. Which left Antoney, Simone, the twins and The Wonder, a fragile, disconcerted crew. They never did find Bluey.

Antoney's final conversation with Oscar took on a greater significance. He had said goodbye, but it was a bigger goodbye than he'd let on, which Antoney would for ever hold against him. The night before the European tour, the two of them had had a farewell cigarette together in the church backyard, beneath a misted sky, a dull pink lulling behind the clouds. The left side of the moon was smoky.

'Where would you go,' Oscar had said, 'if you could go anywhere? What would be the last place?'

'Cuba,' said Antoney.

'What's in Cuba apart from dancing?'

'Some people I used to know. Where would you go?'

'I've been thinking about that lately,' said Oscar. 'I've been hearing seagulls. I've been thinking I'd go to the first place I ever knew.'

'Where's that, New Orleans?'

'You know, sometimes, Antoney, I can barely remember, it's been so long. I'd have to use my instinct, I guess. I'd have to take a step in the better direction and have faith in where it led me.'

Oscar pulled on his smoke. He'd recently acquired a brass-tipped cane, which he used less as a walking stick than an adornment to his walk. His skin was whiter by now, saggier, melting downwards. The rheumatism had stolen the dance out of his left leg.

'A word of advice while you're away, Antoney,' he said with a note of scolding in his voice. 'Share yourself more, my dear. Look after your troupe. If you hold on to the dream too tightly you'll crush it with your own fist. Vaslav would say the same, I'm sure.'

Antoney had left through the yard, climbing up the back wall along a drain to street level and jumping over the fence – a last little performance for his teacher. 'See you tomorrow,' he called down.

'Toodaloo,' said Oscar, and went back inside.

After Carla said no, Bluey left the castle with the intention of finding his own way home. He didn't take anything with him except cigarettes and the cash he had in his jeans. It was daylight when he left. He walked along the main road for many miles feeling no tiredness. His arms hung at his sides. He felt weightless, like a waste bin newly emptied. Some time during the night he hitched a lift from a petroleum-lorry driver bound for the border. They listened to Radio Luxembourg in silence, for thankfully the driver was German and neither of them could speak a word of the other's language. They parted in Hanover where Bluey drifted around for a time. He walked bridges, motorways, catching rides, sleeping rough. He was generally more comfortable when he was mobile.

On the outskirts of a town near Amiens in France he came upon a circus. He didn't approach them to find work, as he might have done when he'd first run away as a boy. The tents were quiet and abandoned in the small hours of the night. He went into the big top and looked up at the trapezist's swing, so aloof from everything else. It struck him as a good place to sleep, but he couldn't get up there so instead he slept across three metal chairs in the rows of seats, where he was woken in the morning by an extremely old, black-haired woman who wrinkled her nose at him. This old woman took Bluey's clothes and washed them in a nearby stream. She gave him something to eat, then a broom, and motioned him to where the animals were kept. The circus bill featured a lame trick with four rabbits and a hat, and a three-limbed poodle that spun hoops on his hind leg. The trapezist was a young girl with pigtails and narrow hips. Instead of sleeping in the tents or caravans with the other human beings, Bluey preferred to lie down with the animals in their tiny, strong-smelling, wheeled house. That way he found he didn't think of Carla at all during the night.

The humans were mostly Gypsies, Albanians, aside from one or two other stragglers like Bluey. They had no running water, which was why they set up base close to streams or lakes. The circus ran five nights a week. Despite its shabbiness a small crowd did trickle in, increasing towards Saturday. Bluey kept himself to himself, sweeping out the animals' quarters and the seating area after the audience had left. He was followed around everywhere he went by two skinny boys of eight or nine, duet contortionists, who between them smoked thirty cigarettes a day. The largest proportion of the circus's revenue was spent on the world's cheapest beer and tobacco. During his stay there Bluey smoked more cigarettes than at any other time in his life.

By autumn two of the rabbits had died and also the trapezist's one-year-old daughter, who was the great-granddaughter of the black-haired old woman. There was talk around the camp that the trapezist's father was also the father of her baby. The day after the infant died a fight broke out between two men, whom the contortionists told Bluey were the trapezist's father and uncle. It was a vicious and deadly fight, both men using knives, a crowd coaxing them on. The father was stabbed in the stomach and leg. While this was going on Bluey stood away from the crowd. Through the window of one of the caravans he could see the pigtailed trapezist sitting in candlelight, unmoving, her mouth opening at intervals into a contorted crying shape, which was then quickly sucked back inside. A few days later, Bluey left the circus and went home.

He couldn't go back to Shropshire because of what had happened there before, so he returned to his uncle's place in Ealing, where he spent days watching TV reports on Vietnam (death toll 35,000), until his uncle asked him wasn't he planning on working rather than expecting a free ride through life? He returned to the bakery. Winter went by, spring was unpretty. Where before he was weightless he now became heavy, and where the lightness had been empty the heaviness was full of things to carry. Behind the counter in his white paper hat he became aware of something particularly heavy sitting next to his heart. It spoke to him in a frightening voice, for it was not of a human sensibility, and it spent all its time looking around inside him for interesting objects or occurrences. If Bluey ate something sweet, like a jam doughnut, it would grunt at him. It was the same with gingerbread, which in the past he had always enjoyed. He stopped eating those foods and stuck to savoury pastries and unseasoned rice.

There were some days when the creature sitting by his heart got especially bored with him and tried to open the red door into his centre. It was always locked, though, and the creature would get frustrated. Look at your veins, it said, your veins are so dull. Look at your bones, they're so pale and nondescript. Let me come and look inside your heart. Bluey refused, but each day was more difficult than the last. Here you are again, said the creature as they woke up together in the mornings. Another day hanging around inside your ribs. In order to drown out the voice Bluey drank vodka from his uncle's drinks cabinet, and when he wasn't working he read the newspapers, filling his head with murders, rapes, bombings and politics, which was such a different reality from the life he'd imagined living with Carla. He'd imagined an island life, a musical existence with like-minded seekers of peace, where babies would know no danger and each day would be nothing more and nothing less than a desire to do the same thing better. Where is the peace? he asked the creature scratching at the door. In there, it said, Let me in and I'll show you.

One day he ran into Ricardo in Acton. 'Where you been, man?' Ricardo said. 'You don't look so good.' He asked Bluey why he'd taken off like that and filled him in on what had been happening with the troupe. Antoney and Carla were living on a barge of all places, and had a gorgeous baby girl, cute like her mum, but things weren't going well with getting shows. Bluey didn't talk much because whenever he spoke now the creature said something like, Oh! Your voice, your lungs, your *vocal cords*! When Ricardo asked him whether he was planning on coming back and gracing them with his cowbell anytime soon, he replied that he'd lost the ear for it.

About three weeks after that he decided to just let the damn thing in. It pushed open the red door and rubbed its hands in glee at all there was to do in there. To Bluey's relief the complaining stopped. There was lightness again, pure silence. He could see colours, the summer, so brightly, as if he was watching everything through a special intensifying screen. He wanted to be outside all the time and found the bakery unbearable as a result. One Thursday, the day before Jimi Hendrix overdosed on a street off the dividing hill, he took off his white paper hat and went out to study the sky, which was turning its face to autumn. He remembered that autumn was Carla's favourite season, and he walked with this memory, as well as the other, older one, through the west London streets, through the brown colours, into the evening. It started to rain. He shed tears to match the rain. He was on the A40, coming towards the new Westway section, when the creature that was residing in his heart suddenly began to shout at him. It was too terrible to listen to. He would have to do it after all. He looked out for a large vehicle, like the petroleum lorry that had given him a lift in Denmark. It had to be big and hefty enough to crush him outright, without a doubt, without a chance, the bones, veins, as well as the heart, which was now lost to him. When he saw a suitable vehicle coming, with two pairs of wheels at each corner, he established his position on the hard shoulder. He kept time. He went under it with a singing shout, a nausea, just as it was too late for the driver to see him, and so it went over him. Upon hearing the news the following day, his uncle said to the police, 'He was at work yesterday serving apple turnovers. He seemed all right to me.'

When Bluey opened his eyes again he found himself on another road, a pasture on one side, on the other side a city square. In the pasture he saw his father kneeling next to the hut where Bluey's mother had been found suspended from the ceiling. Bluey said goodbye to all that, and went in the other direction into the city square, the last place he'd go (in answer to Oscar's question) if he could go anywhere in the world. He sat down on a bench before a flowerbed and waited for the indefinite future.

As Lucas was leaving Riley's flat one evening, Riley said he had something for him. It was a cassette tape containing a conversation he'd had with Antoney in 1970. (Antoney had given Riley permission to record their interviews and late-night talks at will.) 'I thought you might like to hear his voice,' Riley said. Lucas took it as a sign of the old man's increasing trust in him. But the idea of actually hearing the voice was unsettling. He took it home and asked Denise to listen to it with him.

Denise had heard about the critic in Holland Park with the drooping bookshelves and porcelain ballerinas. She'd heard about his project, his archive, his old-time décor, and frankly she was with Jake on it – it was weird. She had also heard about Nijinsky in the war, his leap, his sister, the brother who fell out of the window, Charlie Chaplin's worry that being in Nijinsky's company would destroy his comical ability, Nijinsky in a straitjacket, Nijinsky jumping around in a cell, Nijinsky smearing shit on the walls. She even knew about the Tyrolean hat. But this was crossing the line.

'Why on earth would I want to hear his voice?' She was sitting in Toreth's side-split bluebell armchair. He'd interrupted her in her reading, a book on England's top flower shops. It often occurred to Lucas that Denise wasn't very chilled out for a florist. Weren't they supposed to be peaceful folk? Serene in their contact with nature, softened by the petals, happy like sunflowers? Wasn't she supposed to understand about the human need to know your roots? She was a twenty-nine-year-old woman in an old lady's zone. She'd never been to Subterranea. She'd never seen Bone Thugs-n-Harmony. She'd never drunk Strongbow in a car park at sixteen for the hell of it. It was possible she'd never even been to a pub. Didn't she want to escape too, to have a bed to herself? Lately Lucas had become disgusted by the weight of her body on the mattress next to him, the hush of her breathing and the sound of her dressing in the early morning. She was thorny. She was dry. He sometimes wanted to take one of her buckets, fill it with cold water and drench her with it in the hope that a looser, moist Denise would emerge from the puddle, a Denise who didn't nag and pick and talk of building societies, a florist, an independent flower girl, who practised the colourfulness and wisdoms of her field. The canal beneath their feet was still tonight. It was a lonely summer stillness built from decades of cocoonment and the perpetual unfleshing of bones beneath the soil on the other side of the graveyard wall.

'Because you've never heard it before,' he said.

In fact Denise had heard it before. She thought she might have heard it shout, in this very room, but it was too far back a memory to be certain. In the past weeks she'd been suppressing her growing guilt at having burnt Florence's letter. Now it flared up at her as she challenged him.

'And that suits me fine,' she said.

'If you heard it it might change you.'

'Don't you dare.' There he was, standing before her in his washed-out Stevie Wonder T-shirt, his hair formerly a close grade two now pushing up in uncombed knots like grass that needed cutting; asparagus thin, dole-queue shamed, holding a ghost on tape as if it was divine guidance. 'I'm not the one in need of a transformation here,' she said. 'I'm not the one stuck in a rut. Don't you dare try and drag me into this.' She turned away.

'Please, Denise. Just listen with me for a minute.'

'No. I can't.' She stood and went to the counter with her

empty mug. The boat was becoming unpleasant to her. When she came in from work some days the saloon was a dark wooden tunnel with spiders on either side of it, instead of simply the place where she lived. The objects disturbed her – Antoney's records, the ripped drum by the door, which they'd also never thrown out. She pictured her father's face sometimes. She hated Lucas for it. She hated her father even more, for becoming visible again. The only place on the boat where she didn't feel troubled was the bluebell chair, which was what it had always been, a seat of infinite comfort, though it was getting smaller and smaller in the gathering of shadows.

She slammed things as she proceeded to wash up. Washing up was Denise's way of avoiding, but the sink bothered her, the cistern. Lucas watched her from across the room, refusing to change the subject. She was wearing her usual long cotton dress from Shepherd's Bush market, something he had always thought would be more suited to a repressed Victorian housewife. Her elbows jutted from it violently as she slammed.

'You know something, don't you?' he said.

She was careful not to show any lapse, any giveaway sign. 'What do I know?' she replied sarcastically.

'You're keeping something from me. I can tell.'

'Now you're being paranoid.'

'Then why are you so resistant? How can you be so blank? It's like you're made of stone or something.'

'I've had enough of this.'

She wouldn't look at him. She wiped her hands on a flaw-lessly folded tea towel and made towards the wine-coloured curtain, which frightened her, the memories.

'You're fucking up-tight just like him,' Lucas blurted.

'Who?'

'Riley.'

Denise had the urge to rip down the curtain from its hooks, yet she contained herself and held on to the edge of the counter instead so that her fingertips became incandescent. 'If I hear

218

that name one more time—' she shouted. 'I am giving you an ultimatum now, Lucas.'

He kicked at his floor cushion. 'Ultimatum what – you ain't my mother.'

She'd *taught* him how to speak. She'd *taught* him 'ain't' wasn't proper English. You're *not* my mother, you're *not*. He was doing it on purpose to provoke her.

'And the ultimatum is this!' She was close to tears (though to this day Lucas had never seen her cry). 'Don't ask me another question. Don't tell me another name I don't like. Get your act together, get down off my back – or get out.' Before tossing the curtain to the side and retreating, she paused, and glanced at him with a small compassion.

'I'm going to bed. You're a poor excuse for a Lucas.'

'You can't kick me out,' he muttered after her.

So him alone. He waited until she was asleep. It was a voice, only a voice. A smoke on deck with the yellow-eyed cat to settle the nerves. Biscuits and sherbet pips as a kind of last supper, for something was about to end. The absence was going to speak, to change its nature, like a long-still body turning in the soil. *You're free – nothing to repeat – why spoil it for yourself*? Okay, Jake. But freedom was a deeper prison, a place of doubt. The knowledge, the sound, would make him certain of himself. He craved a second smoke but decided he should stay shallow in case of shocks. A voice, only a voice. He'd heard it already, rising from Riley's ink.

He positioned his floor cushion next to the stereo, from which he took away a slim ledge of dust with the tip of his finger. The brown sheen of the walls leaned inwards from the gunwale to listen. The August spiders folded themselves inside their webs. Sycamores breathed in, buckthorn bushes breathed out. The pigeons on the balconies listened. The last thing Lucas did was check the door was locked, because he couldn't shake that image of Antoney walking into the saloon in his trilby. The boat rocked from side to side as he sat down. He waited until it was still again. With his finger finally resting on the button, he wondered whether this was what it would feel like to detonate a bomb.

First came the loud fuzz of old cassette reel. A quiet, anonymous interior, no background noise – Riley's study perhaps. A voice quickly entered. Lucas turned it right down so that he could barely hear it, increasing the volume slowly as his courage grew. This first voice was Riley's; it was the same inflection, the same well-heeled accent, though it was much gentler and had sharpened since then. The other voice, his father's voice, was low-pitched, significantly deeper than Riley's, with a soft, Jamaican lilt. For a fleeting instant it was like Jonah hearing the voice of God, so pumped Lucas was with trepidation and the twists and turns of all he'd learnt so far. It sent a shiver through him. Then just as quickly it settled into something quite ordinary, a guy's voice, a guy who might rock up at the Breadfruit takeaway for a curry goat roti, or have a pint of Guinness outside the Duke of Wellington while talking to a friend about the bastards at Kensington and Chelsea council. These two aspects of the voice were difficult to marry and he listened with a sense of confusion.

Riley said, 'I thought evictions took years to carry out anyway.'

Antoney said, 'It has been years, Riley. That church is no use to anyone. These people have got too much fucking time on their hands.'

'I could lend you some more money.'

'We can't just live off your pocket.'

Riley asked whether Antoney had heard back about an Arts Council application and Antoney said he hadn't. The conversation went on in this mundane way, punctuated by the knocks and movements of cigarettes being lit and glasses being placed on a tabletop. Lucas couldn't see why Riley had selected this particular tape – he knew he would have done so carefully. But eventually they did come to something more interesting. Antoney, while expressing frustration with his situation, said that he wanted to travel again, further afield this time to Cuba, that Oscar's leaving had increased his desire to do so and now it seemed urgent that he went. He began to relate to Riley some of the things his father – whom he referred to as Mr Rogers – had told him about the island, how you could walk all the way across it under the shade of trees and how in clear weather Jamaica and Cuba could see each other. The tone of his voice shifted as he talked about this, revealing more of that murmuring, anxious quality Riley had mentioned to Lucas during their first meeting. He told Riley a story about his grand-mother in Baracoa, a quiet and feline lady who'd lost her tongue after being deserted by her lover in Havana. Antoney said he wasn't sure, but he thought that the baby his grandmother was carrying at the time was Mr Rogers.

'You've never talked like this to me about your dad before,' Riley said.

'Maybe it's Denise. I've been thinking about him lately, since she was born.'

He had never forgotten that story about his grandmother, because even though he knew nothing more about her than Mr Rogers had told him that night on the bus, he'd always felt an affiliation with her, for he too had looked out to sea expect-antly. By this point Lucas had his ear close to the speaker. He was aware of nothing else but the low-pitched see-saw voice.

'After he left,' Antoney said, 'I used to sneak out of the house during the night and go down to the beach to see if I could spot him. I'd stare at the horizon looking for the Cuban lights, and I did see them, when the sky was clear – a yellow glow on the edge of the sea. Times like that it seemed to me my father was still quite close. I used to picture him, arriving in Baracoa by foot to see his mother, with his hat on his head and every intention in his heart of coming back for me like he said he would. I still don't know if he did or not, Riley. I don't think I've ever stopped looking out for him. I'm that feline lady walking up and down the Malecón all day waiting for her seaman to come back, and it seems like I'll always be waiting. I won't be able to let go of it until I've walked in those lights myself. Do you follow me? It's not about finding him. It's about getting rid of the duppee.'

'What would you say to him if you did find him?' asked Riley.

One of them struck a match. 'I'd tell him that I get his drift,' said Antoney. 'Sometimes when I look at Denise in the cot I feel like running too.'

Lucas had intended after his fight with Denise to sleep in the saloon that night, but he sat for a while in the strange new silence, then passed through the curtain into the bedroom. Before lying down he put the tape away in his private drawer with the toy bus from his father. He dreamt of his mother, the same dream he'd had on the eve of his interview with Simone, though a different version of it. He dreamt that he was woken by the sound of running water. He listened, eyes wide open in the dark. Mustering the courage, he got out of bed and went through the curtain to see. His mother was over the bathroom sink, wearing her same dress, washing her hands. Lucas had shrunk in size by several feet, and he looked up into the forest of her hair which had once brushed his newborn skin. In this version of the dream, she turned off the tap, sensing someone behind her, and wiped her hands. She turned to face him. Her expression was one of strong disapproval, as if she was unhappy with something he'd done. He noticed with a small horror that the front of her dress was torn and stained with mud. He couldn't bear the thought of his mother being angry with him, so he tried to tell her he was sorry for whatever it was that he'd done wrong – he assumed she was annoyed with him for reading her diary. But when he opened his mouth to speak he found he couldn't. No matter how hard he tried no voice would come out. He woke up making croaking noises, Denise roughing him at the shoulder. She turned her back to him and went back to sleep, and when her breathing was deep, he moved closer to her and cradled her in his long arm, making the same shape as she did on the mattress with his body.

9

Carla found out about Bluey in a messy, roundabout kind of way. She and Antoney were passing a cold November evening in their seafaring living room in 1971, Carla on the right in her mother's donated chair not yet side-split, Antoney on the left in the valley of thirteen Moroccan cushions bought wholesale in Golborne Road. From the top of a cabinet next to her Carla took at intervals a pair of silver scissors for the working of a mitten-to-mitten cord through the sleeves of Denise's coat. Antoney was busy with another project, the creation of a written dance code with which to record his ballets. Occasionally he stretched over to the record player to move the needle to a specific section of a Maytals LP. He was wearing two jumpers.

Carla said, 'Put Candi Staton on, I love her voice.'

He was focused on the backward overhead reach in the twelfth bar of Blues House, which required a new addition to the code. 'Let me just finish this section. Her voice will distract me,' he said.

'Oh, yes. I forgot.'

She had on a navy linen dress she liked to wear at home, beneath a thick plum cardigan that complemented her skin. Motherhood had altered her appearance very little. She'd gained minimal weight and quickly lost it after Denise was born. Her ankles had not thickened or lost their shape. The only clear difference was the fatigue around her eyes, and she was less concerned

223

about looking fly wherever she went. Antoney liked her in this maturer, slackened guise. He liked coming home to her and kissing her warm cheek – although he didn't feel that way every day. She stretched the child's coat across her lap and pinned the cord to the inside middle. 'Are you at Oscar's tomorrow? We could pass by and see you.' The mention of Oscar's name still sent a shard of tension into their conversation, but it never seemed right to refer to the church in any other way. Antoney had heard nothing from him and had given up hope he would.

'I'm going to Riley's at two. He wants to interview me for his—'

'Gosh,' said Carla abruptly. 'If Riley wasn't so shy he could've been a quiz host!'

Ignoring this, Antoney continued with his work. Earlier that day he had heard some important news, which he'd so far forgotten to mention. Carla rose and went to the counter to make a hot drink. He declined when offered. The noise she made with her mother's crockery broke his concentration once and for all. Toreth had become a regular feature in their everyday life, be it through her donations (a wall clock, a tablecloth for the dining booth, a laundry service) or her visits, during which she always made some comment about the inappropriateness of raising a child on a boat. It vexed Antoney how it was that you became knitted to otherwise strangers on account of marrying their pickney. He'd finally managed to extract himself from his own mother, her put-downs and her complaining – Florence also couldn't understand the boat idea and rarely came on board – only to find himself in the path of someone else's. Actually he had no plans with Riley tomorrow, but he resented Toreth's presence at the studio and he knew that she and Carla were spending the day together. He put his notebook to one side, leaning back into the cushions on his elbows. It was now that he remembered his news and he looked over at her in antic-ipation. Again she spoke first, with a strained lightness. 'Are you seeing Simone this week?'

'That's the second time you've asked me that. I told you Friday.'

'Will anyone else be there?'

'Why not come and watch?'

She dipped her head in acquiescence and stirred her tea, which unlike her mother she would leave uncovered to let it cool down. Her mother liked to cap it so that it would still be warm if she forgot to drink it. He'd heard them bicker about this.

'She doesn't like children. She never has,' Carla went on. 'That's why she never comes round. I hate the way she coos at Denise, it's so fake.'

'She coos?'

'Yes. She coos.'

A cough was heard from the bedroom and Carla turned towards it. Summer with this water-life was fine; there was deck-basking and special experiences of sunshine. It was good to be away from the grotty streets, the litter, the overcrowded terraces, to exist at an altered pace and pass easy conversation with the other boaters who sailed by or moored next door for a while. It was a peaceful kind of nowhere. But autumns, winters were lived in the icy line of draughts. Denise was often sick. They sniffed and sneezed their way through the winter months. In addition to this Carla was afraid of spiders, a cluster of which were huddled unmentionably behind the records. The cough did not repeat.

'What were you saying?' she said.

'I ran into Ric this morning.'

'Did you? How is he?'

A second cough. A pause, an avalanche of coughing and then a cry. Carla glanced at Antoney as if expecting him to take action but she was already in motion. 'I'll go.' Ten minutes of soothing, mumbling, snivelling sounds and she re-emerged through the curtain carrying Denise, a fierce, thick-legged two-year-old who was born conducting an orchestra.

On that remarkable-sunset night of 1969, after Antoney had

sailed Silver down from Greenford and parked opposite the Kensal Green gasworks without a word of warning, the first move Denise had made in Carla's arms at the hospital was an expansive flinch, her tiny hands throwing themselves up into the air around her ears. Carla recognised the movement from the way it had so recently felt inside her stomach. 'Hello, Little Mystery,' she'd whispered in amazement, Antoney at her side. 'How strange it is to look at you, when I'm still imagining you.' They'd gazed at her, the eyelids, purple and fretfully thin, Carla's father's jet-black hair. Every flinch, every twitch of the mouth and rise and fall of the chest as the baby slept was a fascination, a happening. Her thoughts, Carla sensed, were the white of milk. She loved the feel of her new and fragile spine. At three months old Denise's favourite toy was a weird-faced lilac teddy that she'd liked to crush against her mouth while waving her legs in the air. Antoney had showed fatherly enthusiasm until the need for extreme gentleness had lifted, at about four months. The fact was he didn't understand why children did the things they did. He didn't understand why Denise had wanted to eat yoghurt and put her foot in her mouth at the same time.

'Take her for a minute while I get the medicine.' Carla lowered the child towards him. 'She'll only cry,' he said. 'Yes. Sometimes that happens. She's half asleep, just take her.'

Father and daughter entered a noncommittal embrace. Denise resumed her crying.

'Rub her back. *Comfort* her!'

'I'm *trying*.'

'Pass her to me.' She left the medicine on the cabinet and lifted Denise back into her warm, plum-coloured haven. The medicine was a sweet, spectacular thing. She sighed and slouched upon her mother's moving lap.

'Does Bluey know where we live?' Carla said suddenly.

Right at this moment the Maytals LP unhelpfully came to an end.

Antoney began, 'That's what I was—'

'I miss him. I just don't know why he—'

'Will you let me speak for a damn minute?' he said, alarming her. 'I've been trying to tell you something and I can't get a word in edgeways. Ricardo told me Bluey's dead. He got himself run over on purpose.'

For a few seconds she simply stared at him. As he was speaking she'd hugged her arms tighter around Denise in reflex.

'On purpose? What do you mean? . . . You mean – no. Bluey? No, that's wrong.'

'That's what he said. He could be wrong.'

Carla pictured Bluey in the sunroom that day at the castle, as she often had since. She remembered his dirty hair and clothes, the way his face had darkened when she'd said no, how disgusted she'd felt by his hand scratching at her knee. Somehow she knew it was true. She had a gruesome image of him being crushed on the tarmac and was shocked into tears of guilt and regret, not helped by Antoney's blunt delivery of the news. He went to her chair and tried to console her. He hadn't expected her to get so upset.

'How long ago was this?' she asked after what seemed like a long time.

'Last year, so he said.'

'Oh poor Bluey. It's too late, it's too late.' His hand up and down her back, up around her neck was no comfort at all. 'And when did you find this out?'

'Just today. I was going to tell you earlier but . . .' (he knew he was heading for something here.) 'Well I guess it slipped my mind.'

'It slipped your *mind*? How could it slip your mind?' She shrugged him off, getting up with Denise, whose sticky hand on her ear was a better solace. 'Didn't it occur to you I'd want to know straight away?'

'I'm telling you now, aren't I?' he said angrily.

'I can't believe you,' she said. 'I just cannot believe you

sometimes, Antoney,' and she flashed through the curtain with Denise.

With Oscar gone the church was too quiet. There were no students, no classes. There were echoes previously unnoticed. Antoney had moved rehearsals down into the basement, as the broken windows of the upper hall and the adjacent steepled chamber made him feel lonely and insignificant. He was still doing construction work, more so with the demands of keeping a family. In his spare time he came here, to the high-windowed studio where he'd first found his feet, and practised alone to recorded music, experimenting with new ideas. But he missed the cushioning, the regular stimulation of other dancers around him, other bodies, real instruments. He looked back on the company in its former glory with a sense of nostalgia, blaming anyone but himself for its collapse and believing he would never be able to achieve the same level of success – which at twenty-nine he felt was a premature fate. He wore this disappointment badly, often expressing it by being sharp and impatient at home.

After the tour he'd tried to get gigs wherever possible, but London, it seemed, in the fickleness of cities, had forgotten the Midnight Ballet. It was as if Oscar, Ekow and the other departees had taken the fire with them and the theatres could sense it. One manager had implied that dancing of their kind, the drums and all, was limited and *passé*, that people preferred the classical form. Recently there had only been sporadic slots in places like Surrey and the Isle of Wight, muddy outdoor festivals and shared stages. So he'd been grateful to receive an offer of a short run at an obscure theatre off the Edgware Road, a chance at last to revive the troupe to its former status. The run was programmed for the following May. He and Simone spent the spring making a new duet, to be accompanied by The Wonder and a stand-in drummer. Ricardo and Rosina were also performing.

The opening night was not well attended but the second was

better, though it took place on the same day that Antoney received a rejection letter from the Arts Council about the funds he needed to keep the troupe going. He danced well anyway, strengthened by an adequate amount of rum, a vice to which he was returning after a hiatus. The voice, as usual, went fifteen minutes before.

When the show was over a feeling of despondency followed him to the dressing room. He felt sure he could sense the same melancholy in the others. No one wanted to go for a drink with him. Simone changed quickly and went to catch a bus with The Wonder, the others followed shortly after, and he was left sitting before the mirror in his eyeliner, which he randomly decided to leave on. He could see two grooves across his forehead. He had no desire to go home to the unsailing boat – they'd only been to Camden and the Limehouse marina and hadn't raised anchor for more than a year. He put on his trilby and a played-out nylon jacket, disliking his image in the mirror, and went alone through the dingy back of magic to the stage door, with no idea of where he might end up except maybe at Riley's. Stepping out onto the grey side-street he paused to light a cigarette. The air was freshly scented, perfumed, despite the steamy kitchen of a Chinese takeaway two doors along. As the Pall Mall caught the flame, he heard a voice next to him.

'Mr Matheus.'

Suggestive. Confident.

He lifted his head and she turned to him.

She had tumbling apricot hair. She wore a green dress, a rich, specific green, with large fabric-covered buttons of the same colour ending at her mid-thigh, leaving an opening from which one tall leg protruded as it reclined across the other. Tight green ruffles stitched into the ends of her sleeves and at two levels circling the skirt gave off an adolescent readiness for fun, as did a wrist purse in the guise of a goldfish hanging from her folded arm. Her sandals were also gold. The richness of colour put an arrogance into her very pale skin, its chilled pinkness gliding up her legs, disappearing into the crevice in the dress and resurfacing at the hollow of her neck, where evening shadows collected in the clearing of her hair. She held up her wide, masculine jaw to him. The corners of her mouth sloped upwards into a gentle smirk at the pressure of full, varnished, parted lips that swelled and glowed towards the centre. Light blue makeup was coated around her little watchful eyes, again setting off the cool blush of her skin. She was perfectly arranged. A stern, assembled beauty.

'Audrey Callaway.' She extended her hand.

'Do we know each other?'

'I think you'd remember if we did.'

Where she leaned against the wall half of her was caught in streetlight, and that part of her hair was also gold. It was bewildering, ravishing, dancing hair, had drape and curl, alive in her collarbones.

'Although,' she said, 'I've watched you dance many times before tonight, so perhaps I do know you. Nice Shango by the way.'

'Thank you.' He looked away uncomfortably. 'Are you waiting for someone?'

She watched him, that pretty smirk.

'Do you want to come to my party?'

'When is it?'

'Now.'

'So what are you doing out here?' he said bemused.

'I came to get you.'

She wasn't the same as the girls who used to wait in the lobbies. No flutter, no bashfulness, no request for a signature. She was a different breed, and something about her excited him. But she was too sure of herself for his liking.

'Maybe some other time,' he said.

'Oh, come on, you'll love it. We can walk it from here.'

And she began to, moving past him with her scent, turning

back to lure him on, her golden purse swinging. 'It's this way. You're my guest of honour – we can't let everyone down.'

He really had nothing better to do, he supposed. Sooner or later his feet took her lead, unable to refuse.

They went down Praed Street past the hospital where Denise was born, then through the back-streets leading to Lancaster Gate. She had a bold, steady stride, four inches off the ground in her shoes. She'd watched the evening's performance, she told him, through her new opera glasses. She always used opera glasses at the theatre because she liked to zone in on the details. 'You have a most attractive muscle there,' she said, gesturing to it, 'just where your hip is. It's very well cultivated, I must say. Do you want to see them?' The opera glasses came out of the purse. They were jewelled with butterflies. She'd found them at an antiques place in Kensington. She collected them. Antoney was craving a drink and wasn't much interested in the glasses but he liked her stride, her hair. Her voice was clear and privileged. 'It's not far now. I've got all the booze you could want. Have you always moved the way you do?'

Around half past twelve they arrived at a stately apartment block on Bayswater Road overlooking Hyde Park. The lift took them up to the seventh floor, at which voices and music floated into earshot as they came out. Audrey's door was ajar. They plunged into a smoky crowd where revellers greeted her on either side; a drunk woman in a see-through top flung her arms around her. 'Oh Gwen, your mascara's run,' Audrey said. 'Look who it is!' She pulled Antoney by the hand into a turquoise room the size of three Silvers, full of people lounging on chairs and poofs and dancing around to the Yardbirds. A short, stout man in a ruffed Swiftnick shirt and lacy scarf came rushing forward.

'Audrey,' he said (an American accent), 'Is this who I think it is? Oh you *didn't*. What a dream!'

'Leave him alone, he's mine.'

'He looks even better up close. I am so *honoured* to meet you, Mr Matheus, so very, very honoured.'

231

Antoney didn't like the way they were talking about him. He returned a lukewarm greeting while thinking about stepping out. He'd have one drink and then go. The man was rattling his hand. He snatched it back.

'Ignore Harvey, he's just a sex-crazed queen,' said Audrey, as she dragged him away to the drinks table. 'What's your thing? Beer? Spirits?'

'Rum.'

She handed him a whole bottle, laughing loudly when she forgot the glass. He thought she might be high on something or perhaps it was just the atmosphere, the noise. After pouring himself a glass he replaced the bottle on the table. 'Do you know all these people?' He took a lush, extended swallow, enjoying the heat sliding down into his chest.

'Only half of them,' she shouted. 'They're all off their rockers – That girl in the tie-dye? I went to school with her. She married an actor, divorced last month, she's *devastated*. That's Francesca over there with that ridiculous mask on.' She lowered her voice. 'The guy standing next to you used to play drums for Mick.'

'Mick?'

'Jagger.' Antoney took a look at him, a guy with a fringe wearing a velvet blazer. He couldn't see another black man for heads. There were a couple of girls, one of them reminded him of Carla, but no fellas. He did come across one later in the dope room next door but they didn't say much to each other. 'Don't you mind having strangers in your place when you're not even at home?'

'What's to mind? It's only stuff. I can replace it.' She stroked his waist, near that muscle she'd been talking about. 'I keep the important things locked away in my bedroom.'

He eased away from her and downed his drink. He wanted another, which she predicted. 'I better be going.' 'Oh, no, no, you only just got here! Come and dance with me,' and she pulled him rum-spilling to the place by the balconied window where the people were swaying. She had a silly way of dancing, which was a surprise after the lovely strut. She did a funny, picking-up thing with her fingers and bounced too much, the goldfish dangling off her. Then she tried to copy him and things got worse. But her hair. They were joined by Harvey, who used his scarf as a prop and flicked it in Antoney's face once, which really pissed him off for a minute. He had another drink.

It was one hell of a party. Guys and girls got higher and higher and tongue-kissed in corners. Time went out. Whichever way you looked at it, it was the middle of the night in the dope room and the atmosphere was somewhat tranquil. It was a dining room or something, deep windowsills. The first thing visible as you walked in was a bright red lip-shaped sofa – you sat on the bottom lip and leant back against the top lip. 'Is that thing a sofa?' he said. 'It's my best thing,' she replied. 'If someone tried to thieve that I'd have them up in court. Do you hear that, everyone?' 'Aud, come and sit over here, you trollop,' someone called.

'*Paul*, don't *talk* to me like that in front of my guest of honour! Stick with me and you'll be safe,' she whispered. 'Are you partial to line?'

'Line?'

'You know. *Charlie*.'

'I don't do drugs.'

'But you like a joint, no? It's no different, just better. Can I have my sofa back, please?' The people moved aside and let her sit and he sat next to her surrounded by strangers. He was passed a joint. He couldn't remember whether he'd actually finished that whole bottle of rum. He didn't like to take weed with strangers usually, it made him paranoid, but everyone here was on it and who cared? He dragged and passed. 'What do *you* do for a living?' a girl to his left asked. 'Don't you know who this is?' Audrey shouted. 'No,' said the girl with the shiny button nose. 'This is Antoney Matheus, the greatest dancer on earth, you fool!' 'She's exaggerating,' said Gwen, who was lying on the floor. 'She's always, always exaggerating.' Audrey took

233

a line. The girl with the shiny nose enquired as to what type of dancer he was; he explained modern, of Caribbean and African influences. 'Groovy,' she said, passing back the joint. 'I saw Alvin Ailey once. Is it anything like that?' He jumbled his words while trying to explain the distinction. He didn't sound like himself. He glanced at the other black guy across the room, who was laughing.

A small crowd gathered around him. The Mick Jagger fellow was sitting in a window alcove talking quietly with someone. ('Sex is about being willing to be amazed,' said Gwen, as if she'd said it many times before. 'Being high is confirmation of the truth of all things,' said another.) The fellow kept turning his face towards him and he sensed he was being talked about. Everything he said felt scrutinised, awkward. 'You're from Jamaica? Wow!' He had a fleeting, disconnected thought of Bluey staring into the upper hall that very first day. He became quiet. The blood quickened. He worried that if he spoke his voice wouldn't be his and if he laughed it would come out as a horrible, high-pitched noise, making the whole room stop and stare. He thought he heard Bluey's bell, or Carla's voice. He wanted to get out. The green-gold girl whispered into his ear, at just the right time, 'I feel like a walk. Do you feel like a walk, Matheus?'

She'd finally let the goldfish go. The early morning air was cool on his face. The rolling open space stretched on forever. They held hands like children, laughed like children as they ran through the drifting blossomed park. 'I feel like we've known each other always,' she said, and that stage door back there did seem like moons ago. Her hair rolled and tumbled as they went, she looked as if she was in flames, the green of her merging with the grass, her sandals gone. They didn't stop running until they came to a shaded place of fragrant bushes, and there he took his first line ever. He lost himself entirely, they started kissing but he didn't really mean it he was so far out, her lips were quicksand soft and it felt good the way she massaged that muscle. She wanted him closer so she went beneath his shirt with her cool porcelain hands, unzipped his fly, his blood went higher. You're amazing, she hissed, amaze me, Matheus, you're perfect, oh please. So he went inside her to a moment of pure splendour while a voice within was faintly protesting. She drenched him, sucked him in deeper. He closed his eyes. But the moment passed quickly. The bushes started to smell bad, like a regular place for this kind of fucking. Their mouths were full of party smoke. Lift me up, she moaned. She was heavier than she looked. She wrapped her meaty arrogant thighs around him and breathed hotly into his neck, then she got so heavy that they sank to the ground where he momentarily slipped out of her. I didn't mean it, he thought. I really didn't mean that.

One night at home alone with Denise, Carla was woken by the sound of screaming nearby. She went to the window, then out on deck to see what was going on. There was no one in sight. Coming back inside she took Denise out of her cot and laid her next to her on the bed. I want you to be here, she said to Antoney in her mind. I want you to be here properly. Two days later a report appeared in the newspaper about a murder that had taken place in Ladbroke Grove along the Grand Union Canal. The victim was a young woman who had been dragged there and raped while walking home from work.

Antoney did not see Audrey Callaway again for several weeks and hoped he never would. The Edgware Road shows roused no further interest. In July she waited for him again, this time in the lobby of the Sphinx in Earls Court after he'd performed a solo as part of a line-up of modern dancers. This time she was dressed in white, a filmy blouse caught in at the waist with a red belt; a red handbag and shoes. Riley had come along to show Antoney his support. She strode up to them as they were mingling.

'Matheus,' she beamed. 'How lovely to see you again.'

The conversation stalled. Riley and another critic had been discussing Antoney's interesting choice of music, which Riley felt suggested a new direction in his work. Antoney was in agreement and was about to elaborate, but on hearing Audrey's voice behind him he lost his thread and stiffened like a deer at the sensing of a rifle.

'Was I interrupting something? I'm sorry. I just wanted to congratulate this gifted man on an excellent performance, wouldn't you say?'

The other critic referred again to the music, after which everyone fell silent. Riley acquired a delicate, foolish smile and glanced expectantly at Antoney, while Audrey looked from him to Riley with growing amusement, pressuring an introduction. In the end she introduced herself, first to Riley then to the other journalist.

Antoney couldn't stand it. 'Riley, I'll call you,' he said. 'We need to go over some – publicity things here.' Audrey flicked her hair. 'Terrible me, dragging him away like this. Showbiz never sleeps.'

He led her away with a firm clutch on the elbow. 'What do you want?' he said when they were outside.

'How's that for a welcome?'

'Embarrassing me like that – what the hell you playing at, girl?'

'Antoney, you're being very rude, you could hurt my feelings. Was that a friend of yours in there? I dare to think he's sweet on you. Obvious queen. Can't say I blame him, though. How are you? I've missed you.'

'Listen—'

'Haven't you missed me too?'

'*No.*' He drew her further up the street. 'I didn't know my face from my feet that night, all right? It didn't happen. I was out of it.'

'Yes, I know,' she said disappointedly.

'So let's just leave it at that. I'm going home to my wife.'

'Have a drink with me first.'

'No.'

'A farewell drink. As friends, I promise. I know a place.'

What was it about her? Was it *just* the hair? Or did she have some magus power to persuade? Or maybe it seemed the only way to get rid of her.

'You better hold to that,' he said. 'I mean it.'

A bar in a basement. White stools, red lights. Audrey co-ordinated perfectly with anywhere she inhabited, as if everything was made in her image. It was just a friendly drink after all. She was well behaved, less haughty, even slightly humble, if such a word could be used of her. This time she talked about her four uncles, all men of business, one of whom owned a string of nightclubs in Soho. Dempsey was her favourite, she said. He let her help out sometimes with interior design, which she loved, shaping the surroundings for a fabulous night out. She was actually quite good company if you didn't want too much depth, upbeat and nice to talk to. As the conversation roamed towards Antoney's life he found himself confiding in her about the difficulties he was having reviving the company, the looming eviction from the church, what a burden a family could be for a man in his line of work.

'That sounds really tough,' Audrey said. 'I don't know how you do it, living hand-to-mouth like that. What would happen if you lost the church?'

'I'd have nowhere to rehearse, nowhere to make new dances. I can't afford rent. It's my place, you know? It would be the end for me.'

She became thoughtful, diving through the ice in her cock-tail with a straw. 'Actually, Dempsey has a thing for churches. He likes old ecclesiastical buldings, ruins. Holy structures, he always calls them. What kind of church is it?'

'It's beautiful. It's got a door like Notre Dame.'

'Maybe he should have a look at it.'

As a child Dempsey had wanted to be a priest, she explained.

237

He'd always thought priests were the most powerful people in the world – that is until he'd realised how much money there was to be made in vodka. If he liked the place enough he might even be interested in investing in it, 'which I suppose would make him your patron or something? Would that get the bastards off your back?'

'It would help,' said Antoney.

That night he arrived home buoyant, and kissed both Carla and Denise where they lay together on the bed. Whenever he got home late these days he found them like this, stomach to spine, though Carla had formerly been adamant that a child should learn as early as possible to sleep in his or her own bed. 'I feel safer when she's next to me,' she'd confessed to him. 'It's so dark out there on the towpath.'

Dempsey sent Audrey to assess the building first. She was punctual and professional, in purple flares creased sharply down the middle. She arrived at the gate in an open-top sports car with peach upholstery. Only once she was inside did she remove her sunglasses.

'So, this is the place. I know what you mean about that door.'

Antoney smiled in agreement but he wasn't altogether comfortable with her being there. What would Oscar think of someone like her coming down those steps, with her expensive perfume and her cocaine dust? It didn't seem right. He hoped this would be short.

'What are all these pictures?' she asked, peering at Katherine.

'Dancers, mainly.'

'Oh look, there's Gene Kelly.'

'Yep.'

The Petrushka Nijinsky above the kitchen door she said was ghastly.

She walked around, inspecting ceilings. 'There's a funny smell in here.' Not wanting to jeopardise his chances he kept quiet as she strode into the studio in her heels, mistreating the floor.

238

Bright mid-morning light was falling in from the windows, draping itself over Oscar's board and vaults, which had been respectfully hoarded in the corner. His lecture stool also remained. Antoney was surprised by how much emptier the hall seemed in Audrey's presence compared to how it felt when he was there alone. There was a bleakness about it, despite the light. It felt like somewhere that had passed on, a yesterday place where not much more was going to happen. The idea that he could dance, work and exist in it without really noticing the bleakness saddened him. It did not occur to him that it might be Audrey making it seem this way.

She liked the wall of mirrors. 'I've always thought that must be one of the best things about being a dancer – you get to look at yourself for hours on end. Do you think it's true that all dancers are vain? They do lack personality sometimes, I think. They're all in their bodies, you know?'

'I don't have much of an opinion on that,' said Antoney. She smirked. He was starting to dislike her again.

'I think Dempsey will adore it,' she said, lifting her wide chin and walking to the back of the room. 'It's got a feel to it, an atmosphere. I like it especially down here in the basement.'

'Down here's mine, as I said. Your uncle can do whatever he wants upstairs.'

'Yours, heh?' She came back towards him slowly. 'Don't worry, darling. He probably won't *do* anything with it, at least not straight away. All I'm saying is I *like* it here, seeing where you make your moves . . . I'd hope, as I'm being so helpful, that I'd get a special pass or something.'

'A pass? What are you talking about?'

As his panic rose she positioned herself behind him, and proceeded to slide her hand over his hip, looking at their reflection in the mirror. 'Be nice, Matheus. You're so much more interesting when you're nice.'

'Will you get it into your blasted head I don't want anything to do with you? We made an arrangement!'

239

'Yes, and arrangements can be *un*made.' She tossed her hair and swaggered past him to the entrance hall.

'Are you interested or not?' he said following, 'because if—'

'I'm just not *sure* any more,' she said. 'Maybe it's not his taste after all. He can be quite particular, and there's that *smell*. When was it last decorated?'

'Not long back.'

'Oh come on, these walls haven't seen fresh paint in decades.'

At this point Antoney sat down on one of Oscar's sofas. He couldn't believe the gall of her. She was draining. She was stronger than he could manage. All he wanted was for her to leave, but with a slight chance still existing that this might turn out well he couldn't quite bring himself to order her to go. 'Just tell Dempsey to come and see it for himself.'

'I will. You can be sure I will.' She sat down next to him. 'And there's no need to be so glum. It'll work out fine.' Then she started talking figures. Did he know how much the building was worth? Dempsey was so loaded he wouldn't even notice it gone, she said. He was forever looking for things to throw his money at. She took a cigarette out of her handbag.

'You have to smoke outside. By the back,' he told her.

'Are you serious?'

'Of course I'm serious.'

'But I never smoke outside. I only smoke *inside*.'

'Well, you'll have to smoke *outside*.'

'Antoney. You're going to have to be a bit less precious about things if you want this to go ahead, you know. Don't ruin it for yourself. Did I mention I'm Dempsey's favourite niece?'

'No. You told me Dempsey would like it. You told me he wanted to be a priest.'

'I said he'd like it – but I didn't say he'd buy it. That's for him to decide when he comes.'

Crossing her legs in his direction she reached over and stroked the back of his head, as she might a cat's, her face very close to his.

'Just cool it,' he said weakly.

240

'Darling, we really couldn't get much cooler. I do so hope you don't get thrown out of here. It would be such a blow, as you said.'

She lit her cigarette, her palm now pressing firmly on his thigh. 'I think it's these sofas that smell,' she said exhaling. 'Leather doesn't age well. I've never been partial to it.'

Well, her bedroom housed a bust of Freya (a love goddess, Audrey said) and a huge, elaborately framed mirror of brass quills and curlicues, which on closer inspection revealed tiny fishes and seahorses tipping their heads towards the glass. He avoided his reflection in it. Audrey didn't. She wore her clothes better than she wore her nakedness. He discovered that without her hair she would be commonplace.

Once a week he went there, never staying a night as he was eager to get home. The sight of Carla brought him back to himself, though he was newly timid around her. They rarely made love during this time and when they did he found it difficult to look her in the face. Audrey threw frequent parties to which he declined invitations. Sometimes the Gwens and Harveys would come while he was there and sit in the dining room doing line. After three or four months he and Audrey started going out occasionally, at his reluctance and her promise of discretion, to one of Dempsey's clubs in Soho where they drank cocktails and watched dancers performing striptease routines. Audrey leaned over once and said to him drunkenly, 'That's something *you* could do, with a body like yours.'

'Why the fuck would I want to do that?' he said.

The affair went on indefinitely. He came to see Audrey as a gross inconvenience of his work, while also being aware that the only reason he was in this position was because he was too weak, shady, stupid, milk-livered, desperate, cheap, to get himself out of it. If he got angry with her for any reason she'd say, 'But darling, whatever would Dempsey say?' and he'd remind her with increasing emphasis that her uncle still had not come to see the church. 'He's so busy at the moment,' she'd say. 'As soon as he's free.' The only good thing happening in his life was another run approaching, this time for two nights back at the Ledbury in March '73. He threw himself into preparing for it, revising the ballets, staging a large publicity campaign with Simone's help. It was just the two of them dancing now – the twins had finally lost interest – so they were packaging themselves as a duo, the two brightest stars of the Midnight Ballet returning to the theatre where they'd first made their name.

As summer slipped into autumn and Antoney seemed constantly to be working, Carla began to suspect strongly that he and Simone were having an affair. They couldn't be spending all that time with each other just rehearsing, and after a chance meeting with her friend in the street Carla felt sure she had detected something telling in Simone's demeanour, a kind of smugness. Could it have been going on since Paris? She did not confront Antoney with her suspicions, but watched and waited.

Out walking in Holland Park with her mother one afternoon in December, she asked, 'Mum, were you always sure about Dad, when he was alive?'

'Sure about what?' said Toreth. She was pushing the pram, having prised it off Carla as she always did. Denise was busy putting three disused makeup sponges into a net bag whose drawstring posed complications. They were approaching the flower garden.

'Were you always sure that he loved you?'

Toreth said no, she wasn't, not at first. 'There were times when I wasn't sure at all. But then I discovered the flash of light. A marriage survives on a flash of light.'

'What's that, Mum?' Carla was less patient than she used to be. She'd learnt during childbirth that her mother was a liar. You don't forget the pain. The pain is unforgettable.

'It's a film I saw once,' (pronounced 'fillem'), 'about a javelin

242

thrower who lost his arm in a car accident,' said Toreth. 'He was married to a wonderful woman who nursed him through his recuperation, I think her name was Charlotte, and once he recovered she encouraged him to try and throw again, with the other arm . . . Let's sit down here for a bit.' Denise was unbuckled. 'But he didn't want to, you see, because the poor man was broken. His name was Bobby. Crestfallen and fearful, he was. It was an American film.'

'Will you please get to the point?'

'I'm getting to it, Carla, aren't we curt today?' Toreth pressed at her woollen scarf, tucking it under her chin. 'Well, Bobby wouldn't,' she continued. 'He wouldn't try and throw. For months and months he just refused – Denise, don't pull the flowers! – until, here's the point, until one day Charlotte told him that the memory of his javelin flying through the air was to her like a flash of light. That's what did it. That's what got Bobby practising again. He learnt to throw with the left arm, and even won prizes again! It's such a moving film, I wish you'd seen it.' She became silent.

'I don't see the connection,' said Carla.

'I haven't quite finished,' Toreth said. 'I'm talking about your father and me. It was after seeing that film that I started to think of the love we had for each other as a flash of light. Time goes by. I washed his socks. He had too many socks and it used to upset me. I'd find his toenails on the floor by the bin and I'd feel nothing for him.' She took Carla's hand in her lap as if to warm it with her better gloves. 'But then it always came back, that feeling, that special feeling. And whenever it did I'd think to myself, Ah, the flash of light, there it is. As long as it keeps coming back, love, even if it's only for half an hour or so on a Tuesday morning, and you can see it in his eyes when it does, that's when you know he loves you. That's when you know it's all still worth it.'

Carla watched her daughter perched on the edge of a tulip spread, touching the petals with her mitten then taking the mitten off. This was where it all began for Denise, when she was three, when she was pushed in the pram until she was milkshake and brought to witness the kingdom of flowers, where every colour lived.

'How long do you wait?' Carla said.

'How long?' said Toreth.

'What's the longest you should wait for the flash of light to come back?'

Toreth thought hard about this but provided no clarification. 'That,' she said, 'is an impossible question to answer.'

It was starting to rain so they headed for the orangery. 'Is everything all right,' she asked, beneath their big umbrella, 'between you and him?'

On 8 March 1973, the morning after the first of Simone and Antoney's two performances at the Ledbury, Bunty Tate published a review in *The Times*:

> *It's been a long while since we've had the chance to see the tremen-dous Midnight Ballet in their full splendour, and sadly their current show at the Ledbury Theatre is not one of them. This troupe emerged six years ago as a ground-breaking spark in British modern dance, with their exciting focus on Negro styles of movement and an electrifying musical ensemble beating the dancers through Antoney Matheus's beautiful and complex choreog-raphy. There is just one musician now and two dancers, Matheus and the ever-dextrous Simone de Laperouse, neither of whom have lost their power to fill a space. De Laperouse is almost mesmerising in her white-feathered solo entitled 'Bird', and Matheus equally powerful in the somewhat snipped 'Shango Storm', but the two new duets are weak by comparison and crying out for more. The pair do not make a pair. The first duet, 'Leaving', is laboured, with its repeated spins and its insistence on both dancers ambling into competitive, private solos, one on each side of the stage – it languishes far too long in its own drifting*

intensity. The second, the reworked 'Blues House', once a spectacu-
lar series of swift and striking vignettes (albeit suspiciously
reminiscent of Alvin Ailey American Dance Theatre's 'Revelations'),
is now nothing more than a flimsy ghost of its former self,
lacking in variation, outshone by its music. Where Antoney
Matheus was once dubbed 'Britain's very own Alvin Ailey', I
would dare to say that in his present form he is little more than
'a lesser Alvin'.

Antoney read the review over lunch with Riley at the
Westbourne Grove café. As Riley would describe it to Lucas,
he reacted silently, folding the newspaper and laying it on the
table next to his coffee, but it was clear from his face that he
was destroyed. His eyes gleamed with hurt. His mouth was
tight and miserable as he stared mutely up at the stained glass
window. It wasn't the first time he'd had a bad review (though
never quite so scathing as this). Four years before he might
have thrown the thing in the bin and gone pompously on his
way, insisting it was wrong. But here there was no arrogance,
only sadness and a sense of doom. It was the signal he'd been
dreading that his efforts to keep the company going were
futile.

'Is that what people think, that I'm a lesser Alvin? I'm copying
him?'

'Of course not. She's manipulating the parallel, that's all,' said
Riley. 'It's not even good journalism. You don't just reel through
a list like that.'

He tried his best to persuade Antoney that Blues House had
been adapted well; far from imitation it had its own charm and
identity. He was inclined to agree that Antoney and Simone
were not made to pair but he didn't say this. He said the new
duet was thrilling and intelligent and Shango was all the more
powerful for being a straight solo.

'Bullshit, Riley. It's dead without the girls. I don't have the
power for it on my own, not any more.'

245

'But that's completely untrue! Shango's your best thing – you've never let him down.'

Antoney ordered a brandy. It didn't matter what Riley said, he wasn't taking it in. He found an opposite argument for every encouragement and went on to a rum and black. After a particularly long silence on his part he said, 'Did I ever tell you about Babalu, Riley? Babalu Aye, one of Shango's crew. He was a leper, had sores all over his body, crutches, gnarled hands, dressed in sackcloth. He has a dance like he's falling down. You could say he's the opposite of Shango, weak, powerless and sick – That could also be me.' He looked off into the distance, stubbing out his cigarette. An eerie mood had settled over the table.

'I shouldn't mix drinks so early,' Riley said. 'Don't forget you're performing tonight.'

After leaving the café Riley did not see Antoney again until later at the Ledbury, when he came on stage as Shango.

Simone arrived at the theatre at five, the words echoing in her mind, 'almost mesmerising' – *almost* mesmerising? Antoney didn't turn up for the light and sound checks so they were carried out in consultation with herself and The Wonder. Despite the bad review she had great hopes for the show. After all, it wasn't her dancing that had been criticised but Antoney's choreography. She would show them, and she was in the perfect place. She loved the familiar interior of the Ledbury, the cosy auditorium and mounted teardrop lamps, the memories it held of her first waves of stardom. This would be the grand finale, her stepping-stone to further opportunity, for Simone had decided, unbeknown to Antoney, to go it alone from here. The Midnight Ballet was dead. Mr Matheus had lost his attraction. Tonight she would shine more brightly than ever before. Her body felt loose and supple, ready to amaze.

Antoney eventually rolled in at seven, half an hour before curtain-up, unsteady on his feet and stinking of liquor. Simone berated him as he donned his costume. He almost lost his balance while taking off his socks and applied his eyeliner in two thick smears above the lashes, giving himself a hideous, heavy-lidded glare.

'Antoney, take the minute,' said The Wonder, but by this time there were hardly any minutes left. The last moments before the lights went down Antoney spent arguing with Simone. It did not occur to him until midway through Shango that such a thing should not have been possible, that there had been no punctual muteness, no silence fifteen minutes before – that for the first time since the Midnight Ballet began, he had not lost his voice.

As planned, Carla was attending this performance. Also present was Ekow, who'd come to support Simone. The two of them ran into each other in the lobby amid a good-sized crowd, many of them curious locals welcoming the company back to the district on closing night. The first thing Ekow noticed about Carla, having not seen her in a long time, was how insecure she seemed. Her greeting was shy and rushed, as if she hardly knew him nor expected he would want to talk to her for long. As they chatted together with a mutual acquaintance he saw that she had difficulty maintaining eye contact – she stared rather than looked, and stared for too long so that the other person became uncomfortable and looked away. It bothered him, because she'd always been so natural with people. They sat next to each other in the fourth row.

Riley was sitting near the back. As soon as Antoney came on stage he could tell he was drunk, although it wouldn't be obvious to everyone. He was simply unmighty, unspecial. He was heavy-footed. There was none of his chameleon, charismatic lightness, and the bassy signature turn was more of a circular lumber. ('What's wrong with him?' Ekow whispered to Carla.) Riley instinctively sat forward in his chair trying to send Antoney some kind of message, some telepathic strength or centring. But once it occurred to Antoney that he hadn't lost his voice, he immediately forgot his steps as if in substitute, badly disguising it and at one point seeming to stumble. Riley willed it to end. When it did the applause was subdued. Things got worse. There was a problem with the lights during the next piece, and to Simone's obvious embarrassment Antoney stopped the perform-ance to address the technician in the lightbox across the audi-torium. 'The blue first, right?' he called, shading his eyes and clearly annoyed. 'Ok. We start again.' He and Simone went off stage and did it again from the beginning.

The interval was volatile. 'You never stop a show!' Simone said, struggling into her feathers in a rage. 'Whatever happens, you never stop a show. Don't you know that? Are you out of your mind? I've never been so embarrassed in my life!' Meanwhile Antoney drank from his flask, unleashing an abusive tantrum on The Wonder when he tried to prise it from him. Out front Audrey Callaway arrived with Gwen.

The audience's faith was restored by Bird, and with it Carla's trust. As Simone flicked her small head to The Wonder's flute with such gentleness and innocence, she felt sure she was wrong about the affair and guilty for doubting her, fighting back tears through the enduring applause. But with Blues House her suspi-cions returned. It was flat and ungainly, groping for coherence. Antoney made Simone look bad by default even while she tried her best to smooth over the defects. To Carla none of this mattered. All she saw was the two of them, the two of them dancing together where she had once been able to find Antoney when he disappeared. Her heart broke when he lifted her up in the red spotlight, a shaky, laboured lift but it didn't matter. It should have been her, only her. Tears fell from her eyes. Simone's waist, her ribs were near his face. He slid his gorgeous arm up the front of her body and Carla couldn't take it any more. She sidled along the fourth row into the aisle and ran out into the street.

She therefore missed the trembling, Simone and Antoney trembling together in the instant before he dropped her. The fall was such that Simone landed on the tip of her left big toe, sending the toenail down into the cuticle. She cried out in pain. Antoney bent as if to lift her again and resume, but then he straightened sharply, staring into the audience in what looked like befuddlement. As he loomed over her once more Simone ran off stage, such as she could. He danced the last two remaining minutes of Blues House alone.

Oscar had always said, and Riley would agree with him, that improvisation should have an idea before it, it should never constitute a performance in itself because that would be little more than a form of laziness. Antoney's closing two-minute dance had no idea behind it. It was nonsensical, hysterical, a bombardment of haphazard spins, stamps and leaps, each trying to go higher than the next, the knowledge in his feet forgotten and a crazed, unhappy expression on his face. His arms made frantic sweeping gestures as if shooting away flies. His knees buckled at the landing of each leap. If Fansa had been there to see it, he would have likened it to a Kumina ceremony he'd seen once in St Thomas, where he'd witnessed with his own eyes a woman, lost to the ghosts of the hollowed cedar drums, bite off the head of a chicken and climb all the way to the top of a palm tree. A footlight got broken in the duration. The spotlight lost and found him as he roamed in and out. When the music finished the theatre was absolutely silent. Antoney was confused by the absence of water fizzing on onions. He took a distracted bow, rose, and waited to see if it would come. The curtain closed on him in that position.

One of the memories that had been resurfacing in Denise's mind of late took place that same night, after Antoney got home from the theatre. Carla was waiting for him with her mind made up. Of all the things she had planned to do as she'd hurried back – to pack his things, throw his records in the canal, destroy his coded notebooks – the only one she'd managed (after finally getting rid of her worried mother) was to split the skin of his djembe across the middle with a penknife. It was a less satis-fying and more strenuous task than she'd expected.

Simone was escorted from the theatre by Ekow, after a screeching tirade at Antoney that began with the hurling of shoes when he entered the dressing room – hers, his, The Wonder's trainers. Simone wasn't normally a swearer, and The Wonder was saddened by it. 'You dropped me, you half-wit, you fucking dropped me! The Wonder, did you see? Did you see it? I can't believe he dropped me. You're a fucking crazy drunk. I deserve better than this, Antoney. I deserved more!' It was possible that she'd stored the shoes next to her in preparation for his return, as she had her foot up on the counter and seemed unable to get about. He was hostile and uncompliant despite her injury, even throwing her a few insults back, so that just as Ekow appeared in the doorway she aimed a bowl of water The Wonder had set beside her at Antoney's head, missing only by an inch and drenching the floor.

After the wound was washed and dressed, she and Ekow slowly made their way through the backstage dim to the exit. Antoney was sitting outside the dressing room on the wooden box that was reminiscent of Katherine's trunk. He listened to their familiar voices fading away.

Back in the dressing room The Wonder was putting the costumes and other items into a plastic laundry bag with an air of finality. Antoney followed his movements as a young child would watch its parent. The Wonder told him to go home to his girl, and the thought of Carla momentarily put a brightness back inside him, which dissipated as he remembered Audrey. He raised the flask to his lips.

'Don't do that,' The Wonder said. 'It's enough now. Go home.'

'What are you going to do?' said Antoney.

'I'm going home also.'

'But what about after that?'

'After that? I'll get on another bus, I suppose. I think this time I'll go somewhere quiet.'

'I've got nowhere else to go, The Wonder,' Antoney said. 'My only home in the world is—'

'No. There's another picture.'

The Wonder left the laundry bag on the counter and hoisted his rucksack onto his back. He paused in the doorway, regarding Antoney with his mild and kind expression. 'My friend,' he said in a cheerful tone, 'we did the things. When we are old men we won't disappoint the children like the silly baroness. We will have tales to tell. We did the sensational things.'

After The Wonder had gone, Audrey herself appeared, a mean, devilish, green-booted vision. She stirred a violent inclination in him.

'I've been waiting *ages* for you,' she said, 'me and that critic friend of yours. That was quite a show you gave tonight, Antoney. Very, um, striking.'

'Fuck you.'

She gasped. 'There's no call for that – golly.'

'Did you talk to my wife? Did you fucking step to her tonight?'

'*No* . . . I *didn't*, what do you take me for? Where have you been anyway? I haven't seen you in three weeks. Am I too much for you, darling?'

Antoney gathered his belongings, emptied the flask into his mouth and threw it in the laundry bag on top of the other things. He told her he never wanted to see her again, not anywhere near him, not in this life or the next, no scent or whisper of her, or he'd drag her by her hair to the bottom of hell. 'God, that sounds boring,' she said.

She watched him march into the darkness with his poor man's bag, calling after him, 'If you change your mind you know where to find me. My door is *always* open.' She sniffed into the dressing room, screwing up her nose, and did a quick line on the counter before she left.

Carla heard his footsteps coming down the towpath slope, felt the rocking of the boat as he stepped onto the deck. She stood, becoming unsure. Her instinct was to bolt the door so that he couldn't get in. *(You shouldn't have to be scared of your fella like that.)* But by the time she reached it it was too late. She was standing in his direct path as he entered, which he interpreted with relief as an expression of love and tried to put his arms round her. She pushed him back. The sight of him made her feel nauseous, the sweat on his face, the smudged makeup, yet at the same time his proximity instilled the same heat in her as it always had, perhaps more so now that it was finished. 'I want you out,' she said.

Denise was fast asleep, dreaming of pink. She woke as the volume of their voices rose and worried pinkly about it until it got too much.

'Do you really think I'm that stupid?' Carla shouted. 'Do you think I can't see it just by looking?'

At first Antoney assumed Audrey had lied, that she had presented herself to Carla at the theatre and told her everything. He denied it. He was faithful. The only woman he wanted was her, always. He pleaded with her, but she wouldn't accept it.

'How could you do that to me? She was my best friend!'

'She was – What? Is this about *Simone*?'

Carla gave a sarcastic laugh. 'Is there someone else as well as her?'

'Baby,' he said, 'there's nothing going on between me and Simone.'

'Liar!' During her wait she'd found a half-bottle of spirit in the kitchen cupboard and had tried without success to get the hang of this drowning-your-sorrows-in-a-bottle business. It came at him. He felt a headache coming on. He wanted no longer to be the kind of man women liked to throw things at. 'I hate the way you talk to me,' she yelled. 'You think you're above me but you're not. You're no better than Fansa, going after anything that winks at you.'

'You've got it wrong—'

'Don't come near me. You're sleeping with her. I know it, I know it, I know it.'

Denise had heard the knock of the bottle against the wall. The boat was rocking with their movements. Pink was long gone. There came a terrible crashing sound, repeated again and again, at which point she climbed down off the bed in her pyjamas and went shivering to the curtain to get with her mum. As she peeped into the horror she saw her father slamming his knuckles into the wall by the cabinet, as if he was trying to make a hole to put things in, like makeup sponges and other things he might want to look after, but it seemed a funny way of doing it. Her mother was telling him to stop. 'You're going to hurt yourself.' It was then that Carla heard her daughter's voice behind her, calling for her, bawling. Denise was clutching the curtain. Carla swept her up. Suddenly she believed Antoney about Simone. She turned from him, shushing and bouncing the child on her hip.

When she looked back, he was holding the penknife. Carla had left it on the counter after ripping his djembe. He was holding it horizontally, pointing out to the right. He was gazing at her full of love, his eyes shining – a flash of light. Her legs turned to mist. He came towards them. There was something he wanted to do, but he wanted to kiss them both first, which he did, next to the eyebrow, first Carla, then Denise. He went back out onto Ladbroke Grove.

Her hair in flames. Her wet orgasmic grimace. Her Freya, her seahorse mirror and her evil butterflied opera glasses. He would finish it good. A swarm of dark clouds was surging across the sky, matching his direction, pushing him on. He did not feel the cold. The look on her face when he cut, when he made the first stroke. The power he would feel with every slash.

'Darling! I'm so glad you changed your mind.'

She was barefoot and sky high. Gwen was with her, no one else. He felt a hot, seething excitement as he went in yet he was also clear-headed, light on his feet, floating like he used to. The two women followed him down the hall. 'Matheus wants to play, Matheus wants to play,' Audrey chanted, skipping in her stockings. 'Look at him, he treats the place like he owns it,' said Gwen. As he reached the dining room he calmly took the penknife from inside his coat.

'Do you want a line?' said Audrey. 'Hey, what happened to your hand?'

Gwen screamed when she saw the blade.

'He's crazy. I knew it. I always knew he was crazy.'

'Put that thing away,' Audrey said.

'In a minute. Come here.'

He grabbed her by the wrist and pulled her towards the sofa. 'Stop it. Stop it or I'll have you locked up!'

If she was scared he couldn't see it. It was just like her to try and be tough until the last second. Only when he made the first slash did she let out a flailing, mortified cry.

He did the bottom lip first, the part you sit on, ripped it every which way, full across the length. Then he did the top, the arms and base, shoving Audrey off when she tried to intervene. It was sweet work and he wanted to concentrate on it fully. The stuffing oozing out looked like bubble bath, the cusps of waves.

'Gwen, call the police!' But Gwen was huddled in an alcove. 'You're going to jail for this, you black fuck.'

The job completed, Antoney put the penknife back into his coat, satisfied with a job well done.

'Ladies,' he said. 'It's been real.'

He returned home the next morning freshly showered, having spent the night on Riley's sofa. Carla held his face in her hands. 'I do love you,' she said, 'I do,' and she gave him a sharp, dry kiss. 'But why is it so difficult to love you?'

That year in May they went sailing. They steered Silver westwards into the countryside and discovered new kinds of silence. Long dappled walks with Denise. Laughter in the mornings.

For the first time, Antoney experienced a pure familial pleasure that suggested itself as something that might be enough for him on its own, as if he'd been freed of the thing that had been getting in its way. He threw Denise into the air in a wild-flower meadow. He and Carla listened to music in the evenings and sometimes would dance together on the deck. She told him she wanted them to move. They were too vulnerable on the canal, and she was concerned for Denise. He promised her they would.

The need for motion remained. He exercised for two hours a day and would disappear for hours on a hired bike. If he ever became sombre, if he complained about not dancing, Carla would say something like this: 'Did you see that bird go across just there? Did you see what colour it was? My love, you should look outside yourself more. You might see something new.'

Lucas was conceived that summer.

10

Every other Sunday morning, Denise went to visit her mother's grave. It was situated to the left of the main entrance of the vast cemetery, a limestone cross at the head of a bordered soil bed. She went as usual three weeks before the carnival in August, with carefully selected seasonal flowers. It was summer; it was dahlias, peppered with chrysanthemums (Denise contested the current theory that chrysanthemums were naff). She washed out the vases first, unsticking a snail from one of the rims with a twig, then replaced the old flowers with the new and cleaned the cross and inscription (Toreth's chosen epitaph: *Carla Lillian Bruce, 1944–1974. We miss you God bless*). Afterwards she sat down on the border of the grave and settled herself in the surrounding stillness. They always left it too long to cut the grass. The blades were almost to her knees.

'I suppose I'm all right,' she said. 'It's him I'm worried about.'

Whenever she had a problem it helped to come here and air it. The rustle of a tree in the wind or the emergence of the sun from behind a cloud at the right moment could bring her clarity, sometimes a solution. She and Lucas had reached a stalemate. They hadn't spoken to each other in four days. He squeezed the toothpaste at the selfish end out of spite, and Denise's guilt about burning her grandmother's letter kept her from saying anything. She was doing the right thing, wasn't she? she inwardly asked her mother. The truth would only unbalance him further, surely. But she was starting to wonder how much further there was to go. He was smoking morning and night; there was no distinction any more. He must be spending all his dole money on it. Sometimes he didn't even bother to go outside and she could smell it in the saloon when she got home. She hated seeing him stoned. She hated the uselessness in his gluey pink eyes, the disjointed speech and floppy arms. He was succumbing to that dangerous trap of searching beyond consciousness for something he couldn't find here, and *she* might be the one responsible for it, the nightmares, that disturbing croaking sound next to her in the small hours.

The sun and the wind had nothing to say on the matter. She wished she wasn't so alone in it all. A wave of ancient anger went through her at the lot she'd been given.

As a child Denise's way of channelling her anger had been to immerse herself in the plant world. Escaping Toreth's ramblings she would spend long sessions on the bank making her garden, planting buds and seeds, staring at the soil in a yearning to see them grow. She had maintained the idea that if she could physically see the flowers growing, standing up tall by themselves, opening their petals, it would give her some reassurance of her own future, a sign that she would one day be free of burdens. But she never got to see it. No matter how much she willed it they never responded to her, never made the slightest movement. She deduced from this that growth must happen when people were asleep, so one mid-spring night while Lucas and Toreth were in bed, she went out onto the bank at half past ten with the intention of staying there till morning if that was what it took.

With the cemetery at her back, she established her position before a row of tulips, her favourite flower. She was wrapped up warm, a blanket beneath her, a flask of tea beside her, her equipment at the ready (torch, magnifying glass, ruler, notepad, pen). She focused on one budding white tulip. Not a moment could be missed. If she needed to pour herself some tea she had to do it while watching. When her neck got stiff she moved her head up and down, side to side still watching. At some point maybe three hours into the vigil, she thought she saw something, a tiny movement in the stem, a secret, a fraction of a thing. The tulip walked up itself. She took a measurement, but the difference was so slight she became unsure and went back to watching. Eventually it occurred to her that if the tulip had walked up itself, maybe she wasn't meant to see it, and that was why she wasn't sure she had seen it. Perhaps she'd only seen it because she wanted to see it, like the way Toreth was always saying how when Lucas smiled it was Carla smiling. At dawn she concluded that she'd seen nothing. Growth, she'd confirmed with frustration, was invisible.

She later found an alternative way of channelling. In a reckless reach for autonomy at fourteen, she became criminal for a minute and stole a shopping trolley from Sainsbury's. She filled it with buckets of her homegrown stock and marched it up the towpath slope, round to the cemetery gates. Eventually (this was a Sunday) the mourners came. They bought tulips, hyacinths, winter pansies. It was freezing cold standing out there for all those hours but she felt emancipated, from Toreth's ineffectiveness, from housework, from Lucas's increasing dependence on her. She got so cold her face wanted to walk away, but she returned home with twenty pounds. The next week she made more. If Toreth should ever retreat from laundry (which soon she would), she had found a way of putting food on the table.

Her professional interest in flora and fauna accelerated from there. Anything that grew was referred to by its Latin name, such as garlic ('I think I put too much allium sativum in that sauce'). If Lucas was unwell she forced him to drink foul-smelling potions (for chicken-pox she gave him a marigold brew, insisting it had been used with noted success to fight the plague). She also acquired a mentor penfriend, a retired authoress florist by the name of Harriet who lived in Carlisle, chosen during a school penfriend exercise in which her classmates went for athletes, broadcasters and trendy fashion designers. She and Harriet wrote to each regularly about invisible growth, plant food and the medicinal properties of roses and mimosa. Their correspondence took on a symbolic, philosophical hue. Whenever the responsibility of being guardian to her brother became too much for Denise, she would air it via Harriet, in a language they both understood. 'I know we should always try our best in the winter months to keep the shrubs in colour, but there's always so much raking and cutting and planning and feeding to do. Sometimes I wish it was possible for the garden to take care of itself.'

It occurred to Denise now, as her eyes fell upon the letters of her mother's name, that Lucas had no such way of channelling his own grievances. The thought came to her with a certain external clarity, that he had no solid thing, no reference point, nothing to help him balance his emotions. Perhaps he would always have come to this juncture, where he found it necessary to delve for something, anything to grasp on to. Would it help him to know? she asked herself, disliking the image of that blue airmail letter returning to her mind. Might he actually benefit from the truth? How bad could it be? Could it be worse than what was happening now, or what might happen with him next month?

But no. It was over. It was dead, buried, burnt, and she should leave it that way. She stood up with the same heaviness with which she'd sat down, a feeling of never-ending exhaustion set to accompany her back home, into another croaky night, another tense week. Her departure from the cemetery was always preceded by a thorough assessment of the grave to check for any maintenance matters that would need to be attended to next time, such as chipped vases or ingrained dirt. It was only at this point that she noticed something was different.

Back in April, Denise had planted some orchid bulbs in the

soil bed in front of the cross. She liked to complement the cut flowers with ones grown here, to add a sense of life continuing. But the orchids had failed to come up. Each visit she'd been checking them, through May, June, July – nothing. A reluctant flower troubled her. She always put it down to something she was doing wrong. She'd watered, treated, massaged, talked to them, with no success. By the start of August she'd given up on them, but hadn't quite been able to uproot them and plant something else.

Now, though, looking down into the bed, she found herself gazing at three confident, dusky-violet orchids. It stunned her that she hadn't seen them when she'd arrived – as if they hadn't wanted to be seen. You grew, she thought. All by yourselves, you grew. They had something to tell her. They'd been waiting for the right moment. She crouched down in the grass and dropped her bag in reverence. Bringing her face close enough to take in their scent, she listened.

'I keep *telling* people, don't try and copy the Americans. Dip into those *genes*, man. I'm sick of the half-baked tunes. I'm sick of the laziness. I'm clamping down on this now, I mean it. Look at my boy Roots Manuva. He's got his own thing, his own style, and that comes from looking inside himself, inside his *manor*, get me, and telling it like it is – Lucas, pass it on, man, stop hogging the zoot – Know what I'm saying, though? Funky DL ain't from New York so why's he putting on the accent?'

'Yeah, like Westwood innit.'

'Right, Crow. He's a chief – still you gotta love Westwood, he plays the tunes.'

The beanbag was spongy, whispering. It contained a trillion spongy pips. How many pips were there exactly in a beanbag? Did the pips have thoughts? Did they whisper to each other about what it was like in there? Lucas let his head sink back into the big sponge spread out on Jake's carpet. Jake's room was dedicated to the advancement of sound, two hulking production desks by the door, along one wall rows and rows of the endangered vinyl species. Jake applied mystical predestiny to the fact that his studio (his *real* work) was situated only a few doors away from where Bob Marley had recorded *Exodus*. It was Tuesday night. Roots Manuva was on the system. The room smelt of toast. Why did the room smell of toast? *I want to live like an unnecessary man*, Vaslav once said.

'I want the homegrown sound, people, the homegrown sound.' Jake was standing.

'Biggie, though. He's bad. Pete Rock. Scarface!' (What was this guy's name who's talking? Nigel, was it? That's why it smells of toast. The dude's making toast.)

'Listen,' said Jake, 'the only thing the Yanks have got on us is history and idols.' Jake always says this. Here it goes. 'But we, *we*, are history, you get me? We're black and white in the making. You can write that down if you want, I ain't possessive with my lyrics. Luke, man, the zoot!'

'Blood, what're you having? Marmite or jam?' Nigel had a duckish, hanging chin and was the shortest guy Lucas had ever met. 'Don't give that boy Marmite,' went Jake. 'Don't even mention Marmite to him. Luke, don't say it.' (The long-established thesis on Marmite: it's a salty black treacle when treacle should be sweet, plus it's for kids who don't know better, plus it makes me feel kinda empty, like chewing jelly when you've got a cold.)

'What's this about Marmite?' said MC Crow, who was skinning up on the bed in his tracksuit, on a vinyl sleeve – as *Touch* magazine had said of the superiority of vinyl, 'It's really difficult to skin up on a CD cover.' Tonight it was skunk, which Lucas wasn't partial to as the few times he'd had it he'd got paranoid, but it was all that was around so what the hell? Shapes, thoughts, collisions. Was one of his feet bigger than the other? Were the beanbag pips moving by themselves? Was Riley at home? 'Yeah, jam,' he said.

Yesterday Denise had broken the five-day silence. She'd said to him singularly on leaving for work, which would've been about five a.m. so maybe he'd dreamt it, she'd said, 'Lucas,' her face looming over him as he opened his eyes. 'Lucas, ask Riley if he knows what happened in Jamaica.' Then she went off before he could ask a question, before he could even grunt. What did she mean? What did she know about what Riley did and didn't know? Were they spars? Were they talking behind his back? There was no use putting it to her. She'd closed again like a food lift going up.

He was due at Riley's tomorrow. He'd been waiting all day yesterday and today to ask him about it, because Riley being Riley, uptight as he was, didn't like it when he turned up unannounced and the man didn't have a damn phone. Couldn't he just get a telephone like everyone else? 'Ask him what happened in Jamaica' – what the fuck *did* happen in Jamaica? It was something in those letters, he knew it. That green leather box that had conveniently disappeared. Riley still hadn't let Lucas read any of the letters and by now the frustration was killing him. He would go first thing tomorrow and demand he let him see them, it was his right, he was entitled to the whole story. He'd take no more wait-and-sees and when-the-time-is-rights – now was the time, '*Now.*'

'Now what?' said Jake.

'What?'

'You just said "now".'

'Nothing, man, sorry.'

Jake gave him a funny look. The toast was accompanied by Smarties and they were talking about the ideal woman. Nigel's was Hinda Hicks, a new R&B waif. Crow said Mica Paris. 'You lie,' said Jake. 'Mica's *baff*.' 'She's all woman,' Crow said licking the Rizla. 'Couldn't say that about Hinda.' 'Lauryn Hill,' Lucas put in quietly, for he felt he should contribute, but he was also worried about the veins in his hands. He could feel them beating, making the toast difficult to negotiate. 'Yeah yeah, I'll give you

262

that one,' said Jake, changing the sounds to A Tribe Called Quest. They marvelled at the opening composition of *The Low End Theory*. They discussed the future of Snoop, the supremacy of the orange Smartie. Lucas lost himself in the helium voice of Q-Tip.

The next time the stuff came his way, due to the distraction with his hands he failed to notice the joint drop off its filter as he was about to relight it, so he lit his nose instead. The other three roared with laughter while he went to the sink for water to cool it down. 'See, that's why I don't smoke,' said Nigel. 'My ex's uncle burnt his house down because of a joint, plus it gets you didgy.'

'I'm not didgy,' said Crow. 'I'm dandy.'

'You won't be saying that when you've lost your memory. That's how the system gets you. They let you fuck yourself up with the weed. Skunk's bad news.'

Jake said, 'The system what? I hate it when people start going on about the flippin system like we're robots living in some kind of machine, as if we're not responsible for ourselves. Like we got no brains, star. We live in a *society*, right, and the society has a government that controls—'

'Yeah. The system.'

'– that controls the *infrastructure*, the apparatus in which we roll, get me. I make my own choices inside the parameters. That's my point.' Jake was walking up and down the room in pontification mode. '*I'm* in control, not them. Tony Blair never told me to smoke. Innit, Luke?' but he burst into laughter again when he saw him holding the damp tissue to his nose, a zoot wound, injured in transit. 'I can't take you seriously with that thing on your horn. You lit yourself up, man, how could you do that?'

The others were laughing too and he was gripped by a hostility towards them all. They were so juvenile. They had nothing important to say about anything. He was tired of seeing their same old faces, the pleasure they derived from making each other look stupid. 'If you rolled the thing properly it wouldn't have fell out, would it?' he said to Crow. 'Chief. You lot talk too much shit.'

'Who you calling a chief?'

'Easy,' said Jake. 'I don't know what vibe you're on tonight, blood. It's all that Nijitski crap you're been reading, it's flying you loose, I swear.'

'Nijitski who?' said Nigel.

'Ni*jin*sky.'

'On second thoughts, don't get him started.' Jake cast a discreet glance at Lucas. 'Let's just say he's got his nose stuck in a book these days – excuse the pun.' Crow sniggered.

'My sister's like that,' said Nigel. 'She reads Iyanla Vanzant like it's the Bible, y'na.'

'*No*, my mum as well! Quotes from it and shit,' said Crow. 'I'm telling you.'

I could go round there right now, thought Lucas. I could knock on the door and confront him.

'Once, right,' Crow said, 'my old man got so vex with her for spouting that spiritual talk he dumped all the Iyanlas in the bin. She clasped him for it.'

'Is it?'

'My mum don't *business*.'

His head was so fuzzed, his neck so hot. The pips in the beanbag hissed. They were evaporating beneath him, the floor was beginning to disappear, the blood racing through his hands. Momentarily his attention was drawn back to the conversation. In a voice that didn't sound like his own he asked, 'Did he hit her back?'

Crow frowned. The room fell silent. 'What you tryin'a say? My dad ain't no wife-beater.'

For a split second Crow's voice had sounded exactly like Antoney's on the tape. It was as though he was suddenly here, in this room. Lucas pulled hard on the draw. They were all staring at him. 'This stuff's going to my head, blood,' he said. *Don't say blood*, he heard Denise from the water. *It doesn't suit you.*

He looked up at Jake through the vapours leaning by the window. Behind him, he saw a shadow in the streetlight coming through the curtain, a broad-shouldered figure, long-necked, a trilby, standing there watching him. He was wearing Vaslav's coat.

'Luke. You cool?' said Jake.

'I've gotta go.'

It was better out in the street, but only for a minute. As he passed the alleyway leading to All Saints Road the murky green of it frightened him and he hurried by, tripping over a broken bottle. He didn't head for Riley's straight away but once he'd come through the square onto Portobello Road he couldn't bear the thought of going home. His feet turned left by themselves. He went past the brasserie and the print shop, veering right onto Elgin towards the dividing hill. Every figure that went by was a suggestion of Antoney. The fabric of a woman's skirt was that of his long leather coat, the after-hours drinkers outside the bars held him in their midst, the pigeons on the balconies and in the trees pierced him with those cautious brown eyes. At the top of the hill a swarm of them flew freakishly blue-winged from a monstrous sycamore, causing him to run across the road in the loom of an approaching 52 that missed him only by a yard. By the time he reached Riley's flat on the quiet, curving street in Holland Park he was panting for breath, brimming with a fearful expectation that whatever was about to happen would send him over the edge to a place he wouldn't be able to return from, yet he couldn't turn back. It was the same fear he'd experienced before listening to the tape, but manifold.

He stood at the gate watching the house. The hall light was on, the curtains closed but a glow emitting from the living room. For fifteen minutes his fear held him there. It was his anger at the idea of Denise and Riley colluding together that made him go in. The overgrown path was wilder than when he'd first come here. He had always thought it odd how the front garden was so neglected compared to the back, as if to preclude any hint of invitation. There was no answer when he knocked. He knocked again, insistently. When there was still no response he thumped on the glass. 'Let me in! Riley, open the door!' He went back up the path into the driveway along-side the flat.

Both the kitchen and bathroom windows were closed so he couldn't climb in. There were two tall wooden doors at the end of the driveway leading into Riley's and his next-door neighbour's gardens. Riley's was bolted from the inside and fenced with more wood across the top, but the other door, also locked, had a gridded wire sheet above it that might be held on to while using the drainpipe next to it to climb up. This he tried, slipping at the first attempt and getting his khakis caught. He'd hoped to get directly into Riley's garden that way but he was forced to land in the other, a landscaped spread of shrubs and nightlights with a children's playhouse near the back. In the corner by the fence there was a tin barrel mounded with discarded lawn. Tormented by the nightlights, he stole quickly along the fence to the barrel and scrambled over into Riley's garden, casting a frantic look back at the windows of the other house. There was no sign he'd been seen. Riley's rosebush gleamed in the moonlight. One of the study doors was ajar, a slip of muslin curtain caught in the hinge. The room beyond it was dark. He went slowly towards it.

The letters, he guessed, were in the room that was always shut, the door to the right as he emerged from the study into the corridor. As a final check that Riley wasn't home he peeped into the living room first, then went back to the forbidden door. To his surprise it wasn't locked. The feeling that Antoney was present, all around him, was stronger than ever as he went inside. It was a small room, with a stripped double bed, a wardrobe and bedside table. There was nothing else visible in the poor light falling in from the corridor, so he dared to turn on the light, a naked bulb.

The room seemed to have no connection to the rest of the flat. It was utterly bare, no green box in sight, only hangers and a lone salt-and-pepper coat in the wardrobe, nothing under the bed. He went back to the living room to hunt shamelessly in dusty cabinets, under the sofa, behind the TV, then in the kitchen cupboards, the bathroom. If it wasn't in the study, or in any of the other rooms, then where was it? He had no choice but to wait for Riley to get back. Restlessly he sat down in his usual place on the sunken study sofa, the moonlight through the wafting curtains casting strange shadows across the floor.

Lucas had come to know every nook and corner of this room, every book title and chipped ballerina on the burdened shelves, every juxtaposed object and piece of furniture, the Victorian magazine rack, the new chair. Most of all he'd never forgotten what the old man had said about the French windows being the place where he remembered Antoney the strongest, the place where he used to lean, the curtains moving around him. It all seemed very sad to Lucas, as he waited there in the dark. What could make a man hold on to someone for so long? He wouldn't like to end up like this, living alone in a dead man's dome, like a fossil.

The desk was untidy, which he wasn't used to – whenever he was here it was clear and neat. On either side of the type-writer there were documents, loose pieces of paper, an open notebook, a couple of folders on the floor next to the chair. The typewriter itself was loaded. Riley must have gone out mid-session intending to carry on when he got back. According to his latest update the book was going well and he was on the verge of finishing. The last section he had allowed Lucas to read was an account of Antoney's work after the European tour, which had alluded to his involvement with a shady society girl. It struck Lucas now that the answers he was looking for might already have been written. He got up, and peered at the script in the typewriter. He couldn't make it out. With an inward breath he switched on the desk lamp. There were only a few lines of text. It was titled at the top, 'The Leap'.

By the time he was thirty, after the Midnight Ballet disbanded, Matheus's performance career had come to an end. He had always hoped to keep to the stage for as long as he was strong and fit and then to concentrate on choreography, working with large companies and theatres, while fuelling his knowledge through anthropological expedition. We might have glimpsed him, white-haired and

Lucas sat down in Riley's chair and searched through the other papers. The loose sheets surrounding the typewriter contained similar versions of this beginning, but each one ended mid-sentence and told him nothing in particular. He read through the notebook – Riley's handwriting was small and upright – which comprised lists and snippets of information, instructions from the writer to himself about craft. Perhaps he was having another block. One list read 'tutor, Carla, widower, Beaumont'. What was Beaumont? Underneath the sheets of trailed-off script he came across some handwritten smaller pages of a darker hue, old-looking, apparently torn out of a school exercise book. The writing was not Riley's. The words were large and sloped, their size inconsistent. Lucas timidly picked the pages up and held them for a time, barely skimming the surface, once looking over his shoulder. Butterflies circled in his belly. The letter began, 'To Dear Riley'. The date at the top was October 1982. Midway through reading it, Lucas heard a noise from elsewhere in the room and almost jumped out of the chair in fright. Riley's grey and white cat had slunk in from the garden. It sat on the rug, observing him.

*I was very happy you replied to my letter, because I want you
to know you are my friend. I feel calm when I heard your voice.
I remember who I am inside and that I am not dead. I smell it
around me. But I know I am alive. I am a living man. I am not
a madman and I don't want you to think like my mother that I
don't know myself. She is ashamed of me, but I am not wicked.
I not the devil. I am making a new dance and practising in the
garden. The others watch me. They think it's a performance and
I'm jumping because of them. But I'm not like them. We are not
the same. I don't say any words to them. I told the doctor I am
me. My soul is whispering to me and telling me what I am. That's
why I don't want to talk. Shango is inside me telling me what
I am. He tells me to carry the cross for my wife to let her know
I love her. I love my children. I love my son. Riley if you see my
son tell him I love him and want to see him. I am Antoney.
I am not Midnight like the others call me. I am Antoney and
one day I going to walk away from them with my cross on my
shoulder. This is not my home because I will carry it out of the
gate. I am not death. I am life. I am above the stars. I know you
understand everything I am writing because you always listen
to me and know what I am saying. I can feel how you listen.
I want you to write to me with the green envelope.*

Your friend,
Antoney

A film gathered in Lucas's eyes at the references to him and
Denise. He could not equate the spirit of the letter with his
father, its truncated sentences, the awkward grammar. Its impli-
cations confused him and chilled his senses. The urgency for
information gone, he picked up the folders on the floor, mechan-
ically, like someone locked in a pursuit whose destination they
no longer wanted to reach. Riley's cat walked over and glared
up at him like an ineffectual guard. He found newspaper cuttings
and photographs, some of which he'd seen before. Two further

269

letters, still in their envelopes, were similar to the one he'd read, one of them less lucid. Within a divider marked 'Beaumont', the questions raised were coldly answered. Beaumont was a psychiatric hospital in Jamaica. A letter with the hospital stamp was addressed to Riley, enclosing in strictest confidence the documents he'd requested for help with his research. Attached was a clinical report monitoring Antoney's progress over a six-month period in 1983, what medications he was given, lithium, carbamazepine, what he ate, when he didn't, how he behaved, the occasions on which he spoke. He was diagnosed as manic depressive. He believed he'd built a man-size cross out of wood, which he walked with in the grounds and one day tumbled into a creek. When asked why he believed he'd done this he said, 'I didn't like it.' The last entry in the report read, 'Discharged'. There was no clue as to what had happened to him afterwards.

'Why didn't you wait?'

Riley was standing in the doorway with a late-night grocery bag. Lucas was too confounded to feel guilty or startled at being caught. The old man looked dishevelled, more ashen and sombre than ever.

'I did wait.'

'Well now you can leave. I don't appreciate you breaking in and going through my things.'

'You should've told me,' Lucas said. 'You've known about this all along, why didn't you tell me?'

'I thought it would be best if you read it in the book.'

'That's a cop-out.'

'Please get out of my chair.'

Lucas did so. He watched Riley's movements as he stooped over the desk and gathered the documents into a pile next to the typewriter, feeling a surge of rage towards him. 'Does my sister know about this?'

'I've never even met your sister.'

'I don't believe you.'

'Be that as it may,' said Riley, 'this is becoming a strain on

270

me. You treat my home like a library or a museum. You can't just come in and rummage through it as you please. How did you get in?'

'It *is* a fucking museum!' said Lucas.

'I'm asking you again – leave or I'll call the police.' Lucas could tell Riley was scared from the way he peeked at the door, probably remembering that he didn't have a phone.

'What d'you think I'm gonna do?'

The zoot burn had left a raised blotch on the end of Lucas's nose, which he'd forgotten about until now. They held each other's stare, Riley craning his neck. In his face Lucas saw all the sadness of Beaumont, the decades of going over and over the same ground, the terrible conclusion. For those few seconds he felt close to the old man for the first time, that they were the same.

'How long was he in there for?' he said more calmly.

'Three years, about.'

Again Lucas shrank from wanting to know more, what exactly had put him there. He was more interested in the hope of that word, 'Discharged'. 'And where did he go?'

'What do you mean?'

'Where did he go when he got out?'

'I'm unsure about that.'

'How can you be? You said you'd almost finished. You can't finish it if you don't know what happened.'

'I . . .' Riley turned away, pulling on his beard. 'I'm using my artistic licence, as it were.'

'What?'

'I'm imagining it.'

'Bullshit, you're not allowed to do that in biographies.'

'That's a bit shortsighted of you, isn't it, to think you should just tell the facts from beginning to end?'

A draught blew the curtains into the room, washing the ghost of Antoney towards them and unnerving them both. Riley went and pulled the doors to.

'But he said he wasn't dead,' Lucas said. 'In the letter he said he wasn't dead.'

'That was an expression. It wasn't literal, how could it be? Given his state of mind at the time I think we—'

'Then where's he buried? Where's his headstone?'

'I told you, I don't know what happened.'

Lucas tipped the documents off the desk with a sweep of his hand. 'All right, then, Mr Biographer. What the fuck is your imagination telling you happened? Is he alive? Is he in Jamaica, France, Putney, what? Is he dead or not?'

'Lucas, calm down,' Riley said gesturing with his hands.

'Tell me what story you've made up about my dad, about *my* family, without even asking permission. Tell me all about the lies I've grown up with, go on. Tell me how it ends.'

'It ends—' Riley said. 'Leave my things, stop it!'

Lucas had cleared the desk of the typewriter, which bounced off the edge of the chair before crashing to the floor. 'I need to know where he went!'

Riley rushed out an answer, tripping over his words. 'I had one more letter from him saying he was heading for Cuba, so that's what I'm building on – that's where he always wanted to go, you remember? He went to a place in the east called Baracoa, by the sea.'

'Go on.'

Riley wasn't sure what to say next. He stammered for a while making little sense, like someone who'd forgotten their lines. 'He took a bus there, from Guantánamo. They built a bridge through the mountains after the revolution, he wanted to find his father and grandmother—'

'Yeah?'

'But he never did, he – he settled there. There's a dance school in Guantánamo where they put on shows, sometimes he—'

'So, what, he's still there?'

'According to my version of it – yes. That's what I've *imagined*. I'm not saying that he is.'

'You liar. You sick fucker.'

'For the love of God!'

Riley's chair was upturned along with the desk, which took some doing. Swoop by swoop Lucas cleared the bowing shelves, ripping one out of its joints. The books, ballerinas and photographs clattered down glass frames smashing. He hurled the desk lamp at the French windows. Riley tried to grab the lamp from him before he threw it but was shoved away and fled the room on the tail of his cat as Lucas shouted curses, accusations and roared like a wild thing, virtually unaware of what he was doing. Everything was fallen. Everything tumbled and him with it. There was no solid ground and there never would be. He was the same as the objects he was destroying, dense yet hollow, unknowable, made up. An unnecessary man. A poltergeist.

Meanwhile Riley was knocking hysterically on his neighbour's door. When the young couple eventually opened it in their nightclothes, they saw Lucas stumble up the path and run away.

On stormy nights, on wild nights, nights when the boat would shiver as lightning crashed, and rock so hard that objects were displaced, as the downpour thrashed against the windows and thunder shook trees and buckthorn bushes all around, there was a voice. Don't worry about the storm, it's just the night clearing its throat. It's just Peterjohn, she'd say.

As Lucas ran he craved her aniseed smell. Speed became home. The coat tails whipped in the wind. Years back, Toreth would say, securing the blankets around his chin, long before you or I were born, the Portobello Road was just a rough country lane. Can you imagine that, walking along through barley fields with the nightingales in your ears, on Portobello Road? It was a long, silent, potholed lane, dusty in summer and muddy in winter and, like most open spaces in the cities at that time, it was prone to highwaymen. What's a highwayman? Lucas would ask, even though he already knew the answer. It's a man in a black mask and cape who stole watches from people when they were out and about. Did they use guns? Sometimes, Toreth replied, but not Peterjohn. Who is Peterjohn? I'm getting to that if you'll let me. Most of the highwaymen, you see, Lucas, were drunkards. They were 'in liquor', as you would have heard it back then, and they were also foul-mouthed and smelly. But Peterjohn was different. He had nine children. Did he? said Lucas. Are you lying? No, I am not lying – I would never lie to a child! I'm telling you, nine children, and he did his highwaying to feed them all. One day one of the children fell ill, the youngest boy, Peterjohn's favourite. The boy was very sick. A storm was beginning and Peterjohn went out on his horse to see what he could find for the child, and do you know what happened to him? said Toreth. What happened? Well love, by a maple tree in a hayfield off Portobello Lane he was struck down by lightning. Did he die? said Lucas. Yes, he died. But what happened to the boy, did he die? No, Lucas, he didn't. At the moment the thunderbolt struck Peterjohn, his favourite little boy sat up in bed and was well again. He grew up to be very, very tall and unafraid of thunderstorms. It is said that there was lightning left over in his eyes. (That bit's probably a lie, though. I'll admit it.)

11

After the Midnight Ballet disbanded, Antoney found work teaching modern dance at a local college, and was occasionally offered more prestigious work at The Place. He didn't enjoy teaching, so he would relieve his boredom by telling stories about Katherine Dunham or Oscar Day's dance commune, or talk about the difference between a Number 11 mango and a Julie mango. He wore fading unitards with loose pants and walked around stretching the unitard straps up and down his arms. The regular, more talented students liked him because they thought he was funny, but others loathed him as he exercised favouritism and was given to damning criticism. 'How old are you, girl?' he'd say. 'You move like you're ninety.' '*Please* stop dancing like an ox in front of me. I can't stand it!' Some people came once and never returned.

St Bernard's church was back in the hands of Kensington and Chelsea. The costumes, tape reels, paperwork and photographs – all except the Petrushka Nijinsky above the kitchen door, left there as an afterthought – were placed in the trunk and stored at Riley's for the time being until Antoney could get a bigger place. The only things he took home were the Shango Storm costumes, the portrait of Katherine leaning against the pillar and, at Carla's request, Bluey's cowbell. He focused his attention on her and the coming baby, which he hoped would be a son. He would take him on the buses. He would take him to the theatre where they'd sit next to each other with their legs crossed and their similar chins tipped up. He'd tell his boy if he dreamt of being a kite that he should aim for that kite, because you only get one chance. He would do it right. Although he felt at times as if he were translating himself in this new undancing life, as if he'd strayed from his nature, his family frequently gave him comfort, and it really wasn't so bad. He bought Carla gifts such as vibrant scarves and bracelets from the market.

Pregnancy was harder on Carla the second time round. She was sick and irritable most of the time. In order to help save money for their new place she'd taken a waitressing job in a café and needed to eat carbohydrates at regular intervals to get her through the day. Hunger would not negotiate. Her skin became greasy. Her ankles swelled because she was on her feet so much. Whenever Antoney looked at them a quiet worry whispered to him that a time would come when Carla's beauty was no longer in front of him but inside her, where it would have to be remembered and looked for, when the effort of love would increase. Carla noticed his affection swing to and fro, which made her feel heavier and unappealing, and subsequently left her more moody. By the fifth month she was forced to give up the waitressing job. One day Antoney brought her home a velvet jewellery box containing three pairs of the same earrings and fourteen hairclips for Denise. 'What's wrong with you?' she said. 'Couldn't you just buy one or two?' He said he'd thought it would make her happy.

He often stopped in at Riley's after classes and aired whatever gripes he had over a brandy. He smelt of studio sweat, a rough, esoteric smell. 'Have you got yourself a fella yet, Riley?' he asked him once, making Riley cough into his brandy with embarrassment. 'I reckon relationships between guys must be easier, less fussing and nagging. I can't do a thing right.' Riley said with poorly veiled diffidence that he was probably right about relationships between fellows.

Carla ran into Simone by chance on Kilburn High Road, near Christmas of 1973. They hugged instinctively – they hadn't spoken in a long time. There was a faint discomfort at the bad feeling that had existed between them, but it dissipated when Carla jovially trashed Simone's 'barefaced lie' that she was blooming. They chatted for half an hour in the street, exchanging news, Simone asked after Denise. She'd had no luck with auditions – Carla noticed she'd lost some of that uppityness she'd acquired in the glory days – but Ekow had done well, landing a part in a West End musical production of *Gone With the Wind* showing at the Theatre Royal, Drury Lane. Carla should come along and see it. They parted warmly, with a vague plan to go to the Rushwood Sauna after the baby was born for a pampering session like they used to.

Antoney feigned nonchalance when he heard about Ekow's part, but he was wildly jealous. 'You could take me to see it,' Carla said. 'You could take me to the theatre instead of buying brooms and maps.' (The maps were the most recent unfathomable buy. There was a stall in the market that sold them in psychedelic frames – so far he'd bought Poland and Cuba.) He took her to see *Gone With the Wind* the day before Christmas Eve, leaving Denise at Toreth's. Carla bought herself a new dress especially, a floor-length, bell-sleeved maternity number in tan. She didn't have the right shoes for it so she wore some comfortable old black flats instead. At first Antoney put on the white shirt, but she told him he should wear the red because he looked most handsome in it. She arranged his collar for him in the bedroom and smoothed down the fabric over his chest, her belly pushing into his. He looked down lovingly at her. 'You're my beautiful quiet man,' she said. 'And you're my empress for true,' he said back.

They took the 23 into the West End, which was tinselled and glittering with Christmas lights. The lights in their so many different colours, the cascading loops of them over Oxford Street, the shop windows and streetlamps reflecting more light onto the pavements – it was the most bewitching kind of London evening where you got to feeling there was nowhere else in the world with so much light. Carla felt that the whole city belonged to them. She squeezed Antoney's hand as they reminisced about their old bus journeys, beaming inside with happiness at how she could still feel so in love with him after all this time. No matter how much he annoyed or baffled her, no matter how self-centred he could be, there would always be times like this, when it felt as fresh as the first months. The deep lines in his forehead and the short, uneven afro that she'd tried to pat down before leaving made her love him more, because she knew that in years to come, when he was grey and withered, she would still feel exactly the same way. It would get better and better with the history they collected.

They had cheap seats in the upper balcony. Ekow's was a chorus part but he stood out for his far-reaching charm. 'I'm so proud of him. I think he's going to do really well,' said Carla in the interval, during which they stayed sitting under the pretext that she should rest her feet. In truth, Antoney was wary of bumping into any of his old dance acquaintances who might ask him what he was up to these days. Being in the theatre was painful for him, such a grand theatre at that, its dressing rooms and back of magic closed to him. He'd managed to engage only with the imperfections in the performance, and commented to Carla that the choreography was basic, the positioning unimaginative. 'Oh don't be such a grouch, it's wonderful.' Watching Ekow only made him feel worse. By the middle of the second half he couldn't take it any more and he excused himself to go to the bar.

The bar was empty except for a group of people talking and smoking in a cluster of Chesterfields and two women sitting on high stools. He grabbed a stool, downed his drink in one shot when it came, thinking about how unjust it was that Ekow was up there and he wasn't even on the scale any more. He was a nobody, a fallen star, forgotten. He wanted another shot but couldn't afford it. There was a time when he wouldn't have had to buy his own drink, when people were falling over themselves to refill his glass. Like an echo of his thoughts, he heard an unmistakable voice behind him.

'Antoney Matheus. Well fancy running into you.' He turned in surprise to find Audrey standing at his shoulder.

They hadn't seen each other since the night he'd slashed her sofa and his first instinct was to blank her. But she was smiling genuinely at him in her playful way. Her hair was aglow in the lights above the bar, her green-coated eyelashes reflecting an impressive emerald pendant around her neck. She was wearing a clinging silver pipe dress and beguiling perfume, classy as ever. 'God, you've aged,' she said, also as tactless as ever. It was then he made to leave but she tapped him on the leg and pulled up a stool. 'Don't worry, I had it reupholstered – looks good as new. How are you? . . . Vodka and lime, please,' she asked the barman. 'Are you having another, for old time's sake?'

'I'm here with my wife,' he said

'Your wife's here? How lovely – is she well?'

Relaxing a little, Antoney replied that she was engrossed in the show, which Audrey said was overrated. He told her of the coming child.

'That must be why you look so haggard,' she said. 'They wear you out, you know. I couldn't stand to have kids, they're such unreasonable creatures – all that whingeing and tugging at your clothes. No thanks. Are you still dancing?'

She ordered him a rum and black. Audrey was a few years older than Antoney but in his present mood he envied her carefree youthfulness. 'I'm teaching now.'

'Really? Somehow I can't imagine you as a teacher. Oh darling, you didn't lose Notre Dame, did you?'

'That Dempsey crap. A fucking priest? You made all that shit up.'

'I did not. He *did* want to be a priest.'

'But he never heard a thing about my church.'

'Don't be angry with me. Desire will drive you to mischief.'

She gave him a flirtatious nudge. 'We had a good time for a bit, didn't we?'

Antoney sucked his teeth. It felt pointless staying hostile towards her, and they went on to talk of other things. He was reminded of what good company she was despite being a crazy bitch.

In her husband's absence Carla had left the auditorium to go to the bathroom. She checked her scooped-up hair in the harshly lit mirror, lamenting her weary eyes and fattened, oily skin. She looked forward to when she could get herself back to normal again. On her way back to her seat she popped her head into the bar to see if Antoney was still there. She saw him from the back, talking to a girl.

The first thing that struck her about the woman was not her flame-coloured hair but a lack of hardship in her, her posture, the way she sat, her clothes, the way she moved her hands. She seemed to have never had something to overcome, to struggle against. Her ankles were contoured and creamy rising up from her high-heeled shoes. There didn't seem anything suspect between them. She wasn't quite jealous – Antoney had always known lots of girls. But as he got to his feet something telling happened. The woman, this no-hardship woman, she looked her man up and down, over his body, with an expression of ownership in her face, and just from that look, Carla knew immediately that they had been lovers. She experienced heartbreak for a second time but this time it didn't make her cry.

When Antoney returned to the auditorium he was not acknowledged. He rested his hand in her lap the way they'd been sitting before. A pain was spreading across her back, deep inside her spine halfway down so that it hurt if she breathed too heavily. Afterwards in the lobby while waiting for him to finish chatting with someone it worsened. She eventually interrupted him to say that she was ready to go home, then walked off towards the exit without him. On the bus back to Ladbroke Grove she was silent, curling her hand from his. He put her behaviour down to a prenatal mood swing.

They came off the bus at the usual stop before the canal bridge, but instead of heading past the towpath entrance to her mother's to get Denise, Carla took out her key and unlocked the gate.

'Denise?' He attempted a joke about forgetfulness during pregnancy.

'Later,' she said. She went ahead of him down the dark slope, her dress billowing after her from the end of her coat.

Once inside she turned on the lamp and neatly hung up her coat. They had a miniature Christmas tree that made the room feel even smaller, if cosier; the shining baubles turned on their strings with the movement of the boat. Her mind was pristine clear. She felt more sure of herself than she had in a long time, and with it there was a sense of relief. When she looked at him, though, in the one instant that she did while he was taking off his coat – she was curious about the flash of light, whether it would still happen – the clarity wavered and she appeared disoriented.

'Are you all right? Have I done something wrong?'

'Could you move your coat, please, so I can sit down?'

He hung it up next to hers but that was the wrong place.

'Not there. Put it somewhere else.'

To avoid an argument he laid it on the ripped djembe by the door, which satisfied her. She did not sit down for long. While Antoney went to the counter for a night shot to settle his unease she stood looking out at the water through the spidered window, holding Denise's lilac teddy, which had been lying on the chair. He offered her tea.

'You never did get us moved,' she said, mostly to herself. 'You never did protect us.'

'What's that?'

Facing him (there was no flash of light), she repeated, 'You didn't protect us.'

'Protect you from what?'

281

'Murderers. Rapes and what-have-you.'

'Is this about moving? Come on now, let's not get into that tonight.'

'Ok.'

'Why don't you get some rest and I'll go and get Denise?'

'No. I'll get her.'

Antoney clutched his liquor mug with both hands as if warming himself in the decreasing temperature. It had never felt quite so cold in here. 'This is weird, Carla,' he said nervously.

She gave a heavy sigh, which hurt her back, but said nothing.

'I was thinking back there, you know,' he was trying to make conversation, 'I could get choreography work on shows like that – it was weak, seriously. Could be easy money right there. Maybe I should talk to Ekow about it.'

'Who was that girl you were talking to?'

'What girl?'

'In the bar.'

'The bar?'

'I know you were screwing her so don't try and lie.'

'What? I wasn't!'

'Not tonight, obviously. Before.'

As Antoney seemed to have lost his tongue, Carla asked him again, 'Who was she?'

'How'd you get such an idea into your head?'

'Are you going to tell me her name?'

'You're accusing me of some—'

She shouted, 'Don't insult me. Tell the truth.' After this she leaned forward with both hands on the arm of the chair and for the rest of the conversation remained composed.

Antoney's fingers shook as he topped his drink. 'So?' she said.

'It was nothing.'

'Her name.'

'It wasn't like that, I can't even stand the bitch.'

'Just tell me her fucking name, Antoney, I have a right to know.'

'Jesus, it's Callaway all right?'

'Callaway what?'

'Audrey. Callaway's her last name.'

Carla appeared puzzled. 'Audrey? What kind of a name is that?'

'Are you in pain?' She was clutching the chair and swaying a little. He started towards her. 'Will you sit down?'

'I don't want to sit down.'

'Carla, I swear to you,' he said, 'I didn't mean it. It was a mistake.'

'How long did you screw her for?'

'This isn't fair!'

'Never mind, have a drink.'

'She was blackmailing me.'

Carla spouted in disbelief, 'She was blackmailing you? What do you mean she was blackmailing you?' (Her second use of the word was employed with extreme ridicule.)

So he explained to her about the uncle who wanted to invest, how afraid he was of losing Oscar's place. The sound of sirens passing by on Ladbroke Grove disturbed her for a moment as she listened. 'I wasn't thinking straight,' he said.

'What, so you were kind of like – her whore?'

'Come *on*, now!'

'A prostitute?'

Her face caught in the lamplight was horrifying in its sternness. He felt as if he didn't know her at all. 'You're being disrespectful,' he said quietly.

'Tell me, how long did you spend working as a prostitute?'

'I refuse to answer that. You could try and understand – you know how important my work is to me.'

'I've always known, Antoney. I wish I'd acted on it earlier.'

'Please, just sit down.'

'Don't touch me. How long?'

'All right.' He wanted to be as nasty and callous as she was being. 'Then why don't you tell me something about you and Bluey?'

'What's Bluey got to do with it?'

'There was something going on between you two.'

'Bluey's *dead*. He was my friend. You should be ashamed of yourself.'

'It didn't look like friends to me.' But he knew he was losing ground. He was only lowering her opinion of him further.

'Are you really going to try and use a dead boy to save you?'

To this he had no comeback. He mumbled his answers as she interrogated him further, scolding him to speak up. When she asked him where he'd 'worked' for the girl he lost his temper and raised his voice. She glanced around her. He thought she was looking for something to throw at him and he became depressed. In fact she was imagining what the room would look like when he was no longer living there, when it was just herself with the children. She sank down on the edge of the chair. The size of the room grew so that there seemed a great distance between them, then shrank to less than it was. 'I never thought this would happen,' Carla whispered, the chill wind rocking the hull.

'Baby, I'm sorry,' he said.

'I know. Just one more question. Did you tell her you were married?'

'I told her from the start.'

'Ok.'

She smiled, but there was no shift in her expression as she did so. Nothing happened in her eyes just then when she smiled.

'It's all right, it's finished. You can go now.' She went to get her coat, leaving him standing by the chair. 'I'm going for Denise. I won't be long. Get your things together. I don't want you to still be here when I get back.'

'Don't throw me out.'

He sounded on the verge of tears but she didn't comfort him, for they were not what they were. 'It's too late, I'm afraid. I warned you.'

'But where am I gonna go?'

'Go to Riley's or something – wherever.' She opened the door.

'Wait, *I'll* get her,' he said. 'At least let me get her and bring her back.'

'No.'

'Will you have some sense, girl? It's not safe out a road at this time!'

'We'll be fine.'

He couldn't hold it back any more. He broke down out of sheer frustration and begged for forgiveness. 'Listen to me. I didn't, didn't mean it. I love you.'

'No, you listen to me.' She returned to where he was standing, her face now animated but with pure hatred. 'You're a user, Antoney, a fucking user. You used me the same way you used that bitch, same way you used Bluey and everyone else, so that you could ride that magic carpet of yours and have something to catch you when it all fell apart. Well, grow up. This is where I get off. I'm not going to let you insult me again.' And with that she stepped out onto the deck.

Toreth insisted on returning with Carla and Denise to the boat. She'd suggested they should stay with her until morning, but Carla was adamant that she needed to sleep in her own bed. That night, on an impulse, she took to sleeping on her side instead of on her back, as the fortune-teller had advised. The three of them spent Christmas together. On New Year's Day the Grand Union Canal froze over for the first time in recent history.

Riley had never liked seeing photographs of himself. He was always smiling in an awkward way or too serious. Often he was looking away from the camera. He sometimes worried that it might be clear to others what he was looking at.

On Riley's brother Jeremy's fifteenth birthday, when Riley was thirteen, their parents had held a party in the garden of their house in Finchley. Their mother, disturbed by a habit of social withdrawal in her younger son, invited two sisters who lived on a neighbouring street. They came wearing summer frocks with bows at the back and ankle socks peeping out of their Mary Janes. The sky was cloudless, a pure, bright blue. The older girl, a pretty brunette, chatted away easily with Jeremy, while the younger, also pretty, with honey-blonde tresses, tried to make conversation with Edward. 'You're not as outgoing as your brother, are you?' she said, looking jealously at her sister. Eyed by his mother, Edward gave a flat smile, eventually escaping to his bedroom.

He stayed there for some time, looking down on the garden. He saw his mother get her heel stuck in a hole in the grass, the honey-blonde alien standing around on her own. As he watched, he noticed quick movements in the grass near her. Unable to make out what it was he opened the net curtain by a fraction for a clearer view. It was a creature of some kind, a dog perhaps, but a shadow of a dog, a shadow cast by nothing. It went round and round in the grass as if chasing its own tail.

The people in the garden began to disappear. He had a sense of time striding on. He grew into a young man, Jeremy left home, the room became bare, but through all this he felt that he was still standing at the window, watching the impossible shadow, fascinated by it and unable to leave the room because of it. What was its texture? What was its solid thing? Through university and into work this strange preoccupation stayed with him. A notion developed that the door behind him had been locked.

Antoney arrived at Riley's flat in the small hours of Christmas Eve with his laundry bag. He didn't go outside for days afterwards, not even into the garden. He drank and smoked continuously. When the alcohol and cigarettes ran out and Riley refused to buy more, he went out in his dirty tracksuit then came straight back. He didn't want to go for a walk in the park.

He didn't want to watch TV, only sleep – sleep, drink and smoke. 'Riley,' he said, 'I been shot down.'

Even with the state he was in, Riley liked having him around. The world outside fell away and the atmosphere in the flat was that of a hushed, marooned sanctuary. If it rained it was far-off music. On the last day of the year it snowed. By this time Antoney was willing to go out into the garden where they trod the white carpet and let the snowflakes fall into their mouths. As a New Year's gift, Riley bought him a book of poems by W. B. Yeats and read it to him by candlelight in the living room where they'd made up his bed. For Riley it was a happy and peaceful time.

Antoney was interested in the way Yeats spoke of nature in his poems, as a mystical force greater than ourselves yet also vulnerable. He said to Riley that maybe God had put us on the earth to suffer, so that we could be brought to a point of noticing his creation and gaining comfort from it. Riley said perhaps, but he believed that structured religion was a method of control; we could notice all by ourselves. Nevertheless, on a crisp Sunday morning in January Antoney put on his smart clothes and announced that he was going to church. It was the most positive Riley had seen him since he'd arrived; he seemed hopeful about the future again. He said he wanted to get back on track. But two hours later he returned newly despondent. The church had reminded him of back home, the times when his mother used to drag him there every Sunday after his father had left. His mother had told him that God was his father now, not Mr Rogers, so he'd looked for Mr Rogers in the coloured window-panes, the altar, the ceiling and the holy cross. Of course he never found him. He'd look up at his mother, singing and praying with her hands on her cheeks, and it had begun to occur to him that God was a way of finding what you were looking for by forgetting for a while that you'd lost it. That was why people went back every Sunday, because by Sunday it came time again that they needed to forget. It was a deceit.

He stayed with Riley for several months with no pressure to

get his own place, though he said he intended to. They settled into a harmonious routine. Riley carried on with his journalism. Antoney went back to working part-time in construction. His body loosened. Riley noticed his arms slackening with the absence of dancing. Although he, Riley, was shy with himself, covering himself up on trips to and from the bathroom, Antoney walked around the flat with his shirt off. Riley would study the dips and slopes in his back as he went down the corridor, coming to know every detail of it, every loosening muscle as if it were his own private mountain. On returning from a show one night he walked in on Antoney relaxing in the bath. He made a fraught apology and practically ran out of the room, but he could not erase the picture from his mind of the beloved chest with its bristly black hair, the strong thighs and the genitals breaking the surface of the water. He found it difficult not to think about it whenever he looked at him. It had felt like watching the shadow in the grass, its shape and texture beginning to reveal itself for the first time.

He was glad there was little talk of Carla. When she and Antoney had arrived back from the European tour married, Riley had been crushed by it. He'd struggled to maintain his composure as the two of them had walked towards him into the Westbourne Grove café for a lunch date that had been planned for just him and Antoney. Their knuckles were touching, pronouncing a fortified intimacy, she in a girlish bloom Riley was about to discover was pregnancy. He'd always seen Carla as someone easy to dissect, shallow, leaning towards independence and self-direction, yet more likely to be led into conformity. They, the newly weds, were blankly beautiful, taller, absolved, muted by the magnitude of their vows leaving only an enormous, glossy radiance that belittled him. They were less than themselves yet more. Antoney had refrained from his usual greeting of enfolding Riley's palm warmly in both of his or throwing his arm around him in a friendly embrace. They shook hands, formally, like acquaintances. Riley was insulted, by both of them, for withholding his right to a proper reunion with his friend.

Antoney seemed to have accepted that the marriage was over for good. Even though it was obvious that he missed Carla, he didn't go on about it. He did mention in March, though, that the baby was due that month and he wished he could be there at the birth. 'You think she'll let me see him?'

'How do you know it will be a boy?' said Riley.

'I know it's a boy. That's my son. You think I could try and see her, it might have happened already?'

'It's up to you,' Riley said, a dread collecting in his gut.

Whenever Antoney spoke of the child Riley was standoffish like that and it became a source of tension between them. For a while Antoney stopped mentioning it, assuming Riley wasn't interested – either he was just dismissive of children or thought he was just barking up a tree. He bought a gift for his son, a little wooden bus that he could roll around on the floor. He ventured with it to the canal one afternoon and saw Toreth sitting on the bow with the baby on her lap. He had a tiny brown face and was kicking up his legs. It made Antoney laugh out loud with a bulge in his throat. Even though he still had a key to the gate, and he ached to pick up the boy and smell him, he couldn't pluck up the courage to go any further to present his gift.

The conflict between the joyful reality of the baby boy and his estrangement from Carla depressed him. Riley realised he hadn't accepted it after all. Some nights he couldn't sleep. From his bedroom next door to the study, Riley would hear him moving about in the kitchen or running a bath. He would get out of bed sometimes and sit with him, because he knew how hard nights could be when a person was very down. Antoney described to Riley on one such occasion an ugly grey mass he could feel floating behind his shoulder, like a mesh of wire, tangled with dust and dirt, following him wherever he went. He could hear a distant noise in his head like the sound of marching, as if his thoughts were wearing boots. It was around this time that he started taking medication. The pills lifted his mood. Riley, as he always had, enjoyed being confided in, the idea that he was the only person who fully understood every aspect of Antoney's personality. Subconsciously he preferred it when he was down, as it brought them closer.

They ran into Carla one morning while walking in Holland Park. She was with the new baby and Denise. Riley's heart lost a beat when he saw them, as did Antoney's. Her hair was fizzing over her shoulders. She looked healthy, her large eyes bright. She smiled when she saw Antoney but it was only a friendly smile and subsided to seriousness as if she meant to clarify an unbreakable distance. She was full and shapely in jeans and a broderie anglaise top, which Antoney said afterwards was new.

'Are you well?' she asked him.

'I'm doing all right. You look good,' he added shyly.

She avoided his eyes, ignoring the compliment. Antoney had grown a bit of a beard and knew he was looking tired and scruffy. He saw her register this in the way she quickly glanced up and down him before telling Denise to say hello to her dad.

'Hello, Dad,' said Denise. 'Lucas got my raisin.'

'He's got a raisin?'

Carla held the pram firm as Antoney bent down. She and Riley exchanged stilted small-talk.

'Lucas,' said Antoney. 'You got a good name there.' The baby stared out at him with pupils almost filling the whites, the star-tled gaze of the recently born. Antoney put his finger into his little hot hand, the one without the raisin, and felt the bulge in his throat as the finger was squeezed. He hated having to ask exactly how old he was (going on three months), whether he was eating and sleeping well.

'Do you need anything?' he said. 'New clothes or such?'

'I'm managing. We've got to go, we're meeting Simone.'

'All right. Ok. Well, maybe I'll see you again some time, around the place.'

She smiled curtly. 'Take care of yourself.'

'Bye, Daddy,' said Denise.

'Wait.' Antoney reapproached them as they moved off. 'I got him something. I don't have it with me but . . . maybe I could pass by and drop it.'

'Oh,' said Carla. 'Look, I really don't know. I'll get someone to pick it up from Riley's some time, ok?'

He watched them go down the lane underneath the lime trees until they were out of view.

'Did you see how she smiled at me?'

'I didn't notice,' said Riley.

The Rushwood Sauna on Fifth Avenue off Harrow Road was not the obvious place to be on a hot summer's evening, which was exactly why Carla and Simone were there, a fortnight later. Mrs Earlene Rushwood had set up the place in 1963 having been appalled by the conditions of the British winter on her arrival from St Lucia, which had led her to thinking a lot about the Finnish. After nine years of toil the sauna was unveiled beneath a banner decorated with palm trees. Like-minded women had come from the surrounding avenues, First, Third, Fourth and further afield, bringing with them shower caps, flannels, scrubs, combs, lemons to cleanse the skin, and an array of oils and creams. They beat themselves with towels, taking great sighs and gossiping amid the pungent smell of the lemons, the debris of which was scattered beneath the changing benches – this was a bone of contention for Mrs Rushwood as she had to pick them up every night after closing, when there were signs on the walls in big bold letters telling people to please put them in the bin. Carla and Simone always avoided the busiest times because it got so loud in there. You didn't want people shouting over you when you were heat-hazed.

'He rang me last night,' said Simone. She was on the top slab, Carla on the lower, both in shower caps and bikinis. Opposite, two other women were lying down listening to their conversation, as you do.

'Who did?'

'Antoney.'

Carla went quiet. They'd just been talking about Simone's damaged foot and how awful a thing it was. It had taken months to heal.

'What did he want?'

'He asked me to bring you round to his side. The cheek.'

'That's a bit childish, isn't it?'

'Exactly. Like a schoolboy. He's never even apologised to me properly.'

'Jesus Christ, it's hot,' said Carla. Simone nevertheless poured water on the coals and smoke flew up with a hissing sound. The ageing woman on the opposite top slab rubbed her belly with a half-lemon. 'I think you should forgive him for your toe,' Carla said. 'Bearing a grudge makes you age faster.'

'That's true enough,' said the belly-rubber.

'Oh, I see,' said Simone. 'Sounds to me like you're already *on* his side. Don't *you* bear a grudge after what he did? If Ekow did that to me I'd cut his balls off.'

'What happened happened,' said Carla.

'What happened?' said the older woman.

'He was unfaithful to her. With a *white* girl.'

'Lard Jesus.'

'I'd rather you didn't spread it around the borough, Simone.'

'But isn't that the unforgivable sin?' Simone addressed the older woman.

'There are several unforgivable sins,' she replied. 'Thou shalt not steal, kill, disobey your parents or commit adultery. But Jesus forgives all, bless His heart.'

'Well I think he deserves everything he got.'

'What he get?'

'He's a loser. Doesn't get to see his kids. Carla, you should rinse him dry.'

'Since when has Antoney had money?' Carla said. She dizzied off the slab and went out for a shower.

'I think you could forgive him about the foot,' said the belly-rubber.

Antoney called Simone twice more and she finally agreed to pass on Lucas's toy bus for him if he dropped it round to her place but don't expect a cup of tea. She was taken aback at how rough he was looking; he'd put on weight. Before she closed the door he apologised for the foot.

Riley was trying to get him back into dancing. He offered to pay for studio time so that he could make new work. Dance was what he needed, he said, not Carla. Antoney wasn't inspired by the idea, and the one time he went to the studio he didn't enjoy it. He wanted her back, he kept saying. He wanted his family back. He was saving all the money he could to help her out with everything, which he was sending through the post. Carla returned it with a polite note. Antoney was convinced her mother had a hand in it but he didn't give up. He even seemed buoyed by this desperate wooing, which Riley found vexing. His boldest move was to badger Simone to ask Carla to meet him for a private, no-strings meeting at the Westbourne Grove café on Thursday 9 August, at 11 a.m., in three weeks' time. Simone said she would pass on the details but that was the end of it; he really was wasting his time.

'She'll come,' he said to Riley. 'She kept that last money I sent.'

'That doesn't necessarily mean anything. She's hard up.'

'All I need is to get her on her own for half an hour so I can talk it through with her.'

A week before the proposed meeting, Riley cooked a special dinner of roasted duck and Austrian red cabbage. Miles Davis was playing in the living room, where he'd set up a table with his best cutlery and candles.

'What's all this about?' Antoney said, coming back sweaty from the building site. 'Cooking again? You trying to become a chef?'

'I'm bored with eating in the kitchen.'

They drank a bottle of wine between them, talking about the early Midnight Ballet days, the first tour around the UK. 'I wonder what Fansa's doing right now,' Antoney said.

'Fishing?' said Riley.

'Yep. That's right. Fishing.' They laughed together merrily. Riley loved the smell of his sweat coming across the table, the glint in his eye, those laughing, cork-coloured lips.

'I like you being here,' he said.

'But I've overstayed my welcome. Thursday. Thursday is coming, my friend. You don't want me hanging around the place forever.'

A long silence settled over the music. Riley was miserable. He was going to lose him and there was nothing he could do about it. Antoney drank the last of his wine.

'Man. I really fucked everything up, didn't I?'

'You're a human being. You've achieved more than most – you still can.'

'The only one thinking that is you, Riley . . . Jesus. Look at me, I don't even see my boy. I don't know what I'll do if I can't get her back.'

'How about a brandy?' Riley got up and went to the sideboard.

'Have you ever made love to a woman, Riley?' Antoney asked. 'I'm just curious.'

'Um—' He almost dropped the glasses. Riley's girl history was an untrodden plane behind God's back. They'd never openly discussed his homosexuality before. Now it was he who was sweating.

'Yes, actually,' he revealed.

'Yeah? With who?'

Visibly uncomfortable, Riley returned to his seat.

'You don't have to talk about it if you don't want to.'

'No, it's all right.'

'So how many?'

'Two. I almost got as far as marrying one of them. That was Helen.'

'And what happened?'

'She turned me down. Said I was a liar. I went down on one knee, the whole shebang – but she saw through me.' Antoney was pouring the liquor with a Pall Mall on his lip. Riley had never told these things to anyone before.

'At least you're not one of them married fellas who have to pretend,' said Antoney.

'No. Thankfully not.'

'Did you like it?'

'What?'

'The sex.'

'I'm not supposed to like it.'

'But did you? Some people like both.'

'It was – warming, I suppose. But it was weird, like I was outside myself.'

'There's nothing as warm as a woman. Carla is *warm*,' enthused Antoney. 'What about a man?'

'What?'

'You ever been with a man before?'

'Have you?'

'Me? Hell, no, that's not my thing. Have you? . . . Ok, ok, I'm embarrassing you, sorry.'

There was a pause. Riley drove his hand through his thick wavy hair. 'Yes,' he said.

'Yeah?'

Antoney didn't quite believe him. He didn't elaborate and he didn't push him on it. 'I think a fella would be good for you,' he said. 'You wouldn't be lonely.'

'Do you think I'm lonely?'

'Yeah. I think you are.'

From the effect of the booze Antoney slept soundly for a couple of hours in the living room but was woken by a nightmare. He was waiting for Carla on a bridge. When he looked down into the water below he saw her thrashing around and calling for Lucas. He jumped into the water and tried to look for him but the baby had drowned. On the banks surrounding him he saw soldiers wearing heavy boots. He couldn't hear Carla's screams any more because they were making so much noise with their boots. When he woke up he could still hear them. The sound was all around him in the darkness and he got out of bed shivering. He hadn't taken his medication in three days. He felt drunk, but in a horrible way.

Riley heard him turning on the kitchen tap, then the light switch in the study. He'd been awake for an hour, his own sleep having been disturbed simply by melancholy. He heard the French windows being unlocked and opened. It was raining. Lulled by the music of the rain he fell into a shallow doze, but was woken again by a knock at the door. 'Riley? . . . Riley, are you awake?' He didn't answer.

Antoney came into the room and stood at the foot of the bed. Riley was too afraid to move. 'Please wake up.'

'What's wrong?' he said.

'It won't stop. It won't leave me be.'

'What?'

'That marching sound.' He was crying. 'It's in my head. Everywhere – even in the rain, I can't stand it.'

'Have you been taking the pills?' said Riley, switching on the lamp. 'Oh. I see,' as Antoney shook his head.

'If I take one now I won't be able to sleep.'

'I'll make a bed up on the floor. Don't worry, it'll be all right.'

Antoney helped him arrange the blankets and cushions on the rug at the foot of the bed. Riley had the disorienting sensation that he was physically back in his old childhood room, the garden a storey below him rather than on the same level. The shadow in the grass was chasing its tail with increasing speed. The pure bright blue of the sky was veiled behind the net curtain. Antoney was jumpy. He kept on looking over at the door as they made the bed. When the task was done they both lay down.

'Will you read me something?' he said.

'Of course.'

He read some lines from Yeats before turning out the lamp:

And I shall have some peace there, for peace comes dropping slow,
Dropping from the veils of the morning to where the cricket sings;
There midnight's all a glimmer, and noon a purple glow,
And evening full of linnet's wings.

Now, for Riley, it was impossible to sleep. Every breath, every movement coming from the foot of the bed he registered. Beyond that the ebbing rain, a lone dog barking, the night traffic along Bayswater Road and the distant city hum. Antoney was snoring lightly. The rain had made the air humid and close. For what seemed like a long time Riley lay there staring across at the window – open by a slit, he never closed the curtains – his thoughts becoming paler and more abstract. He hardly ever thought about Helen, but she appeared in his mind as she had been that day, in the trees of the Buttermere woods, a red cardigan over her narrow shoulders, her ever-expectant glance by the diagonal drop of brown hair. *You're so tactile today, Edward*. He was intoxicated by the glorious rural spring. He'd never seen such a spring, the fresh-leafed glow of tarns and glades, the misty Lakeland fells. On returning to their hotel they were met by an equally glorious wedding moving into the banqueting hall. Riley's brother had married the year before. *Tell me why you love me*. Kneeling he could no longer see the fells or the glades. *Because I can be quiet with you*, he tried. He could see up her nostrils instead. *Oh, Edward*. She broke away. *You're lying*. As she ran out into the corridor a warm breeze drifted into the room. He was aware of being too hot and he kicked away the sheet. There was someone else with him. He heard them breathing, could feel himself being watched. He opened his eyes to find Antoney lying next to him, rolled up like a foetus.

'It's coming back. It's getting louder, Riley. I'm scared.'

Riley remained paralysed on his back but turned his head a little to face him.

'Describe it to me. Precisely.'

'Soldiers, thousands all round coming, waves. Thousands of boots.'

'What kind of boots?'

'Army boots, lace-ups.'

'Try and think of the opposite,' Riley said.

'How'd you mean?'

'The opposite thing. Think of ballet slippers.'

Antoney tried it, closing his eyes. An army of silent, tiptoeing ballerinas.

'Is it helping?'

'I think so.'

'That's good.'

Riley yearned to wrap him in his arms and comfort him as his mother used to do to him when he was afraid of something, but he didn't dare. 'You just need to relax,' he said. 'It'll be better in the morning. We'll go for a walk after breakfast.'

Once again Antoney's breathing deepened. Before he fell asleep, the soldiers replaced by the soundless ballerinas, he murmured something directly from his subconscious, no thought or reflection behind it.

'You're the only one,' he said.

It occurred to Riley that he should maybe go and sleep in the living room to escape the turmoil he was experiencing, yet he couldn't bring himself to. He savoured the weight of the body beside him. He'd imagined this many times since Antoney had been here, what it might feel like to lie next to him in the darkness. It wasn't true what he'd told him earlier. He had never been with a man before. He'd suppressed every desire and had tried to convince himself it wasn't what he wanted. The shadow

298

was coming in from the garden, coming slowly towards him, looming over him. The longer he stayed on his back the more he could feel it bearing down on him, accusing him.

He turned onto his side the same way Antoney was facing. His movements were very stiff, his body unusually heavy. At the conclusion of the turn his hands became locked together in the small space between them and his knuckles brushed Antoney's back. His breath was running away from him, swelling beyond his ribcage in the drowsy heat of the room. Antoney gave a long, audible sigh that sounded erotic to him. He opened out his palm onto his back, but through trepidation the palm drew itself in again. Before he drifted sadly into sleep, he whispered in return, 'You're the only one.'

At some point – a minute, an hour later, he had no conception – he opened his eyes. He remembered there had been something he'd wanted to do before morning, and with hardly a thought in this dreamy state he put his arm around Antoney and held him. Suddenly he was free. The shadow disappeared. Joy washed through him. Although his doubts gathered as he became more conscious of what he was doing, he felt that he'd crossed a threshold and mustn't turn back. He moved his hand lightly along Antoney's upper arm and was surprised at the smoothness of the skin. He thought he would explode with the speed at which his heart was beating. He arrived at his waist, the softness of the cotton vest blending with the softness of the slackened flesh. Riley's hand rested there, gathering courage. Antoney sighed once more as he dared to caress his belly, his chest. This happened over a long period of time, the touching so slow and frail it was hardly there at all. You're unforgettable, he thought, I love you. At one instant Antoney shifted. Riley heard his breathing become shallow and then still, as if it had stopped completely. There was a new silence in the room which was sheer and intense. Riley sensed he was awake. He also stilled. But there was no attempt to shove him away. Antoney did not jump out of the bed in horror or disgust.

He stayed there with him, warm and accepting. So Riley carried on touching him.

Through all of it Antoney was motionless. He pretended to be asleep as Riley lifted his vest and ventured underneath, over his nipples, arousing him. Even as he went further down along the thickening hair Antoney did not stop him. Riley kissed his back, emboldened, trembling. Antoney even seemed to help him as he pushed past the elastic of his pyjama bottoms into the hot place within. He rubbed him at the front of his thigh, gently at first then harder, moving inwards, until the edge of his hand was rubbing against the base of his stiffening penis. Riley felt a bloated vein, and paused fleetingly out of fear. Then he trailed the vein with his index finger. Antoney made a small movement with his hip to open himself to him. But as Riley gently took him almost full in his hand, he quickly drew up his leg and blocked him. Riley moaned. Dread and terror overwhelmed him. His hand was left marooned on Antoney's leg.

The room was invaded by mutual embarrassment. The creeping dawn betrayed it, stifling them both. When Riley found the nerve to lift his hand away he turned onto his back, shot with a violent loathing for himself that would never go away. He would never touch like that again. Throughout his life he would never again find the courage. He lay there worrying frantically about how he'd face Antoney in the morning, but he needn't have, because in the morning Antoney was gone. He woke after ten in an empty bed, to find that he'd packed his laundry bag and left. They never saw each other again.

On Sunday 5 August, Carla and Simone took the children to the summer fair on Shepherd's Bush Green. Denise had been excited about it for days and she chose to wear her favourite thing even though it was far too hot, Carla's old pink feather boa, which her mother kept telling her to lift up as it was trailing on the ground and getting dirty. Carla herself wore a wide straw sunhat and a pleated skirt. Her ankles had returned. Her mouth had the faintest downward turn.

They took a bus down Barlby Road along Wood Lane. Simone by now was accepting of the circuitous route their conversations took in the presence of the children – their talk looped around the amazing sighting of a giant bee on the Gale's Honey billboard, or Lucas dropping his tissue-paper-stuffed book of farm animals out of the pram. He was a won't-sleep-long-enough, late-to-walk, late-to-talk kind of infant. Carla had failed to make it to the hospital this time during labour, and her mother had assumed the role of midwife. Toreth had said of Antoney in the aftermath, when Carla mentioned that they should perhaps let him know the baby was born, 'It's best for all of us you keep him away. I always knew that boy was the type to let a woman down.'

As they came off the bus, Carla carried on talking. 'I'm actually getting to like it. It's different. I'd love to live on a boat if I was a kid, wouldn't you? Anyway I won't be able to afford to move for ages.'

'You should get a job in one of those fancy restaurants in town,' said Simone, 'You can get rich just on tips.'

'Mummy look, a wheel! Pink!'

'Yes, pink!'

'It's *my* pink.' Denise had monopolised pink, as well as purple and the letter D.

'There's definitely no money in café work,' Carla said. 'How did your audition go last week by the way?'

'The usual. Don't call us we'll call you. You know the worst thing about it, Carla? It's not being able to put food on your table with something you love doing.'

'*Most* people can't do that – Lucas . . . I'll take that thing off him in a minute.'

'He'll only start screaming.'

'Denise, pick it up, please.'

'So,' said Simone suggestively, 'are you going on Thursday?'

'I'm thinking about it,' Carla said.

'I knew it. I knew you'd give in to him.'

'He only wants to talk, you said. Denise, what are you *doing*?'

The funfair spread before them. Denise could not contain herself and had stepped into the road. 'Do you want to get run over? Hold Aunty Simone's hand or I swear we're going home right now.' Denise obeyed. She found Simone rather a stern kind of big person, though they were beginning to form a rapport. They had an absorbing discussion about the ferris wheel. 'There's people up there.' 'Yes. They're screaming.' (Simone hated heights.) 'I can scream.' Denise demonstrated a scream. 'You scream.' 'I can't do it as well as you,' said Simone, which Denise was proud about. She pointed out that Simone's pink top matched her boa.

It was three, the Green was crowded. There were scores of prams laden with cardigans, suncaps and bags. Gangs of teenagers sloped around checking out the talent, couples came staggering off the wheel and the hair-raising Dive Bomber. A second sky had descended to eye level in the form of candyfloss.

When it came down to it the carousel was too scary for Denise to try, but she did climb right to the top of the Helter Skelter and whoosh down it three times, which Simone just didn't get. Then there was the Fun House. Then Simone endured eight minutes of imaginary motherhood while Carla took her daughter through the ghost train. Lucas wouldn't settle, in her arms or out, until Carla returned. Teddy bears stared out with hard black pupils from crooked tombola shelves. Simone won a rubber snake.

Carla wanted to be daring. She wanted to scream her head off as mothers sometimes must. So she went on the Dive Bomber, whose capsules spun on their joints while their master wheel also turned – double turning, with added height-fright. Charging through the air screamfully, losing her hat, she could no longer see the others waiting for her on the grass. She emerged dizzy yet purged, wanting more. 'This is like taking drugs,' she laughed. 'It's a shame we can't go on something together.'

'I've got my snake. That's quite enough for me,' said Simone.

'You're such a scaredy cat.'

'Mummy, can I have one?' Denise wanted candyfloss.

'All right, but we'll share it.'

Lucas was given a bottle and Denise her floss. Carla asked Simone if she minded her going on the Waltzers. 'Go on then, one more.'

'He'll be all right, he's got his milk.'

A land-bound thrill, also double turning. The carriages did their circling on a horizontal platform composed of up-down metal slopes. Carla chose a yellow car by the name of Super Dan. She was satisfied as she waited for it to start that this should be her last ride as she had a bit of a headache. Simone was holding her hat, and Denise's hand. A few turns into the ride Denise dragged her away to a neighbouring stall where she'd noticed an enormous plastic sunflower. Carla shared her carriage with three strangers, a man and two women. She was on the end.

Weaving through the Waltzers on the metal slopes was a puny guy whose job it was to spin the cars. He had a special wrist action that gave him the power to turn them with great force so that the passengers' backs were sucked against the leather walls of the carriages. He tended to focus on those containing pretty girls. He'd touch the rim of the car, tease it, give it a whirl, an overture to harder, more serious turning. Carla imagined he must lead a dizzy life, working as he did on a turning world. Every time he approached she reinforced her grip on the silver bar holding them in (which seemed loose). Round and round they went. She got increasingly giddy. Mr Spinner did his fast spinning. She screamed and her ears rang with it. She felt herself drifting away from the present moment, away from the screaming and closer to the ringing sound.

At some point Mr Spinner holding his fag turned Super Dan with such a force that Carla blacked out and slumped forward over the bar. The man sitting next to her tried to haul her up, not sure what had happened but concerned she might fall out. Her head hung limp, flopping this way and that. The guy shouted to the spinner to stop the ride but wasn't heard for several more turns. Only when Mr Spinner got hold of Super Dan's rim once more did he notice he had a faint on his hands. He stopped the ride. Carla remained unconscious. Her aid attempted to revive her, and she did seem to come to for a second but she faded again, so he carried her onto the grass. When Simone turned from the sunflower stall to check on the Waltzers, she saw people getting off. That was quick, she thought, looking around for Carla. A huddle of people was gathered on the grass. Going towards it she glimpsed Carla's brown skirt, her legs, one shoe off. She ran over, momentarily forgetting about the children.

Carla came round nine minutes later, by which time someone had called an ambulance. It seemed to her that she'd been travelling a long time to get back. At first when Simone spoke to her she didn't recognise who she was. She sat up. Actually Denise pulled her up, such as she could. The funfair was distant noise and colours.

'Carla. Are you all right? Carla.'

She drew up her legs, holding the back of her head. 'Where's the baby?' Her voice was drowsed and strange.

'He's in the pram. What happened, did you faint? They've called an ambulance.'

'Did you hurt yourself, Mummy?' said Denise.

'Fine, darling, I'm fine.' Lucas was wailing. 'Pass him.'

'Sit down! Wait for the ambulance, you're not supposed to get up quickly,' said Simone.

Carla didn't register this. 'God, that was so – weird.'

'You scared me.'

She was getting up in a jerky, awkward fashion. Simone couldn't persuade her to wait. 'I said I'm fine. I need to get him out of the sky, it's too hot.'

'At least put on your shoe, woman. I've never liked those Waltzers – you get too squashed. Wait. You've got stuff in your hair.'

'Flowers! Flowers!' said Denise. Carla batted Simone's hand away.

She just didn't want to wait, not for an ambulance, not for a bus. They walked all the way back along Wood Lane and up Barlby Road, Denise holding on to her mother's wrist, looking up at her occasionally as if pleased with her. Carla didn't bother her this time about the boa getting dirty, nor when Denise started to complain about walking so far. She herself stopped at some points, suddenly, lightening her grip on the pram, and would walk on again when Simone made to take it from her. The sun was beginning to set. Its heat was still potent. Nearing the top of Barlby Road Carla was so damn hot, so curiously pressed together inside her head, that she was overtaken by a tiredness that caused her legs to collapse beneath her. It was not a faint, but Simone insisted on calling another ambulance. It came twenty minutes later and took her away. She worried, with a distant ringing sound returning to her ears, that Simone would get the temperature wrong in preparing Lucas's milk.

Toreth received a call from the hospital. By the time she got there Carla had haemorrhaged, a delayed result of accelerative concussion. From her future accounts to Denise of pulling the daisies out of her hair in the off-white room, she would omit the loss of colour in Carla's face, the frightening descent in the mouth, the two slices of crescent-moon white where the closed eyelids ended, unable, as always, to cover the expanse. She would be unable to articulate how all of this had finally cancelled her, and the only place for her to continue to exist in the world was in the gap in her grandchildren's lives. She held them both in the dark night. Simone stood silently, arms folded, looking out of Silver's misty window at the water. Denise asked Toreth twice, thinking of her mother lying on the grass, one shoe on and one shoe off, 'Will she get up again and walk?'

It was later discovered by the Waltzers' owner that Super Dan did indeed have a faulty bar, which may have added to the flopping about of Carla's head during her blackout. The bar was repaired. On Thursday Antoney waited two hours for her, but she didn't come.

Afterwards, when it was clear to her that she would not be able to get back in, Carla watched her mother removing the rest of the daisies from her hair. Then she went to the Holland Park flower garden and picked a tulip for Denise. She learnt that when you reach this plane time changes its nature so that people can be older or younger than they were. It is also possible to travel great distances in a matter of seconds. She placed the tulip on the roof of the boat. Denise was sitting on deck, an older child than before. She had nothing to give to Lucas except a kiss, for she didn't know in which direction he'd live. She left the kiss also on the roof. Briefly she passed over Hyde Park, thinking she'd forgotten someone, though she couldn't quite remember who. She was lured by the sound of a bell and went towards it. When the bell stopped ringing she found herself in the square off the Champs-Elysées in Paris where she'd sat that time with Bluey. She was wearing the metallic ballgown the wardrobe mistress had given her. Bluey was sitting on the same bench where they'd sat that night. Their bench. He stood up as she entered the square.

Gosh, said Carla, as they took their seat. That was a surprise.

I've been waiting ages, said Bluey.

The woman who'd ponced a cigarette off him that night was there as well. She departed soon after with a nod, content that her son was neatly deposited with his safe and always one.

Epilogue

Denise got a place of her own above a chemist in Queen's Park, a bus ride away from the boat. As she couldn't afford a garden she entered the allotment community and smothered the flat with window-boxes, producing a somewhat comic, over-shrubbed sight for passers-by. In the years to come she would open her first shop, which as she'd always envisaged it, featured pails full of tulips in the foreground, calla lilies and candelabrum, and bold anthurium heads. She would go on to find success at the Chelsea Flower Show and see her name listed in the register of notable florists kept by the National Horticultural Association in Montagu Square in central London. Occasionally she would attend their annual dinners at the Dorchester Hotel, by the tree that was always Christmas.

The boat lost weight without her. The buckets, trowels, rakes and bags of compost were gone. The cherrywood cupboard was now empty. Lucas had thrown its contents into the canal the night he'd wrecked Riley's study. The only things he'd kept to remind him of back then were a few photographs, the tape of his father's voice, and the toy bus. Silver no longer leaned to one side against the bank.

Denise gave him enough money to keep him going for a few months. Then he would have to fend for himself. 'Take care,' she said. 'You can come round whenever you want.' As she walked away from him up the towpath slope he saw the expanse of her, her anthem, the sum of all she'd experienced. There was great determination and a sense of lost time. 'Denise,' he called, when she was almost at the gate – he'd shunned her parting request to look after the garden. 'I'll water it sometimes. Enjoy yourself, yeah?'

The next day he drifted through the Notting Hill Carnival. The music emerged early in the morning with a far-off susurrus as the masqueraders gathered at their camps. It crept into the floorboards of the locals, through the windowpanes, underneath front doors. By noon the Grove was under siege and thumping with soca bass. Patties imbued the air, along with woodsmoke off the jerk pans, fried fish and Singapore fried noodles. Parading over the canal came a lifesize foily dragon with a gold mane, followed by a sea-life float of blues and whites, and multitudes of feathered people dressed as fire. Children came out, with their mothers and brothers and lipsticked aunties carrying glitter. On went a troupe of batik butterflies. There passed the samba truck tailed by scores of gleaming bikinis. All along the three-mile route, as lines of police blocked off roads and argued with revellers wanting to pass through, balconies filled up with people watching waves of mass gyration, Trinidad and St Vincent going by, the steely silver music ringing out across the rooftops. Lucas refrained this year from occupying his usual place in the float configuration.

(The configuration: Masqueraders take the front, many hotpanted, often having wings or other statuesque backwear, guzzling from flasks of pick-me-up-and-keep-me-dancing. Behind them are the wearers of the T-shirts associated with the float, their commitment to the party is deep and long-lasting. The final group has no uniform or signature of the cloth. They're too far away to hear the music loud enough to shuck out so they chat among themselves, drifting away at will to get chicken or join another float – Lucas usually belongs to this group. All of the above, if they know what's good for them, are wearing trainers.)

But this year he watched the procession from the railings, like a visitor. He avoided Crow's PA in the Sainsbury's driveway, wove through the thousands of bodies, manoeuvring through thick-spots. On the corner of Portobello and Golborne he stopped for a pattie by the reggae sound and listened to some Sizzla. It was a good pattie, the right temperature and softness, but it was nothing new.

It took him two weeks to find a new tiller. Once he got the wild idea into his head that Silver might sail, brought on by the lightness, her shifted position on the water and his craving to leave the bank, he couldn't get it out of his head. He opened the trapdoor in the stern, which along with the dragons by the cabin doors he'd been afraid of as a boy, convinced that beneath it lurked Freddy Krueger, Dracula and Jim Jones. It came open reluctantly after WD-40, with a long, loud creak, revealing an old blackened machine – the engine – and one of Antoney's snakeskin shoes. The engine and the shoe were opposing objects. One went forward and the other went back. He threw the shoe into the canal to join the Midnight Ballet museum and went to the library to read up. The tiller, which was used to steer the boat, he found in a boat shop. The engine was more complicated because of the age of the model.

He eventually managed to track down an elderly water gypsy in Chesham who collected and restored old parts. In his possession was the engine Lucas was looking for. 'How long did you say it'd been moored?' he said mystified. 'Did you ever get the bottom blacked?'

'What's blacked?' said Lucas.

The old man scoffed. 'You're meant to get the boat onto a hard standing so you can paint the hull with bitumen, the black stuff, to protect it. S'posed to be done every five years – it must be chomped away by algae by now.'

The nearest boatyard to Lucas was in Southall. For a tax-averting cash fee the new engine was fitted by a mechanic friend

309

of Jake's, and with his burgeoning knowledge, Lucas replaced the tiller. In late October, brimming with anticipation, he turned on the ignition switch to head for the boatyard. Not surprisingly, Silver didn't move. Lucas returned to Chesham.

'I thought it was a long shot,' said the old man. 'Your propeller's probably gone too.' He agreed, for a fee, to come down and have a look. It took a large whack of Denise's money, a crane, and four men to get the boat onto the towpath, ruining Denise's garden in the process. The propeller was indeed kaput; the hull was rusted over and had some holes. 'It's a wonder it didn't sink!' the old man exclaimed. In a stab at chance, because more wonders might happen, he helped Lucas block the holes and then restored the propeller. Lucas did the job of blacking the bottom, which inspired him to redecorate the exterior and interior of the boat while he was at it, choosing oranges and peacock blue, so that by the time Silver was set back on the water a few weeks later she looked as if she'd sailed just yesterday. The old man tested everything. He congratulated himself and Lucas as the engine crooned and the propeller began spinning in the water.

It would be a winter wade. He said a misleading goodbye to Denise, planning on calling her from his first mooring to tell her where he was because he didn't want her trying to interfere. His plan was to sail at will and find casual work as and when he needed it. On a Monday morning in December, with provisions on board – tins of food, warm clothes – he put on a Scarface album by way of soundtrack and untied the ropes. Then he took his place at the tiller. It would take some getting used to, the idea of steering from the back, but the old man had told him to just keep a long steady eye and use his judgement, he'd quickly get the hang of it. As he turned on the engine and the propeller began to spin he had a flash of Antoney sitting on the imaginary bus along the mountain road from Guantánamo to Baracoa. Lucas would probably never see that road. He had no desire any more to see that road. He would find his own.

310

He'd take a step in the better direction and have faith in where it led him.

It took him some minutes to notice that he wasn't moving. Silver had advanced towards the bridge, but she was now floating stationary, the engine still surging. Becoming flustered, Lucas hurried down the bedroom hatch through the saloon and onto the bow to check on the propeller. It had slowed down. It seemed devoid of its connection with the engine. As he watched, right before his despairing gawp, there came a final spinning, a shudder, then an ugly noise. The propeller dropped off and disappeared into the depths. 'Oh, fuck, no,' he said.

He sank down onto the bow. The yellow-eyed cat parked itself with non-pressing business on the bank. Pigeons made a dark arrow overhead and a family of ducks squabbled on the opposite shore. 'All I want to do is go,' he told them all. 'Why can't I just go?' Before him the liquid road stretched tauntingly ahead to the first bend, beyond that freedom. It was while staring, emptied of hope, at that first distant bend that he thought of the jetty, the jetty that had stretched out to sea in the baroness's private bay, where Antoney had been told to look for a picture of his future. When it came into his mind he stood up. He fixated on the bend and waited, feeling foolish. All he saw of course was water, the towpath and the edge of another bridge. But when he tried harder to get into the vibe of it, when he tried to imagine The Wonder standing behind him in his dashiki and his incredibly white trainers, he saw something else. He saw a train. A big mainline-station train, pausing on the water and opening its doors to him. The wind was blowing in that direction. Silver, unanchored in her apathy, was gently nudged towards it.

So what did he do? He tied her back up, packed his things, and took a 52 to Victoria.

His destination was Penzance, the most exotic-seeming place on the departure boards. He got very excited as the train pulled out. If Jake could see him now. They crossed the Thames. He saw the

Houses of Parliament and the MI6 headquarters. The council blocks amassed through Loughborough Junction. Then the land began to open and it became a constant, grassy sight flecked by farms, forests, warehouses and motorways. Hours into the journey, there came a point when he was ready to read.

After the wrecking of the study, Riley had sent him the last chapter of his book, with a letter of apology for what he now saw as his 'insensitive presumptuousness in imagining'. He said that he'd decided not to publish the book, and he hoped that Lucas might find some meaning or appreciation in keeping it for himself and his sister to do with as they wished.

It wasn't finished until the story was finished. Lucas read of his father's struggle to win back his mother, his efforts to forge a relationship with his children. After Carla passed on, he moved back in with Florence, and they later returned to Jamaica together. Florence took him to Beaumont when she could no longer bear the ordeal and the shame of looking after him. Lucas read the final section in complete absorption, not looking up from the page. He would only ever read this once.

Antoney entered the church from the rear, over the fence, down the drain, the same route by which he'd left the building after his final conversation with Oscar Day. He was a widower. He had lost his children. The church summoned him as a place of comfort and respite. He arrived there after many hours of walking, a floating type of walk that seemed to him the contrary, during which he let his shirt fall to the ground, dropped his keys and coins also, and bent to remove his shoes.

The church was empty. He ripped the boards off the back door and his hands were bleeding in the entrance hall. He could hear the faint marching. The sensation in his feet was that they no longer belonged to him, as he stepped into the studio.

Evening had fallen. It was most peaceful here. Moonlight

was coming down from the high windows. When he caught his reflection in the mirrors he turned his back quickly, and saw Oscar's horse vaults and sleeping board in the dark corner. There came a compulsion to lie down flat, to sleep. The sound of the marching retreated as he made his bed, positioning the vaults at the right distance and the board across them. It was comfortable, actually. He found the rest that he was searching for.

His dreams were of the dancing, the old times when they'd all danced together in that hall – Carla, Ekow, Simone, everyone. They were running. They were seeing who could jump the highest. Oscar threw off his sweater, No no *no*, he went higher! What a whale of a time they were having. The studio door opened and in came Nijinsky himself. He coughed loudly. The cough was followed by the scrape of a chair, close to where Antoney was resting. 'Who's that? Who's with me?' he asked. A swish of clothing, like someone removing their coat. When Antoney opened his eyes the figure gave a little laugh.

He was small and plump, white-haired, wearing a tatty suit with his coat laid across his lap. He emitted a shine. Antoney sat up, recognising the high cheekbones, the secretive mouth and bone-coloured skin. He looked softly past Antoney's face as if expecting that Antoney might soon begin a conversation with him. Suddenly he leaned forward and said, in a coarse, foreign voice, with his hand covering his mouth, 'We are being followed.'

'Who is following us?' said Antoney.

'The soldiers. We must not delay.' Vaslav straightened again in his chair.

'Are you taking me to the resting place?'

Vaslav, as was his habit, remained silent for a time. 'I will take you to the mountains,' he said. 'I will take you to see your loved ones and I will wash your forehead in the spring at Lourdes. I like mountains, because they are unnecessary.'

So Antoney prepared himself. He did not want to keep the great man waiting and he was looking forward to their walk. Vaslav said it didn't matter that he didn't have a shirt.

'Have you found that thing yet?' Antoney asked spontaneously.

Vaslav knew what he was talking about. 'Not yet. But I continue to look.'

'You think it was while we were dancing that we lost it?'

At this Vaslav burst into deep, convulsive laughter, hoarse from insulin. Antoney smiled. Walking side by side they were vastly different heights, Antoney a full two feet taller than Vaslav. Antoney asked him how his feet were doing these days and Vaslav said they didn't treat him badly. Before they reached the door, he dared to make his one, shy request.

'Vaslav,' he said, as the dancer looked past him but not into his eyes, 'before we go, can I see you leap?'

'Oh, but of course!'

Vaslav's face brightened and he cast away his coat. Antoney watched, full of awe and excitement. A symphony broke through the windows. Vaslav began to dance and jump woodenly, raising his stocky arms. As the music accelerated he broke into a run and soared into the air. The suit and the white hair disappeared, to be replaced by a young man in an elaborate black costume, his legs bare and his head thrown back, one arm outstretched and the other arched above. He went higher and higher, higher than Antoney had flown in any dream, then he began to descend.

Oscar was right. It was true. Before he came down, he did go higher.

It was the most perfect leap Antoney had ever seen.